Lynda Page was born and brought up in Leicester. The eldest of four daughters, she left home at seventeen and has had a wide variety of office jobs. She lives in a village near Leicester. Her previous sagas are also available from Headline, and have been highly praised:

'Filled with lively characters and compelling action' *Books*

'A nostalgic background for its mix of colourful characters fronted by the delightfully strong leading lady' *Lincolnshire Echo*

'It's a story to grip you from the first page to the last' *Coventry Evening Telegraph*

'You'll be hooked from page one' *Woman's Realm*

'As always with Page, the text is rich in Leicester dialogue, there's a wealth of well-drawn characters and a happy ending' *Leicester Mercury*

'An enjoyable read with lots going on to keep you hooked until the very end' *Wiltshire Times*

'Lynda Page creates strong characters and is a clever and careful storyteller . . . She has the stamina not to alienate you as a reader and to keep the story going on a constant flow of purpose and energy . . . A great writer who gives an authentic voice to Leicester . . . A formidable talent' *LE1*

A LUCKY BREAK

Lynda Page

headline

First published in 2005
by HEADLINE BOOK PUBLISHING

First published in paperback in 2006 by
HEADLINE BOOK PUBLISHING

3

Cataloguing in Publication Data is
available from the British Library

ISBN 978-0-7553-0883-5

Typeset in Stempel Garamond by Palimpsest Book Production
Printed and bound in Great Britain by
Clays Ltd, St Ives plc

Headline's policy is to use papers that are natural, renewable
and recyclable products and made from wood grown in
sustainable forests. The logging and manufacturing
processes are expected to conform to the environmental
regulations of the country of origin.

HEADLINE BOOK PUBLISHING
A division of Hodder Headline
338 Euston Road
LONDON NW1 3BH
www.headline.co.uk
www.hodderheadline.com

For Michael Brant

I have watched you grow from a beautiful baby, into
a gawky, unsure youth, and on into a six-foot-two,
strapping, handsome, intelligent man, admired
by all you meet.

No aunt could be prouder than I am
to have you as a nephew.

With all my love
Your Aunty Lynda

CHAPTER ONE

'Dead!'

Captain Reginald Mortimer Fosedyke flashed a hurried glance up and down the long corridor before bringing his attention back to the young woman accosting him. A World War I veteran, Captain Fosedyke was of medium height and wiry of stature, his full head of silver hair cut in a short back and sides, a neatly trimmed moustache visible between his thin lips and long narrow nose. He was immaculately attired in a smart three-piece black suit, stiffly starched high-collared white shirt, and well-worn but good quality black leather shoes.

Issuing an irritated sigh, he gave a disdainful tut. 'Dead indeed! Miss Monroe, have you any idea how busy I am dealing with genuine hotel business without having my time wasted by a hysterical member of staff? Mr Roberts most probably had too much to drink last night and is sleeping it off. And what were you doing entering a guest's room while they were still in residence anyway?' he accused.

Connie Mary Monroe anxiously smoothed her hands down the front of her unflattering old-fashioned black chambermaid's uniform, which despite its shapelessness

1

could not disguise her voluptuous curves. Why did it have to be her who had discovered the man? She wasn't even supposed to be working today as it was her day off. She'd been looking forward to visiting her family but after her room-mate begged her, had agreed to cover for her so she could visit her sick grandmother. Though, knowing Valerie Bates as she did, Connie strongly suspected her grandmother's illness was just a ruse to cover the fact that she was meeting a man friend. The monied, much older type probably. That was the sort Val favoured. Connie had spotted them a couple of times as she had passed by a café window, Val and her man, looking very cosy together, intimate almost. Connie herself could not understand why such a pretty woman as Val would go for the older type when she would have no trouble finding a nice man of her own age who'd gladly take her out and show her a good time.

'Well, I did knock loudly several times, Captain Fosedyke. When I didn't get an answer, I thought the room had been vacated and let myself in.' Connie shuddered at the memory of finding the semi-naked middle-aged man slumped across the bed, stiff as a board, his skin waxen. It was immediately apparent he'd breathed his last hours before, seemingly as he'd been undressing for bed.

The shock of what she had so unexpectedly found hadn't quite registered on her yet in the urgent need to deal with the matter, but Connie felt hurt that her boss hadn't yet enquired after her own welfare. After all, it wasn't exactly an everyday occurrence for a chambermaid to enter a room to prepare it in readiness for the next guest and find the only way the previous one was going to leave was inside a wooden box. It was also annoying that the hotel manager had accused her of being hysterical. She wasn't a silly girl, she was a woman of twenty-three, and not prone to attacks of hysterics whenever any out-of-the-ordinary occurrence presented itself. Boss or no boss she would let Captain Fosedyke know that.

She took a deep breath and said resolutely, 'I did my First Aid badge in the Girl Guides and passed with flying colours. Mr Roberts is dead, Captain Fosedyke, I can assure you of that. When I checked for a pulse I couldn't find one and he wasn't breathing. I held a mirror under his nose to check.'

Before he could respond a young girl came rushing up to them. 'Oh, there yer are, Captain Fosedyke.' A look of relief spread over Mona Biddle's extraordinarily plain face. 'I've bin looking all over for yer. Chef . . .'

'What is a kitchen assistant doing in the main hotel?' Reginald Fosedyke interjected. 'You're well aware of the rules, they were made clear enough to you at the start of your employment. You'd better have a good excuse for venturing in here. Chef might be your immediate superior but the rest of the hotel is my responsibility. And straighten your cap! The Connaught is a prestigious establishment. We have standards to uphold and I will not allow those to be compromised. Is that clear?'

Connie tightened her lips. Captain Fosedyke was obviously blind to the fact that the eighty-roomed Connaught Hotel, a five-storey Georgian building on the London Road in Leicester, a five-minute walk from

3

the main railway station, had long since lost any pretensions to grandeur. The building was impressive enough with its pillared portico and revolving door. It had been commissioned over a hundred years previously by Charles Devonshire, owner of a considerable number of rental properties, who had decided to expand his growing business empire into the hotel trade, seeing the need for a better standard of accommodation for the more affluent visitors to the city. By 1956, however, the Connaught was well overdue for a face lift. Stepping inside this hotel was like travelling back in time to the early-1920s.

Hurriedly straightening her white mob cap, Mona peered fearfully at the hotel manager. 'I'm sorry, Captain Fosedyke, really I am. Chef ordered me to find yer 'cos he ain't got time himself. He's a very busy man is Chef, I have ter do what he tells me or he'll sack me.'

'All right, all right, just get on with it,' the manager snapped.

'Right, yes. I'm sorry, Captain Fosedyke. Chef . . . well, he's in a right temper 'cos apart from the meat delivery being late again, we're short of a washer-upper. Well, kitchen assistant, 'cos that's what I am, ain't it? A kitchen assistant. Sounds posher than a washer-upper,' she said, a proud beam lighting up her unattractive face.

He looked at her, bemused. 'And what has this all to do with me?'

She gulped nervously. 'Well, when I asked Chef for some help he said as you pinched Ivy Bishop off us to train up as a silver service waitress, it's your fault we're

4

short-staffed so it's up to you to give us someone to replace her. He said he ain't got time at the minute to do all the interviewing and whatnot, not with everything else he has to do. I can't manage all by meself, Captain Fosedyke. I've bin at it since six-thirty this morning and I ain't got through all the breakfast dishes yet, let alone all else that's stacking up. Look at me hands, they're red raw,' she said, thrusting them at him.

Whether the staff shortage in the kitchen was in fact down to Captain Fosedyke's actions was immaterial. He was more annoyed at being summoned in this peremptory way by Chef. He looked up and down the corridor to make sure there were no guests observing them and narrowed his eyes at Mona. 'Tell Chef to sort this out himself. Inform him I shall be paying him a visit, he can rest assured of that, but at a time of my own choosing.' He flapped one hand at her in a dismissive fashion. 'Now be about your business.'

Mona scooted off to the kitchen, not at all relishing the prospect of relaying the hotel manager's response to Chef. Amelia Harbin, the head receptionist, was next to join them. She was a tall, extremely thin, formidable-looking middle-aged spinster. As usual she was dressed in a back-belted, mid-calf dress with a white lace collar and cuffs, a cameo brooch pinned to the shoulder. Her thick salt-and-pepper hair was scraped up into a bun which sat on the top of her head like a lump of unrisen bread dough. She ran the reception area like a military operation and woe betide anyone who tried to interfere with her domain, except of course for those who held a superior position to her own such as the Captain, Mr Sopwith, the assistant

5

manager, and Mr Griffin, the aloof proprietor, on whom she'd never set eyes during the thirty-odd years she had been employed at the Connaught.

Completely ignoring the presence of Connie she said to the Captain, 'I need to speak to you, Captain Fosedyke, as a matter of urgency.'

He gave an irritated sigh and his response to her was curt. 'Wait in my office please, Miss Harbin. I'll be with you shortly.'

As the receptionist strode away all thoughts of her recent distressing experience flew from Connie's mind as excitement whirled within her. An opportunity was presenting itself, a situation she had longed for for such a long time. Connie was desperate to improve her position at the Connaught and forever on the look out for an opportunity to prove to the management that she had the potential to be much more than a chambermaid. Despite her having been employed for over two years at the hotel, this was the first time such a chance had presented itself and she'd be a fool not to seize it. But did she have the nerve or not? She was well aware of the consequences should Captain Fosedyke perceive it as a breach of protocol. But should she let this opportunity slip away it could be another two years, or even longer, before another chance like this came along. The thought of remaining a chambermaid for longer than she needed to made the decision for her.

Taking a deep breath, her heart beating rapidly, she blurted out, 'With due respect, Captain Fosedyke, it's obvious you've your hands full. I could call the doctor and the funeral home to come and deal with Mr Roberts for you? I'll make sure it's all carried out discreetly so our other guests don't get wind. Well, as much as I can, of course. I expect we'll need to look through Mr Roberts's belongings, too, to get information about his next-of-kin so we can contact them.' Her face clouded over. 'This is going to be a terrible shock for them, isn't it, Captain Fosedyke?'

He looked at her in irritation. 'Miss Monroe, you have other duties to perform to ensure the comfort of our guests. We're already short of two chambermaids since our former employees are of the mistaken belief they'll fare better as chalet maids at a holiday camp.' He eyed her warningly. 'Now please return to your own responsibilities and leave me to mine. I trust I don't need to remind you there should be no tittle-tattle on the subject of Mr Roberts, especially not within earshot of any of the other guests. Careless talk and all that.' He added wryly, 'If indeed Mr Roberts has departed this world, which has yet to be confirmed.' He looked at Connie appraisingly then, and to her surprise his face softened and he actually smiled at her. 'You've had a shock, no doubt. Go to the kitchen and get yourself a cup of tea. For five minutes, no more. Tell Chef I sent you, and if he has a problem to come and see me direct. Go on, off you go.'

With that the manager strode off. Connie stared after him. After what she had just been through a cup of tea was absolutely the thing she needed. Regardless, though, the kitchen was out of bounds to everyone but catering staff, even the owner himself, unless personally invited by Chef, and she knew that her intrusion was going to cause trouble, whatever the reason. It was well known that the hotel's manager and head chef each felt themself to be the most important member of staff. Each conveyed the impression that the place would fall down without them, and each constantly endeavoured to outdo the other in order to confirm their position as number one in the pecking order. She would like to believe that Captain Fosedyke had acted out of compassion in ordering her to go for a cup of tea but he was probably using her as a pawn in his feud with Chef.

Feeling she ought to inform her fellow chambermaid that she'd be absent from duty for a few minutes, Connie hurriedly returned to the second floor. As she turned into the corridor she heard her name being called and saw Dorothy Smith's head poking out of the bathroom at the end. 'Oh, there yer are, Connie. Where yer bin?'

'I had to find the Captain and inform him of a problem.'

Dorothy's eyes sparkled keenly. 'Problem? What sorta problem? Must be bad to have ter tell Fossie about it?'

'It was something and nothing,' Connie said evasively. 'Did you want me for a reason, Dot?'

'Yeah, the lavvy chain is broke in here. The last person who used it didn't flush either and it ain't a pretty sight,' she said, wrinkling her nose in disgust.

Connie shuddered at the vision she was conjuring up. This morning was proving to be one of the difficult ones. She sighed. 'Well, do what we normally do in such circumstances, Dot. Put an "Out of Order" sign on the door and we'll report it to Sid along with the other repair jobs we found needed doing this morning.

I've got to run an errand, I'll be a few minutes.'

'Errand? What sorta errand?'

'Just an errand. And get a move on, Dot. We've only covered half what we're supposed to do by now and time is wearing on.' In truth, Connie had covered more than her fair share but as always when unfortunate enough to be on a shift alongside Dot was hindered by her slowness.

Dot snorted, ''Tain't fair, Connie. We're expected to do far more than chambermaids in other hotels.'

'Yes, well, this isn't any other hotel, is it? In fairness to the Captain we are short-staffed at the moment and at times like this we all need to pull our weight. And we do have a choice, remember. Put up and shut up or else get out.'

'Well, as soon as I can find summat else suitable, I'm getting out,' Dot announced. 'I can't understand why I got turned down by the Bell. I thought they'd snap me up, me being so experienced like.'

Connie understood only too well. Dorothy Smith was lazy, only doing what she had to, and even then her work wasn't really up to scratch and she had to be constantly monitored. Other establishments where she had tried to get a job had obviously detected this trait in her at interview and declined to have her work for them.

'I can't understand you, though, Connie,' Dot continued. 'You ain't the normal type that skivvies for a living. You could do much better for yerself.'

'I intend to, Dot, but to get to the top you have to start at the bottom. Now, as I said, I won't be long. By the time I get back you should have finished that bathroom and made a start on the next lot of bed-rooms.'

After making sure that the door to the deceased man's room was safely locked, Connie hurried off down the back stairs to the kitchen.

CHAPTER TWO

Gordon Stimpson, his stained cook's whites straining alarmingly over his monstrous girth, was firing out orders like bullets as he stomped around the kitchen, flailing his arms wildly.

'I said cut finely, you blithering idiot, not chop like you're hacking at firewood!'

The young man to whom he was directing this verbal abuse gulped audibly. 'The knife's blunt,' he offered by way of excuse.

'Then sharpen it, you cretin,' Gordon hissed sarcastically. Still reeling out insults about the state of the kitchen, he manoeuvred his huge bulk towards the stove dominating the back wall of the large room and stared, appalled, into a big saucepan of puce-coloured liquid being stirred by Melvin Jones, a gawky young commis of seventeen. 'Good grief, what on earth is that?' he bellowed.

Melvin looked at him, terrified. 'Br . . . br . . . Brown Windsor soup, Chef.'

'If that's Brown Windsor then I'm yer bleeding Dutch uncle,' Gordon screamed, grabbing up a wooden spoon to slap it down hard across the back of the young man's hand. 'Chuck it all away and start again.

The food that leaves this kitchen is my responsibility and I won't have my reputation tarnished by your incompetence. Get it right next time or you can kiss goodbye to any hope you have of qualifying as a chef. You'll be washing dishes for the rest of your life, boy, so be warned.' He threw up his hands in despair, giving each of the three young apprentices a look of utter disdain. 'I've had some stupid commis in my charge during my time but you lot take the biscuit! What makes you think any of you has what it takes to make a chef, eh? Now, I'm warning you all, you'd better pull yer socks up or yer'll be out on yer ear. I'd have no trouble replacing any of yer. Jones, get a move on with the vegetables then start gutting the chickens for dinner.' He slapped one paw-like hand to his forehead, letting out a despairing groan. 'Oh, damn and blast, you can't, can you, because that clot of a butcher hasn't delivered yet. Get on the telephone and ask where the hell our order is. I've a lamb casserole to prepare for lunch or we'll only have a fish course to offer the guests at this rate. Now where's that excuse for a hotel manager? You did give him my message, didn't you, Biddle?'

Mona, who had slipped in unobserved while Chef had been ranting and was back at her place at the enormous pot sink, tackling the ever-increasing mound of dirty dishes and greasy pans, gulped in trepidation as she turned to look at him, eyes fearful.

'Er . . . yes, Chef.'

'And?'

'Eh? Oh, he . . . er . . . said he'd be along to see yer shortly.'

'He'd better. I'll teach that jumped-up little upstart

to pinch my staff,' Chef fumed. 'By the time I've finished with him, he'll think twice about doing it again.' He moved swiftly to the side of the young man next to Melvin at the stove and slapped his hand across the boy's head. 'Oi, stir gently, don't beat! The roux for the fish sauce will separate if you carry on smashing it to death like that.'

Using all his will-power, Neal Richmond stopped himself from retaliating equally violently. A tall, carrot-haired, pleasant-faced young man, at twenty-three he was only months off qualifying as a fully fledged chef in his own right. Chefs were notorious within the trade for being generally bad-tempered, treating their apprentices as though they were brainless idiots, even slapping them when the mood took them. Sixty-year-old Gordon Stimpson lived up to the stereotype. Many times in the past, as Neal had painstakingly perfected his skills under the guidance of this foul-mouthed, temperamental man, he had quashed his own anger. The injustice of it was what hurt him the most. Neal had in fact been carefully stirring the roux, not beating it as Chef had accused him of doing, but the other man never, ever paid a compliment for a job well done, always finding fault whether there was any to find or not.

But tyrant though Gordon Stimpson was, with few commis chefs actually managing to complete their apprenticeship under his capricious tutelage, and boringly unimaginative though his menus were, Neal had long since realised he was better under this man's charge than that of some others in the trade with the nerve to call themselves chef. Their culinary qualifications had in truth been gained working in transport cafés or low-grade hotels where the quality of food offered was uniformly abysmal. Stimpson was better than that, on a good day anyway.

Neal had a bright future planned for himself. After putting up with what he had while he gained his qualifications, he wasn't about to jeopardise it all just for the satisfaction of putting Chef in his place.

Stimpson was looking at him fixedly, a mocking smile on his thick lips. He was well aware that Neal wanted to stand his ground but if he dared then Gordon Stimpson would have grounds to sack the senior apprentice – just what he wanted to do. 'Something to say, have you, Richmond?' he goaded.

Reminding himself of his future plans, Neal glanced back at him blankly. 'No, Chef.'

'Sure, are you?'

He smiled politely. 'Absolutely, Chef.'

Disappointment that he had failed to rile Neal was evident on Gordon's face. 'Huh. I bet you'd like nothing more than to have a go back at me, wouldn't you, boy?'

Neal pretended to be hurt that Chef could even think such a thing of him. 'I'm here to learn from you, Chef, and you've every right to chastise me should you feel I'm not coming up to scratch.'

Gordon glared at him. He didn't like Neal Richmond, not one bit. It wasn't anything to do with his sturdy resilient character but the fact that Neal was a far better cook than Gordon was himself; in fact, if he was honest, the lad was a natural. Gordon had very quickly seen the potential in this young man when he had agreed to take him on as an apprentice over four years ago. To begin with the Head Chef had welcomed his presence.

14

For the first time that he could ever remember he'd showed a commis what to do, and not only did Neal remember exactly what he had been instructed down to the last detail, he also made improvements to tried and trusted recipes, even coming up with completely new ones of his own.

Gordon soon put a stop to this. He was no fool. He knew full well that he'd been lazy about keeping up with changes in culinary taste. But, fortunately for him, his place of work was stuck in a time warp so it didn't matter his own range was strictly limited. He might be a cut above some in his profession, but an outstanding chef he certainly was not and never would be. He didn't need a commis showing him up. He was well aware he wouldn't fare well should it ever come to having to seek another job in a decent establishment. He'd managed to secure this one by the skin of his teeth because he was the only chef who had applied for the position when it became vacant after the last incumbent retired after forty-five years' service. Gordon Stimpson had created an easy life for himself here at the Connaught and also bene-fited from a very lucrative sideline; he wasn't going to have all that whipped away from him easily. The likes of Neal Richmond he kept firmly in their place.

As Gordon stomped off, he grunted under his breath, 'Smart arse.'

The sound of the back door opening caught his atten-tion and he spun round to see Gertrude Braddock entering the room. 'You're early,' he hurled accusingly at her.

The elderly woman flashed a scowl of annoyance at the fat man who with his monstrous rolls of blubber and completely bald head always reminded her of a sow about to give birth. 'Oh, and that's a crime now, is it?' she shouted back at him.

'It is when you're expecting to take over part of *my* kitchen.'

She was already several years past the age when most women retire but nevertheless Gertrude Braddock was reliant on her job, needing her small wage to eke out the widow's pittance she received from the government. Having lost her only son in the last war she was alone in the world now and the daily contact with people that this job afforded her gave her existence some meaning. A shame it had to be in the same kitchen as this odious man who was the bane of all who served under him. She wasn't alone in wishing vehemently that something would happen to cause him to leave and then they'd be able to work for a more amiable boss. But until that happy day she'd sooner sell cakes on street corners in a howling blizzard, naked as the day she was born, than let Gordon Stimpson ever have the satisfaction of getting the better of her.

'*Your* kitchen! Listen here, you,' she replied, wagging a finger at him as she kicked shut the back door. 'You might be under the impression you're king pin in this kitchen, Chef Stimpson, but I'm a cook the same as you and you'll give me the respect I deserve.'

Hands on hips, a sarcastic smile twitching his lips, Stimpson replied, 'A *pastry cook* can hardly be classed in the same light as *Head Chef*. Eh, and remember, I'm the boss,' he warned her.

'*Pâtissière*, if yer don't mind,' Gertrude snapped back, then sniggered. 'Yer might be me boss, and yer can sack me if yer want, but you know as well as I do that you'll not get another *pâtissière* of my calibre that'd last one shift in this hellhole with you. The only reason the two breakfast chefs have stuck it so long is 'cos their shift finishes before you come on and they have no contact with you.'

Gordon knew she spoke the truth and fought desperately to save face before the staff who were witnessing this ferocious exchange. He needed to put the old bag in her place once and for all. He was just beginning to worry that he wouldn't succeed when his attention was caught by the inner swing doors opening. He turned his head, eyes nearly popping out to see a chambermaid entering his kitchen.

'What the hell is a skivvy doing in here?' he bellowed across at Connie. 'Get out! Out!' he screamed, gesticulating wildly.

'Give the gel a chance to explain herself before you bawl her out,' Gertrude shouted over as she waddled across to Connie. 'For all you know she could have a perfectly legitimate reason for presenting herself here. What is it, lovey?' she asked, reaching the girl. She smiled at Connie kindly. 'Never mind Chef, he just likes the sound of his own voice,' she said softly.

Connie smiled gratefully at her. 'Captain Fosedyke ordered me to present myself in the kitchen for a cup of tea.'

'Oh, he did, did he? Well, he knows very well the kitchen is out of bounds to the likes of yerself and that Chef would cause a stink about it. And it's not like the Cap'n to excuse anyone from their work without a damn' good reason. What is it then?'

'Oh, er . . . I've had a bit of a shock.'

'A shock, eh? Must be more than a bit of one for the Cap'n to offer tea and sympathy. What kinda shock?' probed Gertrude, her eyes sparkling keenly.

Connie looked at her awkwardly. 'I'm not at liberty to discuss what happened, Cook.'

Gertrude's face clouded over. 'Oh, I see.' Her curiosity was aroused, though, and she intended to find out just what shock Connie had suffered. Putting a friendly arm around the girl's shoulders, she said, 'I'm early today so come with me into the room service kitchen and I'll mek you a cuppa meself.'

The small room Gertrude guided Connie into adjoined the main kitchen. Here room service orders were prepared on a small separate stove: tea and coffee, toast and sandwiches. The ever-boiling blackened kettle was already singing merrily. Whenever possible, the restaurant staff would sneak in here for a crafty cigarette or beverage.

The on-duty room service waiter was setting trays when Gertrude and Connie entered.

'Have you 'ote else yer can be doing?' Gertrude addressed him as she stripped off her coat to drape it across a chair.

The young man shook his head at her. 'I'm ahead of meself today, Cook. Just got to finish getting these trays ready then I'm all set for anyone ringing through their orders.'

'Meks a change for you to be in front, Bernie. What's up? Someone stuck a rocket up yer backside? Or more than likely the Cap'n gave yer a warning to pull yer socks up else yer for it. Well, yer might have thought you was going to sit here with yer feet up reading the paper while yer waited for the telephone to ring, but you ain't. You can finish off the trays later. For now give me a hand by getting all me stuff ready for me baking. It's me own helper's day off today, and me knowing Chef as I do, I doubt he's allocated anyone else to assist me. Don't look at me like that or I'll give you cause to regret it, young man. If any guests ring down for room service, I'll let you know. Now skedaddle, we want some privacy.'

'I really ought to be getting back myself, Cook,' said Connie, aware that the five minutes Captain Fosedyke had allocated her were almost over. 'We're short-staffed ourselves. Until the Captain gets new staff in, we've two maids less than usual.'

'You sit yourself down,' Gertrude ordered as she put leaves in a huge brown tea pot and gathered crockery. 'Shock is a funny thing. Yer might feel fine but it can have a delayed reaction. And the Cap'n ain't fool enough to think the five minutes he said yer could take was long enough for you to make yer way down to the kitchen and drink a cuppa.'

A minute or so later Gertrude put a cup of tea in front of Connie and, armed with her own, sat down opposite her at the table. 'This could have done with a bit longer to mash but it's wet and warm. I've put a good measure of brown sugar in. Just the thing for shock is a cup of sweet tea.'

Gertrude took a sip of her own and eyed Connie keenly. 'You don't seem the flibberty-jibbet type who's easily shocked, gel. Not that I know you that well, if at all in fact, our paths hardly crossing 'cos of our different

19

lines of work. But you seem the sort to have her head screwed well on ter me. So . . . this shock yer've had . . . one of the male guests expose himself to yer, summat like that, was it? It has been heard of, yer know. A few years back, for instance. Priest it was an' all. 'Course, *he* reckoned it was all a mistake but I ain't so sure, and the poor chambermaid he flaunted himself in front of was adamant he was lying in wait for her. But then it was his side that was took, and the poor gel was dismissed and him let off without paying his bill. Summat odd about priests, if yer ask me, what with them vowing to abstain for life from *you know what*.' She put down her cup and folded her arms under her matronly bosom. 'Well, it ain't natural, is it? So . . . er . . . is that what happened to you? Guest exposed himself to yer, did he?'

Connie vehemently shook her head. 'No, Cook, nothing like that.' The Captain's warning to her not to tittle-tattle still rang in her ears and she felt it best to steer this woman off the subject. 'Have you worked at the Connaught a long time, Cook?'

'Long time! Oh, my dear, I've bin here that long I'm part of the fixtures and fittings. Started as a kitchen hand at the grand old age of thirteen.' Cradling her cup of tea, Gertrude leaned back in her chair, eyes glazing over distantly as memories of long ago surfaced. 'I was lucky enough to learn me trade under Ethel Stubbs. What that woman didn't know about baking wasn't worth knowing! Her pastry was as light as a feather and her cakes so delicate you had to tie them down for fear they'd float off. And her puddings were to die for. She had a kindly disposition too: I never heard her raise her voice in all the time I worked for her, and the patience of a saint. Just after I finished me training she went off to run a tea shop with her sister in Bournemouth. I expect she's long dead now, bless her. I was fortunate, though, to have the likes of Ethel teaching me my skills. Can't claim to have inherited her extraordinary talent but I could certainly give Mrs Beeton a run for her money.' Gertrude gave a sigh. 'Goodness me, it seems like a lifetime ago . . . well, it *was*, I suppose. Things were different then, let me tell yer. Well, the calibre of our guests at any rate. Royalty stayed here, yer know.'

'Royalty? Really?' Connie was impressed.

'It was before my time, mind, 'cos it was in the middle of the last century and I might be getting on a bit but I'm not *that* old. The then Prince of Wales stayed here overnight when he came to Leicester to launch a venture for Thomas Cook at the railway station – yer know, him who's the travel pioneer. He hails from Leicester,' she said proudly. ''Course, that was in the hotel's heyday. Oh, it was posh then, let me tell yer. Luxurious. Only the cream of society stayed here, could afford to, in fact, and the hotel employed enough staff to pander to their every whim. In those days you chambermaids would have been under the charge of the housekeeper. Good at her job but a right tartar she was. Nothing got past her and she ruled the cleaning staff with a rod of iron.

'We had a commissionaire then too. What a sight he was! Great big burly chap dressed in a braided coat who'd meet the guests and escort them up the steps and into the hotel. Some guests used to bring their own maids to help them dress for dinner. Oh, that's when yer saw all the finery! The men in their penguin suits, and women decked out in their best evening frocks weighed down by diamonds and pearls. While they were dining, a string quartet played chamber music in the restaurant. Yes, them were the days, ducky. Though I suppose the sort of guests we get now are a cut above some, they can't be classed as the top brass we had staying in those days ... far from it ... despite them acting as though they are. Nearest they have to servants these days is a daily, if they're lucky. Servants are a bygone thing, the war saw to that. Women want more out of life today than cleaning up other people's muck and fannying around after their every whim. And who can blame them?'

She pulled a face. 'Though it ain't just the guests who act above 'emselves, is it? Chef Stimpson carries on as though he owns the place and has a right to treat all his underlings as village idiots *and* get away with it. The Cap'n too won't compromise when it comes to adhering to hotel rules and regulations, trying to keep standards the same as they ever was despite the fact this place is slowly sinking into a decline. As for that head receptionist ... well, if she stuck her nose any higher in the air she'd get altitude sickness, and I pity the poor young girl that works for her as an assistant. I suspect she's not allowed to breathe unless Miss Harbin gives her the nod first.

'Mind you, it ain't like when I was young. Then yer were expected to put up with yer job no matter what, with a thick ear from yer folks should you even mention changing it. Smallest thing they don't agree with now and staff are off, whether they've got another job to go to or not. Years ago, tell people you worked in the hotel trade, especially at a place like the Connaught, and you was looked on with respect. Nowadays they look at yer like yer stupid and ask if you can't get anything better.

'I met my husband working here, God rest his soul. Head porter he was in the days when there were three porters to run after the guests and they had enough money to hand out decent tips. He died ten years back from a heart attack he got lugging a guest's trunk up the stairs when that dratted lift was out of order. Still, I suppose he passed away doing a job he loved, not that he got any recognition from the owner for his years of loyal service. Not even so much as a condolence card did I receive and we both worked here all our lives. Yet when Mrs Griffin herself passed on, all us staff were expected to pay our respects.

'Mind you, sad day for the Connaught Hotel was the one Roxanne Griffin died. She might have been a toff but a lovely woman she was too, the sort you could go up to and say "Howdy do?" and she'd say "Howdy do?" back. Good-looking, a real beauty, with a new baby daughter and a husband who looked like Rudolph Valentino and doted on her. Knew all us staff by name and always showed an interest in how we were getting on in our jobs. I got the feeling she really wanted to know we was happy in what we did. As far as I know Edwin Griffin hasn't been near this place since the day she died, nor the daughter. Wonder what she turned out like? Obviously far too stuck up to show her face in this rundown place.' Gertrude frowned thoughtfully. 'Forty years since her mam died . . . well, it must be. I was only in me twenties at the time. Good Lord, how time flies! It seems like yesterday.'

She looked wistful as she took a sip of her tea. 'My

Lawrence would be so sad to see how this place has been left to go to rack and ruin despite poor old Sid Makepeace doing his best to keep up with the repairs. Sid tries his best, but he's only an odd job man when all's said and done. The Connaught should have been treated to a face lift years ago to stay in competition with the likes of the Grand and the Bell. Mind you, neither of them is what it used to be either, what with two world wars causing havoc in more ways than one, but they're still a damned sight more upmarket than this place is now.'

'I must admit the Connaught is a bit old-fashioned,' Connie agreed. 'But it has got character.'

Gertrude looked bemused. 'Has it?'

'Oh, I think so, most definitely. It's a beautiful building and these high ornate ceilings are really stunning. That sweeping staircase too ... well, I can just imagine all those dressed up ladies gliding down it in the past. The furnishings and décor might be showing their age now but you can still tell they were top quality when new.'

Gertrude was looking at Connie agog. 'I never knew you young 'uns these days took much notice of things like that.'

Connie smiled. 'Think all that catches our eye is a handsome face?'

'Well, that's all that caught *my* eye when I was your age,' Gertrude laughed. 'Actually, I was married by then with a baby on the way. Why aren't you?' she asked bluntly.

'Because I've not found the right one yet, Cook.'

'Oh, I've no doubt yer will, lovey, an attractive girl like you.'

'I'm no beauty, Cook. I ain't so blind as not to know that, even though my mam keeps telling me I am. My nose is too big, my mouth's too wide and my eyes are too far apart. *And* I'm big-boned. I'm what the Scots would call a "bonny lassie".'

Gertrude put down her cup and looked at her hard. 'Well, yes, now yer come to mention it, you have got a big nose, haven't yer? Anyway, yer might be big-boned, but them bones of yours are nicely covered. On the whole men like a woman who's got some meat on her, gives them something to cuddle up to. My Lawrence did. He used to tell me that my bosoms were like two soft cushions. Well, a man can't tell a skinny woman that, can he? There's a nice lad waiting for you, my girl, and he's just around the corner, you mark my words.'

Connie laughed. 'Well, if he is then he'd better have something more about him than knowing what position Leicester City is in the Football League, and keeping his eye on the clock for when the pubs open.'

Gertrude chuckled. 'There's about a million to one chance of that, I'd say.' She looked at Connie, impressed. 'Well, you're certainly a girl who knows what she wants. It does me heart good to meet a young-ster not hell-bent on snapping up the first man who gives her the wink. I've really enjoyed talking to you.'

She leaned forward and fixed Connie with her eyes. 'So . . . er . . . this shock that you . . .' She stopped her flow abruptly as a noise from outside reached her ears. 'That's a vehicle drawing up. Car by the sound of it. What's a car doing round the back?' she questioned, rising to look out of the window into the yard. 'Oh, I say, it's a hearse! What on earth . . .' She turned to look at Connie, a knowing expression filling her face. 'Oh, so that's what shook you, is it? Yer found one of the guests dead. That's it, ain't it? Well, no wonder you was shook up, gel, not every day yer comes across a body. Who was it?' she asked, a spark of excitement in her eyes as she waddled back to join Connie. 'What was the cause, d'yer know?'

'I'm sorry, Cook, Captain Fosedyke warned me not to talk about it. Oh, goodness, is that the time?' exclaimed Connie, catching sight of the clock on the wall. 'I've been here nearly twenty minutes,' she cried, jumping up. 'Oh, I hope Captain Fosedyke hasn't clocked how long I've been gone.'

'Stop worrying yerself, gel,' Gertrude scolded her. 'If he has, I'll back you up – say that you fainted. Finish yer tea, for goodness' sake. The old duffer is more than likely far too occupied trying to get the body out without any of the guests getting wind, in case they think we're responsible for the death in some way, to notice how long you've bin gone.'

Just then the door into the main kitchen swung open and Gordon Stimpson sauntered in. He looked at Gertrude, a sneer on his face. 'There's a meat wagon outside being loaded with the body of a guest and rumour has it it was one of your French fancies that choked him.'

Gertrude's face blackened. 'You nasty man! May God forgive you.'

Connie cringed and decided it was best to slip out now before she found herself in the middle of a battle zone.

CHAPTER THREE

Connie woke from her doze with a start. Pulling herself upright in bed, she stared across at Val who was stripping off her clothes. Smaller than Connie by a couple of inches and two dress sizes slimmer, twenty-two-year-old Valerie Bates was not what a man would deem beautiful but regardless was a good-looking woman, blessed with unblemished creamy-white skin and thick wavy flaxen hair. Sometimes she wore it up in a fashionable French pleat; other times pulled into an American-style ponytail which was all the rage at the moment; or else like it was now, resting loosely on her shoulders in what she called her 'sexy Diana Dors look'.

'Your gran any better?' Connie asked her.

Having hung up her red boat-necked, full-skirted dress on the flaking picture rail, Val was now sitting down on her own bed about to take off her seamed stockings. Without raising her head she responded, 'Yeah, thanks fer asking. She's out of danger now.'

Connie looked at her enquiringly. 'What exactly is wrong with your gran, Val?'

'Oh, yer know, old age,' she said evasively as she rolled her stockings into a ball tossing them on to their cluttered shared dressing table. Standing up, she pulled a shabby pink quilted dressing gown over her brassiere and panty girdle and sat down again, crossing her shapely legs. Taking a file from her handbag, she began to file her nails.

Watching her, Connie sighed as she eased herself back more comfortably against her lumpy pillow, the ancient springs of the single bed squeaking loudly as she did so. 'It's not true you've been with your gran today, is it, Val?'

Her room-mate lifted her head and looked across at Connie, a defiant glint in her eyes. 'So where *do* yer think I've been?'

'Dressed as you were? With a man friend.'

Val gave a nonchalant shrug, returning her attention to her nails. 'So what if I have?'

'Why didn't you just tell me the truth, Val, instead of making up a story?'

'And would you have swapped days off with me if I'd told you I was spending my time with a bloke?'

'Yes, I expect I would, as you usually do manage to fob me off with one of your cock-and-bull tales.'

Val raised her head and smiled across at her. 'Yer a good mate, Connie.'

She gave another deep sigh. 'I wonder if I am such a good friend, Val. I've caught a glimpse of the type of men you go for, and if I was such a good mate I'd do my best to stop you seeing them. They're old enough to be yer dad! What on earth do you see in that type when yer could get a nice man of yer own age to take you out?'

'Who I choose to go out with is me own business,'

her friend snapped. 'If yer so bothered then don't cover for me.'

'Oh, don't be like that, Val. I don't mind covering for you. It's just that . . .'

'Just what?'

'Well, I'm worried you're going to land yourself in serious trouble.'

'If I do get caught for being out after lock up then the worst I can get is the sack for breaking staff rules. That wouldn't be such a bad thing, it's a crummy job I've got here anyway.'

'I don't mean that kind of trouble, Val.'

'What kind of trouble do yer mean? Oh, *that* kind of trouble. Stop worrying, Connie, I can take care of meself.'

'Thousands of women have said the very same, Val, and look where they've landed.'

Val looked at her for a few moments and it seemed to Connie that she was on the verge of saying something, something important judging by the look on her face, but then she obviously changed her mind and just said offhandedly, 'I told yer, I can take care of meself.' Her face softened then and she gave Connie a winning smile. 'Come on, Con, don't let's fall out. Maybe if yer got yerself yer own fella you wouldn't have time to worry so much about mine. What about that head waiter? He's not a bad-looking chap.'

Connie gawped at her. 'He's got to be forty if he's a day! Are you trying to tell me that a much older man is the only type I could hope to land?'

'No, 'course I ain't, yer daft 'a'p'orth. Anyway, Mr Lofthouse might be fortyish but he's in good nick for his age.'

'I expect his wife thinks so too,' Connie said blandly.

'Oh, he's married, is he? I didn't know that. How do you?'

''Cos we have a chat sometimes when we cross paths in the staff room, mostly about his four kids. Three boys and a girl he's got, all under the age of ten. He's a devoted family man.'

'Oh, well, that's him crossed off me list then.'

'Oh, Val, you weren't . . .'

'About to make him one of my conquests?' she sharply interjected. 'If yer must know it was my list of possible men for *you* I was referring to.'

Connie's face twisted in a mixture of shock and hurt. 'I didn't realise that getting a man for me was a mission of yours. You make me feel like I'm incapable, one of those women with no chance unless her friends fix her up with a blind date.'

'Oh, don't be stupid, Con! It's just that since you dumped that barman . . . what was his name now? Brian . . . from the Rose and Crown on Loseby Lane, you've not been out with anyone else.'

'I didn't dump him, it was a mutual agreement as we found we didn't get on all that well. And besides, we hardly saw each other 'cos of the shifts we both work. Since then I've just not come across anyone who takes my fancy, that's all. Maybe having a boyfriend is not top of my priorities like it is for you, Val. Maybe making something of my life is.'

Val looked at her mockingly. 'Being a chambermaid is making something of your life, is it?'

'It's a means to an end, Val. I don't intend being a

chambermaid for much longer.'

Her friend gave a secretive smile. 'Nor do I.'

'Oh, and you think the types that you go out with are going to take you away from all this, do you?'

'Oh, yes, most definitely,' she said with conviction. Val decided she did not want to carry on with this conversation, fearing where it was heading. Connie wasn't the only one who had a plan for herself but Val was not proud of the way she was executing her own. Despite her outward couldn't-care-less attitude about what Connie and others thought of her choice in men, it was better than their knowing the real truth of what she was up to so she continued to let them think what they did. 'Not like you to have a nap in the afternoon,' she commented.

It was apparent to Connie that Val did not want to discuss her social life any further. 'It's been one hell of a day,' she filled her friend in, 'what with us being short-staffed ourselves and having to help out in the laundry room as Kathleen is laid up with a carbuncle on her bum. Apparently it's the size of a melon so until it bursts she'll be out of action. Then, to top it all, finding Mr Roberts like I did . . .'

'Finding Mr Roberts? What d'yer mean?'

'Thinking he'd vacated, I let myself into his room to clean it and found he'd passed away. Hours before, by the look of him.'

Val stared at her, horrified. 'Oh, my God, if I hadn't swapped days off with you it coulda bin me who found him. Was he murdered?' she asked excitedly.

Connie tutted disdainfully. 'Sorry to disappoint you but according to the doctor . . . well, not that I was told by him personally but rumour is going around it was a heart attack.'

Val tutted. 'Oh, I see. Wasn't Mr Roberts due to book out today anyway?'

Connie looked at her, puzzled. 'Er . . . yes, he was. Why?'

'Well, I just wondered if yer'd checked to see if he'd left out a tip for us chambermaids before yer raised the alarm.'

'Oh, Val, how could you?'

'I was only asking. He promised he'd see me right after I said I wouldn't report the fact he'd burned a hole in his sheet with a cigarette.' She sighed with disappointment. 'I was hoping for half a crown at least.'

'Well, he might have kept his promise if he hadn't died before he got the chance! But you shouldn't take for gospel what guests promise, Val. You know as well as I do they express their gratitude verbally for the extras we manage for them, strictly against hotel policy, but when it comes time to show their gratitude to us, nine times out of ten they conveniently forget. All last week, after being asked, I persuaded Bernie on room service to put an extra helping of toast on 106's breakfast tray, saying I'd split the large tip I was promised with him. And what did I find for my trouble when I entered the room after the guests had vacated but the dregs of a bottle of Evening in Paris and the remains of a bar of Camay, all covered in hairs? Bernie's got the hump with me, he thinks I'm holding out on him.'

Val scowled. 'Well, he should know better than to think you'd do something like that. I'll put him straight when I see him next, yer can count on that.'

'Val, there's enough animosity between us staff as it is without causing any more unnecessarily. Anyway, I'm quite capable of fighting my own battles.'

'I've no doubt you are but I ain't having that little shit spreading rumours that you ain't to be trusted, not when you're one of the most honest people I've ever met. Look at that time yer found that gold necklace behind the dressing table after those guests had left. You could have pocketed that and flogged it and no one would have been none the wiser, but you handed it over straight away to Fosedyke and he never even had the courtesy to commend you for yer honesty. Yer never got a thank you in any form from the woman who lost it, did yer?'

Connie shook her head. 'No, I never.'

'Huh! Us chambermaids are treated like muck, Connie. People click their fingers and expect us to do their bidding without a by your leave. Sooner I get out of this godforsaken hole the better, as far as I'm concerned.'

Connie eyed her questioningly. 'You're thinking of leaving then?'

Val rose and grabbed up her toiletry bag and threadbare towel. 'Not today, but sooner rather than later. You'll be the first to know when I do decide to give me notice.' She flashed a glance at the tin clock on the floor beside her bed. 'I'd better get a move on or I'll be late,' she said, heading towards the door.

'You're off out again? But you've only just got in.'

As she pulled open the door, Val turned and glared. 'It *is* me day off, Con, so of course I'm off out. I've a date,' she said, disappearing off to the bathroom.

Was this an arrangement with the same man she'd been with today or someone else? Connie wondered as she eased herself off the bed. Other matters filled her mind then. It was time for her to go and get her evening dinner in the staff room, then straight after that begin the evening round of turning down the beds and answering guests' requirements before they retired for the night. Being a chambermaid was a laborious and boring job for the most part, and those who did it certainly had to work hard for every penny of their wage.

CHAPTER FOUR

Irene Monroe's homely face lit up in pure delight on spotting her elder daughter walk through the back door the next afternoon.

Number 44 Wykes Road was one of four prefabricated single-storey dwellings at the end of a path which branched off Aikman Avenue, a suburb of Leicester where similar two- and three-bedroomed properties had been temporarily erected to accommodate families moved out of city-centre slum terraces being cleared by the council. The small community was approximately three miles from the centre of Leicester, situated at the top of a hill on the edge of New Parks Estate, a far larger council development of several thousand brick-and-steel-fronted family homes built in the early-50s. It was understood that the prefabs' tenants would in due course move into houses becoming empty on the estate. Their prefabricated dwellings were not expected to last more than five years or so.

Each prefab, or Nissen hut as the locals nicknamed them, boasted a bathroom with hot and cold running water, and a kitchen with electric cooker and bow-fronted Frigidaire, all included in the rent. Luxury indeed considering that most residents had previously had to make do with an antiquated range to heat their damp crumbling homes and cook all their food on, and a cold place in the larder would hopefully serve to keep food fresh – the summer months always proved to be the housewives' nightmare. The family scrub downs were weekly affairs held in a tin bath in front of the range, an exhausting operation since numerous pans of hot water were needed to replenish it constantly until each member had taken their turn.

Despite reservations about leaving the house they had lived in all their twenty-five years of married life and getting used to new surroundings, leaving behind old neighbours and becoming acquainted with new ones, the senior Monroes embraced the offer of these much-improved living conditions and made their supposedly temporary home as comfortable as their assortment of well-used furniture and slim supply of money allowed.

Despite his limited decorating skills, Connie's father Victor Monroe, a tall, well-built, kindly but no-nonsense sort of man in his late-forties, had made a reasonable job of wallpapering the living room and two bedrooms with inexpensive but tasteful floral paper. The bathroom and kitchen he'd painted in pale blue emulsion. His home-loving wife Irene had made the nets and curtains for all the windows on her temperamental Singer treadle from material bought off the market. She had chosen blue gingham for the kitchen to help brighten it, and with what was left over made a screen to hide the cleaning materials and household tools kept under the sink. Using the remainder of the blue paint,

Vic had spruced up two old kitchen cupboards bought cheaply from a second-hand shop on the Narborough Road in which to keep pots and pans and pre-packaged food.

'I was beginning to think yer wasn't coming today either,' Irene said, wiping her wet hands on the bottom of her faded blue apron. 'Well, yer here now so tek yer coat off, sit yerself down and I'll mash you a cuppa,' she continued, picking up the ever-boiling blackened kettle off the electric stove to the side of her.

Connie went up to her mother and, minding the hot kettle she was holding, gave her a kiss on her cheek. 'You did get my message, Mam?'

Irene nodded. 'Mrs Gill delivered it herself. 'Course then I couldn't get rid of her until after she'd downed three cups of tea and two slices of me fruit cake, *and* I had to listen to her rattle on about her poor son and the miserable life she believes he's living with his nasty wife and two brats of kids. I've met the wife and she's nothing of the sort, and the kids are the most polite you'll ever meet. I know for a fact it was the wife who insisted they had the telephone installed at her mother-in-law's to keep contact between them in case of emergencies. Mrs Gill just doesn't want to believe that her son's found happiness away from her apron strings. Mind you, letting Mother Gill go on while gobbling down tea and cake is the least I can do in exchange for passing your messages on to us. They feeding you proper at that hotel 'cos yer look thinner to me?' she asked, giving Connie a scrutinising glance.

She tutted. ''Course I'm eating properly, Mam. One good thing about working at the Connaught is they feed us staff well. We have three hot meals a day. You say the same thing every week.'

'I'm yer mother and I've a right to check that me little girl is being cared for proper. And yer look tired. They ain't working you too hard, are they?'

'Maybe a little at the moment, Mam, as we're short-staffed, but you have to muck in in situations like that in any job. And I was up early this morning as it was my turn to clean our room and I wanted to get me weekly bits and pieces in town before I caught the bus to come and see you all.' In truth taking her share of the room-cleaning was low on Val's list of priorities and inevitably she wheedled her way out of it by making some feeble excuse, leaving Connie no choice but to tackle it herself unless she wanted to live in what her mother would deem a pig sty. Amongst the many things Irene had taught Connie was the belief that no matter how short of money you were and how few possessions you owned, there was no excuse for slovenliness. Household soap and water were cheap enough and elbow grease was free.

Connie delved into her shopping bag and pulled out a brown paper bag which she handed to her mother, smiling brightly. 'I got you a present.'

'Oh, yer shouldn't, lovey,' Irene said scoldingly, although her eyes sparkled in delight as she accepted the bag. 'You don't earn that much yerself. Oh!' she declared, opening the bag and pulling out a gaily coloured rayon head scarf. 'Ain't that pretty? How did yer know I was in need of a new one?'

Connie grinned. 'Because you dropped enough hints when I was here last week.'

She grinned back. 'Nice to know me hints didn't fall on deaf ears, and I know it ain't Easter yet but it was more for a Christmas present I was hinting at. Thank you, lovey. Hopefully yer dad's taking me down the club on Sat'day night and I shall wear it then and let everyone know me daughter bought it for me. The moths have got at me other scarf I used for best. It's got so many holes a bag lady wouldn't be seen dead wearing it.'

'It's only off the market,' Connie said apologetically.

'Don't matter where it's from, ducky, it's the thought that counts. Now, a bit of cake with yer cuppa? But not if it's going to ruin yer for yer dinner. You are stopping for dinner? Only asking in case yer've a date or summat. Got yer favourite – steak and kidney pud, and bread pudding with lashings of custard for afters.'

''Course I'm staying for dinner. Sounds grand, Mam.' The meals the staff were provided with at the Connaught were plain but appetising, the portions adequate. They might be prepared by professionals but for Connie they could not compare to her mother's cooking. The meal-time atmosphere around the staff table at the Connaught depended on who was on what shift and their mood at the time but nine times out of ten they were friendly chatty occasions, albeit with much grumbling over management and staff conditions. For Connie, though, nothing was better than sitting down with her family around the dinner table, catching up with all their news while they ate. 'How's Dad?' she asked now.

Irene was busying herself making the tea. 'Same as usual, yer dad never changes, God bless him. Long as he's got me to come home to and a warm fire and a hot dinner on the table, he's a happy man. He was disappointed, though, when he walked in from work last night not to find you here.'

'But I did explain in my message that I was covering for Val who . . . er . . .' She felt it best to keep the truth from her mother, not wanting Irene to think the worst of the friend she had never actually met in person and who was not exactly the simple girl Connie had painted her to her mother. 'She had an urgent appointment.'

'Every other week yer seem to be swapping yer day off with yer room-mate for one reason or another,' Irene said, putting the tea things on the well-worn gate-legged kitchen table. 'Seems to me that gel takes advantage of you. You're far too kind for yer own good, Connie.' She stopped what she was doing and looked at her daughter meaningfully. 'We all look forward to yer weekly visits. It's bad enough you're living away from home and I don't see yer daily without having to go seven days without glimpse of yer. I don't know why yer have ter live in.'

'Oh, come on, Mam, we have this same conversation every week. You know why it's best that I do. I have to start at seven in the morning to deliver the breakfast trays to those guests who want to take it in their rooms, so if I moved back home I'd have to be up at five to catch the six o'clock bus to start work on time. In the evening I don't finish sometimes 'til well after nine, depending what's required of me, and by the time I got home it'd be time for bed.'

'Yes, but living in a draughty attic in a shared room . . . well, it's not exactly home from home, is it?'

'No, I grant you, but then nothing would be like your own home, would it, with your mam and dad looking after you?'

'That's it exactly.' Irene looked pleadingly at her daughter. 'I just wish you'd reconsider yer choice of job, Connie, and then yer could come home where yer belong.'

'But I like working at the hotel, Mam.'

She pulled a face. 'Can't see meself how yer like cleaning up after other people, 'specially not after some of the stories you've told me about the state some guests leave their rooms in and how they expect you to run ragged after them during their stay.'

'Mam, we're been through all this so many times. To please you and Dad, when I left school I tried factory and shop work and I didn't like it at all. You know I don't intend staying a chambermaid for the rest of my life. You know I've always dreamed of being a receptionist.' Connie was sensible enough to realise that such an aim was more than likely a fanciful one with her secondary modern education. It didn't hurt to dream, though.

Irene shook her head at her, mystified. 'Of all the jobs you could dream of doing, why you want to be a hotel receptionist beats me.'

Connie knew. Her mother might not remember the incident that had fuelled this longing within her but she could still picture it as vividly as though it had happened yesterday.

She'd been just a little girl at the time, five or maybe six, and in town shopping with her mother who'd been pushing her then baby sister Barbara in the huge

41

Silver Cross coach pram, piled at the bottom with their weekly shopping. While negotiating the crowds on Humberstone Gate after a visit to Lea's department store, Connie had somehow become separated from her mother outside the Bell Hotel. Suddenly finding herself alone amongst a crowd of strangers, fear had consumed her and she had started to howl in distress. Next thing she knew the kindly face of an elderly man – whom she now knew to have been the commissionaire – was trying to soothe her, explaining he would take her somewhere safe while he looked for her mummy. Taking her hand, he guided her into the hotel, leaving her there in the care of one of the receptionists.

After also doing her best to console her, the pretty young woman, smart in her receptionist's attire, sat Connie comfortably in the guests' lounge in a deep-seated chair that seemed to dwarf her. As she took in her surroundings her terror at being separated from her mother was quickly forgotten as the comings and goings in the busy hotel foyer, the whole exciting new ambience, began to fascinate her. The richness of the décor, plushness of the furnishings, the sheer opulence of the guests in comparison to the shabbier world that Connie belonged to, made the little girl feel like she'd entered a fairy story, one she didn't want to leave. Thankfully, due to the endeavours of the commissionaire, mother and daughter were tearfully reunited before too long. Despite her years, it was one experience that young Connie never forgot. She knew from very early on that when the time came for her to earn her living, the hotel trade was what she would choose.

When the time did arrive, neither of her parents could understand why their eldest daughter would voluntarily choose to be what they saw as nothing more than a skivvy. Despite Connie's constantly reminding them it would only be for a short while until she'd proved her worth and was singled out for advancement by the management, they begged her to reconsider and give what they saw as more worthwhile occupations a trial. Despite knowing her beloved parents' motives were of the very best, the time Connie spent toiling in a shop and then in several departments on a factory floor, was purgatory to her. Still harbouring deep longings to follow her own dream, she was mortally relieved when they finally realised how unhappy she was and admitted they'd made a mistake in persuading her to go against her own instincts.

'You know I don't plan to be a chambermaid for ever, Mam,' Connie said now.

Her mother flashed her a dubious look. 'Depends how long you see as for ever, Connie. You've bin one now for two years. Yer family know you're destined for greatness, but your bosses at that hotel don't seem to have spotted your potential yet.

'Look, lovey, when our children came along, me and yer dad both vowed we wouldn't stifle either of yer, would allow yer to make yer own way in the world . . . unlike us who really had no choice but to follow our parents' wishes, whether we wanted to or not. But me and yer dad recognised that the times are changing and we needed to change with 'em. We haven't always succeeded in just sitting back and letting you and Babsy get on with it. Well, yer can't always. Parents are s'posed to guide and protect as well as let their children develop their own characters. We both know you tried those other jobs to please us, Connie, and we both know how unhappy you was. We couldn't let that continue so we encouraged yer to go after what you wanted.

'It's plain to both me and yer dad that you are happy in what yer doing now, but . . . well, it seems to us that despite you having ambitions, they ain't never going to come to fruition if things carry on the way they are. I mean, the hotel must be happy with yer work or yer'd have heard, but stands to reason to me that they ain't just going to take you off that job and risk putting someone else in yer place that ain't so competent, are they?'

Connie stared at her agog. She hadn't thought of that. She'd laboured hard over the past two years, done everything expected of her and more, in the hope of being singled out for advancement, to no avail so far. But she couldn't quite see what her mother was getting at.

'Do you mean I shouldn't do such a good job then and they'll notice me that way?'

Irene vigorously shook her head. 'No, not at all. They'd sack you then, wouldn't they? What I mean is, maybe it's time you told them that you're keen to improve your position and if they ain't keen to encourage you, then you'll go to another hotel that will.'

'Oh, I see,' Connie said thoughtfully. 'Blackmail, you mean?'

Her mother shrugged and gave a chuckle. 'When

yer put it like that, I suppose it is, gel. You won't be the first to try bettering their position by that means and I doubt you'll be the last. You've just told me yerself the Connaught is short-staffed, and if that fusspot of a manager is worth his salt then I doubt he'll want to lose any more by not allowing his workers the opportunity to better themselves. The least they can do is give you a try and, if you don't work out, demote you back to chambermaiding. Worse thing that can happen as far as you're concerned is that you have to start again somewhere else, but then maybe another hotel won't be so short-sighted and keep you a chambermaid for so long.'

Connie didn't like the thought of starting elsewhere. She had been overwhelmed to be offered chambermaids' positions at several respected Leicester hotels on first applying for the work. But for Connie there had been no agonising as to which to take. In the prevailing trend for modernisation many traditions were being lost, especially in the hotel trade, but not at the Connaught which despite its slow decline over the years due to the owner's lack of investment still insisted its methods of operation and commitment to its guests' welfare were the same it had prided itself on when first opening its doors over a hundred years before. Connie wanted to learn the hospitality trade inside out, no corners cut, and felt she'd be best served there. Despite experiencing its rigid staff rules and regulations for the last two years, some so antiquated now they were laughable, she had not changed her mind. Trouble was, though, she hadn't really told her parents just how formidable Captain Fosedyke was. He wasn't exactly the most approachable boss but always busy, rushing around here and there, and catching him with some spare time in which to discuss her prospects would be hard. Her mother's advice was sound, though. It didn't appear Connie was being noticed like she hoped and needed to be, and she could not risk being continuously overlooked.

'You're right, Mam, I need to let Captain Fosedyke know I want to better myself or he might just think I'm happy staying as I am.' She gave a deep sigh and added distractedly, 'In a way I did try yesterday morning when I found Mr Roberts's body, but the Captain dismissed my help out of hand.'

Irene gawped at her. 'Body? You found a guest's body? God love us and preserve us!' she exclaimed.

Connie flashed her a guilty look. 'I wasn't going to tell you because I know you worry about me, Mam. It was yesterday. It wasn't very nice, awful in fact, but . . . well, it's one of the hazards of the job.'

'I don't know how you can make so light of it. I would have screamed blue murder and run a mile if I'd have been in your place.' Her mother wagged a warning finger. 'You know as well as I do it's best not to mention one word of this to your dad or he'll have a dicky fit and have you out of that hotel whether you like it or not.'

Connie knew her mother had highly exaggerated her own probable response to discovering such a thing. Just like Connie, she'd have pushed her own revulsion aside, confirmed the situation, then raised the alarm with the proper authority. Her father, though, would do exactly as her mother had predicted. He'd instinctively want to shield and protect his daughter and Connie didn't want him making her look weak and helpless. 'I'll keep my lips pressed tight,' she told her mother. 'How's my little sister?'

Irene gave a disdainful click of her tongue as she put the tea pot and cups on the table along with a plate containing the remains of a fruit cake and a knife to cut it with then sat down, motioning Connie to do likewise. 'That sister of yours is acting the devil's child at the moment.'

'Babsy is?' Connie said, shocked. 'What has she done?' she asked worriedly as she pulled a chair out at the table and sat down opposite her mother.

'It's not what she's done, it's what she wants to do,' Irene said, sighing heavily. 'She thinks she should be allowed to come and go as she pleases without me and yer dad asking where she's going or who with. She moans that all we do is bombard her with questions we've no right to ask. Oh, I've forgotten the sugar. Will you get it, lovey? The basin might need filling up. The bag is where I usually keep it, at the back of the bag of self-raising in the cupboard.'

Connie fulfilled her mother's request and sat down again, putting a spoonful of sugar in the cup Irene passed across to her and stirring it. 'I never felt you blasted me with questions, Mam, I wonder why Babsy does?' she asked thoughtfully.

'We never had to ask you anything, you always volunteered the information. Popping round to Della's or Rita's or whoever it was you was going to spend time with, and you'd be back at the time we'd set you, which me and yer dad felt was reasonable for a gel your age. You never was late, even when yer went to the youth club or a dance. Ten o'clock is late enough for a girl of Babsy's age when she's to get up fer work in the morning, don't you agree, Connie? And ten-thirty at the weekend.'

Connie nodded.

Irene gave a despondent sigh. 'You had such a nice group of friends and so did our Babsy, 'til we moved around here. Now she's got herself involved with a family that live down the bottom near the Co-op, and a right rum lot they are, if yer ask me. Three kids, two girls around our Babsy's age and a lad a little older. All allowed to come and go as they please. What the dad does for a living I've no idea as he always seems to be at home but the mother works in the Co-op and a right loud mouth she is. Never looks clean to me. She's upset several of the customers by her rudeness. What they were thinking of when they took her on, I can't imagine.

'But it's Babsy's friendship with the offspring that bothers me and yer dad. She's changed since she started hanging around with them. She used to be such a lovely girl, always polite and obliging, a credit to us. But now . . . well, she's abandoned all her old friends and is downright nasty to me at times. If yer dad heard how she speaks to me sometimes then he'd . . . well, yer dad's never raised his hand to either of his daughters, but I couldn't trust him not to if he caught our Babsy saying some of the things she does to me.

'I've tried talking to her, tried to make her see that she's lowering herself associating with those Lowdens, but she won't listen to me. Tells me she's old enough

48

to make her own friends and to stop interfering. I would never have dared speak to my parents in such a way. Your gran would have knocked me to Kingdom Come if I'd dared to back-answer her. I do miss yer gran in many ways but especially at times like these. Yer dad's mam too. They both had a way with 'em. They'd have taken their granddaughter to task and found out why she felt she could behave in this way, and they'd have soon put her straight.'

Connie was staring at her mother, horrified. 'I can't believe our Babsy is behaving like this. As you say, it's not like her.' She gave a mystified shake of her head. 'Er . . . do you think it would do any good me having a word with her, Mam? Try and find out what's going on with her?'

Irene gave a grateful smile. 'She might listen to her older sister. She's always looked up to you, Connie.'

They chatted for a while longer, discussing what had happened over the intervening week since they had last seen each other.

'Oh, my goodness, is that the time?' Irene said later, looking at the kitchen clock and pushing back her chair. 'I'd best get the dinner on the go.'

Having helped her mother prepare some vegetables, Connie was setting the table when the back door opened and her sister appeared. Babsy was an extremely pretty, slim young woman of seventeen with a mane of blonde hair which she wore in a ponytail while working at her job as a trainee overlocker at the Richard Roberts factory on the Fosse Road. Under her work gabardine coat she was wearing a pink-flowered full skirt and fitted short red cardigan with embroidered flowers down the front, flat pump-style shoes and white bobby socks – her imitation of an American teenager she'd seen in one of her favourite film magazines.

'Hello, lovey,' said her mother, smiling a welcome at her. 'Dinner won't be long. Steak and kidney pud, your favourite.'

'It's Connie's favourite, not mine, as you well know,' said Babsy, flashing a scowl over at her sister. 'I don't want any, I'm not hungry,' she announced as she crossed the kitchen to go to her bedroom.

''Course yer hungry,' remonstrated Irene. 'Yer a growing girl.'

Babsy turned and looked back at her mother. 'Maybe I don't want to grow any more and end up fat like Connie.'

This was most unexpected. Despite the age gap of nearly six years Connie and Babsy had always got on well together, never really exchanging cross words, unlike many siblings who fought like cat and dog. This derogatory comment was so out of character it deeply shocked Connie.

'Yer sister is not fat,' snapped Irene. 'She's womanly, that's what she is. I'll have you know that one of your idols, Marilyn Monroe, is the same dress size as yer sister – though thankfully Connie hasn't such a big chest to flaunt.'

Babsy gave a nonchalant shrug. 'I said, I'm not hungry and I don't want any dinner.'

With that she stormed from the kitchen and seconds later her bedroom door was heard to slam shut.

Irene looked helplessly at Connie. 'See what I mean? It's like overnight she's a different person. Like she went to bed the Babsy we all know and love and woke up a . . . well, you've just seen for yourself, our Connie.'

She hadn't liked what she'd witnessed. 'I'll go and have a chat with her.'

She found Babsy lying on her bed, arms folded under her head, staring up at the ceiling.

She looked across at Connie blankly. 'What do you want?'

Connie eyed her, taken aback. 'Do I need an excuse to come and talk to my sister?'

'I don't feel like talking,' she said dismissively.

Undeterred, Connie shut the door behind her and perched on the single bed opposite her sister's which was her own, all made up ready should she ever need it. The painstakingly hung pink rose-patterned wallpaper had mostly been covered by magazine pictures of popular young film and singing stars: James Dean, Marlon Brando, Montgomery Clift, Marilyn Monroe, Jayne Mansfield, Elizabeth Taylor, Elvis Presley, the Everly Brothers, to name a few, all gazed down at them.

'You've made the room look very snazzy,' Connie said, smiling approvingly and secretly wishing the management at the hotel allowed the live-in staff to do something similar as it would do much to improve the drabness of their rooms.

'Better than having to look at those old-fashioned roses,' her sister said offhandedly.

'Dad did his best to try and brighten up the room.'

'I suppose,' said Babsy flatly.

Connie looked at her for several long moments. Her sister's manner was most uncharacteristic. Normally

Babsy would be eagerly asking her questions about what had transpired during the week, being particularly interested in the comings and goings at the hotel, and in return would willingly impart to Connie all that had gone on with her.

'So . . . how are you?' Connie asked.

The answer was curt. 'You're not blind, are you?'

Connie was most taken aback. 'I'm sorry.'

'Oh, for God's sake, why ask such a stupid question? You can see for yourself, I'm fine. I'd be even better if people would just leave me alone.'

'People! I'm your sister, Babsy,' she snapped.

'Just because you're my sister it doesn't give you the right to interfere in my life.'

'Interfere!' Connie exclaimed. 'Asking after your welfare isn't interfering, Babsy, it's showing I care about you.' Her sister's offensive manner suddenly got the better of Connie and she snapped, 'What's the matter with you, for God's sake?'

The girl swung her legs off the bed and sat up, glaring at Connie. 'I'll tell you what's the matter with me. I'm fed up with everyone treating me like a kid, that's what.'

'And in what way do you feel you're treated like a child?'

She looked at Connie as though she was stupid. 'In what way am I not? I can't do anything without Mam and Dad wanting to know every detail of where I'm going and who with, then dictating what time I've to be in.'

'You don't think they want to know what you're up to because they care about you, and ask you to be in at a reasonable time because they want to sleep easy in their beds, knowing you're home safe.'

Her sister scowled at her angrily. 'Does no one care how stupid I'm being made to look in front of my friends?'

'Oh, so this is what all this is about, is it? Mam said you'd palled up with some kids down the road who are allowed to come and go as they please.'

'You've been discussing me?' she snapped accusingly 'And for God's sake, my name's Barbara, not Babsy. Babsy is so childish!'

'Mam's worried about you, Babsy – sorry, Barbara – so of course she's talked to me about you. I'm worried about you myself now. I mean, look at the mood you're in. You're not normally like this.'

'I thought at least you'd be on my side, Connie,' she hissed. 'I can see I was mistaken. Shut the door on your way out.'

Connie stared at her. 'I beg your pardon?'

'You heard me. This is my room. You don't live here any more, remember? Lucky you,' she added sardonically. 'I bet the real reason you chose to live in at the hotel was so you could do what you pleased, away from Mam and Dad's prying eyes.'

'You know very well that wasn't the case.'

'So you say. Now, if you don't mind, I've a headache.'

Connie sprang up from the bed and headed for the door, but before she departed said to her sister, 'One word of advice. If you want to be treated like an adult then you have to act like one.'

Her mother, who was checking boiling pans on the stove, turned to face her as she walked back in the kitchen, an expectant look on her face. 'Did you have a good chat?'

'We had a chat, Mam, but it could hardly be classed as good. She's got a bee in her bonnet all right. I agree with you that her so-called new friends are behind all this. I told her that she can't expect to be treated as an adult when she's acting so childishly. I'm sorry, Mam, I've probably made matters worse but I couldn't help myself.'

'Don't worry yerself, lovey. Hopefully she'll tire of them before long and go back to her normal self. Yer dad'll be in any time now, so fancy mashing the spuds for me?'

Vic beamed in delight to see Connie when he walked through the back door a few minutes later. 'Hello, me old ducky. I missed you yesterday.'

'I missed you too, Dad,' she said, laying down the fork she was using to mash the potatoes and going over to kiss his cheek. 'How was work?'

'Same as usual, ta, ducky.' Vic didn't particularly enjoy his job as a machine operator at the Premier Screw factory on the Woodgate. He found it laborious although he got on well with his workmates there and was well respected in return, but the wage he received helped him provide for his beloved family – not in the manner he would have liked to, but nevertheless the rent on their house was always paid promptly as were the bills, and there was a little left over, provided overtime was plentiful, to treat his wife to a night out once a week and to save for a week's holiday at the seaside each year now that his two girls were earning for themselves. Although he gave his wife due respect as his

54

life's partner, loved her dearly and admired the fact that she had opinions of her own, Vic nevertheless felt himself to be head of the household. 'Glad to get home to my ladies,' he said, and went over to peck his wife on the cheek. Then he looked appreciatively at the dinner she was putting out. 'Looks good and smells even better. Done us proud as usual.' He noticed the table had only been set for three. 'Who's not having any, Rene?' he asked his wife.

'Babsy says she's not hungry.'

'What does she mean, she's not hungry?'

'Well, maybe she's not, Vic,' Irene said by way of excusing her daughter's behaviour. 'I'll put her a plate up, maybe she'll fancy it later.'

'You will not,' he ordered. 'I'm getting a bit fed up with our Babsy's faddiness of late. Set yer sister a place,' he instructed Connie, and before Irene could stop him he'd left the room.

They both heard raised voices then moments later Vic returned with a sullen Babsy in tow. 'Now sit down,' he ordered her. 'If yer mother's bin good enough to cook yer dinner then you'll be good enough to eat it. You'll not leave this table until yer've finished every morsel. Let's the rest of us sit down and do justice to this good food.'

Despite Babsy's sullenness and blatant unwillingness to join in the conversation, the rest of the family enjoyed what they ate and chatted away happily.

As soon as she had finished what was on her plate, Babsy scraped back her chair and stood up.

'Where are you going? her father asked her.

'Out,' she replied to him frostily.

'That you're not. You've been out every night this week and it won't hurt you to stay in and enjoy the rest of the evening with yer sister. I can't remember the last time you offered to do the pots for your mother. You can do them tonight.'

Her face clouded over anxiously and she blurted, 'But I've arranged to meet . . . my friends. They'll be waiting for me.'

'I'll do the pots, Dad,' Connie offered.

'You will not. Today's your day off. I'm sure Babsy's friends will understand she'd family commitments when she sees them next.' He smiled at Connie. 'Maybe you'd like to mash me and yer mam a nice cup of tea while yer sister's doing the pots, then we can hear the rest of your news.'

The murderous look her sister gave their father before she began to clear the table was not lost on Connie.

'What a bleddy day I've had,' groaned Val as she burst into their room that night, flopping down on the bed.

Connie, who had arrived back from her visit with her family only minutes before and was in the process of taking off her clothes to ready herself for bed, stopped what she was doing and looked across at her. 'Just busy or something out the ordinary happen?' she asked, reminded vividly of the incident of the previous day and wondering if something equally awful had happened to Val.

'Huh! I don't know what's normal and what ain't about this place,' she grumbled, kicking off her shoes and lifting a foot to rub it vigorously. 'Me feet are killing me. The new arrival in 210 has had me fetching and carrying for her all afternoon. Mrs Cedric Wainwright, the old bat is called. She acts like she owns the place, the *Lady Duckmuck* sort. She's got a voice like a fog horn and her chest is so huge it's a wonder she can stand upright. She's up in town from the country for a shopping trip with her daughter for her wedding trousseau and if one thing weren't right with her room, nothing was. To top it all, there was a tiny black mark on the eiderdown, what it was I've no idea, just a mark which I'd defy anyone else to have noticed, but *she* did and had me changing the whole bed then the towels as she wanted to be sure they were fresh ones, wouldn't accept our word for it. After all that, she decided she didn't like the room anyway as it faced the front and she thought it would be too noisy as she was a light sleeper. She insisted she was moved across the corridor to a room facing the back. Lucky for her one was free. I was hoping there weren't any and she'd bugger off to another hotel.

'The old cow then had me changing all the bedding and towels in *that* room as well, and then in her mealy-mouthed daughter's room. What a bitch *she* is! She just stood silently by all the time her mother was booming out her orders with this sort of smug smirk on her face. It took me all my will-power not to smack it off, believe me. 'Cos of Lady Duckmuck's shenanigans I never got me break this afternoon so I couldn't have five minutes' shut eye before my shift started this evening. I've been on the go for fourteen hours straight and no special thanks, not that we menials ever expect management to notice all we do above and beyond the call of duty. Oh, roll on the time I can get out of this Godforsaken hole. It can't come quick enough for me.

'Anyway, had a good visit with yer folks? Did yer mam send any goodies back with yer?' asked Val, her eyes sparkling in anticipation.

Connie smiled. 'Yes, to both questions. There's a tin on my bed with the remains of the bread pudding we had tonight. Mam made an extra big one so there'd be plenty of leftovers.'

'Oh, goody,' said Val, licking her lips. 'The only good thing I have to say about the Connaught is that we get plenty to eat, but yer can't beat proper home cooking. Your mam's bread pudding is just the best.'

Connie smiled. 'I'll pass on your compliments when I see her next week.'

As Val moved aside and upturned objects on their shared dressing table in search of the knife they kept in their room for such occasions, she noticed Connie had grown quiet and turned her head to look across at her. 'What's up, Con?'

'Eh? Oh, nothing . . . well, actually, I was just thinking about my sister.' She gave a heavy sigh. 'She's not acting her normal self at the moment. Far from it, in fact. I don't think my dad is fully aware of just how badly she's behaving towards my mother. What's got into Babsy – oh, Barbara as she's insisting she's called now – I've no idea.'

Val had found the knife and was cutting a wedge of the bread pudding. 'In what way is she misbehaving?' she asked, taking a large bite. 'Oh, this is good,' she said appreciatively as she flopped down on her bed.

The huge piece of bread pudding Val had cut herself registered with Connie. 'I hope you've left some for me?'

She grinned. 'Stop worrying, yer mam sent enough to feed an army. You were telling me about yer sister?'

'Yes, I was. She's behaving in that *stop treating me like a kid* way. She's seventeen so she still *is* a kid, but seems to think that now she's at work and paying board she should be allowed to come and go as she pleases without Mam and Dad asking any questions. Interfering, she calls it.'

'Oh, I see. Sounds to me like that sister of yours needs to open her eyes and take a good look around to remind her just what she's got in her family. Some people don't realise how lucky they are.'

This brusque response had Connie looking at her friend quizzically and she noticed the strange expression on her room-mate's face, a look she could only describe as regretful. 'What do you mean by that, Val?'

'Eh? Oh, nothing,' she said dismissively as she took another bite of the pudding.

Connie frowned. Her instincts told her that something about her own concern for her sister had struck a raw nerve within Val, must have done to evoke such a display of emotion from her. Then suddenly something else struck her, something that in all the time she and Val had been sharing a room and working closely together had never struck her before. She went across and sat down beside her, looking at her in concern.

'In all the time I've known you, Val, you've never talked to me about your home life, not really you haven't. It's striking me now that whenever the subject of your family has come up, you've changed the subject. I never thought much of it at the time as some people don't talk about their families as much as I do mine, but now I'm wondering if there's a reason for you not doing that? You never visit them on your day off. Well, not so far as I know you don't.' She took a deep breath and despite not normally being the prying kind, asked, 'Is your home life not so good?'

Val stared at her for several long moments before exhaling loudly and throwing back her head. 'If yer must know, Connie,' she said, almost defiantly, 'I never had one.'

'Never had one? What do you mean?'

'I was brought up in a children's home.' She took the expression on Connie's face to be one of disgust and snapped, 'Now you can see why I never tell anyone about me background. You think I'm scum, don't you?'

Connie was appalled that Val could think such a thing of her. 'What! No, I don't think that of you at all. I'm just shocked by what you told me. I can't imagine what it must be like to grow up without your family around you.'

Val's face softened. Her voice lowered almost to a whisper as she said, 'Well, it ain't easy, let me tell you.'

'No, I expect not.'

Val let out a long despondent sigh. 'At least your sister knows where she comes from, who she takes after, her mam or her dad, and what other relatives she's got.'

'You mean, you don't?'

Val looked away, her face wreathed in a mixture of hurt, anger and bewilderment. 'I was found on the home's doorstep, Connie. Only hours old I was apparently, and no clue left to who'd abandoned me there. I was named after the woman who found me, a cleaner at the home, just arriving for the start of her shift.' She gave a sardonic laugh. 'Thank God she wasn't called Ermintrude or Griselda or summat equally as awful, eh, Connie?'

She smiled wanly. 'Valerie is a nice name. It suits you.' She looked at her room-mate enquiringly. 'What was it like in the home?'

Val shrugged. 'As children's homes go, I suppose it weren't bad. The people who ran it, the Wilkinsons, tried their best considering they had fifteen kids of varying ages to look after. They were strict but they didn't mistreat us, not like some who run homes do, so I suppose you could say I was lucky. We were fed good plain food and it filled us up. We'd shoes on our feet and clothes on our backs, mostly donated by well-intentioned locals, but you never got anything that fitted properly so we orphans always looked a proper jumble sale, stuck out like sore thumbs even though the other kids at school weren't that well dressed either. At Christmas the Wilkinsons always made sure we got a present. Never anything new, mind, again it was all donated and whatever we got usually had something a bit wrong with it. I suppose the people who donated the things thought it wouldn't matter as we were only orphan kids and should be grateful for anything. Mrs Wilkinson would make us a cake on our birthdays and we'd get jelly and blancmange for tea.'

She gave a sad sigh. 'But they never thought to give us kids a cuddle. All kids need a cuddle, don't they?'

she said wistfully. 'You learn to do without, though. I know it's pathetic but for years I used to fantasise that me mam was from a rich family and for some reason . . . I dunno what . . . she had to abandon me. But one day she'd come back and claim me and take me to live with her and I'd find out I'd lots of other family, grand-parents, uncles, aunts, cousins, all of whom would dote on me. Most of the kids had a similar fantasy and we'd talk about it to each other as though we really believed it was true. Deep down, though, we all knew the truth, that there was no fairy-tale ending ever going to happen for us.

'The worst thing about being brought up in a home is never feeling your mother's arms around yer and hearing her tell yer she loves you. I don't know what that feels like, Con, having a mother telling me she loves me. In the home your fellow orphans become your family. If you're lucky a special friend gives you cuddles when you need them and you do it for them in return.'

Stunned at her revelation, Connie was listening to her friend's tale with a lump forming in her throat. 'Did you have a special friend in the home, Val?' she asked softly.

Her face softened and she nodded. 'Her name was Beatrice. She came to the home when she was three, same age as me. Her gran had been raising her 'cos her mam had run off just after she was born and no one knew where she was. She had no idea who her father was. Her gran died and there was no one else who would take Beatrice in so she landed in the home. Ugly kid she was, thin as a stick. If that wasn't bad enough she'd got a lazy eye so wore glasses with a patch over one lens to try and correct it. Some of the other kids took the mickey out of her, plagued her something terrible. I felt sorry for her so took her under my wing. We grew really close, supported each other through all you go through while growing up with no family of your own around. Best day's work I ever did was taking pity on Beatrice.'

'What happened to her?' Connie gently probed.

'Same as what happens to all orphaned kids when they leave school. Turfed out of the home to fend for theirselves. Now yer know why I chose to do chambermaiding for a living, 'cos it offered accommodation with the job and three decent meals a day.' She glanced around the room. 'This place ain't much, Connie, but it's better than a damp, freezing bed-sitter or a tiny room in a house that's hardly big enough to swing a cat in, with a landlady that looks down her nose at yer as though yer should be grateful she's charging the earth for her rotten facilities and food that's no better than pig swill. Not saying all landladies are like that but most of the ones I met when I was a trainee in a factory before I landed this job certainly were.' She gave a sigh. 'Beatrice works as a . . . well, glorified dogsbody is all you can call it, for a professor and his wife who live in a big house in Humberstone. Us chambermaids aren't well thought of, Connie, but Beatrice's employers treat her like dirt. Expect her to be at their beck and call twenty-four hours a day. They think they've done her a favour, see, taking in an orphan girl. I expect they think she's with them for life, Beatrice not being exactly blessed in the looks department. And besides they hardly allow her any free time in which to pursue a relationship, so in truth what chance has she got anyway?' Val's face screwed up angrily 'Huh! Well, they have no idea that Beatrice and me vowed to look after each other always. Some day in the not-too-distant future her employers are going to get a shock.'

Connie frowned quizzically. 'Oh, how?'

'When I honour my vow to look after Beatrice and take her away from her life of slavery to give her the sort of life she deserves, that's how, Con.'

'How do you propose to do that, Val?'

Her lips curled into a secretive smile. 'I'm working on it.'

Connie wondered what she could possibly have planned by way of honouring her vow to look after her friend. She knew how much Val earned, being on the same wage herself, and even taking into account tips when they got them, after paying out for personal necessities and an occasional night out, not much was left over for saving.

'I've never told anyone at the Connaught me real background, Connie, not even Fosedyke when I applied for the job. Well, as far as I'm concerned, being raised in a home has no bearing on whether I make a good chambermaid or not. I never meant to tell you either – not that I didn't trust you or anything, you've been a good friend to me, Connie. It's just that I've had enough of people looking down on me all my life without purposely inviting more insults.'

Connie laid a reassuring hand on her arm. 'What you've just told me about yourself makes no differ-ence to our friendship. I feel very honoured that you've trusted me with it all, Val, and you have my word it will go no further than these four walls. What you've told me, though, does make me appreciate my family all the more.'

'Yeah, well, let's hope your sister realises what she's got too before she causes yer mam any more grief.' Val's face suddenly lit up as a thought struck her. 'Oh, by the way, a bit of good news. I heard on the grapevine that Captain Fosedyke has taken on three experienced chambermaids today, so that puts us back up to speed on the staff front which will make our lives a little easier. Now, I'm gonna have another piece of yer mam's bread pudding. You want a bit too before I eat it all?'

In bed that night Connie could not get Val's story out of her mind. How dreadful it must have been for her as a child, growing up without any knowledge whatsoever of her parents and having to survive without any parental affection, something she herself got so much of from her own parents that in truth, she took it for granted. How did Val cope each time she passed someone who remotely resembled her in the street? Did she wonder if they could possibly be the person responsible for her being in this world? It was a pity, she thought, that their shifts did not allow them to be off on the same day, then Connie could have taken Val home with her to introduce to her own family, give her a taste of proper home comforts. Her friend Beatrice too. Maybe if she managed to convince Captain Fosedyke to give her promotion she would be able to do just that. Her family would make them both welcome, she knew they would.

Her thoughts then focused on the fact that with the

coming of new staff now was as good a time as any to approach Captain Fosedyke about improving her job prospects. She hoped he would take her seriously but dreaded that he wouldn't. It was quite a while before Connie fell asleep.

CHAPTER FIVE

Mid-morning next day found Connie hesitating outside the hotel manager's office. She knew Captain Fosedyke was in there, had just physically jumped on hearing the telephone being banged down in its cradle. Was it normal for him to replace it in such a way or had something angered him? If the latter was the case then Connie feared she had not picked the right moment to approach him. But then, how would she ever know when was the right time and when wasn't? Her mother's warning that she could forever be overlooked if she did not bring attention to herself had her rapping purposefully on the door.

A few seconds passed during which Connie wondered whether her knock had been heard or not and she was on the verge of announcing her presence again when she heard a voice boom: 'Come.'

Hoping that the fact she was shaking was not apparent, she turned the knob on the solid wooden door and entered.

Captain Fosedyke was seated in a well-worn brown leather chair behind a highly polished mahogany desk which almost filled the small ante-room to the side of the main reception area in the hotel's foyer. On the right of the desk sat a black telephone, to the left a filing tray stacked with paperwork. Centred exactly with the Captain's chair was an ornate Victorian silver ink stand complete with fountain pen set. Squarely at the front of the desk was a brown leather-bound blotting pad. A tall, wide bookcase ran the length of the side wall, filled with files holding all the paperwork related to the running of the hotel, going back decades.

The whole office was as neat and tidy as the man occupying it. He was looking at Connie expectantly.

She clasped her hands in front of her. Despite having checked her appearance in the staff cloakroom mirror before she had come in, she worried now that something might be out of place and then his beady eyes would notice it and he'd reprimand her and that wouldn't get the interview off to a good start.

He gave an irritated sigh. 'I have a hotel to manage, Miss Monroe, what is it you want to see me for?' A look of trepidation filled his eyes as he added, 'Not discovered another deceased guest, I hope?'

'No, no, Captain Fosedyke. Everything is shipshape in my section. Well, not exactly, it never is, but the list of repairs that need doing I've already given to Sid . . . Mr Makepeace . . . to attend to. I . . . well, I hope you don't think I'm being impertinent but what I've come to see you about, Captain Fosedyke, is . . . well . . .' She gave a gulp. Come on, girl, she inwardly scolded herself. Spit it out before he throws you out. 'It's . . . it's about me getting on at the Connaught.'

He frowned at her, non-plussed. 'Getting on?'

'What I mean is . . .' Connie inwardly groaned. She was babbling, coming across like a blithering idiot, and if she carried on like this wouldn't blame Captain Fosedyke for seeing her as unsuitable for working on reception or anywhere else apart from the guests' rooms. She took another deep breath. 'Please don't get me wrong, Captain Fosedyke, I like being a chambermaid but it's not my intention to stay one.'

'I see.' He looked at her enquiringly. 'So what is your intention?'

Before she could answer there was a knock at the door and the assistant manager, Gerald Sopworth, entered. He flashed a superior glance at Connie then, completely ignoring her, addressed his boss. 'There's a representative from a company called the Snow Flake Laundry in reception. He'd like to see you about a quote for handling all our requirements. Shall I send him in?'

Connie did not think much of Gerald Sopworth and knew she wasn't on her own in her feelings. He'd been in his post a little over a month, having taken over from Henry Aldwinkle on his retirement after sixty-two years' service with the hotel, starting off as a porter and slowly advancing through the ranks to become second-in-command to the manager. Everyone had liked Henry Aldwinkle, a kindly patient man who had displayed great respect for all the staff regardless of their rank, his own detailed knowledge of the hotel trade making him appreciate just what each member of staff undertook in their labours to make the guests' stay at the Connaught a comfortable one. It sometimes proved extremely difficult due to some of their demands and expectations, and of course the staff were also hindered by the antiquated hotel rules they were obligated to adhere to. They were aware that lots of matters, some of them even sackable misdemeanours, were kept from Captain Fosedyke by Henry Aldwinkle in his efforts to foster a harmonious atmosphere between management and staff. All of them had been sorry to see him go, despite his being long past the normal retirement age and it being blatantly obvious to all that the elderly man had suffered extreme discomfort from severe arthritis for a number of years.

Gerald Sopworth was nothing like Henry in any way. The thin, fair-haired young man had a permanent look of scorn in his pale grey eyes, especially when dealing with staff in Connie's lowly position. Whenever they approached him with a problem that needed managerial intervention they were always greeted with a dismissive, 'Well, I'm sure you can deal with it if you try.' According to staff gossip, he'd been assistant manager at a hotel up north somewhere before joining the Connaught, but on his performance up to now it seemed to them all that he appeared to know very little about the proper running of a hotel. The staff were very wary of him, careful what they relayed back to him as it was generally felt he was the type that in their words 'arsehole creeped' to the boss, and was not to be trusted. His whole persona now as he stood before Captain Fosedyke's desk reminded Connie very much of the character Uriah Heep, portrayed in *David Copperfield*, which she'd read as a child.

Captain Fosedyke was looking at him in frustration.

'Sopworth, I can't be expected to drop everything every time a rep calls in on the off chance. Nine times out of ten they make elaborate promises they're well aware the company they represent has no chance of delivering in an effort to secure our business. The service we already get from the laundry company we've been using for years is more than satisfactory. The Connaught is not in the habit of dropping loyal business associates without damned good reason and I would have thought you would have learned that during the time you've been here.'

'Oh, I have, Captain Fosedyke,' he said, an unctuous edge to his manner. 'I am aware, though, that it is our duty to the proprietor to keep down the hotel's outgoings – without, of course, compromising the comfort of the guests. I thought you'd be interested in what this company might have to offer as a possible cost saving.'

'Oh, well, yes, that is very true. Er . . . I suppose it wouldn't hurt to ask the representative for a quote for me to consider. Make sure he's left in no doubt, though, what standards we expect and that we're not prepared to change suppliers unless he can prove his company's worth to us. Now, have you contacted Evans Lifts yet to ask them to send an engineer in to check out that noise coming from the lift? And have you checked on the new chambermaids to see how they're settling in? Did you speak to those guests, as I asked you, about the rumpus they were making in their room last night? It disturbed some of the other guests in adjoining rooms, the night porter reported to me this morning.'

Sopworth was bowing his head as he was backing out of the office. 'It's all in hand, Captain Fosedyke.'

It seemed to Connie that the manager gave the young man a look that said 'I just wish I could believe that' before he returned his attention to her and asked, 'Now where were we? Oh, yes, your job prospects. So just what was it you had in mind for yourself, Miss Monroe?'

Once again before Connie could respond they were interrupted. Sid Makepeace entered. He nodded a greeting at her before addressing the Captain.

'The sink in 152 needs a proper plumber's attention, Cap'n, it's hanging off the wall. I've done what I can to prop it up and turned the water off to that room. The chambermaids are clearing up, and a right bloody mess it is too! Seems to me the guest must have sat in the sink to bathe 'emself, the damage they caused.'

In other circumstances Connie would have laughed aloud at the vision Sid was conjuring up, but thankfully she managed to keep her mirth in check.

'The boiler's playing up again,' he continued. 'According to the chambermaid on the top floor, the guests there are complaining their rooms are freezing cold while the ones on the second floor are saying they're being roasted alive. That right, Connie?' he said, looking to her for confirmation.

She nodded.

'Whole antiquated system wants replacing, if yer ask me,' Sid said matter-of-factly. 'We've managed to keep it going by foul means rather than fair but there's only so much yer can do before the whole lot blows us all to Kingdom Come.'

Captain Fosedyke sighed heavily. 'Mmm, yes, well, I do appreciate that you've done an exceptional job in keeping it going, Makepeace, and I will broach this matter again to the owner's representative at our next meeting. In the meantime, I trust you'll work your usual miracle on it?'

'Yer can rely on me, Cap'n,' he said, giving a respectful salute. And leaning close he whispered to Connie just before he departed, 'The miracle being a few choice swear words and a good kick!'

Captain Fosedyke said to Connie, 'You were telling me . . .'

Before he could finish his sentence the head waiter appeared, a very worried expression on his face. He flashed a smile of greeting at Connie, then focused his full attention on the boss. 'Excuse me, Captain Fosedyke, but I've just been down to the wine cellar to fetch a bottle of the special reserve '39 to let it breathe in readiness for Major Brindle who's requested it be served at lunch today, and I'm very concerned to note that three bottles of the Château Pétrus appear to be missing. There were nineteen when I did a stock check yesterday and I know we've only served two since then. Now there are only fourteen bottles. As you know, all the orders for wine come through me so I know they haven't been sold.'

'You're saying they've been stolen?'

'I can't come up with any other explanation for their disappearance, Captain Fosedyke. This is the second time this month I've had to come to you on such a matter, and I can only draw the conclusion that someone is helping themselves, though who I can't fathom as, apart from the master cellar key which you hold, I'm the only one who carries a copy and I can't stress enough how careful I am with mine. Whoever it is is being very careful only to help themselves periodically. They're probably under the impression it goes unnoticed.'

Captain Fosedyke looked thoughtful. 'I don't like to think of any of the staff pilfering. It puts everyone under suspicion, doesn't it, although in an establishment such as ours it does happen, unfortunately. It's catching them at it that's the problem. The master keys are kept in the safe so whoever it is must somehow have got a copy of the cellar key, though God knows how. There's nothing else for it but to get the lock on the cellar door changed and hope that will put a stop to these thefts. I'll get Sopworth on to it. Any other immediate worries?'

'I can see that you're busy, Captain Fosedyke, so nothing that won't keep.'

'Now you were saying?' the manager addressed Connie as the head waiter departed.

She hadn't fully appreciated before just how demanding the manager's job actually was. So many things could go wrong which needed immediate action to ensure the smooth running of the hotel. No wonder Captain Fosedyke came across as being abrupt when he was constantly bombarded with such problems as he had been during the five minutes she had waited in his office. Realising now just how hard pressed he was, she was grateful to him for finding the time to hear her out.

Taking a deep breath she said, 'Captain Fosedyke, I'd really like to be considered for a receptionist's position.' She couldn't tell whether the expression on his face at her announcement was one of shock that she should even consider herself suitable for such an important job or respect for the fact that she wanted to better herself. She was suddenly very worried it was the former and before he could respond to her had blurted, 'I know I haven't had any reception experience but I am very willing to learn, if you'd only give me the chance. I . . .'

She was interrupted by Amelia Harbin striding in then and, much to Connie's indignation, completely ignoring her presence.

'Captain Fosedyke, that imbecile of a girl who was taken on last week as my junior has just walked out without a by your leave. It is of no consequence in that she was quite unsuitable anyway, but the lack of consideration really rankles. I did express my reservations when you informed me of your decision to employ her, after hearing of her shop assistant's background. Well, I cannot imagine what type of shop girl she made as her manner towards our guests left much to be desired. She insisted on addressing them all as "ducky" despite my reminding her more times than I care to remember that guests are referred to as "sir" or "madam". And her arithmetical abilities when tallying the bills . . . well, from the number of mistakes I've had to rectify, I can only conclude she could not add up even the simplest of amounts. I really feel I should have a say in who we take on as my assistant. Someone who has at least been educated beyond the bare minimum and certainly not a young girl. Someone of maturity, who knows her place, is my recommendation.'

Hands clasped, Captain Fosedyke was looking at the head receptionist through narrowed eyes. It struck Connie then that she probably wasn't mistaken in thinking he had an intense dislike for this woman. She could only conclude that he too seemed momentarily to have forgotten her presence when he sighed heavily and to her shock said in an irritated tone, 'That's the third girl that's walked out in nearly so many weeks under your charge, Miss Harbin. In fact, since Wilhelmina Birch retired three years back the staff turnover in reception has outstripped that of every other department of the hotel.'

Amelia Harbin's face tightened so alarmingly her beaked nose seemed to grow several inches longer. 'What are you implying, Captain Fosedyke?' she demanded stonily.

'Just stating a fact, Miss Harbin.' Without giving her a chance to respond he looked at Connie and asked her, 'How are your arithmetical abilities, Miss Monroe?'

'Pardon? Oh, I can add up a list of figures accurately if that's what you're asking me, Captain Fosedyke. I got a prize at school for memorising my times tables.'

'If you had a queue of guests demanding your attention at the same time, how would you handle that situation?'

She was wondering why he was asking her these questions. 'Same way I do now, Captain Fosedyke. We chambermaids are constantly being badgered by guests asking us for one thing or another and we do what we can for them, as quick as we can. We can't always please them, of course, 'cos some of the guests push their luck if you understand me. But ... er ...' She was worried she was going to get herself and the other chambermaids in trouble but continued regardless. 'We do try and keep the guests happy, Captain Fosedyke, even though we know that sometimes we could get into trouble ourselves for doing it. Well, the aim is for our guests to enjoy their stay else they'll go to another hotel next time and that wouldn't do, would it?'

He was looking at her in surprise. 'No, it most certainly wouldn't.' Then he focused his attention on Amelia Harbin. 'It seems we've found you a replacement for your junior receptionist, Miss Harbin.'

Connie's heart thumped. Had she really heard Captain Fosedyke right? Had he just recommended her as the replacement for the receptionist who had walked out without her even having to beg to be given the opportunity?

Amelia Harbin stared at Connie in disgust. 'You're surely not serious, Captain Fosedyke? She's just a cleaner, hardly suitable to be considered for a prestigious position on reception.'

'Miss Monroe has expressed a keenness to improve her status, which is very commendable in her, don't you think? She certainly appears to possess the qualities you have just outlined in a receptionist apart from maturity, but we can't hold her age against her. We don't want to risk losing good staff to another hotel by our own shortsightedness in not giving those who wish it a chance of advancement. The least we can do is give Miss Monroe a trial, don't you agree, Miss Harbin?'

Amelia Harbin knew without doubt that she was being given no choice but to accept Connie. 'A trial it is then,' she snapped as she about turned and marched out.

As Captain Fosedyke then focused his attention back on Connie she could have sworn she saw a twinkle of amusement in his eyes. 'Report to Miss Harbin tomorrow morning at eight o'clock sharp. We'll review the situation in a month.'

'Oh, thank you, Captain Fosedyke,' she blurted, her face full of delight and excitement filling her. 'I'm so grateful to you. It's a dream come true to be given this chance, it really is. I won't let you down, I promise I won't.'

'Yes, well, run along now and attend to your duties until your shift finishes this evening.'

Connie was beside herself, couldn't comprehend her own good fortune or wait to tell Val her news. The moment she walked into their room during the break that afternoon she blurted it out to her.

Val stared at her agog. 'Bloody hell, Connie, from chambermaid to receptionist in one fell swoop! Talk about going up in the world ... I'm flabbergasted. You'll be too high and mighty even to talk to me now, let alone share a room with me.'

'Don't be daft, Val. And you're not the only one who's flabbergasted. I'm still having trouble taking it all in; I have to keep pinching myself to make sure I'm awake and not dreaming. At the most I hoped Captain Fosedyke would tell me he'd consider giving me a promotion at some stage in the future. I never dared hope for a second he'd hand it to me on a plate today. Oh, Val, I hardly slept last night for worry about picking my moment to tackle him but it appears I couldn't have timed it better, what with the receptionist walking out like she did.'

Val looked at her. 'Yeah, but it's *why* she walked out that troubles me. Have you stopped for a moment and thought how you're going to cope with working for that stuck-up old bat?'

'I want this job badly, Val. I know it's not going to be easy with her as my boss but I'm prepared to kowtow to her every whim if necessary to keep it. Miss Harbin made it very plain how she feels about me when Captain Fosedyke gave her no choice about offering me a trial, but if I can prove my worth then maybe she might come to see me differently.' Connie pulled a thoughtful face and said distractedly, 'It was him, though, who really surprised me.'

'Him?'

'Eh? Oh, Captain Fosedyke. I've always dreaded coming across him, always seen him as . . .'

'A bloody bully of a man?' Val cut in.

'Yes, that's it exactly. But, Val, if the number of problems landing in his lap during the short time I was in his office today is anything to go by, then no wonder he comes across as abrupt with all he has to deal with, keeping the hotel running smoothly.'

Val arched an eyebrow at her. 'You ain't showing sympathy for the management, are yer, Con? We all know they sit on their fat arses while we menials do the donkey work. And when praise is dished out it's them that get it not us. They're paid a damned sight more than us too.'

'All I'm saying, Val, is that after what I witnessed today I'm not so sure the management do have it as cushy as we all think, that's all.' Renewed excitement suddenly surged through her at her own sudden good fortune. 'Oh, Val, I can't wait 'til I tell my mam and dad about my new job, they'll be over the moon for me. This calls for a celebration. If you hadn't eaten all my mam's bread pudding we could have had a cup of tea and a slice of that to toast my success.'

Val winked at her. 'Oh, I think I can do better than tea and bread pudding on this auspicious occasion.'

Blankly, Connie watched as she went to the chest of drawers – the bottom two of the four being hers – to delve inside the last one. Concealed under her jumble of underwear, knitwear and other odds and ends, she triumphantly pulled out a quarter-bottle of gin.

'Where did you get that from?' Connie asked her.

Val grinned mischievously. 'Ask no questions and you'll be told no lies. Just get the glasses.'

Probably given to her as a present from one of her dubious boyfriends, thought Connie.

The glasses she was referring to were the ones that held their individual tubes of SR toothpaste and brushes. After rinsing them out in the communal staff bathroom further down the corridor, Connie sat down on her bed and took the glass holding the measure of gin Val handed her.

A thought struck Val then and she screwed up her face, very put out. 'I've just realised, your new job'll mean you won't be able to cover for me in the same way as yer have been doing or swap shifts with me.'

'No, I won't, will I?' Connie grinned at her. 'You'll just have to bribe one of the other chambermaids to do your dirty work. With your charm, Val, I doubt you'll have much trouble.'

She laughed as she raised her glass in the air. 'Here's

to you, Con. Good luck – and believe me, yer gonna need it.'

Connie was well aware that she had a lot to learn before becoming as adept at reception work as she wanted to become. Had absolutely no doubt Amelia Harbin was not going to make it easy for her. But she was adamant she was going to make a success of this job whatever was thrown at her. A new chapter in her life was beginning and she couldn't wait to get started.

CHAPTER SIX

Across town in an area of Leicester called Stoneygate where only the wealthy of the city could afford the enormous upkeep of the huge gabled houses with extensive grounds surrounding them, Miss Edelina Griffin stepped breezily into her father's study. Anyone meeting Edelina for the first time would never have guessed that this petite, strikingly attractive, smartly dressed woman had just entered her fortieth year. She could easily have been mistaken for at least a decade younger. Pulling black kid gloves over her manicured hands as she walked across the room, she was saying, 'I'm off, Father. Not sure what time I'll be back. By the time Phee and I have had lunch then I've quite a bit of shopping to do for our holiday next week, it'll probably be after six. I hope you enjoy your game of golf with Uncle Harvey today.' She added, smiling, 'I'm sure you'll beat him, you usually do.'

Edwin Griffin, a tall, well-made man with a shock of thick greying hair, still remarkably handsome despite his sixty-six years, was seated in a comfortable leather chair behind his big, highly polished mahogany desk. Two walls of his study were lined with shelves filled with an assortment of books ranging from the classics of English literature – which Edwin, a great reader, had read several times over – to books about Ancient Egypt, a favourite topic of his. Across the room by the large Victorian fireplace were two brown leather wing-backed chairs, a small walnut side table standing beside each. The floor was carpeted in blue-patterned Axminster.

Edelina was at the side of him now. She leaned over to kiss his cheek affectionately. As her lips touched his skin she noted he was perspiring and straightened up to look at him enquiringly. The fact that he was staring at a letter clutched in his hand registered with her but not so strongly as the expression on his face. It looked like death.

Frowning deeply, she asked, 'Father, what's the matter?' When he did not respond she repeated her question in a louder tone. 'Daddy, what on earth is the matter?'

His head jerked. He looked at her blankly for several long moments before he finally uttered, 'I trusted him, Eddie. Trusted him completely. I've never had reason not to.' He snatched several sheets of paper off his desk, waving them frenziedly at her. 'Why has he done this to me? What was it he thought I'd done to him?'

She was staring at him, stupefied. 'Father, who are you talking about? Who's done what to you?'

Just then there was a tap on the door and Mabel Jones, the Griffins' middle-aged maid of all work, appeared. 'Mr Crankshaft has arrived, sir.'

To Eddie's stunned surprise Edwin dropped the papers he was holding and jumped up from his chair, crying hysterically, 'I can't see him. I can't face anyone.'

Then, like a man demented, he launched himself across to the window, flinging it open to clamber out. She heard him dropping heavily on to the flower bed below.

She stared after him, stunned, then mentally shaking herself, rushed to the window. As she reached it she saw her father racing across the sweeping well-tended lawns towards the old summer house which stood nestled in a copse of trees by the garden wall.

She was aware of someone entering the room. Looking perplexed, she spun round to see Harvey Crankshaft, her father's oldest friend, being shown in by the maid. The same age as Edwin, he was a portly, ruddy-featured, balding man dressed in plus fours and a tweed jacket over a white shirt.

His smile of greeting faded as the look on Eddie's face registered with him. 'Whatever is the matter, dear?' he asked, arriving to join her by the window.

'Oh, Uncle Harvey, it's Father,' she said, dazed. 'He's ... well ... I don't know what to make of what he's just told me. It's something to do with that letter and other papers on his desk he must have received in the post this morning. Now he's just done the strangest thing. When Mabel announced your arrival he started acting like a madman. Shouted that he didn't want to see you. Not just you – anyone. Then he leaped out of his chair, made straight for the window and jumped out of it, then ran across the lawn in the direction of the summer house.'

Harvey looked at her, astonished. 'Er ... er ... we'd better go and check on him.'

On entering the summer house Eddie was stunned

to see her father sitting on the floor, knees bent, arms folded around them, rocking backwards and forwards. He was moaning incoherently to himself.

Rushing across, she crouched down before him. 'Daddy! Oh, Daddy, what's wrong?' she cried. 'Please, please tell me,' she implored him.

She felt a hand on her shoulder and turned her head to see Harvey looking down at her, his face creased in worry.

'Best fetch the doctor, Eddie.'

Many hours later, Eddie was pacing the floor of the drawing room. At the sound of the door opening she immediately rushed across to greet Harvey.

'Uncle Harvey, the doctor says Father's suffering from a mental breakdown. It's awful, he doesn't seem to know me, just keeps mumbling to himself with this sort of wild look in his eyes. They have to do tests and things before they can decide the best treatment for him and can't tell me how long he'll take to recover, it all depends on how he responds apparently. They've told me I can't visit him until they feel he's up to seeing me . . . or anyone. What am I going to do, Uncle Harvey? I can't leave Father in that dreadful place. I can't, I can't,' she cried. 'I want him moved to a private sanitarium. Or we'll have him nursed here at home. Yes, that would be best. I'll get him brought home tomorrow. No, this evening. Now.'

Harvey looked pained as he took her arm. 'Oh, Edelina dear, I'm so sorry. Poor Edwin. But you can't bring him home. A mental breakdown isn't the sort of illness that can be treated other than by properly trained staff in a hospital. I'm sure before you know it they'll be saying you can visit, and soon you'll be bringing him home right as rain. He's in the best place. You must leave him where he is and let the doctors do their job. You need to keep strong yourself or you'll be no good to your father.'

Her shoulders slumped despairingly and she ran a weary hand over her face. 'You're right, I know you are. The staff at the hospital were very kind. They asked me if I'd any idea what had caused his brainstorm. I had to tell them I didn't know.' Bewildered eyes fixed themselves on him. 'Have you any idea?'

His face grave, Harvey led her across to one of the armchairs by the Victorian fireplace. Tasteful china ornaments, vases of dried flower arrangements and several silver-framed photographs of family ancestors adorned its mantel. Flames danced from the coal and logs stacked by the maid just before she had retired to her quarters for the night a while before when Edelina had told her she wasn't needed any more that evening. Mabel had already been informed by Eddie on her return from the hospital that her employer was ill, would be hospitalised for a while, but not given specific details. It was obvious though that the woman was aware the situation was far more serious than Eddie was revealing.

Having seated her in an armchair, despite her troubled eyes still being riveted on him awaiting his response, Harvey went across to the walnut drinks cabinet, pouring them each a large whisky into a crystal tumbler. After handing a glass to Eddie, he sat down in the armchair facing her.

His reluctance to speak was fuelling the terrible feeling of foreboding within Eddie.

Having taken a large draught of his drink, Harvey placed the glass on the occasional table to the side of him then leaned forward. He clasped his hands and said, 'I'm just a simple retired dentist, Edelina, many aspects of business are beyond me so I hope you'll forgive me when I say that after I began to realise the extent of what had been going on, well, it was beyond me to comprehend it fully so I called an accountant friend of mine to see what he could make of it.' He realised she was looking at him, bewildered. 'I'm sorry, my dear, I should explain that after you went off with Doctor Wingate to follow the ambulance to the hospital, I returned to Edwin's study to take a look at the letter you referred to. The one he was reading just before he . . . well, lost control of himself. I was baffled and confused by what it said.'

'Who was it from and what did it say?' Eddie urged. 'I never gave the letter another thought after we found Father like we did. Not until I got back a couple of hours ago and went to look at it and found you'd taken it with you, wherever it was you'd gone.'

'I'm sorry. I should have left word with your maid that I'd be back as soon as I could but, like you, I had my mind on other matters at the time.'

'Uncle Harvey, it's me who should be apologising to you. I haven't thanked you yet for helping me with all this. I wouldn't know what to do, where to start.'

'There is no need for thanks, my dear. Your father is my friend and therefore so are you. The letter was from your father's employee, Harold Stibley, and it said revenge had been a long time coming but it had been more than worth the wait. Now he, being your father, would know how it felt to have what was his stolen from him, his future in ruins.'

Eddie was gazing at him open-mouthed. 'What on earth does Stibley mean by that?'

Harvey gave a mystified shrug, raking a hand through his thinning hair. 'Well, to me it can only mean that in the past Harold Stibley has had an injustice done against him and obviously feels your father to be the one responsible for it.'

'Injustice? What injustice does that man feel my father has ever done him?' she cried.

'Obviously something bad enough to have caused Stibley to take forty years or thereabouts to wreak his vengeance.'

'I've never known my father do anything underhand against anyone.'

Harvey Crankshaft looked at her stolidly as his voice lowered. 'With due respect, Eddie, maybe neither of us knows your father as well as we think we do.'

She looked back at him, appalled. 'I know my father better than I know myself,' she cried with conviction. 'He would never intentionally do anything to cause grief to anyone else. This man Stibley has obviously mistaken him for someone else.' She suddenly eyed their old friend questioningly. 'Vengeance? You said Stibley had taken forty years to seek his vengeance. Just . . . just how has he taken it?'

Harvey clasped his hands and said, 'Enclosed with the letter Stibley sent to Edwin were bank statements which showed your father's personal and business accounts to be empty. Edelina, I hope you don't think it presumptuous of me but on your behalf I decided to pay Harold Stibley a visit to ask for an explanation. To be honest, I didn't expect to find him and I was proved right. I arrived at your father's office in town to find it all locked up but I persuaded the janitor with a ten shilling note to let me in. The office was neat and tidy as if Stibley had left for the night, ready to return in the morning. I had a poke around his desk and found a pile of unpaid bills in one of the drawers, your travel and hotel accommodation accounts for your month's stay in Egypt next week included, along with unpaid tax demands for quite substantial amounts. That's when I telephoned an accountant acquaintance of mine to ask if he would be so kind as to come over and take a look, to see what he could make of it all. In the circumstances, he agreed.'

Eddie was staring at him, frozen-faced. 'And?' she uttered.

'Well, I left him still going through everything to come and find out from you about Edwin, and to tell you what I was up to on your behalf. But from what my accountant acquaintance has unearthed already he's in no doubt that Stibley has been abusing your father's trust in him on a grand scale. He was just checking through everything again to be certain of his facts before coming here to explain it to you himself. I am so sorry to be the bearer of such bad news, Edelina.'

She stared at him trance-like as her mind raced wildly. She couldn't quite comprehend what Harvey was trying to tell her. She was unaware of the maid showing another man in until she realised Harvey was speaking to her.

'Edelina, this is Frank Whittle, my accountant acquaintance.'

Automatically she put down her glass of whisky untouched on the table to the side of her and accepted the hand that was thrust at her.

'I'm sorry we meet in such circumstances, Miss Griffin,' Frank Whittle said to her as he perched himself on the chintz-covered sofa, placing his briefcase on the floor beside him. He was a small man, wiry of stature, in his mid-sixties and smartly suited. He was looking at Eddie with sympathetic eyes. 'I very quickly formed a picture of what your father's employee had been up to. It was obvious Stibley wanted us to know exactly what he'd done. He was proud of his achievements and wished to be accredited with your father's ruination. He kept meticulous records of all his underhand transactions and left them to be found. I doubt *he* will be, though. Long gone abroad under an assumed name where no one can find him and living the high life there is my guess.

'Of course, it's my duty to inform the police of my findings on your father's behalf and I will do so first thing tomorrow. They'll need to interview Mr Griffin. As Mr Crankshaft has already informed me of his mental condition, I should let you know that until he is in a fit enough mental state they won't be able to take matters very far. As I said earlier, I fear Stibley is long gone and I think you should prepare yourself, Miss Griffin, to accept that there's little hope of recovering anything or taking proceedings against him. For him to get away with what he did, it's obvious to me your father unwittingly allowed him access to his personal business, and any investigation will probably conclude that was your father's responsibility.'

Harvey spoke up here. 'In fairness to Edwin I do know that when Stibley was first employed, Edwin had not long lost your mother, Edelina, and was in a terrible state. He could hardly bring himself to dress in the morning, let alone anything else. It was a terrible time, just terrible.' His eyes glazed, and he said distractedly, 'Your mother was a wonderful woman, very special, and her loss . . .'

Frank Whittle gave a discreet cough. 'I should really conclude my findings to Miss Griffin.'

Harvey looked at him, startled, and seemed to shake himself mentally. 'Oh . . . oh, yes, I apologise for interrupting.'

Whittle directed his words to Eddie who was sitting woodenly, her eyes blank. 'Stibley had been in your father's employ for about a year or so when he became aware of his employer's disinterest in the business. That's when he started wreaking his havoc. His first act was to get rid of the two junior clerks. I assume he convinced your father they were surplus to requirements as he was capable of running the office by himself. He then began skimming off small amounts from the rental income on the properties he managed on your father's behalf. I suspect his success there fuelled further bravado and he started helping himself to more. There were also rent increases made on the properties and I have a feeling Stibley put his own cut on top of what your father had agreed they should be raised by.

Also he was accounting for bogus repair work on the properties, some invoices for quite considerable sums. The more underhand dealings he got away with, the braver he got. He was making quite a tidy sum for himself. I should explain to you that Stibley kept two sets of accounts books. One showed the real picture, the other was for your father's eyes whenever he requested to see them, with doctored figures.

'About twenty years ago it seems your father, whether on advice or having decided it himself, started selling off properties and investing the money in various projects, mostly abroad, mines in South Africa and such like, having been lured into doing so by promises of high returns on investments, far in excess of that his rentals here were bringing in. I should explain to help you understand why he and others like him chose to go this way. In the 1930s the country went through a dismal time and being a landlord was far less lucrative than it had been previously. Unemployment was rife and getting rent money out of destitute people nigh on impossible. To add to the burden, property prices plummeted. Fearing he could lose everything or being advised he could, whichever way it happened, like so many other people in your father's line of business he decided to diversify.

'Trouble was, Mr Griffin's money wasn't being invested in these companies despite his believing it was, nor was it making the healthy profits the set of accounts books Stibley was presenting him showed. Stibley was obviously making the money work for himself and only transferring monies into your father's personal bank accounts when Edwin himself requested it. He kept a certain amount in the business accounts in case your father checked the statements, but Edwin himself believed the bulk of his money was safely invested. In fact, the last of the properties he owned were disposed of only a few months ago. I found a portfolio of supposed company investment documents for varying sums of money, some quite large, that are in fact forgeries and not worth the paper they are printed on.

'Stibley cleverly manipulated your father, duping him into believing the business was prospering under his management when all the time he was slowly bleeding it dry. The only way he could have got away with as much as he did was also to become adept at forging your father's signature on documents and bank drafts. He probably passed himself off as your father in some instances, as he must have done to attain the hefty mortgage taken out against this house three months back. I presume Stibley got hold of the deeds from your father's solicitor on some pretext or other. I really don't wish to add to your burdens, Miss Griffin, but I cannot find any record of repayment of this loan either, though I did find several letters from the bank requesting an explanation for non-payment and threatening foreclosure if payments are not brought up to date.'

Eddie was still staring at him, stupefied. She was having trouble following his account of Stibley's dealings, inexperienced in business matters as she was, and was unable fully to comprehend the significance of it all. 'What does foreclosure mean exactly?' she asked him, bewildered.

'It means the bank will sell this house to the first buyer who offers enough to repay their debt in full.'

'What?' she cried, alarmed. 'Why? Why has Stibley done this to us?'

Harvey looked at her helplessly. 'Maybe Edwin will be able to shed light on the matter when he recovers his faculties.' He sighed heavily. 'I was hoping you'd find it wasn't as bad as we first feared, Whittle. This is just terrible . . . terrible. No wonder Edwin reacted like he did when he realised what Stibley had done to him. Oh, how I wish I was in a better financial position myself to help bail you out, but unfortunately my dental practice never earned me the wealth I hoped it would and what I have now is just enough to see me through my retirement, as long as I'm not too frivolous.' Something suddenly struck him and his face lit up. 'Of course! The hotel. Thank goodness Stibley wasn't able to get his hands on that.'

Deep hatred for a man she'd never even met swamped Eddie. 'What will become of us, Uncle Harvey?' she cried.

He sighed. 'Maybe the sale of the hotel will help clear the debts and leave you with something,' he suggested. 'What do you think, Whittle?'

He pulled a face. 'I assume you're talking about the hotel whose income was shown on the books? In the accurate set of accounts Stibley kept, it didn't seem to be making much of a profit but if a buyer could be found quickly, before the vultures descend, the sale could help salvage something out of this terrible situation. Depends how much it's worth. I happen to know a property valuer who'd give an opinion. I could also put out word in the right quarters that it's up for sale, which might bring forward a buyer. That's if you wish me to, Miss Griffin?'

'Seems your only option to me, Edelina. Edelina? Would you like Mr Whittle to do what he can for you in getting the hotel sold?' Harvey urged.

She was still trying to fathom what possible grievance Stibley could have had against her father to warrant taking such terrible revenge against him, and stared at him blindly. 'I'm sorry? Oh, yes, thank you. I'd appreciate anything you could do.' She wrung her hands tightly, her face contorting with rage. 'It isn't fair Stibley should get away with what he's done. Somebody *must* know him. Must know where he's gone. There must be something I can do. If my father is guilty of some misdemeanour against this man, then, yes, he deserved to be punished, but not to this extent.'

'Edelina, let the police take care of this. I'm sure when they're armed with the evidence Mr Whittle will furnish them with tomorrow, they'll do whatever they can to find him and bring him to book. But I wouldn't bank on achieving justice as I agree with Mr Whittle that Stibley's long gone, leaving no trace of his whereabouts. Let's face it, Edelina, he's been so clever in fleecing your father over the years he's obviously not stupid enough to stay around and risk being caught. And unfortunately you can't be of any help to the police as you had nothing to do with Edwin's business. You need to concentrate your efforts on anything that will spur him into getting better, my dear.'

Her shoulders sagged in despair. 'You're right, Uncle Harvey, I do need to concentrate on Father. Hopefully the hotel can be sold for a good price, and we might even have enough to pay off the debtors and the mortgage on the house.' Her face screwed up worriedly. 'What we're going to live on with no income coming in, I've no idea.' She suddenly looked at him enquiringly. 'What hotel are we talking about?'

He looked at her, surprised. 'Edwin never told you about it?'

She shook her head. 'Father's never mentioned a word about us owning a hotel. Not that he really discussed business with me. We always had an unspoken agreement. Father took care of the financial side of things while I took care of the home.' She paused and looked at him quizzically. 'I am ignorant in business matters but it does seem odd to me that as Stibley managed to get his hands on everything else, he failed to gain control of the hotel.'

'Because your father doesn't own the hotel. You do, Edelina.'

She was stunned. 'I do?'

'Your father signed it over to you when you were a small child, after your mother's death.'

Frank Whittle stood up. 'It's getting late, I hope you'll excuse me?'

She raised her eyes to him. 'Thank you so much for what you've done, Mr Whittle. I need to recompense you for your expertise and time today. I do have a small amount of cash as I was going shopping, but I don't carry much as I usually charge my purchases.'

He smiled at her kindly. 'I won't hear of payment. It's a rum business, a rum business indeed. Makes me feel ashamed of my profession when the unscrupulous few in trusted positions take advantage. Maybe my help today, and any I can give you in the future, will go in some way to restore your faith in human nature.' He looked at Harvey knowingly. 'I'll get things moving then?'

Harvey nodded.

Frank Whittle saw himself out.

Harvey then smiled at Edelina kindly. 'Now, I don't mean to press you, dear, but we'll need the deeds for the hotel if we're to proceed with the sale. Have you any idea where your father might have kept them?'

She could not take any more. Her mind had gone blank and she felt as if she was standing in the middle of a fog.

'Please don't think me rude, Uncle Harvey, but I'd like to be on my own now. I can't think straight any more. I can't deal with this tonight. Doctor Wingate gave me a sleeping draught should I need it after seeing how upset I was over Father. I certainly do need it after hearing all this! I want to sleep, just shut this all out. Hopefully I can think more clearly in the morning and be more able to deal with things then.'

He patted her hand affectionately. 'Yes, of course, my dear. I'm so sorry if you feel I was pressing you but I do want to do all I can for you. As your father's friend I feel it my duty to be of as much support to you as I can in his absence.'

'Thank you, Uncle Harvey. You can come tomorrow? Hopefully the hospital will have some good news for me when I telephone first thing. I pray they will. They might even tell me I can visit. In case they do, maybe we should make it the afternoon that you come?'

'I'll call about two,' he promised.

Immediately Harvey left, she tipped the sleeping draught into the glass of whisky he'd given her earlier, the possibly dangerous effects of doing so not registering with so much else on her mind. She'd hardly climbed into bed before the effects took hold and Eddie blacked into oblivion.

CHAPTER SEVEN

'Miss Rymmington-Smyth, Miss Griffin,' Mabel Jones announced, then departed.

A distracted Eddie looked up to see her friend Sophia gliding towards her in grey suede peep-toe court shoes. She was immaculately dressed as usual, looking stunning in a light wool grey fitted jacket and matching straight skirt, the hem of which ended just below her knees, the whole outfit showing off to perfection her very shapely figure. Her naturally ash blonde hair was cut fashionably short and expertly permed, waves framing her strikingly attractive face. She looked every inch the elegant, pampered, thirty-nine-year-old daughter of an affluent father and indulgent mother.

'I hope it's at least a death,' she was saying as she sat down gracefully on the leather chair before the desk, peeling kid leather gloves off her manicured hands and crossing long silk-stockinged legs. 'Even then, it really is unforgivable of you, Eddie darling, leaving me in the Grand without a word, and no message of explanation or apology when I got home either. You've never done that to me before.' Her face suddenly lit with a roguish smile. 'Mind you, a rather nice man did make himself acquainted with me and ended up buying me lunch. I've agreed to have dinner with him one evening when I can find time to fit him in. He's something in the city. A banker, I think. An executive certainly. Anything less and our dinner date will be the last time he takes me for an evening out: I do have my reputation to think of. So what did keep you from meeting me?' She paused long enough for her pink-lipsticked mouth to form a shocked 'O'. 'Gosh, you look positively dreadful, darling. What on earth is the matter? Someone has died, haven't they? Anyone I know well? Oh, I do hope not. I'm wearing a Norman Hartnell red gown for Lady Frear's charity ball for unfortunate children at the Bell Hotel on Saturday evening and I couldn't bear to have to abandon it for black. I don't suit black. Being so fair-skinned, it makes me look insipid. What are you wearing? Your jade? No, the blue. It brings out the colour of your eyes. You have such wonderful peacock blue eyes, darling. Or have you had a new gown made? It's not red, is it?'

'Oh, Phee, please shut up!' cried Eddie.

Her friend froze, stunned. 'Did you just tell me to shut up, Eddie?'

'Yes, I did. I am so sorry, I didn't mean to shout at you, and I certainly didn't intend to leave you waiting yesterday but . . . well, you see, the most dreadful thing has happened and I really don't know what to do. We're in such a terrible mess. I was hoping I'd have a clearer head this morning to get it all into perspective but the sleeping draught I took last night has left me still feeling dopey.'

'A dreadful thing has happened to you? What sort of dreadful thing, darling? And just what are we doing in your father's study? Mine won't allow the women of the house into his, not for anything. He says it's the only place he can escape women's nagging. Nagging indeed! My father can be so common sometimes, and he a senior judge in the Crown Court. You were going to tell me something, weren't you? Oh, yes, darling. So what is this dreadful thing that has happened?' She looked at her friend knowingly. 'You can't come to the ball for some reason? Oh, Eddie darling, don't tell me it's that? I've managed to get us seated at the table next to Lady Frear and her entourage.'

A good while later, Phee stared at her friend aghast. 'Goodness me, you poor dear. I've heard of these types of things happening but never to anyone I know. Mind you, come to think of it, I do remember one of Daddy's acquaintances blew his head off after losing everything in the 1930s crash. Anyway, I hope when they catch that despicable little man who has done this to you, he comes up before my father. Don't you worry, dear, I'll have a word in Daddy's ear and make sure the book is thrown at him and he rots in jail for the rest of his life. As for your poor father . . . well, I'm not surprised he's gone a little potty. It's understandable, isn't it, suddenly finding out you've been made such a fool of by an employee?

'Now don't worry that the hospital didn't have any good news this morning. I'm sure it won't be long before he starts to respond to treatment.' Phee's face puckered thoughtfully. 'Electric shock treatment is all the rage at the moment, isn't it, dear? Yes, I'm sure I heard Mummy telling one of her friends that another friend of hers was given it because she went a little queer after she discovered her husband was carrying on with their chauffeur. I'm sure once they've plugged your father in and given him a good dose of it, he'll be as good as new.

'I did have a relative once who was completely bananas. She should have been locked up, of course, but her family wouldn't hear of it. I suppose they thought if they turned a blind eye she would grow out of it. She never did, just got worse as she grew older. Most embarrassing for me when people realised I was related to her – only distant cousins, but still related. She used to do some very strange things, like wring birds' necks because she said their tweeting disturbed her, and dance naked down the street in broad day-light wearing bright red lipstick. The men loved it, of course, and would pray she would do it when they happened to be around. Their womenfolk weren't so pleased, let me tell you. She did have the most won-derful big breasts . . . like melons they were. I *did* envy her those. Of course I am quite happy with mine but it would be nice to have been blessed with a little more. Cecilia was only twenty-six when she killed herself. Drove her brother's car into a wall. One of those sporty things it was. The poor car was a write-off. Her brother must have been most upset as I understand he hadn't had it for long.'

She stretched her arm across the desk and patted Eddie's arm reassuringly. 'Look darling, don't worry about money. The bank will give you some if you ask them nicely. That's what banks are for, isn't it? Anyway you can just charge what you want like we normally do. And since we couldn't shop yesterday, are we going today? I've seen a lovely negligee in Marshall and Snelgrove I just must have.'

Eddie was looking at her friend, flabbergasted. She had known Sophia for ever it seemed, the girls having first met as pupils at the same exclusive school when they were eleven years of age. They had instantly hit it off and been close ever since. Sophia had been a loyal and trustworthy friend, and Eddie to her. Both women came from affluent backgrounds and had been coddled by their fathers. The trouble was that Phee had her own peculiar way of viewing life and handling situations and nothing ever seemed to burst her bubble, unlike Eddie who did possess a sensible side to her character.

'Phee, how on earth can you expect me to go shopping after what I've just told you? You were listening to me, weren't you?'

'Of course I was listening to you,' she snapped, hurt. 'But you've had a terrible shock, darling, and shopping is always guaranteed to cheer one up. It certainly managed to do that for me after my three divorces.' She opened her handbag, fishing inside for a gold cigarette case and matching Dunhill lighter. 'It's a pity I married all of them for their looks not their money or by now I'd be a wealthy woman in my own right, with huge settlements when the marriages ended and then I could have helped you out.' A suddenly triumphant expression filled her face. 'Oh, problem solved! I could ask Daddy for some money for you. He loves you, darling, you know that, and thinks so highly of your father. I know he'll want to help you out of your hole when I tell him about it.'

She took a cigarette out of the case she had now found and, after attaching a long black holder, lit it, blowing wisps of smoke into the air. Then she frowned. 'Oh, but then asking Daddy for money just now might not be such a good idea. He was rather grumbling the other day that Geraldine's school fees and incidentals were becoming extortionate. But then, as I said to him, if he doesn't want his granddaughter going to a local authority school, he has to stump up for her education. I can't, can I?'

She gave a disdainful click of her tongue. 'I would never tell him, of course, but I do fear Daddy's money is being totally wasted on Geraldine. Her latest announcement is that she's decided to become a top fashion model. She says she doesn't need to learn algebra to be one. She spends most of her time with her friend, closeted in her bedroom, both of them parading up and down with books on their heads. I caught them smoking too. "That will stunt your growth," I told Geraldine, which actually might be a good thing as she's five foot seven already and only fourteen. Her comment back to me was that it obviously hadn't stunted mine! I would never have spoken to my mother like that . . . still wouldn't dare to, actually. But I do fancy having a model for a daughter rather than one who's only into horses. Backside spreading and all that, and those girls do tend to resemble their beasts in time, don't you think, dear? Especially in the teeth department. Or maybe they just had big backsides and big teeth in the first place. Are we going shopping then?'

'Oh, Phee, for goodness' sake,' Eddie snapped,

shaking her head at her. 'I do love you dearly but sometimes I wonder . . .'

'Wonder what?'

She gave a heavy sigh. 'Oh, nothing.' She looked at Phee enquiringly. 'Where does your father keep deeds? I've had a look through Father's desk drawer, in fact that's what I was doing when you arrived, but I can't find anything deed-like at all.'

'Deeds? What sort of deeds?'

'Property deeds.'

Sophia shrugged. 'How would I know? Daddy deals with that kind of thing. I wouldn't know what a deed looked like. Oh, do you mean you are so hard up this house will have to be sold to pay off the debts that nasty little man left you with? Oh, Eddie, such a beautiful house too. Will you have to end up living with relatives? But you haven't got any relatives that I know of who you can park yourself on and beg for mercy. I would hate to have to go cap in hand to any of mine. I know they'd take great delight in making me skivvy for them, especially cousin Susan. She's always been jealous of my good looks, and quite openly so. She does so remind me of a hawk with her beady eyes and hooked nose. Or do I mean vulture? Anyway, I know she'd take great delight in seeing me as governess to her brats of children in order to pay my way.

'Do you regret not marrying Percy Steadman or Hilary Jamieson now, Eddie? They were both so taken with you, and both of them were loaded. I know it quite broke their hearts when you refused their proposals. You wouldn't be facing a problem now financially if you'd settled for either of them, would you? Oh, what about the safe?'

Eddie looked at her, non-plussed. 'Safe?'

'For the house deeds.'

'Of course! It's obvious I'm not thinking straight, that's the most obvious place. It's not the house deeds I'm after, though.' She added thoughtfully, 'Though I suppose I will need them if the hotel doesn't sell quickly, or at all even. I do hope Mr Whittle can help there. I'm so worried that at any minute a bailiff will call to throw us out if I can't settle the mortgage or at least pay some of it off immediately. And there are so many unpaid bills that Uncle Harvey found in Stibley's desk drawer. It's urgent I find those deeds.' She looked perplexed. 'Now where do you think my father keeps the safe key?' she said, pulling open the middle drawer of the desk and moving items aside in her urgent search.

'Try taped underneath. That's where Daddy keeps his. Mummy tipped me off. I'm not supposed to know, of course, but sometimes one has to help oneself to cash when one's father is being particularly stingy for no good reason.' Sophia laughed, an infectious sound. 'Mummy doesn't need to as she's plenty of her own with all my grandmother left her, but she still does it too. We've both been at it for years. He's never once twigged, though. Poor Father. What we put him through! He *is* rather a dear. Men are silly when it comes to finding places to hide things from wives, daughters, burglars even. They never think to ask their womenfolk who are experts at knowing where best to hide things they don't want found. Mummy has kept letters and tokens from her string of lovers hidden from Daddy over the years despite his constantly turning the house upside down in his efforts to have his suspicions confirmed. It would never cross his mind to look right under his nose at the small table to the side of his armchair where he places his glass of port every night after dinner. The top is hinged, you see, and lifts up to reveal a boxed-in area underneath. So handy for keeping all sorts of things. That's why Mummy bought it in the first place, and Daddy was with her when she did. She's always saying he never takes any notice of her and it does seem that sometimes she's right.' Phee smiled triumphantly when Eddie produced a long silver key she'd found taped under the drawer. 'See, I have got my uses.' Then she frowned as a thought struck her. 'Hotel? What hotel are you selling?'

'The one I apparently own.'

Sophia gazed at her in amazement. 'You own a hotel? Oh, Eddie, how thrilling. How come you own one? Why have you never told me about it, you dark horse, you?'

'I didn't know myself until last night when Uncle Harvey told me about it. According to him Father signed it over to me after my mother died. Father's never mentioned a word about it to me, though. It's not like we're not on good terms, so it's strange he never has.'

'What is the name of your hotel?' Phee asked keenly.

'Pardon? Oh, I've no idea.'

'Didn't you ask last night when Harvey told you about it?'

'Phee, can you not begin to understand how I was

feeling last night? Not only was I dealing with my father being the way he is and having to leave him in that terrible place, hoping they can make him better, I'd just learned that his employee, a man he'd trusted beyond any reproach, had helped himself to everything of ours he could get his greedy little hands on. What the future holds for us now I have no idea. The last thing I was concerned with was the name of a bloody hotel I'd not until then known the existence of.'

Just then there was a tap on the door and Mabel Jones appeared. 'Can I get you anything, Miss Griffin?'

'A brandy,' answered Phee. 'It will do you good, Eddie.'

'That's the last thing I need. I must have a clear head as Uncle Harvey's coming this afternoon to collect the signed deeds so the hotel sale can be rushed through as soon as a buyer is found. I really don't know how I'd cope without him or his friend Mr Whittle. A pot of tea would be nice, please, Mabel,' she called across.

'I'll have a brandy,' Phee addressed the maid. As she turned her head back she saw the look that Eddie was giving her. 'Well, I don't need to keep a clear head, do I? And I do need something to help calm me after what you've just told me, dear. It's all so dreadful, it really is. I just wish I could be of more help. Oh, I do have some jewellery I can sell. Great-grandmother left it to me. It's worth quite a bit, I understand. I'm sure Geraldine will become a hugely successful model and marry into royalty and won't be needing anything I might leave her. I'll see about it tomorrow.'

Eddie was overwhelmed by Phee's unselfish gesture when most times, completely unaware that she was, she acted so single-mindedly. Jumping up from her chair, she rushed around the desk to throw her arms around her friend, giving her a fierce hug. 'You will not sell your jewellery, I will not hear of it! But thank you so much for your offer,' she said, kissing her friend's cheek affectionately.

'You'd do the same for me, darling, I know you would. If you do need me to sell my jewellery then I will, just let me know. Now come on, you're creasing my suit. Look for those deeds. I'm desperate to know what hotel you own.'

The safe was behind a picture on the wall at the back of Edwin's desk. Eddie opened it to reveal a small bundle of five- and one-pound notes, totalling fifty pounds, which Phee said would come in handy; a black velvet box containing jewellery which Eddie assumed had belonged to her mother and which brought a lump to her throat; and under the box a long brown envelope with her own name on it in her father's handwriting. With that in her hand, she relocked the safe, put the key back where she had found it, then sat down in her father's chair again, holding the envelope in her hands and staring at it.

She was unaware of Mabel returning with a tray of tea for her and a large brandy for Phee, unaware of her departing too.

'Well, open it then,' urged Phee, taking a sip of the brandy.

'Pardon? Oh!' Eddie slowly turned the envelope over and lifted the flap, pulling out the contents to open them before her. 'The Connaught,' she said.

Phee frowned. 'The Connaught?' Then her face lit

up. 'Oh, the Connaught. You own the Connaught. Well, I'll be damned.'

'I've never heard of it,' said Eddie.

'You must have. It's that large hotel . . . well, it's nowhere near as big as the Grand or the Bell but it's not small either. It looks rather in need of a face lift, but oh, darling, Mummy always enthuses about the Connaught. She says a better high tea can't be had anywhere else in Leicester and she meets her friend there every Friday afternoon. According to Mummy they serve the most scrumptious cakes. Proper muffins, and tea cakes with raisins oozing butter, and real seed cake. You can get any type of tea you want *and* coffee.' She jumped up from her chair, looking excited. 'Let's go and have lunch there. Come on, Eddie. As you own the place, we won't have to pay for it either.'

Eddie tutted at her disdainfully. 'I can't just swan off for lunch, Phee.'

'Why ever not? No matter what problems you have, you still have to eat.'

Phee had a point, she supposed. 'But Uncle Harvey is coming . . .'

'Oh, he could be hours yet. Anyway, he's an old dear and won't mind waiting for you if he arrives before you get back. Oh, darling, you need cheering up. Having lunch is the next best thing to shopping in my opinion. Besides, aren't you just a little interested in seeing the place? I mean, it's not every day one discovers one owns a hotel. Now go and make yourself respectable while I ask your maid to telephone a taxi for us. Come along, dear, hurry up. If you're not curious about the place, I certainly am.'

Eddie supposed she couldn't do anything until Harvey arrived except sit and brood and work herself up into a worse state than she was already, if that was possible. She suddenly realised how much she was relying on her father's friend to help her sort out this terrible mess Stibley had landed them in, hopefully leaving them with at least something her father and herself could build a future on. Going out with Phee, who was certainly good company, would be a welcome distraction for a while. And she found she did want to visit the hotel she'd suddenly found herself acquiring just once before it was sold.

'Give me five minutes,' she said.

CHAPTER EIGHT

When she arrived in the foyer of the Connaught, Eddie experienced an overwhelming feeling that she had stepped back in time to the 1920s. Bombarded by Phee's constant chatter during the five-minute taxi ride there, her friend lurching from one subject to another, all of them seemingly unrelated except to Phee herself, Eddie hadn't had an opportunity to imagine what the hotel would be like beforehand.

The mahogany-panelled, high-ceilinged foyer was surprisingly large. An assortment of faded but obviously very expensive Chinese rugs adorned the highly polished wooden floor. To the right was a long reception desk behind which she could see a severe-looking older woman, dressed entirely in black but for a cameo brooch pinned on the shoulder of her dress. She was dealing with an elderly couple who looked as if they'd just arrived as they had luggage with them. A young blue-uniformed porter was hovering nearby, waiting for her instruction to show them to their room. Also behind the reception desk sat a much younger woman, telephone clamped to her ear, head bowed, writing a note on a pad of paper. Opposite the reception desk, double wooden doors led through to the restaurant.

Further along another set of doors led to the bar.

Facing Eddie across the foyer was an impressive sweeping staircase. To one side of it, a shaft partly masking it, was an ornate iron-gated lift. To Eddie's left, on the far wall and despite its being a warm April day, a fire was blazing brightly in the grate. To one side of the hearth stood a polished brass coal scuttle and companion set, on the other a huge dried flower arrangement. A wide archway led through into the guest lounge, writing and reading room, and a library leading off that. Against the long windows hung sun-faded gold velvet drapes, with long tassels hanging from the pelmets. Potted palms and other plants in colourful jardinières were placed about the public rooms. From the ornate ceilings hung huge crystal chandeliers.

Waitresses dressed identically to the Lyons' Corner House Nippy girls of the 20s in calf-length black dresses, edged around collar and cuffs in white lace to match their aprons, hair hidden under white caps, were hurrying back and forth carrying silver trays laden with Queen Anne-style silver tea or coffee pots and Royal Worcester Blind Earl tea sets for the gathering of guests in the lounge.

'Gosh,' said Phee, staring around, an amazed expression on her face. 'This place is positively archaic, and so are most of the guests I can see. No wonder Mummy loves coming here. She's nearing her seventies but I suspect she feels like a young girl compared to some of the people here. This is one place I'll cross off my list of where to meet husband number four.'

An elderly man smartly dressed in a black three-piece

suit, obviously the concierge, seemed to materialise before them from nowhere. 'Can I be of assistance, ladies?' he asked them.

It was Phee who took charge. 'Ah, my good man, allow me to introduce you . . .'

With horror Eddie realised that Phee was about to announce who she was. Grabbing her arm, she pulled her aside. 'Don't dare tell him who I am,' she whispered.

Phee looked taken aback. 'Don't be absurd, darling. Why ever not? We'll get the royal treatment when they know the owner of this establishment is on the premises.'

But Eddie didn't want anyone to know the actual proprietor was paying a visit. Then the manager would descend on her and she'd find herself in such an awkward situation should he ask questions regarding the running of the hotel, its future even. She was trying to deal with unimaginable problems, the likes of which she had never had to face before, and could not cope with anything else. She was conscious that the concierge was beginning to look at her and Sophia questioningly, if not a little suspiciously.

'Phee, I suddenly feel very uncomfortable about being here. I think we should go,' Eddie murmured.

'Go? Don't be silly, darling, we've just got here.'

Just then a man entering through the revolving door caught Phee's eye. One of her perfectly shaped eyebrows arched in appreciation as she noted his handsome profile and smart attire, his whole air of assurance. 'Well, this place has suddenly gone up in my estimation,' she said, eyes riveted on him as he took a long look around then made his way slowly into the guests' lounge.

'We'd like a table for lunch,' said Phee to the concierge. 'But first we'll have an apéritif in the lounge.'

'Very good, madam,' he responded, respectfully bowing. At a click of his fingers a waiter came hurrying up. 'Please escort these ladies to the lounge. A table by the window.' He returned his attention to Phee. 'We start serving in the restaurant at twelve-thirty. I will inform you when your table is ready. Enjoy your apéritif.'

Before Eddie could protest Phee was following the waiter through to the lounge and she had no choice but to follow.

The guests' lounge, a large bright room with a fire burning brightly in the wood-surrounded fireplace across the room, was filled with white lace-clothed circular tables, a small crystal vase of fresh flowers on each, surrounded by faded gold velvet-covered chairs in varying styles and dimensions to accommodate different guests. Many of the tables were already occupied. Phee did have a point, Eddie conceded as they made their way through. Not exactly in the first flush of youth herself, nevertheless she was feeling quite out of place amongst the older generation who obviously frequented the Connaught Hotel.

Phee was discreetly glancing around as she followed the waiter and when she spotted her quarry said, 'Over here, I think.' She immediately changed direction, Eddie automatically following, towards a vacant table right next to the one occupied by the man she'd spotted entering the hotel a moment or two before.

The waiter did not notice that his two guests were not behind him until he arrived at the table he'd been instructed by the concierge to seat them at. He prepared to pull out a chair and almost cried out in alarm when he realised they had gone off to another table and he was not there to seat them in accordance with hotel protocol.

As she arrived at the table next to the handsome man, Phee smiled charmingly at him then a look of recognition filled her face as she declared, 'Oh, how nice to see you again, and here of all places. How is your dear wife?'

Mark Gifford could not help but notice the arrival of these two striking younger women amongst a sea of elderly faces. The one addressing him was stunning but the one who really caught his eye was the distracted-looking dark-haired lady behind her who was wearing a very becoming canary yellow swing coat and matching shift dress. Dragging his attention back to the woman who'd addressed him, he stood up politely and said, 'You have me at a disadvantage, I'm afraid.'

Phee looked aghast. 'Oh, so we didn't meet at the Bartons' dinner party a few weeks ago?'

He shook his head. 'Had we met I would not have forgotten. Besides, I'm not acquainted with any people called Barton and there is no Mrs Gifford.'

Phee beamed at the compliment he had paid her but more so at receiving exactly the information she had hoped to hear.

Eddie, who had been watching the scene being played out before her, inwardly groaned. Not that in her present state of mind she was taking too much notice but this man looked intelligent to her and she wondered if he was astute enough to realise that Phee knew very well she had never met him before, this was merely a well-practised ploy of hers to get herself introduced to someone who had claimed her interest. She had a terrible feeling that Phee's next move would be to get them invited to join Mr Gifford. Congenial chit-chat was the last thing she felt like with all she was contending with.

Her fears were realised when she heard Phee say, 'Oh, I fear I can feel a terrible draught by this table.' And looking at Eddie she said with deep concern, 'You positively hate sitting in a draught, don't you, darling?' She then made a great display of looking around. 'Oh, all the other tables seem to be occupied,' she exclaimed, even though several were not. Then looked at Mark Gifford expectantly, smiling charmingly at him.

He took her hint. 'I wouldn't in the least mind changing tables with you.'

'Oh, I wouldn't dream of putting you to such inconvenience, but if you have no objection to our joining you . . . ?'

Eddie noticed the spark of amusement in his eye and knew then that he was well aware of what Phee was up to.

He smiled graciously at her. 'Not at all. Please be my guests.'

Both women sat down in chairs pulled out by the anxious waiter who had now joined them to take their orders: Phee chose a schooner of pale sherry, Eddie ordered a pot of coffee and likewise Mark Gifford. Eddie was well aware that Phee had purposely not introduced her to Mr Gifford because she didn't want to bring Eddie to his attention. This was typical of Phee when she had her eye on a man and wanted to keep him all to herself. Normally Eddie would have been insulted by her friend's selfish action but, in this instance, she was relieved to keep her identity secret because of her association with the hotel.

After the waiter had departed, Phee gave her full attention to Mark, sitting so he had a good view of her shapely crossed legs. 'So what brings you to the Connaught, Mr Gifford? I wouldn't have thought it your kind of establishment.'

'It normally isn't,' he responded, his eyes still holding a spark of amusement. 'I could say the same for yourselves,' he said, looking at Eddie.

Without giving her a chance to answer him, Phee said, 'Oh, we've come to give the place the once over as Edelina has just discovered . . .'

To her horror Eddie realised that Phee was after all about to tell Mark Gifford of her association with the hotel and stopped her in her tracks by interjecting, 'We heard they serve a good lunch, isn't that right, Sophia?'

Her friend raised an annoyed eyebrow, put out at being denied the opportunity to impress this man.

'Is it lunch that brings you here, Mr Gifford?' Eddie asked him hastily.

'No, it isn't.'

His blunt answer told her that his reason for being here was no business of two women he'd just become acquainted with, but Phee was determined not only to keep the conversation flowing but also to find out as much about this man as she could.

She placed her elbow on the table, rested her chin in her palm and looked at him with a hint of seductiveness. 'Oh, a man of mystery, are you, Mr Gifford? Is it a secret assignation that brings you to the Connaught then?'

He laughed, a deep manly sound. 'No, not at all. I'll satisfy your curiosity, Miss Rymmington-Smyth. I've heard through a contact that this hotel could be for sale, and I could be in the market to buy it. As I happened to be in the area, I thought I'd drop in to take a look around before proceeding any further.'

Phee flicked her head back and a look of satisfaction filled her face. 'Well, how fortuitous for you as Edelina just happens to be . . . Ouch!' she exclaimed, having received a sharp kick under the table from Eddie.

'Anything the matter?' Mark asked her in concern.

Eddie didn't give Phee chance to reply. Frank Whittle was certainly proving a good man to have on her side as it seemed he'd wasted no time in laying the foundations for the sale of the hotel. If Mr Gifford was interested enough to buy it then her immediate financial worries would be resolved and all she had to contend with then was getting her father back to his normal self. 'Are you in the hotel business?' she asked him.

He shook his head.

Just then the waiter came up with their order. Eddie waited until he had departed before asking Mark quizzically as she poured herself coffee, adding a cube of sugar and dash of cream, 'So why are you interested in buying this one?'

'For its potential as office accommodation. I'm a property developer.'

She wasn't sure how she felt about this place being ripped apart and turned into offices. But then, what happened to it shouldn't be of any consequence to her. The sale would resolve the terrible mess they were in, that was what was important. 'In your opinion, does it have the potential to make suitable office accommodation, Mr Gifford?'

'From what I've observed up to now it certainly does. It's in a prime location for a start.' He took a look around him, bringing his eyes back to rest on her. 'It's a fine example of its type, and I shouldn't say this in view of my line of work but it does seem a shame to knock it about. I expect this hotel was rather splendid when it first opened its doors. Such a pity the owners have neglected its upkeep over the years. I'm no hotelier but it does seem to me to be very old-fashioned and its clientele not the type to make for a healthy profit. Shame really as I think it could be quite a gold mine with a little modernisation. I think it would suit my needs too. I won't give up trying to get my hands on it.' He gazed at her intently. 'In fact, I'm not a man who gives up easily when I want something. I was wondering whether to get tickets for a performance of *The Pirates of Penzance* at the De-monfort Hall. Have you seen it yet, Miss er . . . ?'

He was flirting with her. Normally the attentions of a good-looking, charming, and most importantly single, man of his obvious calibre would have had Eddie responding accordingly but furthering their acquaintance in that way was not on her agenda at the moment.

Her mind raced, wondering how she could respond without coming across as rude and without giving him her full name.

Before she could make any response, though, Phee uncrossed her legs and stood up. It was very apparent by the expression on her face that she was not pleased. 'Shall we go through for lunch, Eddie? You will excuse us, won't you, Mr Gifford?'

Eddie looked up at her, taken aback. 'But we were told by the concierge we'd be informed when our table was ready.'

'Well, I'm ready to eat now,' snapped Phee. 'Where is that little man?' she said, looking around for the concierge. 'I'll tell him to open the restaurant early for us.'

Just then he miraculously appeared. 'Your table is ready if you'd care to come through,' he politely informed them.

Phee glanced at Mark. 'So nice to meet you,' she said curtly. 'Come along, Eddie,' she ordered, and with head held high walked off.

Eddie put down her cup, gathered her bag and stood up as gentlemanly Mark rose also. 'So nice to meet you.'

'You too,' he said meaningfully. 'I hope we shall do so again.'

Embarrassed by Phee's manner, she gave him a quick smile before hurrying off to join her. Seated at their table in the restaurant, Eddie glared at her friend crossly. 'What on earth got into you? You were most rude to Mr Gifford.'

'I was not,' she denied, looking in her handbag for

her cigarette case and lighter. Having found them she lit a cigarette, looking at Eddie fixedly. 'Did you make an arrangement to meet him?'

'No. Whatever makes you ask that?' Then the reason for Phee's behaviour hit home. 'Oh, Phee, you were jealous that Mr Gifford paid more attention to me than to you!'

'I was not,' she snapped. 'But you did rather monopolise him, darling, which I thought was pretty unforgivable of you since I saw him first.'

Eddie tutted. 'Oh, Phee, you silly thing. I was not monopolising Mr Gifford at all. I was just keen to hear about his possible interest in buying this hotel, for obvious reasons. Don't you realise pursuing a man is the last thing on my mind at the moment?'

'Mmm, I suppose,' she said offhandedly, taking the proffered menu from the waiter. Opening it out, she studied it then looked at the waiter and asked, 'Where's the full menu?'

He looked perplexed. 'Sorry, madam?'

Flapping the menu shut, she thrust it back at him. 'This is obviously for guests who have gastric problems or trouble chewing. I want to see the full *à la carte* menu.'

He shifted uncomfortably on his feet. 'That is the full menu, madam.'

She pulled a face. 'This is all you serve? Roast chicken or cod in parsley sauce? Neither appeals to me. Tell Chef to prepare me some lightly poached salmon with a green salad, no dressing.'

His youthful face reddened in discomfort. 'We only serve what's on the menu, madam.'

'This is a restaurant, isn't it?' Phee snapped abruptly. Then, without consulting Eddie, told him, 'We won't be eating here.' Stubbing out her cigarette and snatching up her handbag, she stood up. 'Come along, darling. I've suddenly lost my appetite. Let's go shopping instead.'

Before Eddie could respond she was stalking off.

Phee's bad humour at her failure to ensnare Mark Gifford, who she deemed more than worthy of further attention soon evaporated as she became embroiled in her favourite pastime. As luck would have it a fashion demonstration was being held in Madame Zena's, an exclusive women's shop, and they arrived just in time to take seats with all the other affluent shoppers there before it began. Mindful of her arrangement with Harvey, if he wasn't actually waiting for her already, Eddie only intended to stay long enough to see her friend happily viewing the outfits being paraded before making her excuses and leaving. She had bargained without their meeting up with several other female acquaintances who, totally oblivious to Eddie's situation, swept her up in their fevered excitement at this chance to view and purchase the latest creations so as to outclass their rivals at their never-ending round of social events locally.

For a while Eddie's problems were temporarily forgotten as she lost herself in watching the latest creations passing before her, at the end of the event placing orders for a dream of an evening dress, two smart day dresses and a suit.

Phee was right. Shopping was just the thing for lifting one's spirits. It had certainly lifted hers.

CHAPTER NINE

It wasn't until Eddie had said her goodbyes to Phee and the other women and settled into the back of a cab at just before six o'clock that evening that her true situation flooded back to her. She felt guilty too for keeping Harvey waiting but hoped he wouldn't be too cross with her and would understand her need for a diversion, considering all she was trying to come to terms with.

At home she was met by Mabel.

'Good evening, Miss Griffin,' she said, helping Eddie off with her coat and folding it over her arm ready to hang up. 'Mr Crankshaft is waiting in the drawing room for you. He's been here quite a while and was getting rather anxious about your whereabouts.' She gnawed her bottom lip worriedly. 'Please excuse me for asking, miss, but is everything all right? I mean, I know Mr Griffin is hospitalised after his turn but I ... er ... well, forgive me, Miss Griffin, but a funny thing happened today and me and Cook were a bit bothered about it as it's never happened before. Well, not while we've both bin working for Mr Griffin it ain't.'

'What sort of funny thing?' Eddie asked her.

'Well, Miss Griffin, yer see, the groceries never got

delivered and when Cook telephoned to ask where her order had got to, she was told that until the outstanding bill was settled we wouldn't be getting no more credit as they'd heard Mr Griffin was bankrupt. Cook told him that was just a vicious rumour. Mr Griffin bankrupt indeed! But Harrington wouldn't budge. Stuck to his guns he did. No more deliveries until the outstanding bill was paid, and until further notice no more deliveries unless paid for up front. Me and Cook then got to talking and . . . well, we wondered if there was no smoke without fire, so to speak, Miss Griffin, what with what happened to Mr Griffin and him being in hospital.

'Cook's gone home as she'd her husband to see to but she left you a tray made up with sandwiches as you never left instructions on whether yer wanted dinner or not, and besides with no delivery she hadn't any fresh stuff to prepare. She's really worried, though, same as me about our positions if this rumour has any substance. I promised her I'd have a word with yer when yer got home. There's no truth in the rumour, is there, Miss Griffin?'

Eddie was staring at her blindly. How had word spread already about their situation? As far as she was aware only she, Harvey, and Phee knew. And, of course, Mr Whittle. Phee was the most likely culprit, perhaps unwittingly saying something to one of her numerous acquaintances, her tongue running away with her as it was apt to do. But Eddie had only imparted her terrible situation to Phee herself that morning and had been with her until only a short while ago, so she knew it couldn't have been her friend. It had also been very remiss of her not to realise that their maid and cook would have to be blind and deaf not to sense something was not right in the household, though up to now she had kept them in the dark over the fact that the hospital her father was in was actually a mental institution. It suddenly hit her then that she had mentally accused Phee of not fully appreciating her situation when the truth was she herself hadn't realised the severity of it.

She was aware that Mabel was looking at her expectantly, waiting for her response to her question. Eddie didn't know what to say to her.

Thankfully she was saved by the appearance of Harvey who came out of the drawing room. He smiled as he came over to greet her. 'Ah, there you are, Edelina. I was getting rather worried about you. How are you, my dear?'

She looked remorseful as together they walked back into the drawing room and over to the armchairs. 'Please accept my apologies for keeping you waiting, Uncle Harvey. It was most thoughtless of me to go out, but I was in need of a distraction.' She clasped her hands in her lap, her face assuming a deeply worried expression. 'My maid has just informed me that rumours are spreading already about Father's financial situation. The grocer has refused us any more credit until his outstanding bill is settled and in future he's demanding payment up front before he'll send anything. This is so humiliating! I've never been refused credit before. Thankfully I did find some money in Father's safe this morning. I assume he kept it there for paying household bills so I can hopefully take care of what's already owed, but what do I do without any more to replace it . . .' Her expression deepened. 'I've suddenly realised I have no idea how much it costs to run this house, or even what the staff are paid. Uncle Harvey, how long will it take, do you think, to get the hotel sold so this mess can be sorted out and we can return to normal? A couple of days, do you think? I've really no idea how long this sort of thing takes.' Her face clouded over with sorrow then, tears glistening in her eyes. 'I telephoned the hospital this morning. I was so hoping they would tell me there were signs of improvement in Father and that I could go and see him. But there is no change whatsoever and neither would they give me any indication when I'd be able to visit. What if he isn't aware that the hospital is stopping me from seeing him and thinks I've abandoned him? I can't ever remember a time when Daddy and I were separated. I don't feel safe without him close by. I miss him so much,' she cried.

'Eddie, please stop upsetting yourself unnecessarily. I did try and warn you yesterday, dear, that it could take a while for your father to show any signs of improvement. You must have patience and faith in his doctors' abilities. If they feel it to be the case that visits from family will hinder Edwin's recovery, then you have no choice but to be led by them. Look, I know this must all be very daunting for you, but please rest assured that you're not on your own. I will do all I can to help you. I'm not your father but I will try and take his place in whatever way you wish me to.'

She smiled gratefully at him. 'I don't know what I'd do if I didn't have you to guide me through all this. I appreciate what Mr Whittle is doing too. Oh, has he reported back to you on what the police had to say? He did report this terrible crime to them this morning, didn't he?'

Harvey nodded. 'Whittle telephoned me just before I set out to come here. It's as he predicted, I'm afraid, Edelina. The police are taking this very seriously, doing what they can to uncover Stibley's whereabouts, but it's really your father who has to bring charges as the crime was committed against him. When Edwin is in a fit enough state to be questioned the police have requested we let them know. Hopefully that won't be long and this matter can then proceed.

'I would also reiterate what you were advised last night, Eddie, and that's not to build your hopes up on bringing Stibley to justice. It's the future you need to concentrate on.' He leaned forward and looked at her expectantly. 'Now, did you find the deeds for the hotel?'

She had really been convinced that the police, on learning of Stibley's hideous crime, would immediately have launched a nationwide manhunt and within hours, a day at the most, arrested him and regained all Stibley had fraudulently taken from her father and then her situation would be resolved. She realised, feeling rather embarrassed, how naive she had been to have thought it could be that simple. 'Yes, I did. They were in Father's safe.'

'Ah, good. I was concerned Edwin may have put them in a bank deposit box for safe keeping and then we wouldn't have been able to get our hands on them until he was well enough to fetch them himself. That would have meant we could not sell the hotel, and I dread to think what your situation would have been by then. Still, you've got them, that's the most important thing. Now, we need you to sign the deeds and then let me have them so everything is at hand to complete a sale as soon as a buyer presents themself. Then you can stop more interest accruing on the mortgage than is necessary, pay off all your other debts and restore Edwin's good name.'

'Oh, yes, it's most important I clear Father's name,' she cried. 'I just hate to think what people might be saying about him. I'll go and fetch the deeds and a pen.' She made to rise then stopped, looking at him in concern. 'I'm not sure what I think about the hotel possibly being turned into office accommodation, though. What will happen to all the staff?'

He looked back at her quizzically. 'What makes you think it will be turned into office accommodation?'

'Oh, just something someone said. A man I met said he was considering it when he visited the hotel to take a preliminary look around today after hearing it was for sale. I was shocked at first by how quickly word had got around that it was on the market then I realised I should be grateful to Mr Whittle for wasting no time.'

Harvey was frowning, clearly bewildered. 'This person came to see you personally? But how did he know you were the actual owner? More importantly, Edelina, you have no experience in this sort of thing and I wouldn't wish you to be duped in any way by any unscrupulous person. It really would be in your best interests to let myself and Mr Whittle take care of this for you. If anyone should call on you personally again, direct them straight to me, my dear, and I will take care of them. You have enough to worry about.'

'Thank you, Uncle Harvey, and let me assure you I wouldn't do anything without you or Mr Whittle checking it out first and giving your approval. Not after what has happened to Father.' Her eyes narrowed darkly. 'I'm still having difficulty believing he has been taken in all these years by Stibley, but one thing it has done for me is to make me realise I cannot trust anyone. Except, of course, for yourself and Mr Whittle. The man showing interest in the hotel today didn't come to see me personally. We just happened to sit at his table at the Connaught and it came out in conversation. I didn't tell him I was the owner.'

Harvey was looking closely at her. 'You paid a visit to the hotel?'

She looked worried. 'It wasn't wrong of me to do that, was it? It was Phee's ... Miss Rymmington-Smyth's suggestion. She said I ought to see the place before it was sold, and I must admit I was intrigued.'

'Oh, yes, I suppose that's understandable. I'm just concerned you don't become too attached to the place. You have to sell it, Eddie, you have no choice.' He looked at his watch. 'Look, I don't mean to pressure you but I do have a dinner engagement so if you'll fetch the deeds ...'

His voice trailed off as a tap sounded on the door and Mabel Jones appeared. 'Sorry to disturb you, Miss Griffin, but a Mr Waddington has called to see you.'

She stared at Mabel blankly. She couldn't remember the last time her father's solicitor had called personally at the house. It was obvious to her why he had called tonight. He must have heard the rumour about her father's bankruptcy which meant it had spread far wider than the local grocer already. The culprit behind the spreading of that rumour had to be Stibley. Not content just to ruin her father, he obviously wanted everyone to know what he'd done so as to cause the utmost humiliation he could. Her hatred of the man intensified. Not generally a violent woman, she would at this moment have had no hesitation about causing him physical harm. She inwardly groaned. Ralph Waddington would obviously want to know all the sordid details and the last thing she felt like was going over it all now. But she couldn't think quickly enough of an excuse not to see him, and besides Mabel would have already informed him she was at home. Resigned to his visit she said, 'Please show him in, Mabel.'

As the maid departed, Eddie looked at Harvey to offer him reassurance that she would endeavour to make this visit as short as possible so they could resume the task in hand. She frowned on noticing the expression on his face.

Realising she was looking at him, he said, 'Oh, I'm ... er ... just annoyed that Waddington's arrival has prevented us from getting on with things.'

'Won't we need Father's solicitor to act for us in the sale of the hotel? We ought to inform him on what's going on, surely?'

He leaned over and eyed her intently. 'Eddie dear, I should tell you that although your father and I rarely, if ever, discussed business, I did ask if he could recommend a solicitor when I was selling up my dental practice on my retirement. He said that he couldn't as he needed to find another himself. He was considering dispensing with Waddington's future services. When I asked him why, he said he feared the man's mind wasn't what it was any more. I did find a solicitor myself and was very pleased with him. I have to say that since then I have heard talk of Waddington at my club and the impression I have is that he's not so well respected as he once was. He must be nearing ninety and should have retired long ago. He's renowned for being very slow, and I don't want to alarm you but if you allow him to handle the legal side of this sale you could end up losing this house because of his dithering ways. The solicitor I found I can highly recommend. He's really on the ball and will push this through fast. Nor will he charge an extortionate fee for his services either, as I know Waddington does. I don't want to remind you but you need to salvage as much as you can financially from this dreadful situation, and time as they say is money.'

Eddie sighed. 'Thank you for your advice, Uncle Harvey. I wouldn't like to offend Mr Waddington, though, so I'll be careful what I say to him.'

He smiled reassuringly. 'If I anticipate the conversation is heading towards dangerous ground, I'll chip in to steer it in another direction.'

She gave him a grateful smile. 'I apologise for the way I keep repeating myself but I really don't know what I'd do without you.' Then a thought struck her. 'Oh, but you have to leave as you've a dinner engagement?'

'Don't worry, my dear. I'll telephone and make my excuses. I wouldn't dream of abandoning you at a time when it's obvious you need my help.'

'But I wouldn't hear of it. I've already disrupted your

day by my thoughtlessness, I wouldn't rest easy knowing I'd messed up your evening too. Oh, the deeds . . .'

She paused on hearing the door opening and turned her head to see Ralph Waddington shuffling in, leaning heavily on his walking stick. Mabel hovered just inside the doorway, obviously waiting for instructions about refreshments for the new arrival.

Eddie glanced at Harvey and murmured, 'Oh, dear, it will look very rude if we both disappear into Father's study to deal with the deeds just as Mr Waddington has arrived, and you really do need to get off, Uncle Harvey.'

'Yes, yes, I wouldn't like to upset the old boy. I'll call around in the morning. You will be at home?'

She nodded. 'I promise. Now you get off. If your hostess is anything like me she'll not be pleased at a guest arriving in the middle of a course.' She saw his hesitation and added, 'I'll be very mindful of what you've advised me, so please don't worry.'

'Good evening,' Harvey said to Ralph Waddington, politely standing up as the old man drew level with them.

Ralph Waddington looked at him searchingly. 'Oh, er . . . ah, yes, it's Crookshank, isn't it? Can't remember the last time we met. A good few years ago now. Not long after . . . er . . . Edwin lost his dear wife. Yes, that's when. I came around for Edwin's signature on some papers and you were the one who told me he was having a particularly bad day and wouldn't see anyone but that you'd get them signed and despatched back to me as soon as you could. You were in . . . er . . . pharmaceuticals if I remember right?'

Harvey flashed a look at Eddie as though to say, I told you the old man was going senile, then grasped the gnarled hand that was being offered him and shook it. 'Actually it's Crankshaft, and I was in dentistry before I retired.'

'Oh, of course. Yes, yes, that's right, I remember now. I had a bad tooth a few years back . . . just dreadful it was, wouldn't wish it on anyone. My own man was on holiday. I tried several others but they couldn't see me urgently. I was desperate by that time and remembered Edwin had a friend who was a dentist so I telephoned him and he said that although he didn't use you as you were not keen on mixing business with pleasure, he could give me the address of your practice. I visited but there seemed to be no one there, and if I remember correctly it was mid-morning during the week when I called.'

'Well, I was obviously on holiday myself. You must have missed the sign on the door. Obviously slipped Edwin's mind too that I was away, that's why he sent you. You're still practising yourself, I believe?' Harvey enquired.

'Oh, I just take on a few things now for old clients as a favour and to keep the old brain cells active.' He chuckled. 'Not so ga-ga as not to know when it's time to take a back seat and let the younger ones take over.'

'Uncle Harvey, you really ought to be off or you will be late,' Eddie urged him.

'Oh, yes, I must. If you will excuse me, Waddington, I've a dinner engagement. So good to have seen you again.'

'Please do take a seat, Mr Waddington,' Eddie said

to the old man after Harvey had departed. 'Can I get you anything?' she asked him

His aged face lit up. 'I never say no to a malt,' he said, looking at her expectantly as he propped his walking stick against the arm of the chair and carefully eased himself down into its seat.

Eddie addressed Mabel as she walked across to the drinks cabinet. 'I'll see to this, I shan't be needing you again tonight.'

The maid had not yet received a satisfactory answer to her question. Her mistress's obvious procrastination was adding fuel to her concern that there really was something behind the rumour of her employer's bankruptcy. Then her job as well as the other staff's was under threat. 'Oh, but . . .' She sighed, realising such matters could not be discussed while visitors were present. 'All right, Miss Griffin. I'll see you in the morning then.'

Ralph eagerly accepted the generously filled tumbler that Eddie handed him before sitting down herself in the armchair opposite. 'Ah,' he sighed, looking at it in appreciation. 'The Scots are famed for many things but to me they are best at producing this.' He took a sip, sighed in satisfaction, then looked at Eddie through rheumy eyes. 'The last time we met, my dear, you were in your perambulator asleep in the garden when I'd called on your father to sign some papers. You were a very fetching child and you've grown into a beautiful woman. You bear a strong resemblance to your mother. She was beautiful too. I'm surprised you've not settled down yet. I assume you would not have been short of proposals?'

Eddie smiled at his compliment. 'I've received more than one,' she said without conceit.

'But you didn't accept any?' he asked bluntly. 'Why?'

She gave a shrug. 'I got close to marriage a couple of times, Mr Waddington, but none of the men had that special something that would entice me to give up what I already have here at home.'

'Well, I suppose that's a good enough reason. I'm glad to hear it wasn't because you felt you couldn't leave your father on his own.'

'My father had never made me feel the slightest bit obliged to him, Mr Waddington. We have always been very close, enjoyed doing lots of things together, but Father always encouraged me to have a life of my own and has been very supportive in anything I've wanted to do, even when I let him down badly. Such as the time when I was nine years old and decided I was to become a famous concert pianist. I pestered Father unrelentingly until he caved in and bought me a baby grand piano and hired a first-class tutor. He would patiently listen to me painfully practising every day even though the noise I made must have been excruciating to his ears. After a year it was glaringly apparent even to me that I'd never master a recognisable rendition of "Chop Sticks", let alone anything by Chopin – something the tutor had tactfully warned Father after my first lesson! Never once did he berate me for how much money my folly had cost. His words were, "Well, at least you tried and I can't fault you for that." The grand piano was donated to a worthy cause so at least someone got the benefit of it.

'He's been a wonderful parent, Mr Waddington, I

couldn't have wished for better. I know I've been very fortunate not to have wanted for anything.' She gave a small sigh as her present worrying situation occurred to her. 'If I have any complaint at all it's that I fear he's looked after me too well, not preparing me at all for what I'm trying to deal with now.'

At her admission the old man leaned forward in his seat, his face screwed up in concern. 'Ah, so the information I heard at my club today is not the mere rumour I was hoping it was then?'

Her father, thought Eddie, might have been a little hasty in his judgement of this old gentleman's mental capabilities. He seemed sharp enough to her. 'Not if the rumour is that Father has been robbed blind by a trusted employee and has suffered a mental breakdown as a result.' She clasped her hands and took a deep breath then proceeded to inform Ralph Waddington fully of what had transpired.

At the end he let out a deep aggrieved sigh and drained the last of his whisky, putting his empty tumbler on the occasional table to the side of him. Sadly shaking his head, he uttered, 'Oh, dear. It's worse than I feared. I was so hoping that the rumour I heard was just that, a rumour.'

'I suppose you think my father a foolish man for allowing this to happen to him?' Eddie said quietly. She rose, picked up his tumbler and went across to the drinks cabinet. When she had retaken her seat, after placing the refilled tumbler on the small table to the side of Ralph Waddington, he sighed heavily. After thanking her for his whisky he said, 'Too trusting . . . naive, that is what I'd brand Edwin, my dear.' He leaned back in his chair, clasping his hands before his chest, his face thoughtful. 'Employers have to trust their employees, but a wise employer will still keep a wary eye out. In fairness to him, he wasn't experienced enough to run the business at the time of your mother's death, though I have no doubt he would have become adept in time had your mother lived and instructed him in its intricacies.'

She gazed at him. 'I don't understand what you mean? Was it my mother who started the family business then? I'd always assumed it was my father.'

He looked at her, taken aback. 'Edelina, do you know anything of your family history?'

She shook her head. 'Very little. Not much, in fact. I learned when I was quite young that it upset Father to talk about the past. I realised he loved my mother very dearly from the odd times I got him to talk about her, from the way his eyes lit up for a brief moment before sadness filled them again. And of course the fact he's never married again. I always assumed he'd never really recovered from her death. I knew we made our money from the letting of properties which were managed from his office in town. Father seemed to manage very well just by paying a visit to the office once a month, sometimes less, to check how it was all going and deal with what he had to. I thought I was lucky to have a father who could be at home most of the time especially while I was growing up. Many of my friends hardly saw their fathers who were away on business such a lot.'

A memory resurfaced and she smiled. 'Father and I were out once when I was a little girl. I can't remember now where we were going but as we were driving along he took a wrong turn. We passed a row of houses and

Father said, "We own all those and a lot more besides that people pay money to us to live in. When I'm no longer here, they will all come to you."

'I had no idea until yesterday that Father had in fact sold off all our rental properties over the years and that we were no longer landlords but our money now came from investments. I don't really understand what investments, stock markets and those sorts of things are all about, and anyway I felt it was nothing to do with me how Father made our living. He looked after that side of things while I ran our home. I was more than happy with our arrangement. Felt I was looking after him as I know my mother would have done.' She paused and looked at the visitor a moment before she asked, 'Was the business started by my mother and not, as I have always assumed, by him?'

'It was actually started by neither of them. Roxanne inherited it from her own father on his death, along with this house and most of the contents. When your father married your mother he had nothing of his own.' The old solicitor's face took on a distant expression. 'I was very fond of Roxanne who was a lovely woman and not just to look at. I was the Devonshires' – that was your mother's maiden name – family solicitor, a good friend of the family too, and Roxanne and I grew close when I helped her through the pain of losing her father, her mother having died some years before that. As their only child by then, she was sole beneficiary of her father's estate, which even after death duties made Roxanne a moderately wealthy woman although most of her assets were tied up in bricks and mortar.'

Eddie stared at him, fascinated by this detailed

account of her parents' life together. Several faded photographs in an album in her room had afforded Eddie a facial likeness of her mother but her personality had always been a mystery due to Father's reluctance to speak of it. Now through the memories of this old man her mother was coming alive for Eddie and she found herself hungry to learn more about the woman who'd died after giving birth to her.

Ralph Waddington continued: 'Roxanne herself knew very little, if anything, of business matters when she inherited the firm at seventeen years of age. Her brother, who had been groomed to take over from his father, had been killed in action in the Great War, and Roxanne and her widowed father barely had time to recover from their grief at his death before Mortimer Devonshire himself died unexpectedly from a heart attack. Roxanne was beside herself with sorrow at losing her father and brother in such quick succession, leaving her on her own in the world. But despite her age and inexperience, being the woman she was, Roxanne was determined that the business her grandfather and father had worked so hard to build up would become even more successful under her ownership. She had a keen brain and was a quick learner. Within a short space of time she was heading the business almost as well as her father had. In fact, already adding to it by successfully negotiating an excellent price for a row of houses badly needing restoration before they could be filled with tenants. She herself found builders who would carry out the necessary repairs for a sensible price and do the work properly. Her father and grandfather would have been so proud of her, I know.

Had she lived, the business would have gone from strength to strength. As it was . . . well . . .'

A brief smile lightened his grave expression. 'I clearly remember the day Roxanne flew into my office announcing she'd met the man she was going to spend the rest of her life with. I've never seen a look like that on anyone's face before or since. Radiant nowhere near describes it. Roxanne had never been short of admirers and prior to meeting your father she had, I know, been stepping out with a gentleman for a few weeks, more in a friendly way than a romantic one. I never knew who he was or anything much about him as he wasn't a serious contender so Roxanne didn't feel the need to go into detail. Regardless, she wasn't relishing the prospect of telling her friend about Edwin as she knew he was very fond of her. She was a very thoughtful woman.

'I must admit that in my capacity as self-appointed father substitute to her, I was dubious about meeting Edwin for the first time over the lunch Roxanne had arranged. She had already informed me Edwin was an orphan like herself, but my concern was that his background wasn't really what I would have deemed suitable for a woman of Roxanne's station in life. She herself was very free-thinking and to her Edwin's background was not important. The man himself was. She told me he was everything she could ever have hoped for in a future husband and father of the many children she wanted to have. I still had my concerns but they were soon dispelled when I was first introduced to Edwin. He was in every way the man Roxanne had said he was. He would make her a good husband and never let her down, I was so sure of that. I never had any doubts about their feelings for each other. They were totally in love.

'They were married only weeks later. Though money was no object, it was a small affair for a few close friends. I was gratified to be included in that circle. That day Roxanne looked the most beautiful I had ever seen her. Edwin moved into the family home and they settled down very quickly and easily together, as if they'd been together years. Their relationship was a wonderful thing to see. They were naturally attentive towards each other.

'Your father's family was of working-class origin and he himself was a plumber by trade. But if I'd had any concerns at all that Edwin had married Roxanne for her money they were unequivocally quashed when he insisted he keep on his job so as to contribute towards providing for his new wife and future family. He could very easily have given it up straight away and lived an easy life on Roxanne's money. It was she who persuaded him into taking a more active role in her business, or rather their business as she insisted it was now they were married. He only agreed to do so on the proviso that he learned all he could before he was given any responsibilities. He enrolled in night school to learn bookwork and would sit for hours with Wilfred Murgatroyd, the family's old head clerk who oversaw the day-to-day running of the business and kept the accounts, gleaning what he could from him. Edwin told me himself none of what he was learning was coming easy to him and he was struggling to understand it all, but he was determined to succeed and become a full partner to his wife so as to honour her total faith in him. Roxanne was delighted with what her new husband was doing and told him that as soon as he was ready she was going to hand over the property side of the business to him while she concentrated on the hotel.'

Waddington paused for a moment to take a sip of his drink, then continued. 'The building of the hotel had originally been commissioned by your great-grandfather in the middle of the last century. At one time he'd planned to have several of them. Unfortunately that plan didn't materialise due to lack of funds. Buildings of such size and quality were even in those days costly undertakings, so instead he decided it would be best to concentrate on building up his business around house rentals. Roxanne, though, had always had a soft spot for the hotel and would have liked nothing more than to fulfil her grandfather's dream of owning several like it.

'By the time she inherited the Connaught it was early-Victorian in its décor and operating methods and badly needed upgrading to 1920s standards. Only a matter of weeks after Edwin had given up his plumbing job, she left him and Murgatroyd to get on with the letting and concentrated her own efforts on the hotel's modernisation, even though she had just received the exciting news that she and Edwin were to become parents. I never doubted she would complete the task she'd set out to do and do a first-class job. She personally oversaw every stage of the renovations, checking every detail of the work to ensure it was all completed to her high standards. She then set about finding a manager to run the place. The upsurge in the hotel's profits was extremely healthy. By this time your birth was imminent and she retired home to await your arrival. Edwin, though, was still struggling to get to grips with accounting procedures, finding out how the business was run overall, determined not to let it beat him.

'I cannot describe to you, Edelina, how elated they both were by your birth. It was as if they'd both been granted their dearest wish. Even a crusty old bachelor like me with an aversion to children appreciated what a beautiful, sweet-natured child you were. Your mother chose your name. If you'd have been a boy she would have insisted you be called Edwin, in honour of your father. Edelina is perhaps unusual but Roxanne felt it reflected his name while still being very pretty and feminine. It was she who nicknamed you Eddie. Your parents had hired a nursemaid but she hardly had any work to do as Roxanne couldn't bear the thought of someone other than herself looking after her child.' He paused and his aged face was drawn with sorrow. 'I still cannot believe that only three weeks after your birth she was gone from us through complications after your birth. Such a tragedy. All through the oversight of a doctor.

'As if Edwin wasn't suffering enough with the shock of your mother's death, only days after her funeral Murgatroyd fell down the office stairs, was seriously injured and couldn't continue, meaning Edwin was left without anyone to take care of the business while he not only came to terms with his wife's death but was also still learning how it operated.' He paused momentarily and his face set grimly. 'That's when Harold Stibley first came on the scene. He turned up the very morning after Murgatroyd's accident, like an answer to a prayer for your father. He'd just arrived in Leicester from down south, chancing his luck after hearing that work here was plentiful and better paid than where he'd come from. He was calling on all the local firms in the hope of being offered work, he told your father. Although barely twenty-five, too young really to be considered for such a responsible position, he came so highly qualified, had such excellent references, that Edwin didn't see the need to look any further. He was just relieved to find someone capable of taking responsibility for the business while he dealt with his own grief.'

His grim expression was replaced with a look of deep thoughtfulness. 'It makes one wonder now . . . yes, it certainly does. But no, Stibley couldn't possibly have masterminded Murgatroyd's accident to get himself employed by your father. It's just too incredible. Must just be a coincidence, his turning up looking for work at that particular time, it has to be. Now where was I . . . Oh, yes. Grief-stricken, my dear, doesn't go anywhere near to describing your father at that time. He was a broken man. The whole sorry tragedy utterly confounded him. He showed no interest in anything but his need to care for you. He was determined you should not suffer by the loss of your mother. Those around him, including myself, were of the opinion that your existence was the only thing that kept him from doing something terrible to himself, gave him his reason for living in fact. We were all convinced, though, that once Edwin had come to terms with your mother's death he would pick up his learning, eventually take over the complete running of the business, and indeed build on it.

'Edwin's enthusiasm never did come back though. Whether he didn't regain the desire because he never got over Roxanne's death or whether Stibley was proving so competent it meant he could concentrate all his efforts on raising his child in the manner his wife would have wished . . . well, only Edwin has the answer to that.'

Ralph Waddington picked up his tumbler, took a sip of whisky and gave a heavy sigh. 'It's very easy as I sit here now, looking back, to see how the relationship between Edwin and Stibley cemented itself. And also, I'm sorry to say, the one between myself and Edwin with a view to the business. I dealt with Stibley more and more, especially during your prolonged trips abroad. Edwin was always determined to expand your horizons, Edelina, but I suspect those trips also served their purpose in getting him away for a while from places that were constant reminders of his dear wife.' He looked at her remorsefully. 'I hope you'll believe me when I say I myself found Stibley a highly personable man, was never given any reason to question matters he came to see me about on what I thought was your father's instruction. He came across as very trustworthy and reliable. Now I realise he was a good actor as well as being a first-class crook.' He looked at her earnestly. 'Stibley didn't just fool your father, Edelina, he fooled me too, and others he dealt with on your father's behalf.'

'Mr Waddington, do you have any idea what grudge Stibley held against my father?'

He looked mystified. 'None whatsoever. From what I know of Edwin, I can't imagine him doing anything bad enough to cause Stibley to bring ruination on him over such a long period of time. Mind you, some people's idea of a bad deed would be shrugged off as a minor misdemeanour by others. I never received the impression that your father and Stibley knew each other before Edwin employed him. It's all most confusing. Maybe your father will be able to shed light on the matter when he regains his health.' He paused and gave Eddie a relieved smile. 'I just thank God Stibley couldn't get his hands on the hotel since your father saw fit to sign it over to you on your mother's death. It will be a wrench for you to lose this house but at least owning the hotel will mean you've an income coming in to fund some sort of future for you both, so all is not quite lost, is it?'

A great feeling of loss for the mother she had never known filled Eddie. Ralph Waddington had painted a picture of a beautiful, vibrant, intelligent woman, with a great love for her husband and daughter. Eddie had had a happy life to date but she knew without a doubt she'd have had an even better one if her mother had lived. She looked at Ralph distractedly. 'No, I suppose we should be grateful for that. I was rather shocked to find out only yesterday about my ownership of the hotel. I never knew before then that it actually belonged to the family, let alone myself.'

He looked puzzled. 'You only found out yesterday? Oh, but I took it upon myself to pay Edwin a visit when you were approaching your twenty-first birthday. I brought him the hotel deeds as I assumed he would wish to present them to you personally. I must admit I was aware by his manner that my bringing the hotel back to his attention didn't sit well with him, and I appreciated his reasons because of its association with your mother, but I was left with the impression you would learn of your inheritance on your coming of age.' He looked at her intently. 'Despite everything that has happened and the terrible tragedy of it all, I know without a doubt, Edelina, that your mother would be happy to know her daughter was involved with the hotel after the family's absence for so long.' He paused to draw breath and a spark suddenly glinted in his eyes. 'Maybe, through you, your mother's dream will come to fruition, my dear.' He saw the expression on her face and said with conviction, 'As we sit here now, I agree that does sound far-fetched. But you are your mother's daughter, Edelina, and if you have any-thing of her in you, you will tackle this situation head on, turn it from a potential disaster into a success and let nothing stop you, just as your mother would have done.

'With your father being as he is and your finances precarious, it is up to you to see that the hotel makes you a decent living. Stibley can be blamed for much but he cannot be blamed for the fact that the hotel has been neglected for the last forty years. That state of affairs was entirely down to your father and his wish not to be involved with the place in any way whatso-ever after your mother's death. In truth it's a miracle it still survives at all, considering it has been virtually left to the staff to run it. I know the prospect of taking charge must seem daunting to you with your lack of experience but I wish to offer you my help in whatever capacity you may require of me, my dear, please do not hesitate to call on me.'

He paused, drew breath and, looking at her meaningfully, said, 'Just one more thing, Edelina. I would advise you that the first thing you should do is to stop any hotel funds going into the bank account Stibley had access to while acting on your father's behalf. A precaution, you understand, just in case, even though he's absconded, he's still greedy enough to chance accessing that account. He must have done so before. Stibley has helped himself to everything else, it would appear.' His face screwed up in anger. 'As the owner of the hotel, those monies should have been yours by rights, Edelina. Despite the hotel not achieving its full potential for years, it should have amounted to a tidy sum. So your father's employee not only stole from him, he stole from you too.

'I need you to know that I did suggest very strongly to Edwin that a trust fund be set up for you when the hotel was assigned to you. By the time I'd had the papers drawn up ready for his signature it was very apparent that your father would not have the Connaught's name mentioned in his presence nor have any dealings with it in any capacity. That situation never changed, so the trust was never created. I believed, like your father, that the hotel's profits were safely accumulating in the bank account which Edwin had no intention of ever touching, that it was all there for you whenever he chose to give it to you . . . but we were sadly mistaken.

'I am so sorry, Edelina, that you should bear the

brunt of Stibley's actions. Why he felt justified in doing what he did will remain a mystery until your father is able to clear up the matter. I am sure Edwin will regain his faculties soon under specialist care. He just needs time. Until then I can only reiterate that should you need me for anything, I am your willing servant.

'Oh, yes, one further thing that is urgent and which as your father's solicitor I will take care of for you is to seek temporary Power of Attorney for you while Edwin is incapable of dealing with his own affairs. You will need to have this authority to sign the deeds for the sale of this house, for instance. I will have the relevant papers delivered to you when they're drawn up.' He paused, suddenly noticing the deeply distracted expression on Eddie's face. 'Are you all right, my dear? No, of course you're not.' He picked up his glass, drained it then took up his walking stick and awkwardly stood up. 'I have taken too much of your time. I will take my leave now and await your summons.'

Completely lost in her own thoughts, Eddie was not even aware that the old man had left.

His narrative had utterly drained her, yet in a way she felt liberated now she had a greater understanding of her origins. She also understood how her father had come to be so easy duped by Stibley, since he had never been the worldly businessman she had always assumed him to be.

She took a deep breath. If, however, she had not fully appreciated the Griffins' financial status before Ralph Waddington's visit, she was certainly under no illusions as to its seriousness now. But that fact was not uppermost in her mind at this moment. The old man had made her see clearly that the way she was proceeding, seeking to sell the hotel to resolve their finances, was not the way to go. She should think of it from another angle entirely. Letting the house go and keeping the hotel.

The hotel was, after all, bringing in a regular income, how little or how much was not the issue at present. The house wasn't bringing in any revenue at all; in fact, could eat up whatever money they were left with after the hotel was sold if no other way to earn an income presented itself. Considering her father's uncertain health at the moment and the fact that he was over sixty-five, it was unlikely he'd ever be able to contribute again. The hotel would provide them with a place to live until they could finance the purchase of another house of their own. It would be such a wrench to let this one go, more so now she knew it had been a family home passed down through three generations, but Ralph Waddington had made her see that she had to be sensible; this was not a time to let sentimentality get in the way.

She felt rather foolish that it had taken an old man to point her in the right direction, that she had not thought of it herself when she had learned of her ownership of the hotel but blindly and willingly allowed herself to be led almost into a sale by Harvey in his belief he was acting in her best interests. She realised only too well why Harvey had chosen to put her on the path he had. He was well aware she was in no position to run a hotel. Hadn't the faintest clue in fact. He had spared her feelings by not pointing this out to her.

But she owed it to her dead mother to salvage what

she could of her inheritance. Her father had always cared for and protected her. Now it was Eddie's turn to care for and protect him, show him that Stibley's actions, terrible as they were, were not the end of the Griffins' world.

She felt a great surge of gratitude to the old gentleman for making her see the way forward in a much more clear-sighted way. She lifted her head to thank him and was stunned to find she was alone in the room. She shuddered. It was cold too. The fire had gone out. Looking over at the grandfather clock, she was shocked to see it was well past twelve. She hadn't realised she'd sat so long, lost in her own thoughts.

Then she jumped as she realised someone had come into the room and saw Mabel, dressed in her nightclothes, hair tightly wound in curlers under a hairnet, hovering inside the doorway. She had a worried expression on her face.

'Are you all right, Miss Griffin? Only I came down ter get meself a cup of tea as I couldn't sleep what with ... er ... having things on me mind, so to speak. I noticed the light was on and thought you'd gone to bed and forgot to switch it off. Are yer all right, Miss Griffin?'

She nodded. 'Thank you, Mabel, I'm fine.' It then struck her that this woman was more than just loyally concerned at seeing her mistress sitting here alone at this time of night. She had come down in the first place because she couldn't sleep through worry for her own job if the rumour of her employer's bankruptcy was indeed true. It would be very easy for Eddie to fob Mabel off and deal with this in the morning when she'd had some rest and more time to take on board all Ralph Waddington had told her, but that would not be fair to a loyal retainer. Whether or not Mabel would like what she was going to hear or sleep well after she'd heard it, it was only fair that Eddie should be honest with her, as she expected her employees to be honest with her.

She walked across to stand before the maid. Clasping her hands in front of her, she looked the other woman in the eye and said, 'The rumour you heard regarding Mr Griffin is true, I'm afraid.'

Mabel let out a loud gasp. 'It is! Oh, Miss Griffin,' she exclaimed, mortified.

'The house will have to go, I'm afraid, and . . .'

'Oh, no,' Mabel blurted, horrified. 'It's *that* bad then?'

Eddie sighed gravely. 'Yes, it is. Thankfully all is not quite lost as . . .' she took a deep breath and announced '. . . we have the hotel to fall back on and I shall now be taking an active role in its management.'

Mabel looked at her quizzically. 'The hotel, Miss Griffin?'

'The Connaught.'

'The Connaught?' The maid's face clouded over in surprise. 'Oh, not that . . .' She stopped abruptly and Eddie suspected she'd been about to say something like 'rundown place'. 'Oh, er . . . I wasn't aware the family owned a hotel.'

Neither was I until yesterday, Eddie thought. 'My father, when he comes out of hospital, and I will be moving there as a temporary measure.' She suddenly realised she hadn't considered their staff. 'Er . . . hopefully I'll be able to find live-in employment at the hotel for you and something suitable for Jess, should you both wish it. As for Arthur . . .' She realised she did not know if the hotel had gardens or not but assumed it had. 'I'm sure the hotel could do with another gardener to tend its lawns. Should any of you, though, decide to seek employment elsewhere, I will of course provide excellent references. I'll try to give you all a gratuity payment but cannot promise how much at this moment in time.'

The older woman wiped a tear from her eye. Her bottom lip quivering, she muttered, 'I appreciate that, Miss Griffin. Oh, such a sad day this is for me, it really is. I know Jess will be devastated too, and Arthur ain't gonna be chuffed neither when he hears of it. I thought I'd see the end of me days out working here for you, Miss Griffin.'

Eddie herself had never expected to leave this house under such circumstances and strongly suspected she was about to cry at the prospect. 'If you will excuse me, Mabel, I am rather tired,' she said stiltedly.

'Oh, yes, 'course, Miss Griffin. Good night.'

Considering the world as she knew it had completely disintegrated and that she was now facing challenges probably beyond her capabilities, it was a miracle that when Eddie got into bed and pulled the covers around her, within minutes she was fast asleep.

CHAPTER TEN

Harvey Crankshaft smiled at Eddie warmly when she entered the drawing room. 'Ah, there you are, my dear. I was rather surprised to find you out this morning when you knew I was coming to help you resolve such an important matter.'

She looked apologetic. 'I am so sorry. I trust Mabel explained why I wanted you to come back this afternoon?' Her face then flushed with a hint of excitement when she added, 'But when you hear what I have to tell you, I know you will understand why I kept you waiting.' She took a deep breath and told him, 'I've decided not to sell the hotel.'

He looked stunned by her announcement. 'Pardon? What do you mean, you're not selling the hotel?' He seemed deeply worried. 'Edelina, you need to sell the hotel to get yourself out of a financial mess,' he urged her.

'It's the *house* I need to sell. Please come and sit down, Uncle Harvey, and I'll explain how I came to this decision.' When they had both taken their seats she said, 'I appreciate why you felt it best to advise me to sell the hotel, Uncle Harvey, but after listening to Mr Waddington last night I feel that his suggestion I should look towards the hotel to provide Father and myself with a future is the better course of action for me to take. I am surprised Father felt Mr Waddington's brain isn't as sharp as it used to be because, I have to say, he seemed perfectly coherent to me.'

Harvey's opinion that she was making a huge mistake was plain. 'I think you're forgetting something, Edelina. Your father always made it very clear he wouldn't have anything to do with the hotel.'

A worried expression crossed her face, to be replaced by one of conviction. 'I'm sure he will understand how I came to this decision when he regains his faculties. He will agree that I had to do my best for both of us in his incapacity.'

Harvey gave a deep sigh. 'I'm not so sure he will understand,' he said. 'Edwin's refused to have anything to do with the hotel for the last forty years due to its painful associations with your mother, do you really think he's going to change his mind after all this time? Have you considered that you could cause him to suffer a setback in his recovery by bringing this all back to him when he finds out?'

'I wish I could discuss my proposal with Father before I go ahead but the hospital still won't allow me to visit him and cannot give me any indication when I will be allowed to. They told me on the telephone this morning the same thing as they did yesterday, that it is early days for someone with Father's condition. If he is still adamant he doesn't want to have anything to do with the hotel personally when he comes out of hospital . . . well, I will just have to deal with that situation in the best way I can.'

Harvey looked at her beseechingly. 'I still strongly advise you to sell the hotel and with what's left over make a future for yourselves. You could buy some houses and rent them out . . . start up in a business that way again. I do worry, Edelina, that you are taking on far more here than you realise.'

She wasn't sure if Harvey was aware of her father's true background; his lack of business acumen which meant that, like herself, he was unqualified to start a business from scratch even should the capital exist. Should he not be aware, she loved and respected her father far too much to risk lowering his friend's regard for him.

'I'm worried there won't be enough money left from the sale to start up any sort of business. Until we sell the hotel we won't know how much will be left, if anything, and by that time it will be too late for me to change my mind.' She took a deep breath, clasped her hands together tightly in her lap and announced, 'It's too late now. I have to proceed this way.'

'Too late? What do you mean, it's too late?'

'I've already put matters in motion, approached an estate agent to put this house on the market. He's coming round shortly to take details. I've also had an interview with the manager of Father's bank and explained our situation. I have to say, I was very nervous about seeing Mr Granger as I'd never had to deal with a bank manager before. I needn't have been. When he learned of the fraud perpetrated against us he was most shocked but also very sympathetic. He made me feel a little better as he told me this wasn't the first case of fraud by an employee that he'd come across, though he did say it was probably the worst. He is fairly new in his position and Stibley must have known this when he approached the bank posing as my father. Mr Granger has agreed to hold off calling in the mortgage for as long as he can, in the hope we will find a buyer quickly. He says a house such as this should attract attention, although as we need a quick sale we may have to sell it a little cheaper than we would have liked. When I explained about the hotel he was most relieved Stibley could not purloin that too and very much in agreement that it was to the hotel I should be looking to provide a future for us. He's also closed the hotel's bank account and opened up a new one for me. Stibley will no longer be able to get his hands on any more of the hotel income should he be blatant enough to try.'

'I see,' said Harvey slowly. He stood up and went across to the French windows to stare out of them for several moments before walking back and resuming his seat. 'I still don't think you've thought this all through properly, Edelina. What do you know about the hotel trade? About running any business? Your lack of experience, my dear, is the reason I didn't suggest this way forward to you in the first place.'

'Please rest assured, Uncle Harvey, I have no doubt you acted in good faith after taking everything into consideration. But it is of no consequence that I have no business experience and know nothing of the hotel trade as the manager handles its day-to-day running. I've no intention of interfering in his decisions. I propose to concentrate my efforts on identifying the improvements that can be made to bring the hotel into the 1950s, and that way hopefully up the profits by attracting a different kind of clientele.'

If he was impressed with her plan Harvey did not show it. His face still grim, he said, 'Improvements cost money, Edelina, money you don't have.'

'I do realise that, Uncle Harvey. The sale of the contents of this house should bring in enough to make a good start.' She gave a sad sigh, flashed a look around the room, brought her eyes back to rest on him and added, 'We have some good pieces of furniture and china which I'm sure are worth something. It's going to be heartbreaking for me, seeing all these lovely things auctioned off, but this is no time to be sentimental. I have to push personal feelings aside and use what I have in the best way I can.' She paused, looking at him questioningly. 'I had hoped you'd be more supportive of my plan.'

'I am, of course I am,' he blustered. 'Please rest assured I have only your best interests at heart. I'm just not sure you're up to taking on what you propose, that's all.'

She gave a brief smile. 'Who knows what we have in us, Uncle Harvey, until we are called upon to find out? I've never had to think for myself in this way before and already I have surprised myself with what I've achieved. I must admit, my first instinct was to ask you to help me deal with all this but then I thought better of it. I have to start standing on my own two feet and not keep relying on you to take care of things for me. I am so appreciative of the support and help you've already given me. I know I can count on you in the future to help me if I find myself in a situation

I really can't handle.' She took a deep breath. 'I can't deny I'm frightened of what I'm proposing but I'm also excited. It's like embarking on an adventure. But the most important thing to me is getting Father out of the hospital and back to normal. He's obviously convinced himself there's no future for us. I want to prove to him that there is, and promises are not enough, I have to show him the evidence so he'll believe it.'

He stood up and smiled warmly at her. 'Well, you seem to have everything under control, Edelina. I'd best contact Mr Whittle and advise him you no longer require his help in getting the hotel sold. Not at this moment in time anyway. You know how I can be contacted should you need me.'

After pecking her cheek, he made his way out.

It was clear that Harvey wasn't best pleased by her decision. But she knew he was worried for her, felt that the hotel would not provide the future she was banking on, and feared his friend and his daughter might find themselves in a worse position than they were now. She just hoped she could prove to him that his fears were unfounded, show him her decision had been the right one. She was warmed, though, by the fact that her father had such a friend.

She heard a tap at the door and saw Mabel entering. 'There's two men, Miss Griffin. They asked for Mr Griffin and when I told 'em he was not at home at the moment, they asked if any other member of the family was.'

'Who are they?' Eddie asked.

Mabel looked uncomfortable. 'They said they're from the bailiff's office, Miss Griffin.'

Her face drained. Eddie wasn't so naive she didn't realise what this call signified. 'Please show them in, Mabel,' she said stiffly.

She rose to greet the two burly-looking men who entered the drawing room moments later. 'Good afternoon, gentlemen,' she addressed them politely. 'What can I do for you?'

The older of the two men, not even affording her the courtesy of removing his black bowler hat, said brusquely, 'Well, yer could pay what's outstanding on this bill,' and thrust a brown envelope in her direction. 'Else we're instructed to take goods to the value.'

A wave of humiliation flooded Eddie as she walked towards him to retrieve the envelope from him. Opening it, she extracted the document inside and read it. It was a final demand from her father's tailor for two suits and pairs of matching extra trousers that he'd made several months previously. The total outstanding was over a hundred pounds. 'I'm sure this is a misunderstanding . . .' she began.

'I'm sure it is, Miss Griffin,' he said, a hint of mockery in his voice. 'If you'll just give us the cash to settle it, we'll be on our way.'

She hadn't that amount to hand, nothing like it. The fifty pounds she had found in her father's safe was now depleted by the several pounds she had given Jess to pay the outstanding grocery bill and enough to cover the order she had needed to place this morning. She noticed that the other man was closely inspecting furniture in the room. Humiliation threatened to swamp her. 'I really am sure this is all . . .'

Before she could finish he interjected, 'Look, lady,

we ain't got time to stand here arguing the toss. Now yer either pay what you owe in cash or we're empowered to take goods to the value. What's it to be?'

Her look gave him his answer.

Within less than twenty minutes, while Eddie stood by helplessly watching, the two men had selected the gramophone cabinet and a large collection of records; the grandfather clock; the walnut writing desk whose contents were emptied and heaped on the floor, and several pieces of china. They loaded them onto a van and departed. Despite being too numb with shock and humiliation to say anything, Eddie was well aware that the goods they had taken would fetch well above the outstanding debt. What this turn of events did, though, was bring forcibly to mind the order she had placed the day before for new clothes for herself. She was a regular customer at the store, always charging her purchases, and had a terrible feeling that at any minute the bailiffs would be calling again. She knew she had no choice but to cancel her order of yesterday and also urgently address the rest of the outstanding bills, somehow finding the means either to pay them or to stall payment until the house was sold or this awful situation might happen again.

She was jerked out of her worrying thoughts by a tap on the door again and glanced across to see Mabel standing just inside the entrance.

'Mrs Rymmington-Smyth, Miss Griffin,' she announced before departing.

Phee, dressed in a black knee-length fitted cocktail dress, its low neckline showing off her diamond pendant and the top of her firm creamy-white bosom, was peeling off elbow-length black silk gloves as she sashayed towards the sofa. She sank down on to it, crossed her legs and draped her arm across the back cushions. She looked annoyed, far too preoccupied with her own problems to notice the state of her friend.

'A brandy, dear, that's what I need. Make it a large one,' she ordered as she started to delve inside her bag for her cigarettes, long black holder and gold Dunhill lighter.

Moments later Eddie handed her a bulb glass holding a generous measure of Armagnac. 'What's upset you, Phee?' she asked, concern for her friend overriding her own problems.

Phee almost snatched the glass from her hand and took a long swallow. 'My bloody father, that's who. Oh, and Mummy too. They've cancelled their plan to take Geraldine to the Riviera for the Easter holidays so I have no choice but to take her myself. Daddy has had a big murder case unexpectedly dumped on him and Mummy has taken to her bed with the flu. Oh, it really is too bad! I was so looking forward to a month's freedom from parents and daughter.'

Eddie sat down on the settee beside her. 'It will be nice to spend time with your daughter, won't it?'

'Will it?' snapped Phee. 'I could think of things I'd sooner be doing than entertaining that little madam for a whole month.' She lit her cigarette. 'Nothing pleases her at the moment, and I find it so difficult to talk to her. She and I communicate in different languages, Eddie darling. Being a mother is so much more difficult than I ever thought it would be. Think yourself lucky you have no offspring. It wasn't so bad when

Gerry was younger and the nanny took care of her, but she's too old for a nanny now. My daughter is so moody lately. She complains bitterly that I don't take any notice of her and I'm never around, but when I do make an effort she complains I'm smothering her.'

Phee took a long draw from her cigarette and blew a cloud of smoke into the air. 'I did my utmost to convince Daddy it would be best to arrange for Geraldine to stay with a friend during the school break, that she'd be far happier doing that than spending time with me in France and that I had other plans here at home that I'd be very loath to cancel. He wouldn't hear of it. Said he'd instructed the château's staff to ready it for his arrival, had the car serviced and the chauffeur on standby, and because he and Mummy couldn't go themselves he wanted me to go and check that all was shipshape over there.' She gave a disdainful click of her tongue, pulling a face. 'It really is too bad. I was going to the races on Easter Saturday afternoon, and on Sunday for a trip down the river with Freddy Simpkin in his new river cruiser. He promised me champagne and caviar. He really is an oaf if he thinks I'd ever accept a proposal from the son of a grocer.'

Eddie looked at her incredulously. 'Phee, Freddy Simpkin's father is *the* Simpkin of Simpkin and James, fine food and wine merchants. They have several large stores.'

'Still a grocer, darling, no getting away from it.'

'But you married a croupier! And the man you thought was a financial expert turned out to be no more than an insurance agent. And there was that actor who never actually landed more than a bit part during your six-month marriage. A grocer's son is a little more upmarket than those three, wouldn't you agree?'

'I suppose, in comparison,' Phee said dismissively. 'But it's a man of means . . . his own means, not his father's . . . that I have in mind for husband number four. Oh, and he must be good-looking too. Pity Angela Sudbury snapped up Reggie Greenwood while I was away skiing last winter. Poor Reggie barely widowed five minutes before she had him up the aisle, a diamond the size of a grape on her finger. He would have suited me very nicely. He's in the fur trade, made an absolute fortune from it. Still, no point in crying over spilt milk, as my old nanny used to say. There's got to be another where he came from. A girl just has to keep her eyes peeled and grab him quick before the likes of Angela Sudbury gets her claws in first.

'Anyway, as I hadn't received a better offer for Easter Sunday afternoon other than helping my parents entertain their luncheon guests, I accepted Freddy's offer.' Her face suddenly brightened as a thought struck her and she cried excitedly, 'Oh, Eddie darling, why don't you come to France with me? Oh, we'd have a ball. Get ourselves invited to lots of parties. French men are delicious, darling. They really know how to treat a woman. Our English men seem like immature schoolboys in comparison. I'll arrange for Geraldine to take a friend with her to keep her occupied.' She took another swallow of brandy. 'I feel so much better now that's settled.'

'I can't possibly come to France with you, Phee.'

'You can't? Why not? Oh, of course, you're off to

Egypt with your father. Oh, hell, I'd forgotten about that.'

'What you have forgotten is my situation, Phee.'

Her friend looked at her non-plussed. 'What situation?' Then it came back to mind. 'Oh, yes, of course, the one involving your father's employee. Hasn't that been sorted yet? But I thought your father's golfing friend Harvey . . . whatever . . . was dealing with all that for you? How is your dear father?' Without giving Eddie time to respond she advised, 'The best thing for you just now is to get right away from everything, and a month in France is just the ticket. When you return everything will be back to normal. We'll leave next Tuesday. Oh, we'll have such fun!' She glanced across the room, expecting to see the grandfather clock, and when she didn't asked, 'Where's the clock gone? Oh, in for repair, is it?'

She looked at the dainty gold watch on her wrist before bringing her attention back to Eddie. 'I know I've arrived a little early this afternoon, but hadn't you better start getting ready as we're expected for cocktails at the Fosters' at six?' She pulled a face. 'I don't know whether the play we're going to see afterwards holds much appeal to me. I never have been fond of Shakespeare. I wouldn't admit this to anyone but you, darling, but I can't understand what the actors are saying, despite pretending I do. Shakespearean plays always sound double Dutch to me. I suppose I should have taken more notice in literature lessons at school but the antics of the gardener held much more appeal. A sad day it was when the Headmistress replaced him with that elderly man after the incident involving . . . what was that girl's name now? Oh, I can't remember but she did rather throw herself at him, and I feel it was rather too bad that her father insisted he be dismissed else he'd take matters further, when it was common knowledge amongst us girls that the good-looking gardener was far more interested in the boys in the school next door and that girl had blatantly lied about his taking advantage of her. She even named him as the father of her baby when we all knew her lies were just to cover up the fact she couldn't possibly have known who the father actually *was* as most of the boys in the Lower Sixth had her to thank for losing their virginity.' She drained her glass and handed it to Eddie. 'I'll have another brandy while I wait for you to get ready.'

Eddie took the empty glass from her. 'Phee, I am sorry but it had totally slipped my mind we had an arrangement for tonight. I'll have to cancel, I've so much to be getting on with.'

Sophia looked mystified. 'Getting on with? Such as what, darling?'

'Well, you see, I'm expecting the estate agent to call at any time and I need to be here to deal with him.' Then her mind flooded with all the other things that needed her urgent attention and they all came spilling out. 'Tomorrow morning I have to pay a visit to Father's office. I do hope the janitor will let me in unless I can find Father's office keys because I need to get the out-standing bills from Stibley's drawer, see if I can arrange to stall payment on them until I can start to draw on hotel funds. Then I need to arrange for the auctioneer to call and value the contents of this house. That is most urgent so I can . . .' Momentarily her voice trailed off. Despite Phee's being her closest friend she just could not bring herself to tell her of the dreadful situation she had found herself in this afternoon. 'Oh, such a mountain of things I have to do. I suppose I should make a list so I don't overlook anything. And I must also pay a visit to the hotel to see the manager and tell him to allocate me suitable rooms as I will be moving in. I'm hoping Father will move in too when he comes out of hospital, but if not I am sure by then I will be able to find us a house to rent until we can afford to buy somewhere. That is providing I have made some inroads into the hotel's renovation and it is bringing in sufficient profits to allow for that. So, you see, I can't possibly come to France with you either.'

As she had talked Phee's mouth and eyes had become wider and wider. Eddie suddenly stopped her flow of words and said, 'Oh, my goodness, I sounded just like you then, going from one thing to another without pausing for breath. I can see you haven't a clue what I'm talking about. I'd better explain.' She fixed Phee with her eyes and said, 'I want you to listen to me, and I mean properly, not pretend to like you usually do with your mind on other things. Are you listening properly, Phee?'

Still wide-eyed and open-mouthed, she nodded.

Eddie proceeded to explain in great detail her future plans. She finished by saying, 'And I'll be needing your help.'

'Help?' Phee frowned worriedly. 'Well, that depends, darling, on just what kind of help you mean?'

'The kind that involves coming up with ideas on how to modernise the hotel, bring it into the 1950s.'

Her friend looked mortally relieved. 'Oh, thank goodness. For a moment I thought you were expecting me to get down on my hands and knees and scrub floors, darling.'

Despite feeling the weight of the world on her shoulders, Eddie could not help but laugh at the very thought. 'As if I'd even dare think such a thing, let alone expect you to do it.'

'Well, work and I don't exactly see eye to eye. The thought of getting my hands dirty makes me feel quite faint.' Phee's face creased in polite query. 'Darling, you really *are* serious about selling up everything to move into the hotel?'

'Very serious, Phee. I have no choice.' Her eyes sparkling humorously, Eddie said, 'You will still want to associate with me when I'm a lowly innkeeper?'

Phee completely misconstrued the humour behind Eddie's remark and tutted. 'Hardly a lowly innkeeper, darling. The hotel needs work, I admit, but it cannot be compared to some seedy guest house down a back street.' And she added quickly, 'Not that I've ever been inside one of those places, you understand, so as to be able to compare. I must admit, it will be quite a novelty, my dearest friend a hotel proprietor. No problem now for us or our friends finding somewhere to stay the night or to have breakfast after we've attended a late function in Leicester.'

Eddie looked straight at her. 'Providing we have vacancies and the bills for the rooms are paid, no problem at all.' She saw the look on her friend's face and added, 'This is no joke, Phee, not a momentary distraction that's taken my fancy that I'll drop and move on from after the fun wears off. The hotel is going to provide us Griffins with our living in future. All guests, including friends and acquaintances, will be expected to pay their bills.' She paused and smiled affectionately at Phee. 'Though, as my dearest friend, I will make a concession for you. But only you.'

She smiled back, patting Eddie's arm. 'You are a sweetheart. But should I require a bed for the night, I'll pay like everyone else.' She was being as free with her father's money as always. Then she looked at Eddie with awe. 'Oh, darling, I think you are being so brave. I don't know what I'd do if I suddenly found myself in your position, having to earn a living.'

She might seem it to Phee, but in fact Eddie did not feel brave at all. She wished with all her heart that she could run off to France for a month and come back to find the whole situation miraculously resolved and her life back the way it always had been. That was not going to happen, though. No fairy was going to wave a magic wand and put this all right while she was away enjoying herself. She had to stay here and do it herself the best way she could.

'Whatever I can do to help, darling,' Phee was saying to her, 'I'm at your command.' Then added as an afterthought, 'Oh, so long as it's not this weekend, I already have plans, and of course as I explained I can't get out of going to France. But provided I don't need another holiday so as to recover from spending a whole month with my daughter, I'm all yours on my return.'

There was a tap at the door then and Mabel appeared.

'Miss Griffin, a Mr Froggitt from Froggitt Estate Agents has arrived. He says he's got an appointment.'

'Show him in please, Mabel.'

'Well, I'd better be off,' Phee announced, uncrossing her legs to stand up.

Eddie got up to join her, kissing her cheek. 'I'm sorry for letting you down tonight, but you understand why now, don't you?'

Just then a smartly suited, good-looking man in his early-forties entered. He was armed with a clipboard.

Phee flashed her eyes at him then turned and whispered in Eddie's ear, 'Oh, darling, such a temptation, but I just couldn't bear to go through life being addressed as Mrs Froggitt.'

The poor man beside the door could not understand why the two women across the room were both looking at him so regretfully.

CHAPTER ELEVEN

'Oh, for goodness' sake, girl, don't you listen? That is not the way I showed you how to collate the breakfast requests for tomorrow. I will not have my department's excellent reputation ruined through the slap-dash attitude of someone who should never have been allowed behind this counter anyway, except to clean it. Now do it again – and properly this time. Hurry up!' Amelia Harbin glared at Connie. 'Captain Fosedyke is going to request a report on your progress any time now and it's not going to be favourable. After I tell him of your inability to perform one task correctly, I wouldn't be surprised if you find yourself back where you belong, as a chambermaid.'

Connie fought to control her anger. She had done the job exactly as Miss Harbin had instructed her to do and the woman was blatantly lying by saying she had not followed her instructions. Connie had done so precisely. Amelia Harbin had behaved in exactly the same way with every other job she had given Connie to do since she had taken up her new position four days ago. Right from the first minute in her new post it was apparent to Connie that the senior receptionist was not going to give her a fair trial but would seize every opportunity she could to make Connie look incompetent so as to have an excuse to be rid of her after the trial period.

But Connie had waited a long time to be given this chance to work on reception and was not going to let a dragon of a woman take her chance away from her without putting up one hell of a fight.

She forced a smile to her face. 'I apologise, Miss Harbin, and I will do it correctly this time.' Then a way of halting Miss Harbin's game struck her. 'Miss Harbin, in future when you instruct me to do a task, I will write down your instructions on a pad. I can follow those instructions as I do the job and that way I can't possibly go wrong.'

How Connie stopped herself from laughing at the look the senior receptionist gave her was a credit to her.

Eyes dark as thunder, physically shaking with rage at what she felt was Connie's audacity, Miss Harbin had reared back her head and opened her mouth to rebuke her subordinate when she was stopped short by the arrival at the counter of an elderly woman who banged her hand hard against the desk-top bell for immediate attention. Spinning on her heel, Miss Harbin went across to deal with her.

'Another breakfast order for you, Connie. Room 210 have just rung down with it.'

Connie turned round to see Pamela Wardle approaching. Pamela was the hotel's switchboard operator and constantly wore her earphones around her neck, long cord dangling, ready to plug back into the board on her return. The switchboard was situated in a cubicle to one end of the long reception counter and operating it was something Connie knew she'd be expected to learn in order to relieve Pamela at breaks, lunchtime and on her day off – always provided Miss Harbin hadn't achieved her wish and got rid of Connie first. Pamela was an ordinary-looking, plump, twenty-five-year-old woman with a pleasant personality. The two of them had taken a liking to each other as soon as they'd been introduced on Connie's first morning in her new position.

She smiled at Pamela now as she retrieved the order from her. 'Thanks, Pamela.'

The telephonist looked at Connie knowingly and, flashing a quick look round to make sure Miss Harbin was otherwise occupied, said in hushed tones, 'She likes to be the Queen Bee, don't she? I really enjoy my job but I'd like it better if we had another senior receptionist over us, someone who didn't think we're something she'd need to scrape off the bottom of her shoe. Unless you've come from a monied background with a private education, like Miss Harbin, and been trained in a top hotel in London, she doesn't think you're good enough to join her in what she sees as a prestigious place in the hotel.'

Pamela was suppressing a fit of the giggles. 'Silly old bat acts like this place is the Savoy instead of what it really is and that's a once grand hotel that's now second rate, or even third considering the shabby state of some of the rooms.

'Don't let Miss Harbin get to you, Connie, like she has done all the other girls who've taken your position since Miss Birch retired. The pair of them managed the whole of reception apparently, including the switchboard, even covering for each other on days off. Since I've been here Madam's never had a day off to my knowledge, and I've my own ideas as to why she hasn't. It was the Captain who realised they'd never get another person to take up the old position like Miss Birch did and decided to split it between a switchboard operator and another receptionist. That's when I was employed so I've only been here myself four months. Miss Harbin tolerates me because I'm GPO-trained and you can't get better than that. Even she can't make out I'm not good enough.

'I was under the mistaken impression I'd like a job where I wasn't being watched over all day by hawk-eyed supervisors at the GPO, but I was wrong. Miss Harbin's worse, if that's possible, but I'm not leaving until I'm good and ready to and certainly not when Miss Harbin decides I am. I wouldn't give the old bat the satisfaction.' Pamela smiled at Connie warmly. 'I have to say, I wasn't struck on the other girls who've come and gone since I started here but I've took a liking to you and think me and you will get on well together. Just do your best not to let the old dragon have any reason to complain about your work, and when she does have a go at you, hold your breath and count to ten, like I do. Anyway, I'd best get back before she has chance to say I've deserted my post.'

Connie smiled warmly at her as she hurried back to the switchboard that had just started to bleep, announcing an outside call had come through. She felt better after Pamela's talk to her and was even more determined now not to let Amelia Harbin get rid of her, just as Pamela wasn't. Connie might not have had a privileged background with a private education but that didn't mean she couldn't do this job as well as someone who had. She took a deep breath and began to redo her task.

Several moments later she was aware that someone had approached the counter and looked up to see a cheaply dressed young couple looking expectantly at her. The young woman's eyes were dancing with nervous excitement while the young man with her looked extremely uncomfortable. The woman had a drooping pink carnation pinned below the shoulder of her market-quality coat, the man a red one on the lapel of his off-the-peg suit.

Having been warned very clearly by Miss Harbin that she was not to deal with any guests until she had gained more experience – though how she was supposed to gain that experience if she wasn't allowed to approach them she had no idea – Connie looked across to see that Miss Harbin was now engrossed in dealing with a query from the concierge. Connie felt it wasn't right to keep the young couple waiting until Miss Harbin was available when she herself was free to help them but did not want to risk another severe reprimand so soon after just having one.

She placed a welcoming smile on her face and said, 'Good morning and welcome to the Connaught Hotel. Miss Harbin won't keep you waiting a moment.'

Before she could ask if they'd like to take a seat while they waited for Miss Harbin to become free the young woman blurted out excitedly to her, 'We've just got married.' She delved into her plastic handbag and pulled out a marriage certificate which she proudly thrust out for Connie to see. 'Mrs Wiggins, that's me. I became her a couple of hours ago, I did.'

'Congratulations,' said Connie sincerely. 'I hope you'll be very happy together.'

'Ta very much,' said Mrs Wiggins, putting the marriage certificate back safely in her handbag. She gave her new husband a nudge in his ribs. 'Well, Dennis.'

He looked at his wife blankly. 'Well what?'

'Tell the lady we got a room booked, yer soppy 'a'p'orth.'

'Oh, yeah, we've got a room booked,' he said to Connie. 'Janice's mam and dad booked it for us as a surprise.'

'Yeah, that's right,' said Janice Wiggins. 'They came here for their honeymoon night thirty-eight years ago after me gran and granddad saved up to give them the treat, and they thought it'd be nice for us to start off our married life like they did. They saved up the money and gave it us, and enough for a nice meal tonight too. Me dad's been poorly for the last couple of years and not been able to work so I know saving up for our surprise ain't bin easy for them. We did pay for the wedding ourselves, though, didn't we, Dennis, so they wouldn't have that burden. It were only a small do but it don't matter, does it, when yer marrying the right one? We thought we was just spending our honeymoon night at me mam's, didn't we, Dennis, so this is a real shock for us. We ain't never stayed in a hotel before.'

With an awed expression she flashed a glance around before looking again at Connie. 'It's so exciting! Do we get our bags carried to our room? I can't wait to see it. Mam told me she'd managed to book the same one she and Dad stayed in, and it's got comfy chairs to sit in and a table we can have our breakfast on if we don't want to come down. Or we could have it in bed. Oh, yes, we might do that . . . just like posh people do.'

Connie glanced across to see Miss Harbin still involved with the concierge. This young couple were so touchingly eager to be settled into their room so they could savour every minute of such an unexpected gift, something it was quite possible they might never find the money to experience again. There was no telling how much longer Miss Harbin would be and Connie did not feel it was right to keep this young couple hanging about when she was quite capable of booking them in herself, having closely observed how Miss Harbin did it.

Feeling sure the senior receptionist would appreciate that she was trying to do her best for their guests, which after all was the most important thing about her job, Connie leaned over and retrieved the reservations book. Tracing her finger down the first column, she saw a reservation in the name of Wiggins against room 187. It was one of the hotel's larger rooms on the third floor, sporting a stunning view over the rooftops of Leicester, and was better furnished than other rooms so carried a higher nightly rate. Mrs Wiggins' parents had indeed made sure the newly weds were spending their first night together as a married couple in one of the best rooms the Connaught had to offer.

Picking up a blank registration card, Connie held it out towards Mr Wiggins and was just about to ask him to complete their details when it was snatched out of her hand and she turned her head to see Miss Harbin standing to the side of her.

She was glaring haughtily at the young couple. 'We have no vacancies,' she said brusquely. 'I suggest you try a guest house off one of the side streets further up London Road. More your type of establishment.'

Janice Wiggins gawped at her. 'Eh! But we've a booking. And what d'yer mean by saying a guest house would be more our type of establishment?'

'Miss Harbin, Mr and Mrs Wiggins do have a bo—' Connie was stopped abruptly by the look she received from her superior.

Miss Harbin addressed the young couple again. 'Good day,' she said dismissively. Turning her back on them, she addressed Connie. 'Have you finished collating the breakfast orders for tomorrow yet?'

'Er . . . no, Miss Harbin.'

'Well, I suggest you get on with it. Urgently,' she snapped as she retrieved the reservations book to take it back across with her to the end of the counter by the switchboard cubicle, where she took her seat and appeared to be busying herself tallying bills ready for guests booking out later that morning.

Connie looked on helplessly as, with a look of humiliation on her face, Janice Wiggins grabbed her new husband's arm and urged him, 'Come on, Dennis, I want to get out of here. It's obvious we ain't welcome.'

After they had departed Connie went over to Miss Harbin. 'Excuse me, Miss Harbin?'

She looked up at her blankly. 'Make it quick, I'm busy.'

'Mr and Mrs Wiggins, they do have a booking. If I

184

hurry I can catch them and bring them back. Explain we made a mistake.'

'That you will not. They might have had a booking but the likes of them the Connaught does not encourage.'

Connie looked confused. 'I'm sorry, but what do you mean by the likes of them, Miss Harbin?'

'Oh, come on, girl. I doubt very much they have the money between them to settle their bill and more than likely plan to abscond without paying. And as for their actually being married, well, it's my opinion that is not the case. I will not knowingly allow fornication under this roof. What kind of message would that be sending to our other guests? The receptionist's job is not just about booking guests in and out, it is also up to us to make sure the calibre of our guests will not lower the hotel's high reputation. That particular booking was obviously taken, without my knowledge, by one of your imbecilic predecessors and, if by chance they'd done their job properly, the address of the person who made the booking will be on file. I will write to them and clear up this matter to ensure the good name of the Connaught continues, although I doubt that has any relevance to those concerned in this case. You have a lot to learn, Miss Monroe. It remains to be seen whether you have the capacity,' she said, glancing Connie up and down scathingly.

She was having terrible trouble quashing her anger at this woman's blatant snobbery and despotic decisions as to who should be allowed to stay in the Connaught or not. It wasn't as if all the rooms were booked either. Connie did not know whether the hotel could afford to turn away paying guests but, regardless, felt it was not right that Miss Harbin had turned the Wigginses away just because they fell below her own personal standards. She dreaded to think how hurt and upset the pair were after this woman's nasty treatment of them. She had most likely ruined their memories of their wedding day. 'But Mr and Mrs Wiggins were married, Miss Harbin, I saw their marriage certificate.'

'You were maybe shown a certificate but that does not mean it was genuine.' Miss Harbin glared stonily at her. 'I will make sure Captain Fosedyke is aware of your lack of respect towards me as your superior in questioning my authority. My advice to you is to press your chambermaid's uniform ready for your return to those duties as you won't be in this position much longer.' She stood up. 'I trust you can man reception while I pay a visit to the powder room. Should any guests require attention during my absence, ask them to wait until I return.'

With that she stalked off.

Connie heard Pamela addressing her and turned to look across at her, sitting at the switchboard. 'Remember what I told you, Connie. Don't let the old dragon get the better of you.'

She gave a wan smile. Easier said than done.

Just then a messenger entered through the revolving doors and came immediately across to Connie. 'Hand delivery for a Captain Fosedyke. Sign here for it,' he said, indicating a space on a form on his clipboard. After she had signed he handed her a letter and went on his way.

Connie looked at it. It was addressed to Captain Fosedyke and had 'Urgent' scrawled underneath his name in thick black ink. She looked across to the long corridor where the staff toilets were situated. There was no sign of Miss Harbin returning. Urgent meant immediate, didn't it? As Connie had signed for the letter the Captain could very well query why she hadn't taken it in to him straight away, and possibly reprimand her for her laxness in not doing so. Trouble was, Miss Harbin could also reprimand her for deserting her post for the minute it would take her to deliver the letter to the Captain. She felt as though she was caught between the devil and the deep blue sea. But then the Captain was the hotel manager and his position superior to Miss Harbin's. She checked again to see if Miss Harbin was on her way back. There was still no sign of her.

'Pamela, could you hold the fort for a moment while I deliver this urgent letter to the Captain?'

Smiling, she nodded.

Armed with the letter, Connie hurried to the end of the reception counter, lifted the flap and passed through, replacing the flap behind her. She then hurried across the short expanse of hall to the Captain's office and tapped on the door. When she heard him call out for her to enter, she opened the door and went inside.

As he lifted his head from the paperwork he was dealing with to see who had come in she held the letter out towards him and said, 'Sorry to disturb you, Captain Fosedyke, but this letter has just been hand delivered for you. I thought I ought to bring it to you straight away as it's marked Urgent.'

He accepted the letter from her. 'Thank you, Miss Monroe.'

She flashed him a quick smile and made to leave but was stopped when, much to her surprise, the Captain asked her, 'How are you settling into your new position?'

'Oh, er . . . I like the job, Captain Fosedyke. I've a lot to learn, I know that. I'm sure I can, though, and prove my worth.' Then, before she could stop herself, she added, 'I'm not sure Miss Harbin thinks I'm up to the work, though.' Connie immediately scolded herself for saying what she had.

He surprised her again by smiling kindly at her. 'You haven't been in the job long enough for Miss Harbin to have formed a proper opinion. I am aware that she does have exacting standards. Since Miss Birch retired it's been difficult to find a suitable replacement but Miss Wardle seems to have settled in well and I have high hopes of you yourself becoming a valued member of our reception staff. I was very pleasantly surprised by your request to better your position and your enthusiasm for doing so. I was aware that you were one of our better chambermaids and was sorry to lose you from that position, but thankfully we didn't lose you to another hotel.'

A beam of delight split Connie's face. His words of encouragement were so welcome after not receiving any at all from Miss Harbin. 'Thank you, Captain Fosedyke.' Her need to return to her place behind the desk occurred to her then and she turned and hurried to the door.

Just as she was departing through it the Captain called, 'Oh, just a moment, Miss Monroe.'

She stopped, turning back to face him.

'I'm expecting a Mrs Driffield for an interview for an accounts clerk's position. I am just off to do my morning rounds and should be back before she arrives, but should I not be would you please seat her comfortably in my office and despatch the porter, if he's free, to come and find me? Or if he's not free, please inform Miss Harbin I have given you leave to seek me out.'

'Of course, Captain Fosedyke.'

Connie made to leave again and was stopped when he asked, 'Oh, you haven't seen Mr Sopworth about, have you?'

She shook her head. 'No, I haven't. Sorry, Captain Fosedyke.'

A flash of annoyance crossed his face. 'How long does it take for that man to do a simple job?' Then he mentally shook himself, realising he'd voiced his private thoughts out loud. 'If you do see him, will you tell him I was looking for him?' he asked as he reached over for his letter opener and made to slit open the envelope Connie had given him.

'Yes, of course I will.'

As she made her way back to reception Connie smiled warmly to herself. She really was seeing another side of the Captain. He was far nicer than she had previously realised. Maybe she'd just caught him at bad times before. Maybe his response to her had changed because she had now joined the administrative staff and was working more closely to him. Whatever the reason it wasn't really important to Connie. The fact that she didn't feel quite so intimidated by the hotel manager made her more comfortable within herself. All she had to do now was win over Miss Harbin, though she had a feeling that wasn't going to be so easily accomplished.

She had just resumed her place behind the counter when Miss Harbin returned. 'Anything happened I should know about while I was gone?' she brusquely asked.

Connie flashed a look in Pamela's direction who flashed her a sign back that no guest had sought attention while she herself had been absent. 'No, Miss Harbin.'

'Right, well, when you've finished collating the breakfast orders and logging them into the book for me to calculate the guests' final bills, I want you to do the same with the newspaper orders before we give them to the night porter when he comes on this evening. Do you think you can handle that correctly?'

The look she was giving Connie was telling her Miss Harbin severely doubted she was capable of carrying out such a simple task correctly. She quashed a great urge to shout at her to give her a chance instead of condemning her out of hand. 'I'm sure I can, Miss Harbin,' she replied evenly.

She looked surreptitiously at Connie. 'Well, we'll know the answer to that in the morning by the number of complaints we receive that guests haven't had their newspapers, won't we?'

Connie stared at her as she turned and walked off to address Pamela.

She had finished the breakfast orders as far as she could until any more were received and was totting up what newspapers were required when she realised someone had approached the counter and looked up to see a smartly dressed, very attractive woman looking at her expectantly.

Connie flashed a glance over at Miss Harbin who was engrossed in convincing a middle-aged couple that the taxi that had been ordered to take them to the Palace Theatre that evening at seven-thirty would arrive promptly because she herself had ordered it. She then heard the gentleman ask where in Leicester she could recommend they should visit tomorrow. It was apparent to Connie that Miss Harbin was going to be some time dealing with those guests.

Smiling at the woman facing her, Connie said politely, 'Good morning, madam. Welcome to the Connaught Hotel. Miss Harbin won't keep you a moment, she'll be with you to deal with your reservation in person. Would you like to take a seat while you're waiting?' she asked, indicating a nearby area of high-backed chairs by a coffee table on which was arranged an assortment of quality magazines and a selection of current newspapers. Several of the seats were already occupied by guests or visitors of guests waiting for them to come down from their rooms. 'I'll arrange for the porter to bring in your luggage for you,' Connie said as she quickly scanned around in search of Danny, the young day porter, but he was nowhere to be seen. 'I'll organise that for you as soon as the porter comes back.'

Edelina's mind was fully occupied with how she was going to approach the hotel manager with the news that she was going to be taking an active role here in future as well as living in. She'd decided not to mention her father's possible requirements just now but would deal with that situation when the time came for him to leave hospital, which she dearly hoped would be soon. She did hope she would not betray to the hotel manager the humiliation she inwardly felt at her enforced change of lifestyle, praying that the story of her father's loss and its dire effects on them had not circulated as far as the hotel's management or staff. She wanted her sudden interest in the hotel to be viewed as keenness on her part to become involved in it after the absence of any proprietorial participation for so long.

Since she had made her decision not to sell the hotel five days previously, her every waking moment had been consumed with organising all that was required for a swift sale of the house and its contents, all of which were now thankfully safe in the expert hands of the estate agent and auctioneer, both of whom had promised they'd do their best to obtain good prices for her. In light of Stibley's misdemeanours, she hoped they'd be true to their word. She had then turned her attention to the task of contacting all the people with whom they had outstanding debts, and thankfully had convinced them all to give her more time to settle their accounts. As it was her father's name that was on all the bills, and as he was hospitalised, all of them in truth had little choice but to agree to her terms.

To obtain all the creditors' names and to discover the actual amounts outstanding she had had to pay a visit to her father's office. She hadn't liked the thought of entering the actual place where Stibley had planned and executed his despicable scheme to wreak vengeance against her father, taking forty years to do so. Her first instinct had been to turn to Harvey and ask him to collect the information from Stibley's desk drawer as well as any more letters which might have been sent since his departure, but then she had thought better of it. Upon informing Harvey she was not following his advice but instead that suggested by Ralph Waddington, she had also told him that she could not keep relying on him continually to be at her beck and call, that it was time she stood on her own two feet and dealt with her problems herself, only calling on him when something she was dealing with was beyond her capabilities. She must honour that decision.

Finding her father's office keys at the back of his desk drawer, and blanking her mind against anything other than what she needed to obtain in the office, her visit had been short. She had felt proud of herself after she'd completed her daunting task, feeling that anything she'd face in the future would not be as bad as entering the devil's den.

Finding absolutely nothing left for her to do at home bar pace the rooms while buyers inspected them, she knew the time had now come to inform the hotel manager of her intentions. Visiting the hotel with Phee in the guise of a diner was one thing. Presenting herself as an owner, who before now hadn't bothered to show her face for any reason whatsoever, was another. On entering the foyer, Eddie had been relieved that the concierge was engaged with a guest – the fewer number of staff who knew she was on the premises the better. She wanted to get her interview with the manager over with and leave her introduction to the staff in his capable hands. As she stood at the reception counter, the pleasant young receptionist waiting for her to respond, Eddie suddenly wished she had not come alone but had instead asked Harvey to accompany her, to at least be on hand while she broke the ice. Even the company of Phee, who could not be relied upon to act in a businesslike way, would have been preferable to facing this by herself. But to turn and run could attract adverse attention, she might possibly be remembered when she returned because she would have to come back.

She planted a smile on her face before responding to Connie. 'I'm not booking in so have no luggage. I have come to see the manager . . .'

While thinking this lady looked rather posh to be applying for an accounts clerk's job, Connie cut her short by replying, 'Oh, the Captain's expecting you. He told me to take you into his office as soon as you arrived.' Fired by Captain Fosedyke's instructions and her own great desire to show him she could be relied upon completely to follow instructions to the letter, Connie totally forgot to inform Miss Harbin she would be leaving the counter for a couple of minutes to escort Mrs Driffield into the manager's office. Rushing over to the flap, she lifted it, passed through, and less than two seconds later was at Eddie's side.

Eddie herself was wondering how the hotel manager could possibly have been expecting her as she had only made her final decision to request an interview with him an hour before and had not told anyone where she was actually going, except to inform Mabel, who was packing china ready to be crated for the auctioneer's, that she was off out and wasn't sure what time she'd be back.

'I'll take you through,' Connie said to her. 'Captain Fosedyke said if he wasn't in his office when you arrived I should give you his apologies and go and find him.' As they walked towards the office she continued, 'You'll like it here, I'm sure. I've worked here for over two years myself. I was a chambermaid but I've just been promoted to reception. It's ever so interesting and I can't wait to be allowed actually to deal with the guests. I like the thought of helping them enjoy their stay. The rest of the staff are a good bunch, though . . . well, I suppose I shouldn't tell you this, but if you do take the job it's best you're forewarned, ain't it? One or two of the senior staff can be a bit superior, if you know what I mean. Best to humour them.

'I used to think the Captain was like that but since I've been on reception I've had more to do with him and he's not so bad as I thought. Actually he's quite . . . yes, he's quite nice. Here we are,' she said, stopping before the office door. She smiled at Eddie. 'Best of luck,' she said, giving the door a knock. When she received no reply she said, 'Captain Fosedyke's not returned from his rounds yet so I'll get you settled then I'll go and fetch him.' She pushed open the door and entered to show Mrs Driffield to her seat when the sight that greeted her froze her rigid, her mouth dropping open in shock.

Captain Fosedyke was slumped over his desk. One arm lay under him and seemed to be clutching at his chest, the other hanging limp over the side of his chair.

Quickly regaining her faculties and completely forgetting the presence of Eddie, Connie launched herself over to the Captain and felt for his pulse. Thankfully she found a faint one. She hurriedly picked up the telephone and, as soon as Pamela responded, instructed her to call an ambulance telling them the hotel manager had collapsed, was still alive but his vital signs were weak, and to come quickly. She returned to the Captain, gently eased him up and back against his chair, then loosened his tie and collar and again took his wrist to feel for a pulse.

Just then the assistant manager walked in. His eyes bulged in shock at the scene before him. 'What the . . .'

Connie cut him short. 'Captain Fosedyke passed out. He might have suffered a heart attack, Mr Sopworth. I've had an ambulance called. They should be here any minute. Has the Captain any family, do you know, so we can inform them what's happened?'

He gave a shrug. 'Don't know.'

'Oh, dear.' Without realising she was dishing out orders to her superiors, Connie said, 'Well, someone's got to accompany the Captain to the hospital and as his second-in-command you should be the one. You'll know his details better than anyone else.'

Just then an ambulance man appeared, closely followed by another. 'Luckily, we were just passing by on our way back to the hospital after another call out when we got the radio message we were needed here.' Spotting the Captain he said, 'Right, let me take a look at him.'

As she moved out of the way to allow the ambulance men to assess the Captain's condition, Connie noticed a letter on the floor directly under the place the Captain's hand had hung before she had eased him back against the chair. Realising it was the private letter

196

she had brought in to him earlier, she picked it up and slipped it inside the Captain's jacket pocket.

Her suspicion that he'd suffered a heart attack was shared by the ambulance men and within minutes a still unconscious Reginald Fosedyke had been lifted on to a trolley and was in the back of the ambulance on his way to hospital, accompanied by Mr Sopworth. Connie, having gone ahead to clear a path through the reception area in order for the ambulance men to wheel the trolley quickly through, watched out of the revolving door as it sped on its way. She dearly hoped the Captain would be all right. She sighed heavily as she returned to her station behind reception where she found a stony-faced Miss Harbin waiting for her.

'I should reprimand you, Monroe, for leaving the reception desk without permission for whatever reason it was, but I suppose in these circumstances it was lucky for Captain Fosedyke that you did. Have you finished tallying the newspapers for tomorrow?' she barked.

'Not quite, Miss Harbin.'

'Then I suggest you do.'

With that she strode back to her seat behind the counter to busy herself typing confirmation letters to future guests.

Several moments later Connie's ears pricked as she heard a woman say breathlessly to Miss Harbin, 'I'm ever so sorry I'm late for my appointment but, you see, the bus never turned up and I had to wait for the next which was late . . .'

'What appointment would that be, madam?' Miss Harbin asked the woman.

'For the job as accounts clerk. It's with a Captain Fosedyke. Hang on a minute,' she said, delving inside a bulging handbag, 'I've a letter here somewhere confirming my appointment.'

'Well, I'm sorry, it will have to be rearranged, the Captain has been called away unexpectedly.'

Connie gasped. If this woman was Mrs Driffield, then who was the woman she had shown into the Captain's office a short while ago? A horrible thought struck her. In the confusion of what she had found on entering the office and her urgent need to get the Captain safely off to hospital, she had completely forgotten about the woman. Connie's eyes scanned the reception area. Several guests were milling around, waiters and waitresses toing and froing, but she could see no sign of the woman. So where was she? Then an even more terrible thought struck. She couldn't still be waiting in the Captain's office?

Without further ado she leaped up from her seat, rushed to the end of the counter, yanked up the flap and bolted through it, letting it drop behind her. She made straight for the office and stopped short, not believing her eyes. The woman was sitting in the Captain's chair, looking through the papers in his filing tray.

Eddie looked up as Connie entered and smiled at her. 'The Captain got off safely to hospital, I trust? Has any news been received of his condition yet? Oh, I expect it's too early, he's probably only just arrived there.'

'Eh . . . oh . . . er . . . Mr Sopworth's going to telephone as soon as he knows anything. What are you doing?' she demanded.

At her tone Eddie looked offended. 'I beg your pardon?'

'I asked what you are doing? That's private hotel business you're rifling through. And you're not Mrs Driffield come for an interview for the accounts job, are you, because she's just turned up in reception. So who are you and what are you doing masquerading as Mrs Driffield?' Connie demanded. 'You'd better tell me truth before I call the police.'

'Miss . . . ?'

'Eh?'

'Your name?'

'Connie. Connie Monroe.'

'Well, Miss Monroe, I can assure you I was not masquerading as anyone. It was you who assumed I was Mrs Driffield. I did try to tell you who I was but you didn't give me the chance to while you were herding me in here. My name is Miss Edelina Griffin.' She could see that her name meant nothing to Connie and added, 'I am the owner of this hotel.'

Connie looked at her, stunned, then snorted. 'That's a good one, I have to say! I asked you to tell me the truth. All right, have it your own way. If you won't tell me, then the police will get it out of you.'

She leaned over the desk to snatch up the telephone receiver but Eddie stopped her by placing her hand on top of hers. 'I really wouldn't wish you to look foolish, Miss Monroe, especially not after the impressive way you handled the situation with Captain Fosedyke. I am the owner of this hotel. I can easily get my solicitor on the telephone to confirm it. Would you like me to call him?'

Staring wildly at Eddie, Connie pulled back her hand and straightened up. 'You . . . you really are the owner of the Connaught?'

Sitting back in the Captain's chair, Eddie nodded.

Connie gulped and muttered, 'Oh, hell.'

Eddie smiled. 'Not quite the reception I was hoping for. I'm pleased to meet you too. Please, take a seat.'

Connie sank down in the chair before the desk, the one she had intended to sit Eddie in earlier when she had assumed she was Mrs Driffield. 'I'm ever so sorry, Miss Griffin, for the mix up. I can't believe I made such a terrible mistake. I really thought you was Mrs Driffield, you see.' An overwhelming dread that she was going to lose her job filled her then and she blurted out, 'Are you going to sack me?'

Eddie looked taken aback. 'Is that what I should do, do you think? Would the hotel manager sack you for mistaking someone's identity?'

Connie shrugged. 'Er . . . I'm not sure. If I was doing my job right I should have asked who you were instead of assuming, shouldn't I? So it is misconduct.' And without realising she said out loud, 'Miss Harbin would certainly recommend I got the sack.'

'Who is Miss Harbin?'

'She's the senior receptionist.'

'Oh, the older woman I noticed behind the desk when I came in?' Eddie smiled kindly at the worried-looking girl. 'Well, we all make mistakes. I'm sure Miss Harbin will see that's all you did and choose to over-look it.'

Connie's spirits lifted. She hoped Miss Griffin was right.

Eddie was looking thoughtful. 'I'm not sure what to do now. I really needed to sort out some urgent matters with the hotel manager but he could be absent for a while, depending on how serious his condition is.'

Just then a voice boomed, 'What on earth is going on?'

Eddie looked towards the door and Connie's head jerked round, both of them seeing Amelia Harbin looming in the doorway. She wore an expression of amazement on her face.

'Ah, Miss Harbin,' Eddie said, smiling at her. She held out her hand in greeting. 'I'm very pleased to meet you. You are the senior receptionist, I understand?'

'That is none of your business,' Miss Harbin barked back at her. 'Just who on earth do you think you are, sitting in the Captain's chair . . .' She flashed a glance at Connie then back to Eddie. 'Holding court, by the look of it.'

'Oh, there you are, Eddie darling,' announced Phee, gliding past Miss Harbin while slipping off a pair of grey kid gloves. She flapped them across her handbag and unbuttoned her woollen grey-and-cream-checked swing-back coat, its collar of grey mink, underneath which she was wearing a simple dark grey sleeveless shift dress, a string of pearls around her neck and matching earrings. 'There is no one on reception and the concierge was busy so I had to get a guest to point me towards the manager's office where I assumed you would be. I'm off to France tomorrow which as you know, darling, I'm not at all looking forward to. Geraldine isn't either as she's moping around with a face like thunder at the thought of spending a whole month solely in the company of her mother. So you can appreciate how much I felt in need of cheering up, and who better to do that than my dearest friend?

'I called at your house to see if you could spare the time for lunch, and when your maid said you weren't at home and she wasn't sure where you'd gone, I thought to myself, Eddie will have gone to the hotel, as I do remember your mentioning the last time I saw you that you were rather anxious to put the manager in the picture as to your intentions. And I was right, wasn't I? Here you are.' She looked at Eddie, impressed. 'I have to say, you do rather look the part, darling, sitting behind that desk.'

Connie had automatically stood up on Phee's entrance, and during her monologue had moved across to stand beside Miss Harbin. Sitting gracefully down in the chair Connie had just vacated and crossing her legs, Phee turned to look at Miss Harbin. 'Be a dear and fetch us a tray of tea. Earl Grey.' She glanced at Eddie. 'Tea for you, darling, or would you prefer coffee?' Without waiting for her friend to respond, she turned back to Miss Harbin. 'We'll have both.'

Amelia Harbin was left open-mouthed. 'Well, of all the audacity! Who on earth do you both think you are, commandeering the Captain's office and acting as though you own the place? The pair of you, get out now before I have the police fetched.' She spun round to address Connie. 'Go and find the porter. Tell him we need him to escort two . . . *ladies* off the premises. Quick about it!'

'Stay just where you are,' Phee commanded Connie, Eddie herself desperately trying to interject but Phee not giving her the chance to. Throwing Miss Harbin a look of disdain, she demanded, 'And just who might you be?'

Miss Harbin's face tightened alarmingly and she puffed out her skinny chest indignantly. 'I am the senior receptionist. In the absence of the manager and his second-in-command, I am in charge here.'

'Not quite,' said Phee, a smug smile twitching her lips. 'You're not senior to the proprietor of the hotel, I trust?'

Miss Harbin looked bewildered. 'Are you deranged?' she shot at Phee.

She arched one perfectly tweezed eyebrow. 'I have in my time been accused of being just a little eccentric by some dear friends,' she said, flashing an amused look at Eddie before fixing her narrowed eyes back on Miss Harbin. 'But I can assure you, my good woman, I most certainly am *not* deranged and I take offence at the accusation.' She then addressed Eddie. 'Have you actually introduced yourself to this woman?'

'I have been trying to but you haven't given me a chance.'

A wicked smile danced on Phee's lips. 'Oh, please do allow me the honour, darling.' She turned to look back at Miss Harbin and announced, 'You are graced with the presence of Miss Edelina Griffin.'

Amelia Harbin almost choked. 'Miss Griffin! The . . . the . . . daughter of the owner? That Griffin?'

Even more smugly Phee told her, 'Miss Griffin is not the daughter of the owner. She *is* the owner.'

For Connie it was pure joy to watch the look of sheer horror fill her superior's face.

Bowing subserviently, Miss Harbin blurted, 'Oh, I do apologise, Miss Griffin. I had absolutely no idea at all you were expected. How may I be of service?'

'You can make yourself useful by fetching the tea and coffee I requested when you first so rudely barged in here,' answered Phee.

Grabbing Connie's arm, Miss Harbin pulled her out of the office, shutting the door behind them. 'Why was I not informed Miss Griffin was on the premises?' she hissed, incensed.

The girl was quaking. 'But I didn't know she was expected, Miss Harbin, honest I didn't. I thought . . .' There was no point in lying about what she had done as it would not look at all good should it come out later. 'Well, you see, Miss Harbin, I mistook Miss Griffin for Mrs Driffield, and as the Captain had ordered me to show Mrs Driffield into his office as soon as she arrived, that's what I did.'

Miss Harbin's eyes glazed over maliciously. 'Well, your behaviour is nothing less than I'd expect of someone from your background. If this doesn't bring home to the Captain that he made a grave mistake in thinking you would make a suitable receptionist, then nothing will. I shall be speaking to him as soon as he comes back. And the fact I was not informed about Miss Griffin's visit once you knew of it won't go unmentioned either. Now fetch their tea and coffee then return straight to your duties.'

With that she stalked off.

Meanwhile Phee was smiling triumphantly at Eddie.

'Well, that's put her in her place! What a dreadful woman, darling. You say you're going to make improvements to this establishment? It's my opinion the first problem you should address is doing something about her. The thought of lunch here doesn't appeal, not to me anyway considering the boring choices on the menu, so after we've had our beverages we could get a table at that nice new place that's opened on Belgrave Gate. Teddy Maxwell was telling me at the theatre the other evening that he'd tried it and he said the food was absolutely delicious. They keep a good wine cellar too. Oh, by the way, the play was as dreadful as I thought it would be and I didn't understand a word, not that I let on.'

'Oh, Phee, I can't possibly go for lunch. I don't know what to do at the moment. My situation is just getting worse and worse.'

Phee was delving in her handbag for cigarettes, holder and lighter, and said absently, 'Really, dear? In what way?'

Eddie gave a heavy sigh. 'Without even going into my being taken for an imposter, and your being accused of being a mental case, and both of us being threatened with arrest for trespassing which is all really too bad after I so badly wanted to create a good first impression . . . well, after steeling myself to approach the manager with my intentions, I arrived to find he'd had a suspected heart attack and is now at the hospital along with his assistant manager.'

Phee's head jerked in astonishment. 'What? The assistant manager has suffered a heart attack as well as the manager?'

Eddie tutted. 'No, Phee, the assistant manager has

just accompanied the manager to help with any details the hospital may require. Any hope I had of getting my first introductions and seeing what rooms I'd be occupying is certainly not going to happen today, is it. Now I have accepted the house is going, I just want to move on and try and put what Stibley's done to us behind me.'

Phee lit her cigarette and blew out a plume of smoke. 'It is rather inconvenient, the manager having his heart attack today, isn't it, dear? But you don't need him actually here at the hotel to sort out what rooms you'll take up residence in. You can choose which ones you want yourself and then instruct that sour-faced senior receptionist to get them ready for you. You're the owner, darling, and it's about time you started acting like it.' She pulled a thoughtful face. 'I suppose with the manager indisposed for however long it takes to get over what ails him, you will have to take charge, don't you think?'

Eddie stared at her. 'Take charge! But I have no idea how a hotel operates. I cannot possibly take charge.'

'Don't be silly, dear, of course you can. You just give the staff orders and they do it all. You tell your maid and cook what to do, what's the difference?'

'The difference is, Phee, I know how to run a home.'

'A hotel is similar to a home, darling, just bigger, that's all. Anyway, I'm forgetting the assistant manager who's not had a heart attack, thank goodness. He'll take over during the actual manager's absence so your problem is solved.' A flash of excitement filled her face. 'Come on, darling, I'll help you pick your rooms. Have you actually had a good look around yet?'

Just then there was a tap at the door and Connie entered carrying a laden tray which she set down on the desk.

She was mindful of Miss Harbin's instructions to get back to reception quickly but regardless asked politely, 'Is there anything else I can do for you, Miss Griffin?'

'Yes, there is something else,' Phee answered. 'You can escort us around the hotel and show us the best rooms so Miss Griffin can decide which would suit her.'

'Me?' Connie said, poking herself in her chest.

'Are you incapable of escort duties?'

'No, not at all. I know the hotel like the back of me hand.'

'Well, you'll do perfectly then.'

Connie still looked worried. 'I don't know whether it's my place to. It's Miss Harbin who really should show you around, in the absence of Captain Fosedyke and Mr Sopworth.'

'I don't think so, dear,' Phee said, pulling a face. 'I couldn't stomach any more of that woman's company today. Are you refusing my request?'

'No, not at all, madam,' Connie said hurriedly. 'I'd be honoured to escort you both around.' Wondering if she had understood Miss Griffin's friend correctly and the owner would be taking up residence in the hotel, she looked across at Eddie and asked, 'You're moving in then, Miss Griffin?'

'Yes, she is,' replied Phee. 'Is that a problem?'

'No, no, not at all.'

'I'm glad to hear it. Miss Griffin has decided that to

move here temporarily would only be common sense while she's overseeing the modernisation programme.'

Eddie looked gratefully at her friend who, whether she had realised or not, had actually spared her the embarrassment of coming up with a plausible excuse as to why she was here.

'You're going to oversee the modernisation of the hotel, Miss Griffin?' asked Connie.

'Long overdue as I expect you'll agree,' confirmed Phee.

'The hotel would benefit from being done up, yes, I do agree, madam. I could think of things that would do wonders for this place.'

Phee looked at her keenly. 'Really? Well, you'll come in handy then should we become stuck for ideas. Do you need to get some keys or something so we can view the rooms?' she asked Connie, standing up to announce she was ready to start her grand tour.

Miss Harbin did not hide her fury that Connie had been the one chosen to accompany Miss Griffin and her friend. As she slapped the set of skeleton keys into Connie's hand, the girl was left in no doubt she was going to be made to pay for this rebuff.

A while later, pulling a face, Phee said to Connie, 'This is your best room, you say?'

She nodded.

Phee took another look around. 'Well, if it is then I suppose it'll have to do. You could use this one as your bedroom, Eddie, and the one next door as your private lounge. At least there's a bathroom the other side that you can make out of bounds to anyone else. I would suggest you get the decorators in before you actually move into these rooms, though. That paper is positively dreadful. The design of Chinese birds on that hideous blue background next door . . . well, I presume they're birds. I've never seen anything resembling them fluttering in our garden . . . I mean, that paper was bad enough but this . . .' She peered at it. 'What are those flowers? Orchids, I assume. They look dead, don't they?'

'That's because the paper has faded, Phee,' said Eddie. 'I should imagine this room looked lovely when it was first hung.' It would have been her mother's choice and despite its now being dreadfully outdated, she rather liked it.

'Not quite today's taste though, is it, darling? Some of it's coming off, look,' she said, pointing towards a join in the paper that had come unstuck over the years. 'A nice flock or Regency stripe is what's needed in here.' Phee pulled a pained expression. 'How on earth you're going to cope with just two rooms . . . well, I couldn't. Still, I suppose you have all the rest of the hotel at your disposal too, it's just that a few other people will be sharing it with you.'

'I'll get used to it,' said Eddie with conviction, examining the bed and thinking it would have to go to make room for her own, while at the same time realising she had no choice but to get used to her private living accommodation being grossly reduced, thanks to Stibley. It was really coming home to her that there were many more changes she'd have to get used to in future. She took another glance around. Removing all the furniture from this room, including the terrible monstrosity of a wardrobe which took up such a large amount of space, and bringing in her own chosen pieces would do much to take away the alien feeling of the place. Make it seem more like home, having her own familiar things around her. Phee was right about the bathroom next door. She couldn't bring herself to have to share that with strangers and would be making sure it was out of bounds for any of the guests who were allocated rooms on this corridor. There was a bathroom at the other end, that would have to suffice.

Phee gave a shudder. 'It is rather cold in here, are the radiators turned up?'

Connie went over to check the huge metal concertina-shaped object by the far wall. Although the thermostat was turned up to its fullest, the radiator was stone cold to the touch. 'Sometimes the heating works, sometimes it doesn't. It's the boiler, you see, it's very temperamental. But then it's very old.'

'Just like a certain member of staff,' said Phee dryly. 'Well, thank goodness for the fireplaces. A roaring fire in here on a cold winter's evening, the curtains drawn, and I should imagine it would seem quite . . . quite . . . well, it will do, I suppose.' She looked at her watch. 'Darling, have you seen enough? I mean, there's plenty of time for a proper grand tour when you actually take up residence. I'm sure Miss Monroe can handle having these rooms cleared out for you and supervise your furniture being arranged when it arrives, couldn't you, Miss Monroe? Oh, and don't forget the private bathroom next door, there's a dear.'

Connie smiled politely. 'I could relay your instructions to Mr Sopworth, Miss Griffin.'

'There you are, darling. As I told you, instruct the

staff and they handle everything for you. No need for you to stay any longer. Not like you can do any more today, is it, because I doubt the manager will be back even if his heart attack turns out to be a bad case of indigestion. If we hurry we'll still be able to have lunch in that lovely new restaurant Teddy recommended. My treat.' She pouted her lips. 'I *am* going away for a month tomorrow, Eddie, and I want you to myself for a while before I go as I will miss you.'

Phee was right, Eddie supposed. There really wasn't anything else she could do at the hotel today. Nothing requiring her immediate attention back at the house either. Lunch did sound tempting and it would do her good to get away from her problems for a while.

CHAPTER TWELVE

Connie locked the room behind her and glanced down the corridor. There was no sign of Miss Griffin or her friend and she assumed they'd both made their way out of the hotel and were now on their way to the restaurant for their lunch. How wonderful it must be to lunch at a whim in expensive restaurants, she thought, and also wondered if she herself would ever be able to afford to eat on a whim even in cheap restaurants. She smiled to herself. What a turn of events, the owner turning up so unexpectedly like that. Life in the hotel was going to change drastically in the future, and she wasn't sure yet whether that was going to be for the better or the worse as she couldn't quite fathom Miss Griffin.

She did seem a nice woman, considering she was from a wealthy background. She had her airs and graces but wasn't haughty, not at all, nor did she look down her nose at those below her. Considering she was the owner of the hotel, it didn't seem to Connie that she knew much about the trade from some of the questions she had asked. Connie thought she must be mistaken, though. After all, her introduction to the proprietor could not be classed as having been under normal circumstances. Despite Miss Griffin's being under the impression that her mistaken identity would be overlooked, Connie knew it wouldn't be and wondered if she would still be working on reception or back in her old job as chambermaid when the modernisation got underway. Oh, but hadn't Miss Harbin got her just desserts? If only Connie could have filmed the whole episode and played it back to savour every minute of Miss Griffin's friend putting her right in her place. Miss Harbin's attitude towards Connie herself had been bad enough before this morning's incidents, so what she was going to be like now didn't bear thinking about. Still, Connie knew she had no choice but to get on with it and shoulder it all as best she could.

She headed off towards the door leading through to the narrow closed-in service stairs and hurriedly began to make her way down the three flights to the ground floor, taking two steps at a time in her urgency to face Miss Harbin's expected wrath and get it over with. On turning a sharp corner she slapped straight into someone coming up and jumped back, startled. 'Oh, I'm so sorry,' she exclaimed, rubbing her smarting shoulder where they had collided.

'It was my fault,' apologised Neal Richmond, rubbing his own shoulder. 'I wasn't looking where I was going. Me mind wasn't on what I was doing.'

'No, it was my fault,' she insisted. 'My mind was elsewhere too.'

Neal started laughing. 'We'd best agree we're both to blame or we could be here all day.' He made to move by the woman he'd collided with and, as he looked into her face, suddenly a tingling sensation shot up his spine and heat flooded through him. God, but she was beautiful! Just the type of woman who appealed to him. It was a long time since he'd come across one he liked the look of. Then his mind whirled uncontrollably. Had she a boyfriend? Would she go out with him if he asked her? Did he dare ask her? He took a deep breath and blurted, 'You work here then?' He could have kicked himself.

Connie thought that fact very obvious judging by the dowdy black receptionist's dress she was wearing and the fact she was using the back stairs. 'Just started on reception but I was a chambermaid here for two years before that. Yourself?' Then she laughed. 'Silly question, I can see by your uniform you're in the kitchen.'

She was talking to him at least, that was something. Keep the conversation going, he ordered himself. 'Commis chef. Been here nearly four years. Actually I'm just about fully qualified. Four months to go.' He hoped that would impress her. 'Mind you, that's provided Chef doesn't drive me into the mental home before then. He's not the easiest man to work under.'

'I could be joining you,' said Connie. 'I have the boss from hell too.'

'Seems we have something in common,' he said, his eyes sparkling. Ask her out now, his mind screamed, but the words just would not come, he was so afraid she would reject him. 'I'm . . . er . . . just off up to my room to change my trousers as I split them picking up a bag of spuds. Wouldn't have happened if the hotel provided uniforms that actually fitted properly.'

Connie was well aware of the ill-fitting uniforms

the hotel provided its staff with as nothing she had ever been given had fitted her properly despite her attempts at alterations. 'Yes, well, you consider yourself lucky if you get provided with anything that halfway fits. And these dresses we females have to wear aren't exactly flattering, are they?'

What she was wearing appeared to him to fit her in all the right places.

He seemed very nice, she thought. He wasn't good-looking in film-star terms but he was definitely attractive and she did have rather a penchant for carrot-coloured hair. In her opinion it stood out against the more common browns and blonds. The splattering of light brown freckles across his nose she thought rather sexy. It seemed he had a sense of humour, too. She liked a sense of humour in a man. And she'd noticed that his shoes were polished which meant he kept himself smart. Fancy working here for two years and never crossing paths with him before. But then, she thought, kitchen staff considered themselves a cut above the others and avoided contact with the rest unless absolutely necessary. They had their own staff room where they took their meals and breaks. He must live in if he was on his way up towards the male quarters to change his trousers so it was a wonder they hadn't bumped into each other when leaving or returning to their rooms. But then, the male and female staff quarters might both be in the attics but were sectioned off from each other and hotel rules stated neither sex was allowed in the other's area under any circumstances. So all in all it wasn't that surprising she had not known of his existence until today. She wouldn't mind a chance to get to know him better. If he asked her out she wouldn't say no. Go on, ask me, she willed him.

His mind was racing, desperately trying to find the courage to ask her for a date, find the right words to ask.

Suddenly a picture of Miss Harbin's grim face loomed before Connie and she was reminded of her urgent need to get back to her workplace. It didn't seem she was going to get her wish granted as . . . she didn't even know his name . . . was just standing there looking at her with a sort of blank expression on his face. A nice-looking man like him probably had a girl-friend anyway. 'I'd best be off,' she said flatly, moving around him to negotiate the rest of the stairs. 'See yer,' she called after her.

His shoulders sagged. Why had he stood there like a blithering idiot? What was the chance of crossing . . . he didn't even know her name . . . that beautiful woman's path again when their respective workplaces never coincided under normal circumstances? Not much of one, he guessed. He would so have liked a chance to get to know her better. Well, he'd blown that chance now good and proper through his own inability to ask what he had wanted to ask her. 'Yeah, see yer,' he responded equally as flatly.

Miss Harbin glared daggers at Connie as she slipped back behind the counter and took her place. 'Oh, you do remember where you actually work then?' she snarled. She snatched up a stack of papers. 'I had to finish the newspaper order off for you and telephone it through. File this lot, and in the *right* files,' she commanded, thrusting the pile at Connie. 'I will be checking, so be warned. Then I want you to polish all the brass holders on the sets of spare keys. After that take everything out of the pigeon holes, polish and dust them all out, then put any guests' messages back in their rightful place. Then I want everything under the counter taking out, the shelves polishing and everything put back neatly. Got all that?'

It was most apparent that her superior was giving her the most laborious jobs she could think of and Connie thought it was a wonder she hadn't instructed her to get down on her hands and knees and scrub the floor behind the counter with a toothbrush. She nodded. 'Yes, Miss Harbin.'

'Well, what are you standing about gawping for? Get to it.'

For the rest of the day, every time Connie looked up from her tasks she would see Miss Harbin glaring at her. She wondered how long she was going to demonstrate her acute displeasure at Miss Griffin's show of preference. Connie was mortally relieved when her shift finished at seven o'clock when they handed over to the night porter and she was able to escape to her room, not only to get away from Miss Harbin's murderous looks but so as to relay to Val the amazing events of the day.

CHAPTER THIRTEEN

As it was Connie had to wait patiently until Val's shift finished at nine-thirty and occupied the time by going down to the laundry room and tackling some personal washing which she left to dry on the staff-allocated drying cradles. After a good wash down in the female staff bathroom she felt disgusted at the state the previous user had left it in and wished she knew who it had been so she could express her displeasure.

The female staff bathroom was not a place anyone would wish to linger. Decades worth of limescale, green and blackened in parts, encrusted the taps overhanging a chipped and cracked pot sink. The iron bath itself was heavily mottled with rusting craters where chunks of its enamelling had fallen out. The ancient grouting between the cracked white tiles was mildewed with age. The length of string replacing the cistern chain often broke, and more times than not to flush the toilet the user had to climb on the seat, reach up and man-ually pull down the ballcock handle – or, as some of the female staff couldn't be bothered, leave the bowl unflushed for the next user to deal with. It was always a miracle if the antiquated plumbing system managed to pump hot water up to the attic and mostly a bath was abandoned in favour of a hurried splashdown as the water was too icy. It was in the staff rules that they should clean up after themselves but since the non-replacement of the housekeeper a decade or so ago, this rule was grossly flouted. Connie did not linger in the bathroom long that evening.

As soon as her friend came through the door, Connie pounced on her. 'Oh, Val, you just *have* to hear what happened today,' she blurted out, slapping shut the second-hand paperback she'd been reading and dropping it on the well-worn counterpane.

Sighing heavily, Val threw herself down on her own bed and eased off her shoes to rub her feet. 'If it's about the hotel owner showing up, then I know,' she said dully. 'Everyone's talking about it. You'd think royalty had descended on us, the way some people are going on.'

'Oh, but she *is* like royalty to us, Val, her being the owner,' Connie said, aghast.

Val shrugged. 'If you say so. Some owner though, ain't she, when she's never shown her face in this place for decades, according to gossip. Why is she suddenly doing it now?'

'So she can oversee the modernisation.'

Val pulled a face. 'Modernisation, eh? That's a fancy name for a coat of paint.'

'Oh, I got the impression it's more than that the place is getting, from what her friend said, Val.'

She raised an eyebrow. 'Oh, yeah, I heard you was the one who gave Miss La-Di-Da and her lady-in-waiting the grand tour of inspection.'

'Oh, don't be like that, Val, I've had enough of Miss

Harbin giving me grief over it. Weren't my fault Miss Griffin singled me out.'

'Yeah, well, some of the other staff might see you as her blue-eyed little girl from now on. They probably won't dare speak in front of you in future in case you go running back to tell Her Ladyship.'

Connie scowled, annoyed. 'Now that *is* stupid. For God's sake, I showed Miss Griffin a few of our better rooms for her to choose the ones she wants to have as her private quarters, that's all. And there was no grand tour.' She looked across at her friend quizzically. 'Are you not going to speak to me either now?'

'Don't be daft, I'm just warning yer that some of the other staff might be a bit funny with yer. You know what folks are like.'

'Yes, I do, and they can be as funny as they want to be with me 'cos I know they're just jealous Miss Griffin didn't pick them.' She looked at Val in concern. Her room-mate was certainly in a bad mood and Connie wondered what had happened to cause it. 'What's up with you, Val? Has something more than out of the ordinary happened today to make you so grumpy?'

'There's nothing wrong with me, I'm fine,' she snapped. 'What the owner wants to move into this dump for when she must have her own mansion to live in with servants running after her . . . well, her type do live in mansions, don't they? . . . is what I want to know.'

'Oh, come on, Val, the Connaught's not that bad. A spruce up should make it look a million dollars.' A thought struck Connie. 'Oh, do you think we'll get our rooms done while they're at it? My bed is almost falling apart and I know yours isn't much better. And our bathroom could certainly do with it.' Val's expression gave her her answer. 'Oh, well, we can live in hope, I suppose. Yeah, I wonder why Miss Griffin is moving in? She doesn't really need to live in to oversee the modernisation, does she? Still, I suppose she's got her reasons. I am worried about the Captain, though.'

'He's management so what yer worried about him for?' Val shot at her.

'He's still a human being, ain't he? Mr Sopworth told us when he came back from the hospital that it was high blood pressure that caused the collapse. He doesn't know how long the Captain will be in for.' Connie looked worried. 'It seems he has no relatives so he won't get any visitors, will he? He's no one who cares what happens to him, has he? I told you the other day, I've been seeing a different side to the Captain. I think he's a nice man underneath that gruffness.'

Val pulled a face. 'Well, I've certainly never seen that side to him. He had a right go at me for not noticing a small tear in one of the counterpanes in the room I was cleaning when he came on his inspection rounds yesterday morning.'

'He was right to give you a rollicking. You should have noticed, it's yer job to.' Connie looked at her quizzically. 'Not like you not to have noticed something like that. Dot Smith, well, she's a different matter. She wouldn't notice if the window had fallen out and a bloody gale was blowing in 'cos she's so lazy, but you . . .' Connie looked deeply concerned. 'There is something up with you, Val. What is it?'

'Will you stop going on?' she snapped, and stood up to gather her washing bag and towel.

'Oh, are you going out?' Connie asked her.

'So what if I am?'

Connie had been hoping for Val's company until bedtime, had been going to suggest she herself should sneak down to the room service kitchen to make them both a cup of cocoa and hopefully find some leftover biscuits or cake or maybe bread to make toast. Anything room service hadn't scoffed themselves or thrown away. They didn't clean the kitchen as thoroughly as they were supposed to on finishing their evening shift. 'Oh, you've a date with a man friend, have you?'

Val shot her a look. 'It ain't always a man friend I'm meeting when I go out. I do have other friends, I'll have you know.'

'I wasn't trying to make out you hadn't.' She looked at Val, hurt. 'I had thought me and you were friends yet you're being really off with me tonight, and I haven't done anything to make you be like this with me as far as I know.'

Val's face softened and she gave a heavy sigh. 'Look, I'm sorry, Connie, I didn't mean to take me mood out on you.'

She smiled warmly. 'That's all right, I forgive you,' she responded good-naturedly. 'So what has put you in this mood then?'

Val was looking at her hesitantly and Connie knew instinctively there was something on her mind she wanted . . . no, was desperate to share with her. Something very important. Connie could see she was debating the odds and wondered what it could possibly be that was causing her friend such a dilemma. Val obviously decided that whatever it was it had to remain private as she gave a nonchalant shrug and said evasively, 'Oh, it's nothing.' Then she flashed Connie a quick smile. 'I'd best get a move on.'

Connie felt very thoughtful after Val had left for her appointment, whoever it might be with. She was slapdash about keeping their room tidy, showing little thought for her room-mate and regularly leaving her bed unmade and personal items strewn around, but usually Val was meticulous about how she herself looked when going out. Tonight, after a quick visit to the bathroom, she had hurriedly returned to their room to pull on a pair of old trousers and a jumper, had grabbed her coat and shot off, telling Connie she wouldn't be long but if she wasn't back before the night porter locked the back staff entrance door at ten-thirty then would Connie do the usual for her and unlatch the room service kitchen window for her to get back in?

So who was Val meeting? Not a man friend, not dressed as she was. It was also very late in the evening to be meeting up with a friend or group of friends for a social gathering. Connie knew it was not really her business but Val's mood was worrying her, the fact that she was refusing to discuss the reason behind it when usually Connie had a job to shut her up as she grumbled and complained about guests and management. Still, unless Val chose to open up to her there was nothing Connie could do to help her.

Then a thought struck her. Here she was worrying about Val when she had enough of a problem on her own account to keep her occupied. Namely, Miss Harbin. Connie was well aware that it was most unlikely she was ever going to win the woman over enough to make her working life harmonious, but if she wanted to continue working as a receptionist at the Connaught the price was obviously to be that she must put up with her boss's vile attitude.

Her thoughts then drifted back to her day off two days before. Wanting to witness the full impact of her news about the promotion, albeit for a trial period, when she had telephoned a message through to her mother via Mrs Gill that her day off had changed, Connie had not elaborated on the reason, just left it to be assumed she had obliged a colleague again. She smiled at the memory of her parents' reactions when she eventually told them over dinner. Her mother had sat for a moment with a look of stunned surprise on her face before leaping up to rush around and hug her daughter fiercely, proclaiming her delight. Her father just nodded and said matter-of-factly, 'Well done, gel, yer deserve it,' but Connie knew that inside he was as overjoyed as her mother.

Her sister's reaction had been disappointing. Picking at her food, Babsy had grunted and snarled, '*She* gets to do what she wants while *I* get treated like a prisoner and it ain't fair!' Her father had immediately ordered her to her room and, face thunderous, she had stormed off, slamming the door behind her. Irene had sighed despondently. 'I don't know what to do with her, I really don't.' To which her husband had responded, 'She needs a good hiding. We're far too soft with her, Rene.'

His wife then replied, 'If we were too soft with her we would have given in and be allowing her to come and go as she pleases, no questions asked. I said she could go to the dance on Friday night and even relented and said she could stay 'til the end when you'd meet her out to walk her home safely. That's what any responsible parent would offer, ain't it? But no, she weren't having any of that, said she'd sooner die than be humiliated in front of her friends by her dad meeting her to walk her home. So I said in that case she wasn't going, which is fair, ain't it?'

Connie had thought her mother to be acting very fairly and that her sister's reaction was totally out of order. After helping her mother clear up after their meal she had gone through to have a talk with her sister but had been met by a silent glare. Realising that whatever she said it would fall on deaf ears, and hoping that sooner rather than later Babsy would accept that her parents were only showing how much they loved and cared for her and go back to the lovely girl she had been, Connie had returned to spend the remainder of her visit answering her mother's questions about her new responsibilities, though she was not honest about Miss Harbin's attitude towards her, not wanting to worry her parents.

She yawned now. She was tired after her eventful day but it wasn't yet ten o'clock and she had to wait up to see if Val returned before the night porter locked up at ten-thirty. If not she needed to sneak down to unlatch the window for her friend to come through. She would read her book again.

Just as she had settled down comfortably, or as

comfortably as her lumpy bed would allow, her book opened out before her, a knock came on her door. She opened it to find Dot Smith, dressed in her nightclothes, hair rollered under a hairnet. She was looking at Connie suspiciously.

'It's Val I want to speak to,' she said off-handedly.

For a moment her attitude stunned Connie until she remembered Val's warning that the rest of the staff might act strangely with her because of earlier events. 'She's not here,' she replied, smiling at her visitor warmly. 'Can I help you, Dot?'

'I'll call back later.'

She made to hurry back to her own room but Connie stopped her by saying, 'Some of the others being off with me who don't know me all that well I might understand, but you and me worked together so you do know me, Dot.'

The other woman tossed back her head. 'I don't know what yer mean?' she snapped.

'Yes, you do. You're being funny with me because Miss Griffin asked me to show her some rooms. Now you've got it into your head that I'm going to be running to her to snitch about anything I think she might be interested in. I'm right, ain't I?'

Dot fixed her with her eyes. 'Well, ain't yer?'

Connie's face filled with hurt. 'I didn't realise you thought so little of me.' She threw back her head and said firmly, 'It wasn't my fault Miss Griffin picked me out. You and the others can think what you like but, I assure you, I've never been one to run to the bosses with tittle-tattle and I never will be.'

She then made to shut her door but Dot stopped

her. 'Look, I'm sorry, Connie,' she said remorsefully. 'It's just . . .'

Connie cut her short. 'That you're too quick to listen to narrow-minded gossip in the staff room. Now can I help you or do you want me to give Val a message that you were looking for her?'

Dot shifted uncomfortably. 'I meant to come and warn you earlier, only I forgot.'

Connie's brow furrowed. 'Warn me? About what?'

'Mr Sopworth. I was in the staff room just after dinner tonight and I heard him bragging to the head waiter that being's the Captain's laid up in hospital, *he's* now in charge.'

'Well, as he's the assistant manager I suppose what he's saying is true, Dot.'

'Yeah, well, I ain't the only one who don't trust him. I think he's gonna make it his business to try and catch us staff doing summat we shouldn't so he can suck up to Miss Griffin and make himself look good.'

'Like you all thought I would be?'

Dot looked ashamed. 'Deep down I know it was wrong of us to think you'd be like that, Connie, honest. Anyway, I'm just warning you and the others to watch your backs, that's all, as far as he's concerned.'

'If you want my opinion, that man is more concerned with finding places he can sneak off to for a crafty fag than bothered about much else. The Captain ain't daft and if Sopworth doesn't watch out his days will be numbered. I appreciate your warning and I'll tell Val. Good night.'

As Connie went back inside the room and shut the door behind her, Val's empty bed caught her attention.

It suddenly struck her that should Mr Sopworth, in his new role of temporary manager, take it upon himself to do a staff rooms check without warning – unlike the Captain who always made it known an inspection was imminent, to give the staff a chance to have a tidy up – witness the mess in Val's half of the room and apply the hotel rules literally, they could then both be told to vacate. Connie's parents, especially her mother, would be delighted about her return home but the consequences for Connie, despite her new position meaning she no longer had such early starts or late finishes, would be several hours added to each day, travelling to and from work, and having to find the bus fares out of her wage which would only be raised depending on the outcome of her trial period. But more worrying to Connie was the fact that Val hadn't a home to fall back on and would find herself turfed out on the streets. She sighed heavily. She had no choice but to tidy up her room-mate's mess just in case Sopworth did an inspection without warning first thing tomorrow morning, which Connie wouldn't put past him.

Ten minutes later she had tidied the top of the dressing table and half-filled a discarded brown paper carrier she had found poking out from under Val's bed with empty stocking packets, shampoo bottles, jar of Pond's Cold Cream and several makeup remainders. Having made Val's bed and hung up her nightclothes next to her own on one of two hooks on the back of the door, Connie then set about folding up the jumble of clothing on top of the tallboy. Having made a neat pile of it she went to put it on top of Val's bed for her to put away in either of her two drawers when she realised that, knowing Val as she did, all she would do would be to put the pile back on the top of the tallboy for it quickly to become a jumble again, and then her own well-meant efforts would have been a total waste of time. The sensible thing would be for her to put everything away in Val's drawers herself.

Bending over, she attempted to pull out the bottom drawer but something inside was preventing it from opening much more than a couple of inches. She gave it a good yank, hoping that would dislodge whatever was stuck, but it still didn't do the trick. Kneeling down, Connie eased her hand into the narrow opening and worked it around the object. It felt to her like a large bulky envelope. Easing her fingers over the top of it, she pushed it down against the soft jumble of clothes underneath far enough for the back end, which had wedged itself against the drawer plinth, to free itself. Then with one hand still pressing down the clothes, with the other she gently eased the envelope out. As it came fully out of the drawer the weight of its contents pushed open the flap and they came tumbling out into Connie's lap.

Eyes and mouth wide in shock, she stared down at the pile of five- and one-pound notes, the collection of silver, plus several pieces of decent quality jewellery, her mind whirling. Where could Val have got all this from? She jumped, head spinning, on hearing the door open.

The scene before Val registered immediately and she advanced across the room to loom over Connie. Her face thunderous, she hissed, 'What are you doing rifling through my belongings?'

Connie jumped up, heedless of the fact that she'd sent the objects in her lap flying. 'It's not what you think, Val,' she blurted out. 'Honest it's not. Dot came to warn me a short while ago that she overheard Mr Sopworth bragging he was in charge until the Captain comes back and we'd better watch our backs 'case he caught us doing something we shouldn't be. He could tittle-tattle to Miss Griffin and get us into deep trouble. I got to worrying that Sopworth might take it upon himself to do a room inspection without warning. Well, he's only got to poke his head around our door and see this mess and then we'd both be out on our ear. I've got a home I can always go back to, but you . . . Well, you ain't, have you, Val? Look, I wasn't sure what time you'd get back tonight so I was just trying to help, that's all.' Her face was wreathed in questions. 'Where did you get all that money and jewellery from, Val?'

Her friend's eyes narrowed darkly. 'I didn't steal it, if that's what yer think,' she hissed.

'Val, I ain't so stupid I don't know a decent piece of jewellery when I see it. This is beyond your pocket, and you haven't saved out of your wages 'cos I know how much you earn.'

Val's eyes blazed. 'That's just it, I did earn it.' She saw the look on Connie's face and added, 'And not the way you're thinking. I ain't no prostitute!' She bent down to scoop the money and jewellery back inside the envelope.

'Oh, Val, I wasn't thinking you were,' Connie cried, aghast.

'Yes, yer were,' she accused, standing up and

clutching the envelope to her chest while she glared at Connie.

Her face filled with shame. 'All right, I admit it's the first thought that struck me 'cos I can't think of any other way you'd get that lot. How much have you got in that envelope anyway?'

'Hopefully enough to buy a little eating place in Skeggie that will support me and Beatrice.' Still clutching the envelope to her chest, Val moved across to her bed and sank down on it with a heavy sigh. 'I ain't proud of how I got this money, but the way I did it is the only way I could think of to fulfil my promise to look after Beatrice. She needs looking after, Connie, she ain't like me, can't stand up for herself. She soft and very shy. People put on her, use her, like those people she's working for are now. And if she got up the courage to leave there'd be a good chance whoever took her on next would treat her just as bad. I tried to persuade her to come here and try her luck. I'd help her by putting a good word in with the Captain, hopefully we'd share a room and at least we'd be together that way, but she could never bring herself to put in her notice and was scared that if she just left without word her employers would make sure she got a bad reference so no one else would employ her.

'Beatrice ain't had a day off now for months 'cos her mistress makes up excuses that she can't spare her, telling her she'll get her time off another day, and it never happens. The only time I get to see her now is once a week when her employers go out to play cribbage for the evening and I sneak up to the house. We meet in the shed for half an hour because that's all the time we can snatch. That's where I've been tonight only we barely had a few minutes together because Beatrice's employers came back early and she had to scarper back inside the house before she was caught.'

Connie was staring at her, her mind racing. There was a look in Val's eyes as she was speaking of her friend that was telling Connie this was no normal friendship between two girls who had grown up in a home together, looking out for each other in a com-radely way. There was something more between them. Then she gasped as it struck her: Val loved Beatrice. The kind of love usually shared between a man and a woman. The shock of the realisation had her exclaiming out loud, 'Oh!'

Val glanced up at her, saw the look on her face and knew what Connie was thinking. Her own face clouded over defensively. 'Yes, I love Beatrice and she loves me. I'm queer, Connie, or whatever else they call people like me and Beatrice. Make you feel sick, do I?' She pulled a threatening face. 'You'd better run away from me in case I pounce on you.'

Connie found herself stepping backwards. It was almost as if Val was carrying a disease that she could catch. Then suddenly she realised how stupid she was being. Val was no more of a threat to her now she had come clean about her private life than she had been last night when Connie had been oblivious to her true nature. Val had never compromised her in any way whatsoever during the two years they had shared a room and there was no reason to think she would now.

'Stop it, Val, just stop it!' she cried. 'Look, I . . . Oh, Val, I can't say I'm not shocked 'cos I am. I never had

233

a clue that this is the way you are. I can't say as I understand how you can love another woman because I don't. But I want to understand if you'll tell me, because . . . well, because you're my friend, Val.'

Val stared at her for several long moments then with tears pricking her eyes, muttered, 'It isn't easy being like me, Connie, having to pretend all the time to be like other women, man mad, when in fact the thought of being with a man in that way absolutely repulses me. That's why I was in a bad mood earlier, because one of the waiters was pestering me to go out with him when I was in the staff room having me afternoon cuppa. On and on he was going. He really got on me nerves, making out I should be honoured by his offer 'cos he thought himself God's gift. I wanted to laugh at him, tell him why he was wasting his time, but can you imagine if anyone even got a hint there was something different about me how I'd be treated? Years ago women like me were burned at the stake.

'What you have to try and understand, Connie, is that what I feel for Beatrice, what she feels for me, is normal to us. For me it's the likes of you that are odd because you like men. Can you even begin to imagine how it is for me and Beatrice, knowing we can never show how we feel about each other in public? It's awful, Connie, when we both want to shout to the world how much we love and care for each other, the same as men and women do. The only way we can be together is to be in a town where absolutely no one knows of our background and to pretend that we're sisters sharing a flat or house and a little business together. Even then we'll still have to watch how we are with each other until we're behind closed doors.'

Val's pain filled Connie's being. Sinking down on the bed beside her, she took her hand, squeezing it gently and saying, 'Oh, Val, if you hadn't explained to me I would never have understood. I'm not sure if I do understand properly but, please believe me, I'm trying to.' She stared at Val, bewildered. 'What I don't understand is . . . what I mean is . . . well, you say that being with a man in that way sickens you yet I've seen you a couple of times with them, Val, acting like . . . well . . .'

'I'm mad about them?'

'Yes, that's just how you looked to me. All over them, you were.'

'Connie, I might not like men in that way but that don't mean that men don't like me in that way. I used 'em, Connie, to make money for me and Beatrice.'

'But if you weren't sleeping with them for money, how did you make money from them?'

Val grinned. 'Oh, it's so easy, Connie. Most men will do anything to get you into bed, especially older men, the ones whose wives aren't that accommodating, if you get my drift. Meeting that kind is easy. Pubs are full of them. You've only got to flash a smile at them and the ones that are game are over like a shot, chatting you up. Act girly with them, make out you're a virgin, and you can string them along for weeks on a promise. During that time they buy you presents, hopefully jewellery that can be sold or even better actual money to buy yourself a nice dress or something else you say you desperately want, all the time flashing your eyelashes at them. As soon as I know I can't stall them any longer from doing the actual deed I drop them like a ton of bricks. 'Course they never know me real name or where I really work, and the beauty of it all is that they can't cause a fuss or, I warn them, I'll make sure their wives find out. I told yer before and I meant it, Con, I ain't proud of what I've been up to but it was the only way I could think of to get some decent money together for me and Beatrice.'

Her face screwed up and her clutch on the envelope tightened. 'I've been doing this for over two years now and I thought another six months or so should get us enough to make a good start only as soon as Beatrice met me in the shed tonight I knew something was badly wrong. She told me her boss had been looking at her in a certain way for a while. She'd never told me about it before because she knew I'd be very upset but today, when his wife went out shopping, he got back from work early and cornered her in the kitchen and . . .' Val paused and gulped, lowering her voice to barely a whisper. 'The beast put his hand on her breast. How dare he? How dare he do that to my Beatrice? I've seen her boss. He's an ugly man, like a gnome, and his wife's a goblin. My Beatrice isn't the sort men fall over for but a man like him that most woman would run a mile from would find her attractive. Thankfully his wife came back and he scarpered quick sharp, but not before warning Beatrice that if she should say anything she'd live to regret it. Beatrice is terrified now of what he might do next and that's why she told me. I was hoping for another six months or so to make more money but after what she told me tonight I can't leave her in that place no longer. I told her to pack her belongings and sneak out before her employers get up in the morning and that I'd meet her at the station tomorrow afternoon and then we'll go off together and start our new life.'

'You're leaving, Val? Were you going to tell me?'

She shook her head. 'No. I couldn't give a damn about anyone else here, Con, but I didn't like the thought of leaving without telling you. I just felt it was for the best. Face it, how could I begin to explain to you that you'd been sharing a room for the past two years with a lesbian who'd been conning money out of men to pay for a new start for herself and the woman she loves? How do you begin a conversation like that? You would never have known if you hadn't decided to do a good deed for me and found my stash.' She paused and looked at Connie remorsefully. 'Do you hate me?'

'Hate you? No, of course I don't, Val,' she insisted. 'I just . . . well, I just feel very sorry for what you've had to do so you and Beatrice can be together and how you have to hide your feelings about each other in public. I can't say as I agree with how you've made your money . . . but, Val, I really hope it all works out for you, I mean that.'

She smiled gratefully. 'Thanks, Connie, you don't know how much it means to me to hear you say that.' She gave a sigh. 'It feels strange having actually been honest with someone about the real me after keeping it hidden from people, terrified in fact in case anyone guessed. If only I'd realised you wouldn't react like I was a freak I'd have told you before. Believe me, there've been times, Con, when I'd have given me eye teeth to pour me heart out to someone.'

She got up. 'I might as well start packing now as I don't need to wait until you're out of the way tomorrow. I've nothing to hide from you now, have I? I'll leave early in the morning so Beatrice isn't left sitting for hours on the station platform waiting for me. I'll lose me week's wages but it's a small price to pay.' Giving a brief smile she added, 'And it's not like I'm leaving broke, is it? Will you tell people you woke up to find me gone when they ask, Connie, and any more than that yer don't know?'

She nodded. 'Yes, of course I will. Would you like me to help you pack?'

'Would yer? I'd be grateful.'

'I will miss you, Val. Well, not your mess I won't, but I will miss *you*. Will you write to me, let me know how you're both doing?'

Val looked at her for a moment before saying, 'Yeah, 'course I will.'

Connie knew she wouldn't and she knew why. Val was protecting her in case the truth about her did come out and Connie suffered as a result of their association.

CHAPTER FOURTEEN

Earlier that evening Eddie walked into the drawing room and stopped abruptly as the bareness of the room struck her. Its adornments were crated ready for the auctioneer's staff to collect, and they and the furniture she was keeping would be moved the day after tomorrow. Making the decision to sell the house along with its contents, save for a few choice items which she was taking with her to the hotel, was one thing; to witness it actually happening was another.

It deeply saddened Eddie to think about the sale of the family treasures that had been part of her everyday life since she'd been born, and of her mother's and grandparents' before her. In a way she felt that part of herself was inside those crates. She felt the same about this house. Whoever took up residence here next, she would always feel deep down that it was her and her father's house, that they were just allowing other people to live here as caretakers.

She supposed she should be glad that Mr Froggitt the estate agent had telephoned her just as she had arrived home a couple of hours before after her delicious lunch with Phee in the new restaurant, to tell her that he had received an offer for the house, albeit below the asking price. Aware of her eagerness to sell quickly, he'd vehemently recommended she accept the offer unless she was willing to wait for another buyer to show up, and even then it was far from a foregone conclusion that they would offer her more. She had hesitated before asking who the offer was from, not sure whether she wanted to know or not, but as it was she was none the wiser as the estate agent told her he was not at liberty to divulge that information as the possible buyer was a very private person and didn't want his new place of residence to become common knowledge. Obviously from a well-respected family and Eddie was inwardly reassured the house was being placed in good hands, to be looked after and cared for as much as its previous owners had.

She accepted Mr Froggitt's recommendation to accept the offer along with his promise to complete the transaction swiftly using a solicitor he recommended. Eddie had been thankful to hand it all over to him, freeing herself from the ordeal. She had immediately telephoned the bank manager and informed him that the sale of their house was underway and repayment of the mortgage was imminent. The one thing she dare not think about was how her father was going to respond to all she had done in his absence, when he was well enough to understand. She just hoped to God she had made the right decision and the hotel would provide them with a new future.

A sudden overwhelming desire for the clock to turn back and everything be how she had always known it filled her. A vision of how the room had been before it had been cleared swam before her. She saw her father and herself sitting in the armchairs by a roaring fire, relaxing together after their evening meal, him reading his paper, she a copy of *Vogue*. He looked up and smiled at her, the love he held for her beaming from his eyes. She felt a presence by her side then and her heart leaped. 'Father!' she exclaimed, spinning round to face him, only to find Mabel looking back at her.

'You all right, Miss Griffin?' she asked her mistress.

'Sorry? Oh, yes, I'm fine, thank you, Mabel. What can I do for you?' Her voice was curt although she hadn't meant it to be.

'I wondered if I could have a word with you?'

'Yes, of course.'

The maid looked uncomfortable. 'Well, it's just that I thought I'd better let yer know that I've decided not to come with yer to the hotel, Miss Griffin. I've been offered a position with a Major Pimley and his wife. It's a good position as housekeeper and they seem very nice. I think it'd suit me better than hotel work. They want me as soon as possible so if it's all right with you, as soon as all the furniture and crates have been loaded . . . well, there won't be anything for me to do here, will there, after then?'

'No, there won't be. And I'm pleased for you, Mabel. Jess told me this morning that she had found a job as a school cook and Arthur has got himself gardening work too. I am of course disappointed that none of you will be coming with me. I shall miss you all.'

Mabel smiled wanly. 'We'll miss you, and Mr Griffin too.' Just then the front door knocker sounded and Mabel looked relieved at this chance to escape from an interview she was not enjoying at all. 'Best go and see who that is.'

Seconds later she returned to show in Harvey.

'Edelina, my dear,' he greeted her. 'I was just on the way to my club and thought I'd drop by to see how you are as I haven't seen or heard from you for a couple of days.'

She smiled at him welcomingly. 'I've been very busy but it's good to see you, Uncle Harvey. Have you time for a drink?'

'That would be kind of you.'

Eddie made to go across to the drinks cabinet then stopped short. 'Oh, I'd forgotten, everything is packed away ready for the auctioneer's to collect. We just kept a few items back for immediate use.' She went across to the door and pressed a button on the wall. Moments later Mabel appeared. 'Would you bring a whisky for Mr Crankshaft and a gin and tonic for me, please, Mabel?'

Harvey was looking at her in concern. 'You look peaky, Eddie.'

'Do I? I'm a bit tired. I've a lot on my mind which is understandable but apart from that I'm fine.'

He didn't look convinced. 'I don't think you are, Eddie. I can see this is all far too much for you. Look, my dear, it's not too late to change your mind. I still feel that selling the hotel is the best way to go.'

'I can't change my mind even if I did want to. I've had an offer for the house which I've accepted and the sale is proceeding. I've telephoned the bank manager to inform him that the mortgage will be settled shortly. As you can see, Mabel has been very busy crating up the items ready for the auctioneer's staff to collect on Friday. I've also chosen rooms at the hotel to move into and informed them I will be taking an interest in the place in the future. The household staff have all found other jobs. So you see, Uncle Harvey, things have progressed during the last couple of days.'

He was looking at her, surprised that she had achieved so much in such a short space of time. 'But you haven't exchanged contracts on the house, Eddie, so nothing is cast in stone until then. What you've done towards the move can be undone.'

Mabel came back with the drinks and they sat down.

Harvey leaned forward and looked at her intently. 'Now you've had time to think a bit more about what you're proposing, you must see that it's a huge challenge for someone in your position, Eddie.'

She sighed. 'I'm trying not to think too deeply or I'm afraid I'd kick up my heels and run away as fast as I could. But I can't run, Uncle Harvey. What good would I be to my father if I did? I know I have a huge amount to learn but I'm prepared to and I'm sure the hotel staff will be a great help to me.' She was about to tell Harvey about the hotel manager's illness and the fact that until he returned she would not have the benefit of his experience, but thought better of it. Harvey was concerned enough that she was taking on far more than she could handle, and she didn't want to worry him any more than he already was. And besides, as Phee had said, the assistant manager would oversee everything until he returned. Then she noticed Harvey was looking very pensive. 'Uncle Harvey, is there anything the matter?'

'Matter? No, nothing is the matter. Well, yes, there is. I'm upset I can't get you to change your mind, Eddie. I do very strongly fear that your decision is the wrong one but I can see I'm not going to sway you. All I ask is that you remember it's no humiliation to admit at any time that you were wrong and then Mr Whittle and I would be only too glad to resume our endeavours to sell the hotel for you.'

She wished he would show more faith in her, give her some encouragement at least in what she was facing instead of continuously telling her he felt she was heading for trouble. 'I won't hesitate to turn to you, Uncle Harvey, should I come to that conclusion,' she said quietly.

He patted her hand affectionately. 'I do wish you well, Edelina, I really do.' He looked at her enquiringly. 'No change in Edwin, I take it, or you would have said?'

She shook her head, deep sadness clouding her face. 'They just keep telling me not to expect too much, too soon. I wish they'd agree to let me visit him. I'm sure seeing my face would help bring him out of his mood. All I want to do is put my arms around him, tell him I haven't abandoned him, reassure him that hospital is the best place for him to get better.' She blinked away tears. 'I know it's been not much more than a week since all this happened but it feels like a lifetime to me.'

She forced a smile to her face. 'But you didn't come here to listen to my tales of woe. I'm holding you up from your evening at the club. I do appreciate your coming by to enquire after me, Uncle Harvey. I shall be taking up my rooms in the hotel as soon as the contents of this house have been collected on Friday, ready to be auctioned next week, so that's where you'll find me from then on.'

'I wish you luck, Edelina. You're going to need it.' He downed his drink and rose, going over to her to peck her cheek. 'Don't get up, I can see myself out.'

His parting words reverberated in the bare room. She suddenly felt herself to be standing on the edge of a cliff, ready to jump. She would either plummet down to the rocky depths below or soar skywards. She sincerely hoped it was the latter.

CHAPTER FIFTEEN

It felt very strange for Connie to wake the next morning and not see a bleary-eyed Val staring back at her from the bed opposite, or as was usually the case have to shake her awake so she wouldn't be late for her shift and suffer verbal abuse in return. The only consolation was that the room was tidy, albeit Val had left her bedding piled in a heap in her haste to leave in the early hours of the morning.

Struggling upright to stretch and rub her eyes, she wondered whether Val and Beatrice were already reunited on the station platform, about to embark on their new life together. She still hadn't come to terms with the fact that two people of the same gender could love each other the way those two obviously did, and didn't know whether she ever would. Regardless she really did wish them both well and hoped they would both be happy and fulfilled. She then wondered who her new room-mate would be. Hopefully someone she got on as well with as she had with Val and not someone who was as untidy as her, but time would tell on that score.

Connie entered the hotel foyer a good half an hour before her shift started that morning. The smell of fresh polish filled the air from the labours of the early-morning cleaners and the drone of a couple of vacuum cleaners could be heard coming from the guests' lounge and connecting reading and writing rooms.

Harry Glebe, the middle-aged night porter, gave a tired smile when he saw her coming towards him. 'Hello, Connie lovey. You're nice and early this morning which means I can get off home sharpish.' He gave a wicked grin. 'With a bit of luck might even catch me wife still in bed.' He grinned even more broadly on seeing her blush but thankfully for Connie didn't pursue that topic of conversation and heighten her embarrassment. 'It meks a nice change to see your happy smiling face this morning instead of being greeted by that po-faced old cow.' His craggy face screwed up in an expectant look as she arrived behind the counter. 'I suppose it's no good me hoping the old goat's retired or fell under a bus, is it?'

Connie wondered if Miss Harbin had any idea how much people disliked her, or if she even cared. 'Not as far as I'm aware, Mr Glebe.'

'Ah, well, ducky, I suppose we can all live in hope. Mind you, I only have ter deal with her at the start and end of me shift, unlike you and Pam who have ter deal with her all day. I know for a fact Herbert the concierge keeps his distance from reception as much as he can to avoid contact with her, 'cos he told me himself. Amelia Harbin is the most trying woman I've ever met. How do yer put up with her, lovey?'

As much as Connie would have liked to have told the night porter that it was with great difficulty, Miss Harbin was nevertheless Connie's superior and it was against her nature to act or speak in open disloyalty against her to another member of staff. 'All the morning papers delivered to the rooms, Mr Glebe?'

'Certainly are, ducky. And the boots and shoes all polished and standing to attention outside the right doors like they always are despite that woman doing her best to catch me out so she can have the pleasure of giving me what for. It was a quiet night last night. I only had one guest ring down for attention. Wanted his coal bucket topped up as he said the rads were stone cold and he had to work late on a paper or summat for some presentation he was doing for a company today. What the hell he needed to tell me all that for I've no idea. I wasn't interested despite having to act like I was. I suppose he thought he was making himself look important to me. It's about time that boiler was put out to pasture and a new one put in.'

He looked at Connie eagerly. 'What's this Hubert the barman was telling me after his shift finished last night – that the Captain was rushed off to hospital yesterday? I'm sorry to hear about it, 'course I am, he's a decent enough boss is the Captain, always finds time to have a quick word with me every night before he goes home, even when it's really late. He's not married, yer know. In fact, from the odd comment he's passed to me over the years I've bin working here, I gather all his relatives are long dead and buried.' Harry pulled a rueful face. 'Believe me, there's bin times I wished I wasn't married with three growing daughters, but in times like the Captain's going through just now yer need yer family more than ever. Still, I suppose the nurses will take care of him and I suppose he can afford to employ someone to come in and do for him as he's only himself to spend his money on.

'Anyway, no disrespect to the Captain but what was more interesting was that Hubert told me the owner apparently showed up out of the blue, and a woman too, can yer credit it? According to Hubert she's moving in and this place is getting an overhaul. Is that right, Connie?'

She was very aware she should not be spreading gossip. 'I had the privilege of meeting Miss Griffin and she seems very nice.'

He looked dubious. 'Too much of this about these days.'

'Too much of what, Mr Glebe?'

'Women thinking they can run the show. Not that I don't think it's about time the owner showed an interest in this place before it well and truly goes to the dogs, but why ain't this woman married and at home looking after her husband and kids like women are meant to, that's what I want to know? Let's just hope she ain't another Miss Harbin, eh, Connie, for all our sakes.' He stopped short as the staff entrance door across the foyer was heard to open and shut, and smiled a greeting at the man coming towards them. 'Goodness me, what is it with you day staff this morning, all arriving for work early? Haven't seen you, Neal, since yer had a stint helping the breakfast chefs out when one went sick a year or so ago.'

Neal came up to them and smiled a greeting at Harry and seemingly as an afterthought gave a quick nod of his head at Connie. She flashed a brief smile of recognition back, immediately experiencing a lurch in her stomach that told her she really did like this man which was a pity as she obviously didn't attract him, judging by the way he had only acknowledged her presence as an afterthought.

'Chef's lumbered me with the job of cleaning out the cold store, just by way of meanness because I never gave him any reason to have a go at me yesterday. I thought I'd get up early and get it over with but I'm going to have my breakfast first. I wondered if you'd a spare newspaper knocking about that I could have a look through while I'm eating?'

'You've worked in this place long enough, lad, to know Miss Harbin makes it her personal business to account for every paper, and it's a criminal offence as far as she's concerned should any be unaccounted for. You'd think she personally paid the newspaper bill.' A sudden smile twitched Harry's lips, his eyes sparkling humorously. 'I'm a father of three gels and I'd be a blind man if I didn't see the real reason you've paid a visit to reception this morning.'

Neal looked puzzled. 'I don't know what you mean?'

Harry flashed a quick look at Connie, then back at Neal. 'Oh, I'm sure yer do, lad,' he chuckled, and gave them both a suggestive wink. 'I'll leave yer both to it and go and unlock the outer doors ready for business, then I'll be on me way. See yer tonight, Connie,' he called after him as, jangling his bunch of keys, he made his way over to the counter flap to depart.

Connie and Neal were left looking at each other in embarrassment.

Neal's stomach was churning. Since bumping into this girl . . . Connie . . . yesterday on the back stairs he

251

hadn't been able to get her out of his mind and had lain awake for most of the night trying to fathom a way to cross paths with her again and do what he should have found courage to do yesterday. His ploy to catch her at the start of her shift without the presence of Miss Harbin, using the search for a newspaper by way of excuse, was the best out of a jumble of other lame excuses he'd come up with. Fired up, he'd been jubilant to enter through the staff entrance into the foyer and see Connie as he'd hoped, early for her shift and with no sign of the formidable Miss Harbin. But he'd bargained without Harry Glebe seeing through his guise and passing his most embarrassing remark which had completely put Neal off his stride.

'I . . . er . . . don't know what Harry was going on about, I'm sure,' he stuttered awkwardly.

It was very apparent to Connie that Harry's insinuation that there was something between herself and the good-looking commis chef had caused Neal acute embarrassment. 'No, neither do I,' she said tartly. 'Well, if you'll excuse me, I have things to be getting on with and your breakfast will be getting cold.'

'Oh, er . . . yes, it will.'

With that he spun on his heel and almost ran in the direction of the staff door, leaving Connie in no doubt how keen he was to get away from her. Did she disgust him so much?

Just then Pamela entered through the flap in the counter and beamed a greeting. 'Morning, Connie. Thought I was going to be late this morning as the bus was full and I had to wait for the next one, but at least I've got here in time to have five minutes to myself before old Dragon Face shows herself. Is it worth hoping she might be in a good mood today, do you think?' Before Connie could answer Pamela gave her a nudge. 'You've a customer.'

'Eh? Oh,' she exclaimed, spinning round to face the counter on the other side of which a middle-aged woman was looking back at her hesitantly. Guests usually arrived to be booked into their rooms after twelve o'clock so this woman was unusually early. It struck Connie then how strained she looked, as if she'd suffered a deep shock. Connie smiled welcomingly at her. 'Good morning, madam. Welcome to the Connaught. If you'd care to take a seat over there,' she said, indicating the waiting area, 'Miss Harbin our senior receptionist will be arriving shortly and will be very pleased to see to you.'

The woman eyed her anxiously. Timidly she said, 'Oh, I really don't want to wait. You can help me, dear, can't you? I just want a room. I can have one?' It was a desperate plea rather than a question.

This woman had suffered a bereavement at least, Connie assumed by her whole demeanour, and she felt it would be just terrible of her to add to such suffering by insisting she wait the ten minutes or so until Miss Harbin appeared. By then Connie could have her booked in and already settled. Oh, well, she thought as she went across and picked up the reservations book, better get my chambermaid's uniform back out of store in readiness.

'Just a small room would do me,' the woman said as she watched Connie scan her finger down the reservations book.

'Somewhere quiet?' Connie asked her instinctively, looking up to smile at her.

'Oh, please, dear. Yes, that would suit me. Peace and quiet, that's just what I need. You are most kind.'

'It's my pleasure, madam. The side of the hotel on the second floor is best then. Not much of a view, though, I'm afraid.'

'I'm not worried about a view, dear.' And she added distractedly, 'A view is the last thing on my mind.'

'How long will you be staying with us?' Connie asked her.

The woman looked troubled. 'Oh, I don't know. It depends, you see.'

'Well, how about I book you in for a couple of days and then you let us know whether you wish to stay for longer?'

'Yes, I could do that. But . . . er . . . do you think you could make it a week, dear? Maybe by then . . . Yes, maybe by then . . . Is it permissible for me to book in for a week?'

'Yes, of course it is, madam.' Connie passed her a reservations card. 'If you'll please fill that in, I'll get the porter to show you up and settle you in. Should you need anything, please telephone down and we'll do our best to accommodate you.' She smiled kindly at the woman. 'Would you like me to ask room service to bring you up a tray of tea? Some toast perhaps?'

Connie was taken aback to see tears of gratitude in the guest's eyes. 'Oh, you are most kind,' she reiterated.

Connie spotted Danny the day porter emerging through the staff entrance and beckoned him over. Handing him a set of keys, she asked him to show Miss

Weaver, as she now knew her name to be, to her room and wished her a pleasant stay.

The lift carrying Miss Weaver and the porter had just started to ascend and Connie had just replaced the telephone receiver after calling through to room service with Miss Weaver's order when the staff entrance door opened again and Amelia Harbin strode through, her face a stiff mask as usual.

There was no pleasant morning greeting from her as she joined Connie behind the counter. 'In between doing the breakfast orders and newspapers for tomorrow, you're to make a start on typing confirmation letters, Monroe. Three carbon copies of each, pink for Captain Fosedyke's file, green for the accounts office and buff for our own reception records. Of course, I will need to see them all first for checking and signing.' She paused and there was a spiteful spark in her eye when she asked condescendingly, 'You do type?'

Connie knew instinctively that the woman fully expected her to say she didn't possess such a skill, wanted to ridicule her for expecting to become a competent receptionist without being able to, and use this inability as another reason why Connie was unsuitable for the job. Well, Miss Harbin was going to get a shock and it was going to give Connie great delight to deliver it.

'Yes, I do type, Miss Harbin,' she said proudly. 'I was timed at forty-five words a minute and only one mistake when I passed my Pitman's exam at night school last year. I did realise that to work as a receptionist I'd need to type.'

Connie could see her boss was having to fight hard

not to show her fury. 'Well, the examining board might have turned a blind eye to your one mistake but, I can assure you, I won't,' she snapped. 'The typewriter needs a new ribbon inserting. I trust night school showed you how to maintain equipment? Spares are kept in the stationery cupboard next to the switchboard. While you're in there, do a stationery check for items we're running low on for me to present to . . . well, I suppose it will be Mr Sopworth during the Captain's absence.'

'Yes, Miss Harbin,' said Connie, smiling politely. What Miss Harbin did not realise was that Connie enjoyed typing and would look forward to producing the letters after the far more mundane tasks her superior had been filling her time with. Then she remembered the guest she had just booked in and was very aware of how Miss Harbin was going to react to what she had done. She thought she had better get it over with. Steeling herself she said, 'Oh, Miss Harbin, before you arrived this morning I booked a guest in.'

Her eyes bulged. 'You did what?' she hissed. Hands clasped to the front of her, she puffed out her skinny chest and stated, 'I have given you strict instructions that until I feel you are competent enough to deal with the guests, you are to ask them to wait until I am available to deal with them. You blatantly disobeyed me, Monroe.'

Connie gulped. 'Miss Harbin, I do apologise, but you see . . .'

'There is no excuse for such disobedience,' she cut in harshly. 'I shall have to pay a visit to the guest and apologise for not being on hand myself to take care of her. No doubt there'll be complaints about your hand-ling of her. Once again, this proves to me just how unsuitable you are . . .'

Suddenly Connie had had enough of this woman's unjustified condemnation of her abilities without ever giving her a chance to prove herself. All fears of losing this much-coveted job temporarily flew from her as she blurted, 'Miss Harbin, if you'll please listen to me, I did ask Miss Weaver to wait until you arrived but she wouldn't, wanted to be booked in straightaway. She was very upset about something, maybe a close relative had died and she's come for the funeral, but anyway it wouldn't have been fair of me to make the situation worse by having her wait in the foyer until you arrived for work, with people staring at her. I booked her in properly and Miss Weaver thanked me for the way I'd taken care of her.

'With due respect, Miss Harbin, it's not right that I have to ask guests to wait until you're free to deal with them, sometimes quite a while if another guest is keep-ing you occupied, when I'm capable of seeing to them if you'd just give me a chance to. I'm used to dealing with guests, I dealt with them all the time in my job as chambermaid and I never got any complaints . . . well, not many . . . and they were only when guests were being unreasonable. Please give me a proper chance to prove I can be good at this job, Miss Harbin, and a real help to you.'

Eyes blazing, her superior thrust forward her head like a chicken about to peck crumbs and hissed, 'A proper chance to prove to Captain Fosedyke that you can run reception more efficiently than I can? I know your game,

Monroe, same as I did all the other young chits who thought they could get the better of me. But I'm not going to let you, like I didn't let them. It seems these days that experience is not top of the employer's list any more like it used to be when I was starting out in my career. A job such as this one was a vocation to be taken seriously, like nuns dedicating themselves to God. Girls were chosen because of their ability and show of dedication to their profession, not because they had a pretty face and shapely figure. I saw the way you batted your eyelashes at the Captain to get this job and, typical man, he responded accordingly. I will prove his error to him, as I did with those others he insisted I take on since Miss Birch retired. Hopefully when you have gone back to where you belong he will realise it's best to leave me to choose who I have working with me. Namely a woman who respects my position and does not try to undermine me at every opportunity, as you enjoy doing. I repeat, I will not be forced out of the job that I have given my life to, by you or anyone like you.'

She straightened up and took a deep breath. 'I will allow you to deal with the guests but only when I am otherwise engaged. Woe betide you should I receive one complaint. Forget typing the letters. Until the breakfast and newspaper orders start to come in for tomorrow, you can give the guests' message cubicles a dust and polish, and clean the top of the counter while you're at it. Those cleaners never do it properly. I must speak to the Captain when he returns about their slap-dash ways. Now get to it!'

With that she stalked off to her seat behind the counter to immerse herself in her work.

So that's why she's so reluctant to give me any proper responsibility, Connie thought as she stared after her. Miss Harbin was terrified that Connie was after her job when all *she* wanted was to be allowed to learn to do the one she had. And maybe, when the time was right far in the future, become equipped to take charge of the reception area. Miss Harbin was silly to be of the opinion she was and Connie could only hope that time would prove her error to her then hopefully she'd mellow in her attitude towards her subordinate. She inwardly smiled. Miss Harbin had relented enough to allow her to deal with the guests only because she knew Connie was right and it was wrong to keep them waiting unnecessarily. Oh, well, she thought as she began a task that she'd only done a couple of days before, at least one good thing had come out of all this. Now she would deal with more guests direct.

Meanwhile, having found he'd no stomach for his breakfast, Neal was in the huge cold store with a large metal bucket of hot soapy water. Having cleared a shelf of foodstuffs, he was scrubbing it down while inwardly fuming at Harry Glebe for innocently or not stamping on his golden opportunity to ask Connie out with his embarrassing remark. The only consolation was that at least Neal now knew the name of the woman who'd claimed his attention. But after the dismissive way he had acted after Harry Glebe's comment it wouldn't surprise him if Connie never spoke to him again. He knew he'd be a fool to let this incident deter him, though. All his instincts were telling him that she was the special sort of woman who was rarely encountered and he could spend the rest of his life regretting letting this one slip through his fingers. But at the moment he could not think of a way to put things right without making himself look more of a fool than he did already.

Shelf scrubbed clean, he neatly restacked the tins and packets of foodstuffs on it and proceeded to clear the next, ready for cleaning. The water in the bucket was murky from the grubby shelf so he thought he ought to change it before he washed down the next.

The two breakfast chefs, so opposite in nature from Chef Stimpson, were good-humoured, likeable men who had each notched up over fifteen years cooking at the Connaught. They ribbed Neal mercilessly as, carrying the bucket, he made his way down the kitchen to the huge pot sink by the back entrance door. Wolf-whistling and winking suggestively, they barracked him with female names, such as Sweet Suzie and Sexy Sadie, demanding to know why he wasn't wearing his skirt and pinny and if he was enjoying his promotion to kitchen skivvy? Neal laughed at their cracks and guffawed aloud at the chef who was so interested in ribbing him he didn't notice that his pan had caught fire and the sausages and black pudding inside were flaming.

His empty bucket refilling under the hot tap, Neal leaned back against the sink, his mind once more filled with thoughts of Connie, and jumped like a scalded cat at a thump on the back door. He automatically went to open it. Before him stood a shifty-looking character.

Neal eyed him warily. Tradesmen called regularly with their deliveries, but not usually this early in the morning, and besides this man was no tradesman. 'Can I help you?' Neal asked him.

'Wanna see the chef,' he demanded.

'Which chef?'

'Why? How many you got?'

'How many do you want?' Neal said flippantly.

The man grunted. 'Fucking funny ha-ha. The big fat one. Simpson.'

'Stimpson? He's not due on until ten.'

'Ten? Oh,' the man muttered, disappointed. 'Can yer fetch him? Tell him I'm here.'

Neal gave a scoffing laugh. 'Listen, mate, no one in their right mind wakes Chef Stimpson up, not if they value their life, which I do.'

'Oh, shit,' the man grumbled. 'We'd arranged the meet for later tonight but I can't manage it 'cos summat important has cropped up so I was hoping we could do our business tomorrow night instead.' The man looked at him anxiously. 'I'll mek if worth yer while if you go and fetch him?'

Neal shook his head. 'I've already told you, no.'

'Oh, fuck you then,' the other man snarled nastily. 'Just tell Stimpson Ronnie can't mek it tonight. He knows where he can find me to arrange another time.'

Neal closed the door to find his bucket overflowing. He turned off the tap and added soap powder to the water in the bucket, swirling it around with an old wooden spatula. All the while his mind was racing. Neal wasn't stupid. He felt he knew exactly what business arrangement Chef Stimpson had with this man. He was obviously selling food on the side and would be falsifying his accounts books to cover it. This underhand practice was an easy thing for a chef to operate in a kitchen such as the one they worked in. It would be very difficult for management actually to find out the exact quantities of ingredients used to produce meals for the hotel if Chef didn't want them known. Neal also knew that the portion sizes served up in this kitchen fell short of what would generally be given. If a customer actually complained about the size of his meal, the blame was always firmly placed upon the poor commis who'd prepared that dish, who dare not speak out and say that the portion size was dictated by Chef Stimpson himself. Other food was recorded as wastage but in truth was not sold on as pig swill but disposed of to a queue of people who were always ready to take it off the hotel and sell it on. All in all, Chef's illicit practices must prove a nice little sideline for him.

When Neal had charge of his own kitchen, he intended never to stoop to such underhand dealing, risking his own good reputation and career prospects. When all was said and done such practices were theft. Serve Stimpson right if he was caught, Neal thought.

Then an idea struck him. Chef was a nasty piece of work and made the kitchen staff's lives an utter misery. Neal knew that Melvin Jones in particular was just about at the end of his tether from Chef's bullying ways. Neal felt the young lad had potential, given a chance, but because of his experiences under Chef Stimpson he would most probably abandon all hope of qualifying to work instead in a factory or some-where else where the regime wasn't so harsh. Neal had only stuck his own apprenticeship under Stimpson because of his fixed determination to get his professional qualification. As soon as he did he was off. But if somehow he could catch Chef Stimpson red-handed in his illegal activities he could maybe warn him that if he didn't lay off the kitchen staff, Neal would shop him to the management. He wouldn't, of course, ever do such a thing. If the management were ever to discover the underhand dealings in the kitchen then it would not be through him splitting on a colleague, whether that colleague was detestable or not. In truth, the thought of resorting to blackmail did not sit well with Neal, but if the end result was that their working lives improved then it was something he would resort to. A bit of detection work was called for first, though.

As he ran the gauntlet back through the kitchen, once again bombarded by the two breakfast chefs' good-humoured barracking, his mind fixed on Connie and his own deep desire to find a way to ask her to go out with him.

A short distance away from the hotel, Eddie was just finishing her breakfast and thinking she really ought to get Mabel to help her make a start on her personal packing. She was moving to the hotel late tomorrow afternoon, after the house had been cleared by the auctioneer's. She heard the telephone ringing. A moment or so later she heard it being answered by Mabel and prepared herself to be summoned to take the call. A minute or so went by before the flustered maid came into the dining room.

'Oh, Miss Griffin, that was the hospital with an urgent message. They want you to go immediately!'

Eddie whipped the napkin from her lap, wiped her

mouth, and rose from her chair. She could not disguise her own agitation. 'Did they give any indication why they wanted to see me so urgently?'

'I asked . . . well, I think it was the doctor, it was a man anyway . . . to let me fetch you to the telephone, and he said just to give you a message that you was wanted up there urgently.'

A wave of panic swept over Eddie. Something must have happened to her father. What, though? 'Telephone for a taxi, please, Mabel, while I fetch my coat.'

Fifteen minutes later a highly anxious Eddie was in the back of the taxi, making her away across town to the hospital. What awaited her there she dare not allow her mind to dwell on. She knew she needed to keep herself calm in order to face what the doctor had to tell her. Her father had obviously taken a turn for the worse, that much she did allow herself to admit, or why summon her so urgently?

The receptionist, a thirty-something pale-faced studious man with horn-rimmed spectacles, greeted her coolly through the glass hatch. 'If you'd take a seat,' he said, indicating a row of worn brown leather chairs arranged along the corridor, 'I'll get Matron for you.'

'It was the doctor who summoned me. It's him I need to see,' Eddie urged.

'If you'd take a seat, madam,' he repeated, reaching for the telephone, 'I'll fetch Matron for you.'

Eddie knew she had no choice but to do as she was bidden. It was a good half an hour later before a bulky-looking woman appeared before her.

'What can I do for you, madam?' she enquired starchily.

'I was telephoned and asked to come here urgently.'

'By whom?' the nurse requested.

'I assume by the doctor who's treating my father. My maid took the call.'

'The doctors do not usually see relatives until the afternoon between two and three o'clock, and then strictly by appointment only. I am not aware of Professor Chandler, your father's consultant, telephoning for any urgent family visitors, and I would be aware of it, I assure you. Besides, the Professor would not have telephoned personally, it would always be his secretary who placed calls.'

'Nevertheless I have received a telephone call,' Eddie insisted. 'Whether it was from the Professor himself or his secretary, one of them telephoned.'

'I can only deduce that your maid got the message wrong.'

'My maid is very reliable. In all the years she has worked for my family I have rarely if ever known her to get a message wrong.' Eddie's mind was whirling. *Someone* had summoned her. 'I want to see Professor Chandler,' she demanded.

'I'm afraid that isn't possible. The Professor is lecturing at the University this morning and is not due here until this afternoon.'

'One of his junior doctors then. Matron, I need to know how my father is.'

'The doctors are busy with patient rounds at the moment. I could make an appointment . . .'

'I'm here because I was requested to come and that warrants a personal consultation in my book.' Eddie took a deep breath and added, 'I want to see my father.

I won't leave until I can put my mind at rest about him, see that he's not actually any worse than he was when I brought him in. He's been here over a week now and so far you have not let me see him.'

'That's because it's in the patient's best interest not to allow visitors yet. He's in a fragile state. Mental illness isn't like a headache that can be fixed with a pill. It's a broken mind that's being dealt with here and the mending of it takes professional skill and weeks, months, sometimes years of treatment. And sometimes I'm afraid the patient never fully recovers to what they were before.' A glimpse of unexpected kindness crossed Matron's previously stern face. 'It could be very upsetting for you, Miss Griffin, to see your father at the moment.'

Eddie appreciated her concern. 'I saw how he was when he was first admitted, can it really be any worse than seeing him like that? Please, Matron, let me see him. Just a glimpse through a door, that's all I ask.'

Matron gave a deep resigned sigh. 'Well, it's highly irregular. I could be risking a very severe reprimand myself . . . all right then, just a quick visit, long enough to satisfy yourself he's in good hands. In future you must be patient and await the Professor's call.'

They walked through a maze of corridors, several times stopping to unlock and relock security gates, and up a flight of stairs. Matron briskly led the way. The sounds of wails, screeches, torturous moans, filled the air, as did the stench of human suffering. En route they passed several pitiful human beings, looking lost and bewildered. Selfish though it seemed, others' suffering inside this heavily guarded Victorian fortress was not Eddie's immediate concern. Her father was.

Matron finally stopped by a door in the middle of a long dim corridor, faced Eddie and said, low-voiced, 'Because of your father's position in life he was not put on a ward but given a private room. Not many are so fortunate. You may take a quick look through the observation window.'

Eddie moved to the door and peered through the small square of wired glass in the middle of it. It was iron-barred on the other side. The room she was looking into was small, white-painted, and held a metal-framed bed with a chair beside it. Sitting on the bed, his profile to her as he stared out of a barred window opposite, was her father. He was dressed in the clothes he had been wearing when he had been brought in, over his knee was draped his overcoat, perched on top of his head was his hat. He cut a sorry figure.

Eddie gasped, 'He looks as if he's ready to go out!' She turned to face Matron. 'I suppose I expected to see him with his night clothes on, in bed.'

'He sits like that all day. He's waiting for his wife to collect him.'

'My mother? But she died forty years ago.'

'It seems that to cope with whatever shock your father had to cause this breakdown, in his mind he's reverted to the time when he was happiest and that seems to be before your mother died. I did try and warn you that this would be distressing for you, Miss Griffin.'

Eddie bit her lower lip, fighting to stem the threat of tears. 'He will get better, won't he, Matron?' she whispered.

'The Professor is the one you should consult, Miss Griffin.'

267

'My friend Phee . . . Sophia Rymmington-Smyth . . . well, she mentioned electric shock treatment. Her mother's friend had it apparently when she . . . well, like my father. It sounds . . . oh, it sounds so awful! Will you be giving that to my father?'

'Again, that is a question to direct to the Professor. We really must go now, Miss Griffin.'

'When will I get to see the Professor so I can ask him these questions?'

'We will call you with an appointment when he has something to tell you. Until then you will have to be patient, Miss Griffin.'

The ride back in the taxi found Eddie in a sombre mood. She wasn't sure which was worse: witnessing her father's frenzied state a week ago or this total distancing of himself from reality. All she could do was hope that either via treatment or gradual recovery his condition would stabilise and he'd be able to join in their new future.

As the taxi drew up outside her house, Mabel came running down the steps to greet her. 'I wasn't prepared, Miss Griffin, hadn't made a start on your personal packing . . . but I did my best. Because of your summons to the hospital you obviously forgot to tell me . . .'

Alighting from the taxi and paying the driver, Eddie looked at her maid, puzzled. 'Mabel, what are you going on about?'

'Everything going to the auctioneer's today and not tomorrow as I'd been told. And I was under the impression you were taking some items you'd picked out to the hotel with you, only the man in charge said he'd had no such instructions. He'd been told to pick up everything. Your trunks are in the hall, Miss Griffin. I don't know what I'm going to do, I'm not expected at me new place until tomorrow evening and I've nowhere to sleep tonight unless they let me start earlier . . .'

Eddie was frowning at her, bewildered. 'I wasn't informed that the day for collection had been changed.' She was annoyed. 'Get Mr Adkins from the auctioneer's on the telephone, please, Mabel.'

Ten minutes later, Eddie put the receiver back in its cradle, walked over to the bottom of the stairs and sank down on a step. She covered her face with her hands and let out a groan. 'No! Oh, please, God, no.'

While Eddie had been on the telephone Mabel had gone to the kitchen to make her a cup of tea. She was now back in the hall, cup and saucer in hand, looking at Eddie worriedly. 'Miss Griffin, what on earth's wrong?'

She lifted her head, her face pale. 'Those men who came to clear the house, did you check their credentials?'

'No, I never thought to, Miss Griffin. I did query why the day had been changed but the one who seemed to be in charge just said he was following instructions and asked would I mind if they got on with it as quick as they could as they'd another job to do this morning. Two big furniture vans pulled up only minutes after you'd left for the hospital and before I knew it men seemed to be swarming everywhere. They had the house empty and were off before I knew it.'

'Was there any name on the side of the vans, Mabel?'

She gave a shrug. 'I didn't notice, I was too busy packing your personal belongings, fearful they'd cart those away as well. Why are you asking these questions, Miss Griffin? What's happened?'

She took a deep breath and ran her fingers through her hair. 'What's happened, Mabel, is that I've been robbed.'

'Eh?'

'Those men were not from the auctioneer's.'

'They weren't? Then where were they from, Miss Griffin?'

'Your guess is as good as mine. As far as the auctioneer's are concerned the job is still scheduled for tomorrow, they know nothing about any collection being made today.'

The cup of tea Mabel was holding crashed to the floor. 'Oh, my God,' she cried, clapping her hands to her face. 'I don't believe it, Miss Griffin. You mean, I let those men in and stood by while they took every stick you own?'

Just then the door knocker rapped, resounding eerily around the now empty house. Automatically Mabel went to answer it and let in Harvey Crankshaft.

'Eddie, dear.' He smiled as he strode over to her. 'I wondered if you'd like to go for lunch . . .' His voice trailed off as he registered her agitation and the fact that the house was empty. 'What . . . er . . . but I thought the contents were being collected tomorrow. Eddie, what on earth is wrong?'

She stood up wearily. 'I've been robbed, Uncle Harvey.'

He looked at her, astonished. 'What?'

'Bogus removal men took everything. I was summoned to the hospital urgently this morning, only it turned out to be a ruse to get me out of the house because no one there had summoned me. While I was gone men came and loaded everything on to two vans. They'd gone before I got back.'

'And you let them?' he shot accusingly at Mabel.

'It isn't Mabel's fault, Uncle Harvey. She thought I hadn't informed her that the collection day had been changed.' Then the shocking truth of what had just taken place hit her full force. 'Oh, I can't believe this has happened . . . all our lovely things, ones that belonged to my grandparents and my mother and father . . . I'm not worried about anything I've bought over the years, but to lose my family's things . . . Oh, what am I going to do?' she implored. 'It was bad enough making the decision to sell everything, but to have it all stolen . . . And I was banking on the money from the auction to get the modernisation of the hotel underway. We need to call the police,' she cried urgently. 'Maybe they can catch whoever did this and get everything back for me.'

'I'll telephone them,' offered Harvey.

A good while later, Mabel looked at Eddie shame-faced. 'I'm so sorry, Miss Griffin. I felt such a fool not being able to tell the police anything – well, nothing really. I know that Inspector thought I was stupid to let the burglars in like I did. They don't hold out much hope of getting it all back, I could tell that.'

An ashen-faced Eddie placed a reassuring hand on her shoulder. 'Don't distress yourself further, Mabel. I hold you in no way to blame for this. We can only hope a miracle happens and, as the police said, they'll hear through informants that someone is trying to sell similar items and maybe they can apprehend the culprits that way. Do you think it's as they suspect, Uncle Harvey, and an employee of the auctioneer's took payment to give the burglars the tip off? Is maybe even in on it himself?'

He nodded grimly. 'Seems the most likely scenario.'

'Then I just have to hope that whoever it is will buckle under the strain of a police interview and tell them everything.' Eddie looked thoughtful. 'I'll have to start making a list of all the things for the insurance claim. Will you help me, Mabel?'

'Oh, 'course, Miss Griffin, 'course I will. It's the least I can do.'

'I think you'll be wasting your time, Edelina,' said Harvey.

'I'm sorry, I don't understand?' she replied, looking at him quizzically. Then the truth hit home. 'Oh, no, you mean we aren't insured? Stibley will have ignored the premium payments, won't he, during the last few months, trying to wring every penny out of my father that he could? Oh, that man!' she cried harshly. 'I hope to God everything he's got out of us brings him nothing but misery.' The tears came then, to flow unashamedly down her face. 'Oh, why is all this happening to me? When will it stop? I've informed the staff at the hotel of my plans and I'm going to look such a fool now, having to tell them the modernisation programme isn't going to take place. And I've none of my own furniture to bring with me after instructing them to clear the rooms ready to receive it.'

Mabel looked on helplessly as Harvey went to put his arms around Eddie, pulling her close. 'I'm so sorry, Edelina.'

'So am I, oh, so am I,' she sobbed, burying her head in his shoulder. 'At this moment I envy Father for being oblivious to all this.'

It was all going wrong, her mind screamed. She must have been mad to think she could turn around the fortunes of a failing hotel and make it viable enough to support herself and her father as well as trying to recoup some of the money Stibley had stolen to finance a future for them. Harvey was right: she was far too ignorant of business matters ever to have made a go of it. Burglars had seen her vulnerability and fleeced her. There was no telling if those she came across in the hotel trade, her own staff even, might not take advantage of her ignorance too and she be powerless to stop it. She should have accepted the offer to find a buyer for the hotel and let Mr Whittle handle the sale on her behalf. Her life then would be far from the opulent one she and her father were used to but with careful management of their resources, safely placed in a bank account, a modest, debt-free existence was possible.

She pulled away from Harvey and looked up at him, just about to tell him she had changed her mind and wanted to ask his help in approaching Mr Whittle again, when a vision of her mother swam before her. Roxanne had once been in the same position as Eddie was now, when her own father had died leaving the business in her charge. According to Ralph Waddington she had tackled the challenge by throwing herself into learning all about the business, overcoming whatever obstacles were placed in her path to achieve the success she'd probably never thought possible.

To Eddie it was as if her mother was wagging a

finger at her, telling her to pull herself together, that Griffins rose to a challenge and always did their best. As a proper Griffin so should she.

A surge of determination filled her. She was not going to let this setback quash her belief that the hotel was the key to their future. She'd be damned if it would. It was all daunting, but of course it was all new to her. Nevertheless she was the owner of a hotel and, as Phee had said to her, it was about time she started acting like one.

Head back, voice firm, she said, 'Mabel, please telephone for two taxis.'

'Two, Miss Griffin?'

'One for yourself and your belongings to take you to the Pimleys' to start your new job. If they are not prepared to accept you tonight, you are to come straight to the hotel where I will find you accommodation. The other taxi is to take me and my luggage to the Connaught.' And she added with conviction, 'I have a business I need to start learning to run.'

CHAPTER SIXTEEN

Amelia Harbin almost fell off her chair in shock when she saw Miss Edelina Griffin come through the revolving doors and into the foyer. She jumped to attention, planting a smile on her sharp-featured face, ready to receive their prestigious visitor.

Eddie had been through enough ordeals recently without, she felt, voluntarily subjecting herself to another one. Ignoring Amelia and the approaching concierge, she made straight for Connie, sitting beavering away transferring room service charges to guests' bills.

Immediately sensing a presence on the other side of the counter, the girl looked up. 'Oh, Miss Griffin,' she said in genuine delight, standing up respectfully. 'We weren't expecting you 'til tomorrow but you're here now and it's nice to see you again.'

Miss Harbin butted in and rudely stood directly in front of Connie. 'Good afternoon, Miss Griffin,' she said subserviently, with a slight bow of her head. 'What an honour your visit is to us. How may I be of service?'

Her blatant slighting of her assistant was not lost on Eddie. This woman, she realised, was a thoroughly unpleasant person. 'Good afternoon, Miss Harbin,' she said briskly. 'I would like a word with Miss Monroe, if you don't mind. I wouldn't wish to hinder you from seeing to our guests' requirements,' she added, indicating with her eyes a large gentleman waiting for attention at the other end of the counter, drumming his fat fingers on the top in his impatience to be seen to.

Amelia flashed a look at the man in question and, fighting to hide her own indignation, said evenly to Connie, 'I will be on hand should Miss Griffin require anything that is beyond your capabilities.' She turned back to face Eddie and bowed her head slightly before she stalked off to deal with the guest.

Connie knew she would pay for this incident but regardless she was delighted Eddie had sought her help.

'What can I do for you, Miss Griffin?'

'Could you summon Captain Fosedyke for me, please?'

'Oh, but the Captain's still in hospital as far as I know, Miss Griffin, and no news yet as to when he's coming back to work.'

Eddie's heart sank. This was the last thing she had wanted to hear. She had been banking on the hotel manager being by her side to guide her through the maze of what she needed to learn to justify her status as owner of this hotel. In his absence it would have to be the assistant manager who helped her acquire it and Eddie just hoped he would be as understanding as she had hoped an older and wiser manager would be.

Connie could see the news she had given her had greatly disturbed Miss Griffin. Despite her outward appearance of being calm, in control, Miss Griffin actually wasn't. Connie could see the apprehension, almost fear, in her eyes, and it shocked her to realise Miss Griffin was finding this situation truly daunting. All her instincts told her that this woman needed sympathy and understanding. That was why she had sought out a friendly face and not allowed the formidable senior receptionist to attend to her needs. 'Miss Griffin, is there anything I can do for you?' Connie offered kindly.

Eddie looked into her eyes and instantly realised this young woman knew exactly how she was feeling, was in her way reaching out to her and offering womanly understanding and support. Exactly what Eddie needed at this moment. She smiled at her, deeply gratified. 'I should appreciate your help very much, thank you ... Connie. It is Connie, isn't it? First, could you arrange for someone to collect my luggage from the taxi outside?'

'Of course, Miss Griffin.' Connie scanned her eyes over the people scattered around the foyer and spotted her quarry emerging from the lift. 'Danny,' she called over.

The young lad came hurrying to her. 'Yes, Miss Monroe?'

'Danny, I'd like you to meet Miss Griffin ...'

Before she could finish he spun round to face Eddie, grasped her hand in both of his and vigorously shook it. 'Oh, you're the owner? Pleased ter meet yer, Miss Griffin, very pleased indeed. Yer going to spruce up this place, so I've heard?'

'Danny,' lightly scolded Connie, 'give Miss Griffin her hand back. And could you go and fetch her luggage from the taxi waiting outside?'

'Yeah, 'course I can.' He beamed, tipping his fore-lock. 'Where d'yer wannum?'

'Just bring everything in for now, please, Danny,' instructed Connie, and laughed aloud as he shot off towards the revolving door. 'He's a good lad is Danny, Miss Griffin. Very obliging, nothing's too much trouble. The guests love him.'

'Yes, he seems a likeable young man,' Eddie agreed. She then took a deep breath before saying, 'Miss Monroe, you will no doubt have deduced that my plans have been brought forward. I will be moving into the hotel this afternoon. I won't after all be bringing my own furniture with me and I do apologise for any inconvenience this may have caused but I will need the furniture putting back in the rooms I picked out, with the exception of that monstrosity of a wardrobe. Maybe the hotel has something a little more pleasing to the eye that it can be exchanged with? You did pass on my requests to the assistant manager?'

'Yes, I did, Miss Griffin.' She did not feel it right to mention that Mr Sopworth had not responded with any degree of enthusiasm to organising the removal of the furniture from the two rooms Miss Griffin had picked out for herself or overseeing the arrangement of the furniture she had been going to bring with her. Neither had he looked particularly thrilled at the prospect of the owner of the hotel being permanently on the premises; in fact, had acted more like it would be a great inconvenience to him personally. Whether he had in fact actually remembered to fulfil Miss Griffin's instructions was questionable as normally requests had to be made two or sometimes three times before he actually got around to acting on them.

Just then Connie saw the man in question coming out of the lift, carrying a vacuum cleaner, and immediately heading off in the direction of the staff door to the back of the hotel. She wondered what he was doing with a vacuum.

'Mr Sopworth,' she called to him.

He stopped and glanced across at her. 'What?' he snapped.

Eddie's eyebrows rose at his aggressive manner. She hoped this was not the under manager's normal attitude as it was most unbefitting to a man in his position. In his defence she supposed he must be very busy as he was covering for the manager at the moment.

'Do you think you could spare a moment, please, Mr Sopworth?' Connie asked him.

He looked most put out at being interrupted in what he was doing. After slipping the vacuum inside the staff door and shutting it, he came across to them.

'What is it you want?' he said belligerently to Connie. 'You can see I'm busy.'

'I'd like to introduce you to Miss Griffin, our proprietor,' she said.

The shock he received was almost comical. He immediately spun round to face Eddie, standing to attention. It was then, with a feeling of horror, that he suddenly remembered the request to ready the rooms for Miss Griffin's arrival. Connie had told him days ago and he'd completely forgotten.

Smiling politely, Eddie held out her hand in greeting to him. 'Pleased to meet you, Mr Sopworth.'

He took her hand and shook it. Such a limp handshake from a clammy hand told her a lot about this man, and despite herself she took an instant dislike to him. Regardless, she fought hard not to show her feelings. 'I appreciate this will be an inconvenience to you, Mr Sopworth, as you will naturally be a very busy man while you're covering for Captain Fosedyke. Let's hope he's back with us soon, but my own plans have changed. I will now need to have my rooms furnished as they were.' She proceeded to inform him of her new requirements and finished with, 'I trust you can see to all this for me?'

It was all a very great inconvenience to him as, taking full advantage of the fact he hadn't got his boss checking on his every movement, Sopworth had planned to sneak off early tonight for a date with a girl he'd met in a café up the road. 'Yes, of course, madam,' he said in a dull voice.

'Mr Sopworth, with due respect,' Connie spoke up, 'may I suggest that there's a really comfy sofa on the second-floor landing that's not really used by the guests. Miss Griffin might like it in her sitting room, and I'm sure a couple of the armchairs and a table from the writing room won't be missed.'

He was glad of her suggestion as he hadn't a clue where he was going to commandeer the items Eddie had requested. 'I was just going to suggest those myself,' he lied. 'I'll get on to it now, Miss Griffin.' He made a hurried escape before anything else was landed on him.

As Connie made to address Eddie again to ask her if there was anything else she could do for her, she did notice that instead of heading for the lift to attend to Miss Griffin's requirements, Mr Sopworth had disappeared through the staff door.

Danny struggled up then, pushing a heavy trunk on a sack barrow. Connie instructed him which room to take that to along with whatever else had been offloaded from the taxi. She said to Eddie, 'Would you like me to request a chambermaid to unpack for you, Miss Griffin?'

Eddie smiled gratefully at her. This young receptionist was proving very efficient but also had an approachable warmth to her. She felt she had made a good choice in accepting Connie's assistance to get herself settled into her new home. 'Thank you. When you have arranged that, maybe you would accompany me on a proper tour of the hotel to greet the staff?' She read the expression on Connie's face and added, 'I will inform Miss Harbin that I have requested your company.'

'Then I'd be delighted to, Miss Griffin.'

Early that evening, Eddie stared pensively into space. Her sitting room had been set out quite pleasingly, as had her bedroom – her belongings all unpacked and arranged neatly. She suspected that Connie had had a hand in that as she had excused herself for a good twenty minutes during their walk around the hotel, leaving Eddie in the competent hands of the head waiter who somewhat nervously introduced her to the twenty or so staff working under his charge as he showed her around the restaurant and bar area.

Regardless of the way her rooms had been arranged, though, they did not feel like home to Eddie, despite the added touch of the vase of fresh flowers that Eddie felt sure she had seen previously on a table in the foyer when she had first arrived – obviously another thoughtful touch by Connie. It might have gone some way to making her feel more at home if she'd had some pieces of her own furniture, a few ornaments and bits of bric-a-brac gracing the mantel and a couple of occasional tables to either side of the sofa. But as matters stood, unless the police uncovered the identity of the thieves, someone else would be getting the benefit of her house contents in the future.

Eddie gave a thoughtful sigh. She had become increasingly aware as she had been introduced to the staff on her tour of how cautiously, even fearfully, they had reacted as soon as they heard who she was. Mabel and Jess had never acted this way with her, but then they had known her from childhood and hence always been comfortable in her presence, whereas the staff at this hotel did not know her at all. She was a stranger to them. She must somehow find a way to allay those feelings, let them see that she was not the enemy, or she herself would never feel comfortable amongst them.

The most glaring thing that had struck her, though, as Connie had taken her around, was that the hotel was in a far worse condition than she had first realised on her visit with Phee. If Eddie herself was paying for a stay here she would most certainly not be impressed by formerly white paintwork dulled to a creamy yellow; or William Morris flower- or bird-patterned wallpaper in rooms and corridors, expensive when first hung and stylish then but now outmoded and showing signs of wear, just like the furniture. The staff dressed like characters from a 1920s farce. The expensive plushness her

mother had created forty years before had faded to a
dreadful old-fashioned tiredness.

Eddie could appreciate why the majority of the clientele appeared to come from the older generation. Their
reduced income would not stretch to the higher prices
charged for a more upmarket hotel to stay in or meet
in for a meal. She might be ignorant of business matters but she wasn't so ignorant as not to realise that if
the hotel were to survive for much longer, and more
importantly attract a more affluent clientele, modernisation of some form or other had to take place. If not,
the future of Eddie, her father and the eighty or so
members of staff was in jeopardy.

After silently cursing the mindless culprits who had
stolen her means of paying for at least some of the renovations, she sat and pondered the problem of how she
could now raise the money for the work to be done.
Even doing the whole hotel up one room at a time was
better than letting the place fall into further decline and
the inevitable fading away of the guests as they found
pleasanter surroundings in which to stay.

A wave of hopelessness washed over her and a vision
of her father tormented her. His pathetic figure on the
metal-framed bed in that austere room swam before
her. Oh, Father, her mind screamed, I am trying to give
you a reason to make yourself well, really I am trying.

Thinking of her father and mother, she was reminded
of the jewellery box she had found in her father's safe
and set aside to examine properly when she was on her
own. The contents of the safe she had bundled together
and placed safely in her vanity case ready for the move
while Mabel had been packing up the contents of her

father's study for what they had thought was the impending auction. Eddie cast her eyes around now in search of the vanity case and, not seeing it, realised the chambermaid would have automatically put such an item in her bedroom.

Eddie found it strange to be leaving this room and stepping several yards down a corridor to go next door to enter her bedroom instead of going up some stairs, mindful as well that the rest of the rooms in the corridor were for guests and each time she was there she could be bumping into one of them. Her new living arrangements were going to take some getting used to.

She found the vanity case on top of the dressing table, along with her neatly arranged silver-backed brush and comb set and an array of perfume bottles and face creams. Sitting on her bed, she opened the case. Lifting out the bulky brown envelope containing the deeds to the hotel, she pulled out the black velvet-covered box that lay underneath.

She took a deep breath before slowly opening it up. Inside, carefully placed in plush compartments, were a plain gold band – her mother's wedding ring – and a solitaire diamond ring which must be her engagement ring. To Eddie's expert eye it was not an expensive stone. She knew her father would not have been able to afford a grander one from his plumber's wages. Another plain band she assumed had been her grandmother's; another engagement-type ring had a ruby surrounded by opals, again presumably her grandmother's. There were also several pairs of very pretty earrings and a couple of necklaces. Her mother had obviously not been the sort of woman who had spent lavishly on adornments for herself, nor it seemed had her own mother. The items inside this box, though, were all Eddie had of her mother and grandmother and she would forever treasure them, never, ever selling them even should she find herself, as she almost did now, without a penny to her name.

Then like a bolt from the blue it struck her. How silly of her not to have remembered that the reason she had chosen to keep this hotel was because it was bringing in an income, albeit the profits of which Stibley had been siphoning off until recently. She needed to find out how much the hotel was actually making. That was what she would use to fund its renovations. In reality it would pay for its own regeneration. She would request an interview with the accounts office manager to whom she had been briefly introduced today who had presented himself to Eddie as a quiet, polite man who took his job seriously and was very competent at it. It seemed, however, that his clerk was leaving to get married and a replacement was being sought. Mr Vickers, though, would be the one to know exactly how the finances of the hotel stood.

Emotionally and physically drained after her eventful day, Eddie hadn't any reserves of energy left with which to telephone down for a meal to be sent up or even to eat it. A hot bath and a very early night was all she felt was called for. Tomorrow was going to bring new obstacles for her to face and she needed to be fresh and alert to deal with them.

As Eddie was preparing for her extremely early night, Connie was just finishing her shift on reception. Since her return to her place behind the desk after taking Miss Griffin on her guided tour earlier that afternoon, Miss Harbin had not spoken one word to her or acknowledged her, except periodically to flash her an icy glare. Pamela Wardle, having put the switchboard on night service, had moments before left to catch her bus home. Harry Glebe had not yet shown his face but there were still a couple of minutes to go before his shift started and Harry was never one for starting until exactly the second he was being paid for his time.

Connie had just tidied her working area when she felt a presence at her side and turned her head to see Amelia Harbin staring at her, a cynical scowl on her face.

'You must think I'm a fool not to have seen the way you blatantly ingratiated yourself with Miss Griffin. But be advised, Monroe, she will know the truth about your incompetence as soon as I have an opportunity to inform her.'

Connie had every right to be outraged by this woman's vendetta against her which was all down to her own misguided belief that Connie, and seemingly every other woman younger than Miss Harbin herself, was after her job. Instead Connie felt great pity for a woman who seemed to have allowed herself to be consumed by her job. Connie could beg and plead to be given a fair chance but knew she would be wasting her time. Besides, whatever lies Miss Harbin told to convince either Miss Griffin or Captain Fosedyke of her unsuitability for the position, they would have to believe her as she was the senior employee. Connie was also well aware that Miss Harbin craved the satisfaction of hearing Connie plead with her to keep her job. Connie wasn't going to give it to her.

Smiling politely, she said evenly, 'As you wish, Miss Harbin. I've finished up all my work and tidied my area so I'll wish you good night.'

She picked up her handbag from under the counter, turned and left Miss Harbin glaring furiously at her for not reacting to her tirade as she had desired.

As she made her way upstairs to change out of her working clothes and into a red knee-length straight skirt, white short-sleeved blouse with pretty embroidery on its Peter Pan collar and a pale pink cardigan, before going back down into the staff room for her evening meal, Connie reflected on her future plans. It upset her to think that Captain Fosedyke would believe he'd made a mistake in giving her a chance to prove herself, something Connie felt positive she would have done given a decent boss to work under and the proper training. One thing she had decided, though, and that was that when she received her notice to return to her chambermaiding duties she would leave the hotel and try her luck at another one, hopefully landing a job on reception with a superior who would treat her more favourably.

Thinking of Captain Fosedyke made her wonder how he was progressing. She sincerely hoped he was well on the mend. As she unlocked the door to let herself into her room, a comment Harry Glebe had made that morning came back to mind. The Captain had no family. Did that mean he would have received no visitors during his hospitalisation? Before he'd been taken ill, the Captain had showed her a side of his character that was perceptive and kindly and she felt she owed him a debt of gratitude for that. She did not like the thought of his lying ill in hospital with no familiar faces visiting to enquire after his welfare. Everyone needed to know someone cared about them.

Then a thought struck her. Had a representative from the hotel, Mr Sopworth perhaps as his second-in-command, been to see him and check on his progress, expressing good wishes for his recovery from the other members of staff? She suspected that doing so had not crossed the mind of a man like Sopworth. What *had* he been up to with that vacuum cleaner as well? She couldn't think why he'd be taking one through to the staff toilets and cloakroom because that's all that was down that particular corridor until you arrived at the door that led outside. Connie supposed he'd had his reasons. She gnawed her bottom lip as her thoughts then returned to the plight of Captain Fosedyke. Someone from the hotel should go and see him. Then it struck her, why not herself? It wouldn't be seen as presumptuous of her if she paid a visit to the hotel manager in such circumstances, would it? Too bad if it was. To aid his recovery she felt it was important that Captain Fosedyke be made aware that people he worked with were concerned for him. Whether the rest of the staff were truly bothered about him or not was debatable. She herself was.

Connie looked at the tin clock ticking on the floor beside her bed. It would mean missing her evening meal but if she hurried she could just about make the hospital for the last half of visiting time.

Reginald Fosedyke looked down the ward at seven o'clock to see the outer door open and a herd of people swarm in armed with brown bags of fruit, bottles of cordial, books and magazines.

The old chap in the bed to one side of him struggled to ease himself up against his pillows and gave a wheezing cough. 'Oh, 'ere we go,' he cackled. 'An hour of listening to 'er moaning on about n'ote in particular. I keep telling 'er I came in 'ere for a bloody rest, but will she leave me alone? Will she hell as like! You're a lucky beggar, you, Reg, having no ball and chain chewing yer ear off night and day. Oh, 'ello, dear, brought me some biscuits, have yer?' he eagerly asked the shabby old lady who shuffled up to ease herself down on the chair to one side of her husband's bed.

'Biscuits? Don't you mention biscuits to me . . .'

Reginald listened to his neighbour's wife moan on about the price of a packet of Crawford's custard creams. She'd been to the shop that morning apparently especially to buy some to bring in this evening, only for their glutton of a son to come round on his way home from work and scoff the lot before he went off to his own house to devour the dinner his wife had cooked him.

Reginald sighed deeply. Lucky not to be married, eh? It was his neighbour who didn't know how lucky he was, having someone who cared for him when Reginald had no one. He would have liked nothing more than to have met a lovely woman to settle down and have a family with, but his chosen profession after coming back unscathed from fighting for his country in the Great War, earning his commission and a medal for gallantry for his efforts, had meant working long, unsociable hours and he'd never met a woman who'd put up with his work regime long enough to allow him to propose to her. He couldn't say that the Connaught had been exactly busy over the last twenty years, but by then the time had long passed for him to settle down and have a family.

Reaching over to his locker, he picked up a book. Settling back against his pillows, he opened it and had barely read the title page when he heard a soft voice say, 'Captain Fosedyke?'

He looked up to see a very apprehensive young woman looking back at him. As he stared at her in utter astonishment recognition struck. 'Miss Monroe!' he exclaimed.

There was a long uncomfortable silence before, taking a deep breath, Connie flashed him a nervous smile and blurted, 'I thought I'd come and see how you are, Captain Fosedyke. Well, all the staff are worried about you and send their best wishes.' A worried expression clouded her face. 'I . . . well . . . I haven't brought you anything. I didn't know what you were allowed, you see. I . . . well . . . I haven't done wrong in coming to see you, have I, Captain Fosedyke?'

He cleared his throat. 'Er . . . no . . . no, not at all, Miss Monroe. It's just such a surprise for me to see you. I wasn't expecting anyone. Please, do sit down. It's . . . er . . . very good to see you, really it is. Most thoughtful of you to give up your time and come.'

Unbuttoning her coat, she perched on the chair at the side of his bed, clutching her handbag on her knees. 'I didn't know whether Mr Sopworth had been to see you, Captain Fosedyke?'

'No, he hasn't. I wish he would, though. I'd like to thank him personally for what he did.'

Connie looked at him questioningly. 'What he did, Captain Fosedyke?'

He looked at her, surprised. 'In taking charge of getting me to hospital. It was a suspected heart attack, you know, and if it had truly turned out to be that, Mr Sopworth would have been responsible for saving my life. Didn't he tell you all what a hero he was? I have to say, it was a surprise to me to discover he did have something about him after all. I hadn't thought him to be so quick thinking, you see. Yes, really quite a shock to me, it was. Until then I hadn't been much impressed with Sopworth's performance as assistant manager and was thinking very seriously about finishing him. It's my opinion now that maybe I judged him too quickly and had not given him enough time to prove himself properly. The hospital staff told me he'd explained to them how he found me collapsed in my office and suspected I'd had a seizure. He called the ambulance and insisted on accompanying me to help with any details he could give. Unfortunately I didn't really regain my faculties properly until well after he'd left.'

That wasn't quite how Connie remembered the incident but regardless she said soberly, 'Yes, Mr Sopworth is quite the hero, isn't he? How are you feeling now, Captain Fosedyke?'

'It's very kind of you to enquire. I feel absolutely fine. The medical profession are convinced it was a sudden rise in my blood pressure that caused my collapse.'

'So you'll be back to work soon, Captain Fosedyke?'

'Back to work?' He looked at her strangely, then his eyes narrowed darkly and he gave an ironic laugh. 'No, I won't be back to work at all,' he said gruffly. 'I would have thought that would be common knowledge among the staff by now, knowing how quickly gossip travels around a hotel.'

Connie looked at him non-plussed. 'I'm sorry, what would be common knowledge, Captain Fosedyke?'

'That I've been finished.'

She gazed at him in shock. 'Finished? You mean, you've been sacked, Captain Fosedyke?'

He looked deeply pained. 'Yes, that's about the size of it. I wasn't even given proper notice. Not even told in person. Done by letter it was.'

Connie was looking at him, bewildered. Something wasn't right here. If Miss Griffin had sacked Captain Fosedyke, then why had she asked for him today when she had come to the hotel and seemed genuinely concerned to learn that he was still in hospital. Why say she hoped he'd be back at work soon? Then Connie remembered the letter she had found on the floor by the side of the Captain's desk after finding him collapsed. The same letter that had been delivered by hand and which she had taken in to him a short while before. That letter must have caused his collapse. Miss Griffin had not come across to Connie as the kind of person who would so peremptorily sack an employee who had proved invaluable for so many years. This situation was all very confusing. Something wasn't right.

Reginald Fosedyke was looking at her, embarrassed.

'I profusely apologise, Miss Monroe, it was most improper of me to have spoken to you about all this as I have.'

She looked at him understandingly. 'Oh, that's all right, Captain Fosedyke. You're upset about the way you're been treated.'

'Have ... er ... they got another manager to replace me yet? I expect they have. Obviously had someone in mind, that's why I was dispensed with.'

'No, not another manager, Captain Fosedyke. Miss Griffin herself is taking charge, so I understand. She's actually moved into the hotel. Today, in fact.'

He looked stunned. 'Miss Griffin? Miss Griffin herself? And she's moved in you say?' His face screwed up thoughtfully as he said to himself, 'Oh, I thought she would have had more need of me ... All that worry for all those years trying to keep my promise and now I get shoved aside without a thought.' He seemed to shake himself. 'The hotel is none of my business now, is it?' He looked at Connie enquiringly. 'I would like to ask how you're getting on in your new position, though, my dear?'

Connie could not bring herself to tell him what constant purgatory she was suffering through Miss Harbin's feud against her. Apart from the fact that it would mean her speaking critically of Miss Harbin, which would make Connie herself look bad in complaining about a superior, if the Captain wasn't manager of the Connaught any more then there was nothing he could do about the situation anyway. 'I really enjoy my job,' she said with deep enthusiasm.

He smiled. 'I'm glad. I knew I was right in requesting

that Miss Harbin give you a trial. You will go far, I am
sure, Miss Monroe.'

'Well, I just hope I can prove your faith in me justified, Captain Fosedyke. I really am grateful you gave
me the chance.' She felt it best to change the subject
just in case he should ask how she was actually getting on with Miss Harbin on a personal level. 'So . . .
er . . . when do you expect to come out of hospital?'

'Tomorrow, all being well.'

His grim expression did not escape Connie. 'You
don't look pleased to be going home, Captain
Fosedyke.'

'Oh, I'm pleased to be leaving this place. Be good
to get back in my own bed as hospitals don't exactly
offer all the comforts of a hotel. It's just that when
Matron found out I would be returning to an empty
house, she insisted they engage a woman to look after
me for at least two weeks, just to make sure I don't
have any recurrence of my symptoms. They wouldn't
agree to discharge me until I agreed to their terms. I
can't say as I was overly impressed by Miss Byford,
the woman they found when she came to introduce
herself to me and collect my keys so she could settle
herself in and have the house ready for my return. I
have a feeling it's going to prove a long two weeks.'

He gave a thoughtful sigh. 'For years I've had a
charlady go into the house to clean the place three
mornings a week but she retired herself a couple of
weeks ago and I was in the process of finding a replacement for her. My needs have changed now I've been
forced to retire myself. I had always intended to employ
a housekeeper when I retired as I'm not much good

around the house, not much of a cook either, but I thought I'd have plenty of warning to seek out a lady I could get on with and she with me, considering my home her home, be more a sort of companion to me than a servant. That's what I was hoping for, but life has a habit of not turning out as you expect it to.

'I know from my experience of seeking suitable staff for the hotel that finding the right person can take time, especially these days when not so many women are looking for housekeeping jobs like they used to. Factories, shops and suchlike employ far more women now. Still, hopefully there is someone out there who wants what I am offering. I can but hope.'

It shocked Connie to realise this man was lonely. For whatever reason he had never married – maybe the demands of his job had never given him time to find a woman to share his life with, one who would put up with the unsocial hours he worked. How sad to have to look to a housekeeper to fill the void in his life.

'I'm sure you'll find someone who suits you once you start looking,' said Connie reassuringly. She noticed the book he was holding. 'Oh, what are you reading?' she asked.

'It's a gardening companion. I've always fancied myself as a gardener but never had the time to do it really, working the hours I do . . . did. My garden is rather overgrown. My father would be quite upset if he could see the state it's in. He was a keen gardener himself. Now I'm retired and have plenty of time on my hands, maybe I can get it back to how it was when he died and left it to me. He won prizes for his sweet peas did my father.' Reginald gave a wry smile. 'I suppose at seventy I'm a bit old to be starting a new career, though.'

Connie looked at him in surprise. She hadn't realised he was that age. 'You're never too old, my mam always says, Captain Fosedyke.'

'Well, let's hope your mother is right.' He looked at her appraisingly. 'I've really enjoyed your visit, Miss Monroe. You're a very kind young lady. Not many people of your age would have taken the trouble to visit an old man in hospital.' And he added, a twinkle of amusement sparkling in his tired eyes, 'Especially their ex-boss who I know had a reputation amongst most of the staff of being . . . well, rather a tyrant as far as they were concerned. In my defence, I should say a manager has to command respect from his staff or else a breeding ground for contempt can arise.'

'Oh, I never heard that said about you,' Connie insisted, although she had of course heard all the gripes and groans from the other staff whenever the Captain had felt it necessary to upbraid them, and she'd heard the array of derogatory nicknames they had for him, but 'tyrant' had never been one of them. She noticed he looked pale and more tired than when she had first arrived. Probably her news about Miss Griffin had upset him. Connie smiled cheerily at him. 'I'd best take my leave, Captain Fosedyke, before the nurses accuse me of overstaying my welcome.'

'Oh, they'll do that all right, if they think they have cause. Again, thank you for coming to see me, Miss Monroe.'

As she walked down the ward, Connie felt a degree of sadness for the man she had just left behind in his hospital bed. Unlike Miss Harbin, who was a down-right nasty person obsessed with guarding her own position at the Connaught, regardless of the suffering she caused to her subordinates, Captain Fosedyke's brusqueness towards staff was simply a way of demon-strating his authority so as to ensure they worked to the standard expected of them. Connie felt positive that underneath his outwardly formidable exterior, the Captain was a fair-minded, kindly but also lonely man. She strongly suspected it was going to take him quite a while to adjust to his new life of retirement after the busy and demanding one he had led as manager of the Connaught. She did wish him well, though, and hoped he find a housekeeper who proved more of a com-panion to him and would look after him as conscien-tiously as he'd tended the smooth running of the Connaught Hotel.

CHAPTER SEVENTEEN

The poor woman looked deeply distressed about something and Connie could not help but change her direction to go over and ask what the problem was.

'What on earth is the matter with you, Freda? You look like you've just had your only pair of knickers shredded in the mangle and no money to buy any more.'

The other woman was so consumed by whatever was troubling her that Connie's joking comment passed her by. 'Ah, Connie, you ain't seen it, have yer?' she pleaded. 'I've looked everywhere. Bloody mystery it is.'

Connie looked puzzled. 'Seen what, Freda?'

'Me vacuum. I put it away along with me box of cleaning stuff in the cleaners' cupboard under the service stairs yesterday morning as I finished me shift, and it ain't there now. In fact, it's nowhere. I've hunted high and low. It were a new 'un an' all, Connie, to replace the one that conked out on me a couple of weeks ago. Where the blazes can it have gone to?'

Connie looked at her thoughtfully. Why did a vacuum cleaner ring a bell with her? She had seen someone with one recently . . . Just then the staff room door opened and Mr Sopworth came out. 'Oh!' she exclaimed as memory returned, and without further ado called over to him: 'Mr Sopworth?'

He stopped, tutted in annoyance and reluctantly came over. 'What now, Monroe?'

Faced with him she was reminded of his blatant lie to make himself look good over the handling of the Captain's collapse; not that she wanted praise for the fact that it was she herself who was responsible for saving his life, but she was angered that this man, who in truth had failed to show any degree of gumption during the whole incident, should take the honours through downright lies. 'Was it Mrs Frake's vacuum you had yesterday, Mr Sopworth?' Connie asked him coolly.

He looked at her as though she was stupid. 'I never had any vacuum cleaner yesterday.'

'Oh, but you did, Mr Sopworth. I saw you coming out of the lift with one when I called you over to introduce you to Miss Griffin. You put it inside the staff door before you came across.'

He narrowed his eyes at her and snapped, 'You're mistaken, Miss Monroe. It was not me you saw with a vacuum yesterday. Why would I be carting around a vacuum? I'm not a member of the cleaning staff. Now please excuse me, I'm busy,' he said, striding off towards the manager's office.

She most definitely *had* seen him with a vacuum. Why had he lied to her? Connie shrugged helplessly at Freda. 'Sorry, I can't help you. I'm sure you'll find it if you keep looking.'

'I hope I bloody do, and quick, I'm already late starting in the guests' lounge. See yer, Connie,' she said, shooting off to continue her search.

'Am I to expect any work out of you today, Monroe?' an agitated voice shrilled.

Connie spun round to see Miss Harbin glaring across at her from behind the reception counter. Oh, God, she thought, here we go. 'I'm just coming, Miss Harbin.'

Mid-morning found Eddie with an expression of defeat on her face.

Cyril Vickers had just left, taking his books with him. She had done her best to understand his accounting jargon during the detailed explanations of the incomings and outgoings and overall profit margins of the Connaught. When he had finally got round to giving her the overall profit figure, the information was not what Eddie had been hoping to hear. Some months, it seemed, were better than others but on the whole the hotel's profits had dwindled over the last dozen or so years to the point now where they were just about breaking even.

On hearing this information, Eddie's heart had plummeted. Her idea of using the profits to fund renovations vanished like a magician's rabbit in a puff of smoke. She rubbed her hands despondently over her face. To increase profits and provide herself and her father with a living she needed constantly to fill all the rooms every night. At the moment it seemed the hotel was only half-full at any time. Every table in the restaurant needed diners eating at it each lunchtime and evening, not just the thirty or so it was catering for at a sitting now.

If she hadn't the means to make the interior of the hotel attractive enough to entice the numbers of new customers they desperately needed, how else could she persuade them to come and spend their money here and not elsewhere?

If only the hotel manager were recovered enough from his illness to return to work. With his wealth of experience in the hotel trade, he would surely know of other ways to lure in new business. In his absence she wondered if the assistant manager, Mr Sopworth, would be able to come up with some ideas. She'd barely had more than a brief chat with him on first coming into the office that morning as he'd quickly excused himself to do his rounds, checking all the staff were present and correct and getting on with their work. She hadn't seen him since and knew he wasn't in his small office next door because she'd checked several times. Well, at least he'd seemed eager to get on with things. Eddie was gratified at this show of commitment to his job.

Her head was beginning to pound and she reached down for her handbag at the side of the desk, delving inside for the bottle of Aspro she usually carried with her for the rare occasions she was troubled by a headache. No small brown bottle uncovered itself and she realised with annoyance that she must have run out and not got around to replacing her supply. But it wasn't surprising in view of all she had had to contend with just recently. She knew that the accounts manager's disappointing news was not all that was contributing to her headache. Before her interview with him, she had made her usual telephone call to the hospital to enquire after her father, and as usual had built her hopes up to hear good news about his progress, and once again had them quashed on being informed there was still no change to report to her. Maybe someone would go out and fetch her some

Aspro, though on second thoughts it was possible the reception staff kept a supply in for guests.

As she approached the counter she was gratified to witness Miss Harbin fully occupied in booking in a rather grand-looking elderly woman draped in a fox fur coat and matching hat, her old but good-quality leather luggage stacked nearby, and Connie just about to deal with a loudly dressed middle-aged man who'd just come in.

She saw Connie smile politely at the man as he arrived, placing his well-used suitcase on the floor by his feet.

'Good morning, sir. Welcome to the Connaught Hotel. How may I help you?' Eddie heard her greet him.

'How much for a room, young lady?' he asked. Connie passed him a tariff list which he scanned. 'Bit pricey, aren't you?' he grumbled, taking a glance around the foyer. 'After all, it isn't exactly the Ritz, is it? Still, I haven't got time to seek out another hotel so this one will have to do. What about a discount if I book in for four nights? I've got a bit of business in Leicester and if it comes off, which I fully expect it to do, I could be here for a week at a time every couple of months.'

'I could make enquires for you, sir, if you'd just give me a moment?'

Eddie then noticed that Miss Harbin had excused herself from the woman she was dealing with and was now at Connie's side.

'We have no rooms available,' Eddie heard her say brusquely to the man.

He looked at her, taken aback. 'What, none at all?'

'None at all. The Belgrave Hotel takes in travelling salesmen, I believe. I'm sure someone will give you directions if you make your way down to the clock tower, it's not too far from there. Good day.'

Eddie couldn't believe her ears. Miss Harbin was telling this potential paying customer that the hotel was full when she herself had just been informed by Mr Vickers that it had more vacant rooms than occupied ones. Either Mr Vickers had his facts wrong or this woman had lost her mind.

Without further ado she hurried across to the man who was by now preparing to leave and placed himself in front of him, smiling at him apologetically. 'Excuse me, I believe there's been a mistake and we shall be able to accommodate you after all.'

He looked at her warily. 'And who are you?' he demanded.

'I'm the owner of the Connaught.' She held out her hand to him. 'Miss Edelina Griffin.'

He accepted her hand and shook it. 'Ron Stark. Well, your receptionist just told me you're full so how can you suddenly accommodate me?' He gave Miss Harbin a look of disdain. 'Eh, and for your information, I'm not a travelling salesman – not that I've anything against them. I used to be one and made a decent living at it too. It gave me the chance to go into business for myself which I'm now doing very nicely from.' Then he addressed Eddie. 'Now, either you're full or you're not. What's going on?'

She flashed a look at Miss Harbin then back at the guest. 'I intend to find out.'

'Excuse me, but have I been forgotten about?' the woman Amelia Harbin had abandoned boomed across.

'Please see to the guest, Miss Harbin,' Eddie instructed

her. 'After you have dealt with her, I'd like to see you in my office, and please bring the reservations book with you.' Then she addressed Connie. 'Miss Monroe, would you please see to Mr Stark's requirements?'

'And what about my discount if I stay for four nights?' he demanded.

'I'm sure we can come to an amicable arrangement. I wish you a pleasant stay at the Connaught, Mr Stark.'

Fifteen minutes later Eddie closed the reservations book and handed it back to Amelia Harbin. 'Miss Harbin, over half our rooms are vacant for tonight so just what was your reason for turning Mr Stark's business away?'

She gave a haughty sniff. 'I would have thought my reason was very obvious, Miss Griffin.'

'Not to me, Miss Harbin, maybe you'd care to explain?'

'The Connaught has a reputation to uphold. That type of man is hardly the sort to encourage.'

Eddie looked at her, stunned. 'We are in the business of providing accommodation to anyone who requests it, not turning guests away at a whim of yours. This hotel will cease to function if such practices continue. I appreciate you were probably only doing as you'd been instructed by the hotel manager. I cannot understand why he would give such an instruction, however, I will certainly find out why when he returns. My own ruling is that in future no potential guest is to be treated in the insulting manner Mr Stark was just treated. Is that understood, Miss Harbin?'

Tight-lipped, she said, 'Perfectly, Miss Griffin.'

'Good. By way of an apology to him, give Mr Stark

tonight's stay free of charge and let's hope that is sufficient incentive to encourage him to stay here again. Now something Mr Stark said is bothering me . . .' Eddie felt a certain embarrassment that it had taken a guest to show her one of the ways in which the hotel was not achieving its potential. 'Mr Stark said that in his opinion our room rates are steep. I do appreciate that this hotel's appearance is not of the standard it once was and that being the case we cannot expect to charge top prices for our accommodation. Maybe that's why we're not attracting the amount of business we could be.'

'Just what are you suggesting, Miss Griffin?'

'That we lower our tariffs in keeping with the present standard of the accommodation until such time as improvements are made to justify higher prices.'

Amelia Harbin's eyes bulged. 'I would strongly advise against doing that, Miss Griffin. Our regulars won't like it, won't like it at all, having to mix with the inferior sorts that a cut in room rates will encourage. Our regulars frequent the Connaught because they know we attract a certain calibre of guests, feel comfortable with their own sort. I strongly advise you not to go ahead with any such reduction.'

She inwardly shuddered at the thought of having to deal with the lowly types she felt sure would stream through the doors should Miss Griffin go ahead. Those people didn't know how to conduct themselves in a hotel such as the Connaught. As a result its reputation would suffer, along with her own status as head receptionist. She'd be perceived by others as no better than if she worked in a cheap boarding house. That thought didn't sit well with her at all, indeed it did not.

Eddie looked at her in concern. Miss Harbin had a point. It wouldn't do to alienate the guests the hotel already served and risk losing their patronage. But then Eddie felt she was right to be suggesting a cut in room rates. Something Phee had said to her rang in her ears again. She had told Eddie to remember she was the owner of this hotel and should act like it. Yes, she was the owner and she should be instructing her staff as to how the hotel was run, not the senior receptionist. If her decision was wrong, it was she who would suffer the consequences, not this member of staff. Eddie looked the other woman in the eye. 'Miss Harbin, I appreciate your concern for our regular guests but there are not enough of them staying here at any given time to keep this hotel paying its way for much longer. We must at least give tariff reductions a trial and see what kind of response we achieve.'

Lips even tighter, the receptionist said stiffly, 'As you wish, Miss Griffin. How much do you want the tariffs dropped by?'

Eddie didn't know, she hadn't thought that far ahead. She supposed she should seek Mr Vickers's recommendations but that would mean undermining her own position and giving this employee licence to question other decisions she might make in future. 'By a quarter.' Eddie hoped that wasn't too much. She wasn't an accountant but surely receiving three-quarters of the usual price of a room here was better than receiving none as it was empty?

A quarter! Was this woman mad? thought Amelia Harbin. Horrified, she visualised the riff-raff that such a cut in price could bring swarming to reception. She would be expected to deal with hoi-polloi in future. This woman might be the owner of the hotel but she obviously hadn't a clue that her proposal could ruin the Connaught's reputation all for the sake of filling a few more rooms. Miss Harbin inwardly smiled to herself. Reception was her domain. She could still be the one to decide just who stayed in this hotel and who didn't. She would have to be more discreet in her methods in future, make sure Miss Griffin wasn't around. Word would soon spread that the Connaught Hotel would be more affordable to the lower classes, but *she* would make sure those lower classes knew they were not welcome at all should they try to book in!

She smiled. 'As you wish, Miss Griffin.' She made to ask if that was all Miss Griffin required so she could take her leave then realised this was a golden opportunity for her to do something about the major problem on reception at the moment.

'Miss Griffin, as I am with you, I'd like to discuss the very urgent matter of Miss Monroe's position. I would strongly suggest that in future I be the one to choose my assistant as I'm the one who knows exactly what skills a receptionist needs to possess. I hardly need any longer to assess Miss Monroe's suitability as it was apparent to me from the moment she commenced that she falls far short . . .'

'Miss Harbin, do we carry headache powders?' Eddie interjected. Her head was really thumping now and this woman's monotonous drone wasn't helping.

Amelia did not appreciate being interrupted, and especially not when she had at last found a chance to do something about getting rid of Monroe. 'We do keep a medical chest for guests' emergencies in reception, Miss Griffin,' she said stiltedly.

Thank goodness for that, Eddie thought. In her urgent need for medication she suggested, 'I'll come back through with you, and if you'd be good enough to supply me with something to ease my head, I'd be most appreciative.'

'But . . . about Miss Monroe . . .'

'I don't wish to appear rude, Miss Harbin, but I really am in urgent need of something for my headache.'

As Eddie was standing by the counter, waiting for the senior receptionist to oblige her request, a couple walked past her towards the outside door and Eddie could not help but overhear their conversation.

'Why aren't we eating here?' the woman asked the man.

'I had a glance at the menu while I was waiting for you to come down and I'm not at all impressed with what's being offered. Only a roast of the day and a fish dish to chose from. I don't have a fancy for either. You'd have thought a hotel of this size would have had a more varied menu. I noticed a little restaurant when we drove up here yesterday in the taxi from the station, I thought we'd go there.'

Thoughtfully Eddie stared after the couple as they disappeared through the revolving door. Phee also had complained the choice on the hotel menu was too narrow. Eddie had been too consumed by more pressing matters to take any notice of the menu herself, but when she'd last eaten in a hotel, which until recently she had done quite regularly, she'd expected to have a choice of at least five or six different main courses. No wonder the restaurant tables at the Connaught remained unoccupied. She needed to have a prompt interview with the Head Chef to discuss with him his suggestions for improving the menu. She would request Mr Sopworth to arrange it for her. It then struck her that her guided tour by Connie had not included the kitchen, and she wondered why?

Miss Harbin came over with a fold of paper containing the headache powder which Eddie gratefully accepted from her. 'Thank you, Miss Harbin. If you or Miss Monroe should catch sight of Mr Sopworth, would you tell him I would like to see him?'

'Certainly, Miss Griffin,' she responded stiffly.

Eddie looked at the woman. She reminded her of a formidable headmistress she'd had at the girls' school she'd attended. All the girls were terrified of her. Phee's nickname for her had been Mrs Crippen. She wondered if Amelia Harbin was aware of the impression she created. More to the point, was she the sort of person Eddie wanted in charge of welcoming guests to her hotel? She couldn't think about this now, though, she needed to take the medication before her headache worsened and turned into a migraine. She had suffered one only once and wouldn't wish to suffer so again.

CHAPTER EIGHTEEN

'I'm surprised you're still lowering yerself to eat yer meals with the likes of us now, Connie.'

Forkful of liver and onions poised in mid-air, Connie realised a whole tableful of staff had stopped eating and were looking at her expectantly. She fixed her eyes upon the girl who'd addressed her. 'And why wouldn't I still be eating my meals in the staff room now, Deirdre?'

The silver service waitress smirked smugly. 'Well, what with you being so pally with the owner, I just thought you'd be eating with her in the restaurant.'

Connie eyes narrowed. 'Miss Griffin asked me to show her around the hotel when she first arrived and to help her move in. Someone had to do it, I just happened to be the one. Would you have refused and risked your job if it'd been you she'd asked and not me?'

Deirdre sniffed haughtily. 'Why *has* she suddenly moved in, that's what we want to know, ain't it?' she said, looking at the rest of the gathering for support. 'You weren't very forthcoming when Val suddenly upped and offed, like a burglar in the night. None of us was convinced by your story she'd urgent family business to deal with up North. We're hoping you're going to be more obliging about Lady Duckmuck moving in, aren't we?'

'Yeah, we are,' piped up Noreen Greenwood, a chambermaid.

'Miss Griffin will have her reasons, though I can assure you she didn't tell me what they were. I've told you, I just showed her around,' Connie snapped back.

'Is it true this place is getting done up from top to bottom?' asked Kevin Williams, a waiter in the restaurant.

'How would I know?' Connie responded tartly. 'I've told you already, and I'm getting a little sick of repeating myself, I just escorted Miss Griffin around so she didn't get lost. You all know what a maze this place is. We've all of us got lost a few times when we first started working here.'

'Well, I met her and I think she's ever so nice,' chirped up Danny, the young porter.

Most of the people around the table looked at him as if the lad had committed a mortal sin by admitting he'd taken a liking to the owner of the hotel.

'Why don't you all just eat your dinner and leave well alone?' spoke up George Humphries, the concierge. 'I want you waitresses under my charge ready to serve up high teas as soon as guests start ordering, and we've plenty of things needing to be done before then. And the rest of you need to be back to your own jobs promptly or you'll be getting a rocket from your own superiors.'

Connie smiled at the elderly man, grateful for his intervention. Val had warned her this would happen and she'd been right. Hopefully Connie had now put all the staff right and their unjustified accusations against her would cease. She had enough on her plate, contending with Miss Harbin's attitude, without the rest of the staff turning on her.

Connie rose, picked up her dirty plate and stacked it on the table by the door that led into the kitchen. She had a few minutes to spare before she was due back behind the reception counter when Miss Harbin herself would come through to have her dinner. She never took more than ten minutes instead of the allotted hour over her meal, nor did she come through to the staff room like everyone else for her fifteen-minute morning coffee or afternoon tea breaks, having those served to her as she sat ramrod straight on a hard-backed chair in the switchboard cubicle, much to Pamela's annoyance as during those times she felt the constant boring of her boss's eyes on her every movement, only too aware Miss Harbin was ready to pounce should she make the slightest mistake. It seemed to Connie that Miss Harbin was loath to abandon her position behind reception for any length of time for fear an emergency would arise during her absence, leaving Connie in no doubt that she herself was deemed incapable of dealing with any such happening.

The thought of returning to face Miss Harbin's moods any sooner than was necessary held no appeal for Connie. She decided to spend the remainder of her lunch break taking a breath of fresh air out in the hotel yard.

This usually held a huddle of staff smoking cigarettes, but today for some reason it was empty except for Connie. In the corner of the yard, hidden behind numerous rubbish bins, a portion of the boundary wall had crumbled away forming a U-shaped niche where it was possible to perch a backside, provided it was not too wide a backside, in the gap. Making her way over, Connie eased herself down into the niche, resting her bottom gingerly against the knobbly surface of the crumbling red bricks, then turned her face towards the warm rays of the early-May sunshine. She closed her eyes and imagined she was on a deserted beach, it didn't matter where, just miles of soft golden sands, the lapping of the imaginary sea against the shore lulling her senses. 'Mmm,' she sighed, feeling a blissful peace swamping her.

The sound of a door creaking open reached her ears. Sighing softly at having her moment of tranquillity disturbed, she eased herself out of the hole in the wall and raised herself just enough to peer over the top of the bins and see who was coming into the yard. If it was a friendly face she'd enjoy a few minutes' natter with them; if not, she hoped her presence wasn't noticed. To her surprise she could see a head poking out of the staff door. It seemed to be checking around and then, satisfied the yard was apparently deserted, the whole body emerged. It was unmistakably Mr Sopworth. He was carrying a cardboard box marked 'Bell's Whisky'. It seemed to be a good weight, judging from the way he was labouring under it.

The back of the hotel held several doors. One led down into the huge cellar underneath where broken furniture, old mattresses, and piles of other useless items had been discarded and forgotten about; a door next to the staff entrance led to the kitchen; next to that were several other doors leading into store rooms and a large coal store. The two doors near the end of the building led into flats now long since empty but which had once been the residence of the hotel's housekeeper and manager.

Connie watched, fascinated, as Sopworth lumbered over to the door leading into a small store room. He put the box on the stone slabs by his feet, took a key from his pocket and unlocked the store-room door. He picked up the box and disappeared inside to re-emerge seconds later, locking the door behind him before hurrying back to the staff entrance and disappearing inside.

A look of puzzlement appeared on Connie's face. The assistant manager had seemed to fear he'd be discovered in the process of whatever he had been up to. What was in that box? she wondered. Something there shouldn't be, she had no doubt of that, or why had Mr Sopworth acted so suspiciously? There was no window in the store room and as the door was locked there was no way she could find out without breaking it open, which wasn't an option. That didn't stop her wondering, though. After his denial of ever being in possession of that vacuum cleaner, which as far as Connie knew still had not been found, and now this performance with the box, she strongly suspected the man was up to no good. What sort of no good she wasn't quite sure.

She realised time was passing and if she didn't get back to her position behind reception she risked worsening Miss Harbin's mood, as if it wasn't bad enough already today.

On her way back she stopped by the staff room to snatch a hurried glass of water and there found Mr Sopworth just about to sit down with several other staff members to have his dinner. He didn't acknowledge her presence and for Connie this meant he was totally oblivious to the fact she had just witnessed what he had done. Having poured herself a cup of water from the sink by the door, she drank it down and was taking her leave, passing the chair Mr Sopworth was sitting in, when she remembered something.

'Oh, Mr Sopworth, Miss Griffin was looking for you earlier.'

He looked up at her, non-plussed. 'What for?'

'She didn't give me her reason, just asked me to tell you she wants to see you.'

'Well, she'll have to wait until I've had my dinner,' he said off-handedly, shovelling a forkful of food into his mouth and chomping on it noisily.

Connie was shocked by such disrespect for the owner of the hotel. A similar summons to other members of staff, including herself, would have had them dropping everything to answer the request. It seemed Mr Sopworth felt himself to be more important even than the hotel's proprietor.

Miss Harbin was due back from her lunch at any minute. During her absence Connie had been twiddling her thumbs, having caught up with her work. The reception desk was particularly quiet and she'd had no guests to deal with. Normally she would have taken advantage of the situation to have a chat with Pamela but she had been kept busy with a succession of telephone calls, both incoming and outgoing ones for guests, and with logging all these transactions in her record book. Connie knew the new tariffs had been calculated and the lists were ready to be typed. She would have relished the job but dare not take it upon herself as she knew Miss Harbin would see her well-intentioned act as presumptuous and twist it to use against her.

She did not want to be sitting idle when her superior appeared and cast her eyes hurriedly about for something to do. In desperation she lowered her head to look under the counter and see if it needed tidying. A voice whispering her name had her head jerking up and she gazed in surprise at the woman looking back at her from the other side of the counter.

'Mam!' Connie exclaimed, jumping up off her chair. It was then she noticed the expression of deep worry etched on her mother's face. 'Mam, what's wrong?' she demanded.

'I'm so sorry to visit you at work, lovey, I know you could get into trouble with me coming here, but I'm at me wits' end. I'm hoping you might have a clue . . . well, I'm praying you have.'

Any thought of the trouble she could be in for her mother's visit was shoved aside. 'A clue about what, Mam?' Connie urged.

Eddie had had a continuous trail of senior staff into the office over the last couple of hours, all of them seeming to have assumed that as the owner she was now in full charge and thus the person to consult about any problems they had in running their areas. Despite patiently listening to each individual problem, still Eddie hadn't a clue how to go about resolving them. After assuring everyone their worries would be addressed, she had written them down in list form to pass on to the assistant manager to deal with. She also wanted to question him as to why all these people were seeking her out to resolve their crises for them and not Sopworth himself. As soon as the last person departed her office she seized her chance to head for the foyer in search of the elusive Mr Sopworth.

She automatically went across to the reception desk to enquire if anyone there knew of the assistant manager's whereabouts. With so much on her mind she didn't appreciate that Connie was already dealing with someone. Approaching the desk, Eddie immediately launched in with, 'Connie, have you caught sight of Mr Sopworth at all today? I last saw him myself just after eight this morning. I really do need to . . .' It was then that she noticed Connie was engaged with a woman and immediately apologised. 'Oh, I do beg your pardon, madam, I didn't realise Miss Monroe was dealing with you.' It was then that she noticed the look of worry on the woman's haggard face. 'Is there anything the matter?' Eddie asked her in concern.

Connie gulped. 'Miss Griffin,' she said falteringly, unsure how the owner of the hotel was going to react to this blatant breach of staff rules, 'this is my mother.'

Before Connie could say anything else, Eddie smiled welcomingly. 'How very nice to meet you, Mrs Monroe.'

It was obvious to Irene that this woman was important from her daughter's manner towards her and she blurted out, 'Look, I don't mean to get our Connie in no trouble, I just needed to speak to her very urgently.'

Eddie addressed Connie. 'Why don't you take your mother into the office so you can have some privacy to discuss her problem?'

Connie gulped again. 'Oh, but I couldn't take advantage, Miss Griffin. And besides, I can't leave my post.'

'I'll hold the fort for you until Miss Harbin returns. Where is she, by the way?'

'Having her lunch. She's due back any second.'

Was it that time already? Eddie hadn't realised as the morning had seemed to fly by. She hadn't thought about food herself and now realised she was hungry. As soon as Miss Harbin appeared she would go and see what the restaurant had to offer. Thinking of the restaurant reminded her of the urgent need to speak to Chef about his suggestions for menu improvements. 'Well, I'm sure I can't manage to do too much damage in just a few seconds,' she said, smiling warmly at Connie. 'Off you go. I'll explain to Miss Harbin that you had urgent business to attend to and will return as soon as possible.'

Connie was too desperately worried over what had caused her mother to visit her at work to pay much thought to anything else. Within seconds she was on the other side of the counter where she grabbed her mother's arm and rushed her into the manager's office.

'Mam, what's going on that brings you here so urgently?'

Just as Connie and her mother disappeared inside the office, the staff door opened and Miss Harbin strode in. She was behind the counter before she realised Miss

Griffin was too and immediately dreaded that the hotel proprietor was about to inform her of more changes. 'Miss Griffin, to what do we owe the pleasure?' she enquired frostily.

'I was just covering for Miss Monroe who was called away urgently to speak to her mother. They are both in the office. I don't know what the problem is but I'm sure Miss Monroe won't be away for too long and you can manage without her meantime.'

Relief flooded Amelia that Miss Griffin was not here to propose further changes but nevertheless she felt appalled by what she had just been told. 'Miss Monroe's *mother* is on the premises? Well, really! Monroe is well aware that staff are allowed no visits from family or friends under any circumstances. You can count on me to ensure she is disciplined appropriately, Miss Griffin.'

'There really is no need to make such a fuss, Miss Harbin. I appreciate it wouldn't do to have all the staff's families and friends popping in and out for a chat whenever they felt like it, but this case is an exception. I saw for myself how deeply upset Mrs Monroe was over something. She desperately needed to talk to her daughter about it and couldn't wait for a more convenient time. There is no need for any rebuke of Miss Monroe on this occasion, Miss Harbin.'

Miss Harbin was livid at being denied an opportunity to make a strike against the young woman she had convinced herself was out to take her job from her. 'Well . . . I . . . As you wish, Miss Griffin.'

'Are the new tariffs in place yet?' Eddie asked her.

Amelia was stalling the implementation of the tariffs for as long as she could. 'The calculations have been done and I now have to type the lists out. I would, of course, have enlisted Miss Monroe's help but she is not a competent typist and therefore I could not entrust her with such an important task. I have to find the time to do it myself in between all the other things I have to see to in my capacity as senior receptionist.'

'Well, maybe Miss Monroe would prove of more help to you if you gave her the chance to build up her speeds. I would appreciate if you would give the tariff lists your urgent attention; I want the new prices implementing as soon as possible. I'll be in the restaurant having lunch should anyone be looking for me. I am still urgently in need of a word with Mr Sopworth so I would appreciate your passing on my message to him should he come this way.'

Connie was looking at her mother, stupefied. 'What do you mean, our Babsy's left home?'

'Well, that's what it looks like, Connie. I can't understand why she's done what she has. We were getting on much better this past week. She seemed to have stopped her nonsense over not wanting to tell us where she was going or what she was doing and had been coming in on time and being more or less her old self with me. She was just going out to meet her friends last night, promised me and yer dad faithfully she'd be back at ten, but it came and went, then eleven, and me and yer dad was frantic by that time. Yer dad went looking for her but no sign of her at any of the places she's told us she goes to. Finally I checked her room and found all her stuff gone. I thought you might have some idea where she could be? But why has she gone off without a word when she knows we'll be worried? That's putting it mildly! Have you any idea where yer sister might have gone, Connie, or why even?'

Mystified, she shook her head. 'You said she didn't have anything to do with her old friends any more after moving to the prefabs and getting pally with those two girls and the lad at the bottom of the road, so it's unlikely she'll be with any of her old pals. What about that family down the road? Have you asked them if they have any idea where Babsy's gone?'

'Huh, them! Me first port of call that was. The mother just laughed and said she didn't have a clue where her own kids were most of the time, let alone mine, then shut the door in me face.'

Connie was angered that her mother should be treated in such a way by anyone. 'Have you tried Babsy's work?'

'I've just come from there. Oh, Connie, she gave in her notice and left yesterday! I'm at me wits' end where to look now and that's why I came to see you. I'm so sorry if me coming is going to get you in trouble but I didn't know what else to do.'

This was no sudden decision to leave home then, thought Connie. Her sister had obviously planned it. She could not think of one good reason why Babsy should suddenly uproot herself from her comfortable home, cared for by loving parents, to go off to God knew where and fend for herself. She wrapped her arms protectively around her sobbing mother.

'We'll find her, Mam, and bring her home. We will, I promise you. I'll start tonight straight after I finish work. It's my day off tomorrow and I was coming to see you as I usually do but I'll spend the day trying everywhere I can think of that she might be.' And she'd give her sister hell when she did find her for causing them all such anguish by her thoughtless actions.

Irene sniffed, looking at her elder daughter gratefully. 'Oh, Connie, what would I do without yer? Yer dad's had to go to work, bless him, but how the hell he'll concentrate with this worry about our Babsy hanging over him, I don't know. He'll be out again tonight looking, I know he will, and I will too.'

'You go home, Mam. More than likely our Babsy's realised what an idiot she's been and is in the kitchen right now, making herself a cup of tea.'

Irene looked at her hopefully. 'Oh, Connie, do you think she might be?'

'If she's got any sense she will be. Look, I know it's daft me telling you this, but try to stop worrying because if she's not had the sense to come back yet, between us we'll find her, I promise you we will. If she does come back before I finish my shift at six, will you telephone and leave a message with Pamela on the switchboard?'

'Won't you get into more trouble than you could be already if I telephone you as well?' her mother asked her worriedly.

More than likely, Connie thought, should Miss Harbin find out, but at this moment she didn't care what trouble she herself was in. Finding her sister and putting a stop to all this worry was what she cared about. She desperately wanted to begin her search now, but that would most definitely be asking for the sack.

After seeing her mother safely off the premises,

Connie returned behind the reception counter to find a frosty-faced Miss Harbin waiting for her.

'Miss Harbin, I'm very sorry for . . .' she began.

'I should think you will be *very* sorry for your appalling behaviour in abandoning your post to receive a social visit from your mother. You are well aware of the staff rules on visits from family and friends. Miss Griffin is not impressed by your conduct. She won't let this matter go undisciplined, she told me so herself.'

Connie looked bewildered. 'Oh, but Miss Griffin . . .'

'Don't interrupt when I'm talking, Monroe,' her boss snapped at her harshly. 'It must be plain to you by now that you are not up to the standard required for a receptionist at the Connaught and you are fooling no one but yourself if you think you are. The sensible thing for you to do is to give in your notice before you're sacked. Leave immediately is my advice.'

Connie knew without a shadow of a doubt then that Miss Harbin, for her own reasons, was hell-bent on getting rid of her. She also knew she was lying about Miss Griffin expressing her displeasure at Connie's conduct. If Miss Griffin had been annoyed in any way then Connie felt sure she would have said so at the time and not offered to cover for Connie while she found out what was troubling her mother. Well, she wasn't going to make it easy for Miss Harbin by giving in her notice, she'd be damned if she would. If her superior wanted rid of her that badly, she'd have to work a lot harder to do it.

Connie smiled politely at her boss. 'Don't you think it's about time I started to learn how to use the switchboard so I can relieve Miss Wardle at her lunch and breaktimes and then you won't have to do it any more, Miss Harbin?'

Eddie meanwhile was sitting in the office feeling totally useless. She still hadn't seen anything of the assistant manager and guessed that he, like all the other staff members, was going about his business while she, the owner, sat doing nothing. She couldn't get on with what she had come here to do originally because of her lack of funds, and although she was somewhat proud of herself for coming up with two ideas in her first morning for improving the running of the hotel, actually being on the premises in person seemed point- less to Eddie. When Captain Fosedyke returned she wouldn't even have this office to sit in as he would be needing it. She visualised herself sitting in her room upstairs all day, just hoping enough money was being generated in the rest of the building to support her father and herself. But it would drive her mad, being isolated in that room. She couldn't indulge in any of the pursuits that used to occupy her time because most of those had cost money in some form or other that was not now at her disposal. She suddenly realised how much she had taken her affluent lifestyle for granted and felt ashamed that she had been so complacent in assuming it would always be so.

She gave a deep sigh. From now on, what was she going to do to fill her time? What did other hotel owners do with themselves while the staff they employed ran their business for them? She supposed, though, that those hotels were making enough of a profit to fund their owners' chosen entertainment. She needed to find something to occupy her time that didn't cost money, but what? Taking up knitting or crochet didn't appeal to her. She enjoyed reading but not every minute of the day, every day. She could offer to do some voluntary work, she supposed. When her father came out of hospital he would need looking after. Then it struck her how quickly the morning had flown by because she had been involved in hotel business. She might not have completely understood what Mr Vickers had explained to her, or been able to help the staff with their problems, but the fact was she had wanted to understand what Mr Vickers was explaining to her, had wanted to resolve the staff's problems for them, if only she had known how to.

She felt a sudden great need to know exactly how the hotel operated. It seemed very simple on the surface. A building had rooms which people paid to use. But she was now realising that there was more to it than that, a whole lot more. Maybe with a better insight she could come up with more ways to get the hotel profitable again instead of being reliant on the manager and assistant manager to tell her how they thought improvements could be made. Though considering the decline the hotel had suffered over the years, the manager hadn't proved himself very competent in that respect.

Then another thought struck her. Her plan to renovate would have guaranteed pleasant surroundings for the guests but that in itself was not enough to ensure the overall success of a hotel. It was the people at its helm, overseeing the day-to-day running, ensuring everything was as it should be, having the expertise to know when it wasn't, that was the most important factor. That was why Stibley had got away with what he had for so long, because her father had not been knowledgeable enough about the running of the business he'd inherited to realise shady practices were going on. It was wrong of her to mistrust people as not everyone was like Stibley, but if this hotel were to be their saviour then she would have to know exactly what was going on inside its walls or she risked ending up in the same position her father had done and there would be no hotel to fall back on this time.

Eddie now knew how best to fill her time in future. She got to her feet and went in search of Sopworth.

Still not having learned her way around the maze of corridors she got quite lost, ending up on the back service stairs before eventually she found the assistant manager in the staff room, lounging in a chair, feet on the table, drinking a cup of tea. He almost choked on it when Eddie came through the door and splashed it all down himself in his haste to stand up in her presence.

'Oh, er . . . Miss Griffin, I was just about to come and see you. You wanted me, I believe,' he blurted, wiping spilt tea off his suit as best he could with his hands.

'Yes, I do, and have done for several hours.'

'Well, I've been busy dealing with things,' he said evasively, knowing that if this woman uncovered just what he had been up to all day it was curtains for him. Not that he minded. He hadn't even wanted this crummy position, and certainly didn't care enough about it to learn all the ins and outs of the job. He'd only been offered it because he'd lied very convincingly to the hotel manager about his supposed previous hotel experience. He didn't in fact possess any and knew Fosedyke had been becoming increasingly suspicious of him, and his time in this job was quickly coming to an end. Luckily for him a reprieve had come in the form of the Captain's illness which had afforded him a while longer to make some more money from the highly profitable sideline he had going with a partner in crime who also worked at the Connaught.

'Oh, what things exactly have you been busy doing?' asked Eddie, keen to start learning the business as quickly as she could.

His mind whirled. 'Oh ... well, finding out what things we're running low on so I can re-order and ... er ... checking the staff are doing their jobs properly, that kind of thing.'

'I'm very pleased to see how dedicated you are, Mr Sopworth. There is a list I put on your desk with further details of problems the staff are experiencing. They need your urgent attention. Hopefully I'll soon have the ability to resolve them myself should my manager be otherwise engaged. From tomorrow, Mr Sopworth, I wish you to begin to instruct me in every aspect of hotel management.'

His mouth dropped open, eyes widening in shock at her announcement. 'Eh?'

'Is that a problem, Mr Sopworth?'

'Er ... no, but ... er ... wouldn't Captain Fosedyke be your better bet?'

'My better bet? Oh, I see what you mean. The Captain isn't here, is he? Hopefully he'll be back with us soon and can take over from you in instructing me, but in the meantime I would very much value your assistance. Shall we say in the office at eight? I'll accompany you on your rounds to start with so I can really begin to get a feel for what goes on. Oh, and there is another reason I wanted to see you. Would you ask Chef to come to my office? Now would be a good time.'

He looked at her in concern. 'You want to see Chef? What for, Miss Griffin?'

'Oh, I suppose I should have told you as you're the assistant manager. You should be kept in the know about everything, shouldn't you? I want Chef to make some suggestions for menu improvements. The two main courses we offer at the moment are not enough of a choice to encourage people to dine in the restaurant. Five or six main dishes would be much preferable. Are you too of the opinion that a wider choice would encourage more diners, Mr Sopworth?'

'Oh, er . . . yes, most definitely. I did suggest doing that to Captain Fosedyke only he wasn't keen on making any changes.'

'Really? Oh, I see. Did you suggest other improvements that weren't taken up by the Captain?'

'Er . . . oh, yes, I did.'

'And just what were they?' Eddie asked keenly.

'Oh, I'll outline them for you tomorrow as I'll need time to recall them all. As for Chef, he'll be off just now.'

'Off?'

'On his afternoon break. Probably having a sleep. Chef starts at ten then knocks off at about three as soon as they stop serving lunch in the restaurant. He comes back on about at six for the evening meal and stays until about nine.'

'Oh, I see. Then it will have to be tomorrow I speak to him,' Eddie said, disappointed. 'Please arrange for us to meet as soon as possible then.'

Sopworth was desperate to make his escape for fear Miss Griffin should catch him out on something he was supposed to know about but didn't. It wouldn't take her long, he guessed, to realise that she already knew more about the hotel trade than he did. He was surprised, in fact, that he'd managed to fool the Captain for as long as he had when all the time he'd concentrated only on remembering the things that were far more important to him about the Connaught Hotel.

An anxious knot formed in Sopworth's stomach. He needed to keep his job at least until twelve o'clock tomorrow night. Although he hadn't planned on leaving quite that soon he would nevertheless quite happily abscond then with a good amount of cash in his pocket. Somehow he had to come up with a ploy to stop Miss Griffin discovering his charade for another day or so. After tomorrow night she could find out what she liked about him. By then he'd be long gone.

'Excuse me, Miss Griffin, but I really need to get back to my office and place orders for things we're low on else we won't get them delivered before we run out. And I'd better have a look at the list of things you left on my desk for me to see to.'

'Please don't let me hold you up,' she said. 'I'll look forward to seeing you in the morning.'

She wondered how Phee and Harvey would react when they both found out what she intended to do.

Phee would not take her seriously and would suggest bringing her to her senses by going for lunch or on a shopping trip. Harvey was still of the opinion that she should sell the hotel and live on what she could get for it. He had been worried enough that she was making a mistake by not selling. What his reaction would be when she told him she now proposed to learn the hotel trade and become adept enough to take an active role in it she could not imagine. But she felt sure he would be supportive, knowing he had both her own and her father's best interests at heart.

CHAPTER NINETEEN

Connie's offer to learn the workings of the switch-board was met only with a murderous glare from Miss Harbin. Without a word she devoted herself to her own work, for the rest of the afternoon leaving Connie to her own devices. Consumed with worry about her sister's whereabouts, Connie was mortally thankful she did not also have to contend with her boss's nasty sniping.

Just after six that evening she went bounding up the service stairs to her room, intending to swap her work attire for a pair of blue Capri pants, white blouse and pale blue cardigan, and without stopping even to have her evening meal immediately dash out to begin her search for Babsy. During the afternoon as she had worked away she had gone over and over possible loca-tions for her sister. Where could a seventeen-year-old girl with more than likely only her previous week's wage in her purse go that held so much more appeal than her own home? Connie had no idea. Aware that her par-ents would be scouring their immediate neighbourhood, Connie felt it best to cast a wider net. Coffee bars attracted young girls, she enjoyed going to them her-self, and armed with a photograph of her sister Connie hoped someone might recognise her and give her a lead. It was a start anyway.

About to lock her door, she heard a movement nearby and automatically turned round, expecting it was one of her colleagues. The face before her was so unexpected that she dropped her key in surprise. 'Babsy! Oh, Babsy,' she cried.

Her sister immediately launched herself on her. 'Connie,' she wailed, wrapping her arms tightly around her neck and burying her head in her shoulder. 'I didn't know where else to go,' she blubbered.

As she hugged her sister tightly, Connie's whole body sagged in relief. 'Have you any idea the worry you've caused Mam and Dad as well as me?' she scolded. She was suddenly conscious that no visitors whatsoever were permitted in staff living quarters. The discovery of her sister could heap even more trouble on Connie, maybe even expulsion. Hurriedly freeing herself, she retrieved her dropped key, unlocked her door and ushered Babsy inside her room along with her battered suitcase.

'Did anyone see you come up here?' demanded Connie.

Babsy now presented a forlorn figure huddled on her bed, sobbing hysterically.

She shook her head and hiccoughed: 'I don't think so. I sneaked in the staff entrance this morning and made me way up here. I've been hiding in the bathroom ever since. God, it's awful in there, Connie. Several times people tried the door to get in but I held me breath until they went away. I knew what time your shift finished and was peeping out the door, looking for yer to come up.'

Sitting down beside her, Connie took her hand and held it protectively in hers. 'What on earth were you playing at, Babsy? What did you go and leave home for like that, without a word? Mam and Dad are scouring the streets for you. I was about to make a start looking for you myself as soon as I'd changed my clothes. We were all frantic with worry that something awful had happened to you. So what made you do it?'

A trail of fresh tears rolled down her face. 'Oh, Con, I've been so stupid. I thought he loved me, I really did . . .'

'Who loved you, Babsy?'

'Johnny Lowden.' She swallowed hard to clear the lump of deep distress from her throat. 'I met him through his sisters just after we moved to the prefabs. He's got a motor bike and wears a black leather jacket and has his hair done in a DA . . . he always has girls hanging around him. First time I saw him I fell in love with him, I couldn't help myself, and I couldn't help spending as much time as I could with his sisters just so I could get a glimpse of him. I wasn't daft enough, though, not to realise a man like him would never look at me twice because I was much younger than him for a start, and the sort of girls he knocked around with, well . . . they were sexy, if you know what I mean, and Mam and Dad would never let me dress like the sort he obviously fancied. I thought I'd no hope of ever catching his eye.'

She gave a miserable laugh. 'He knew I fancied him, though, and used to tease me about it in front of his mates and his sisters, saying things like I was still a little girl, having to do what my mam and dad told me, but I was working so it was about time I stood up to them. When I didn't have to be in by ten he might consider taking me out. He said only boys looked at girls like me. He was a man and only looked at women.

'I just so wanted him to look at me as a woman, really wanted that, Connie. I felt like a woman inside. And I started to feel so resentful towards Mam and Dad for keeping such a close watch over me and not letting me dress like I wanted to. I knew I was being rotten to Mam but I couldn't help myself. I just wanted to be the girl on the back of Johnny's bike, for him to be kissing me and not one of those trollops he went with. It was Mam and Dad who were stopping me from being that woman. I was so miserable, Connie. I wanted him so badly.

'One night last week me and Johnny's sisters and a couple of their mates were hanging around the chip shop, just chatting, when Johnny roared up on his bike. I could tell straight away he was in a bad mood. Franny, one of his sisters, asked him what was up with him. He told her to mind her own bloody business, and then she ribbed him that his girlfriend had done something to upset him and by his reaction it was obvious she'd hit the nail on the head. Then, I couldn't believe it, he asked me if I wanted to go for a ride on his bike. 'Course I did, Connie, I'd been willing him to ask me that since the first day I clapped eyes on him.

'Next thing I knew we were racing down the street, the wind blowing in me hair, and ... oh, I can't tell you how I felt just being that close to him! Then next thing I knew he'd stopped the bike and turned around and was kissing me. I was floating on a cloud. I'd never been kissed like that before, not like Johnny kissed me.'

She paused long enough to pull a handkerchief out of her coat pocket, noisily blow her nose and dab her streaming eyes. 'Then he told me him and a few mates were going to Great Yarmouth the following week, to work on the fair for the season, and all his mates were taking their girlfriends. I could go with him as his girl if I wanted to. Oh, Connie, I couldn't believe he was asking me to go away for the summer with him and be his girl! He said he could get me a job on the fair, working with him. It sounded so romantic, Connie, and I wanted to go more than anything so I said yes. Johnny seemed really pleased.

'I couldn't tell Mam and Dad what I'd planned. They didn't like me being friends with the Lowden sisters anyway, and if they'd have found out about me and Johnny, well, I knew they'd put a stop to me going and I couldn't bear that, I just couldn't bear them stopping me from being with him. So I didn't give them any reason to think I was up to anything.

'Every night after that until last night Johnny took me for a ride on his bike and always stopped at the same place as he'd done before. We'd kiss and then he'd drive me back again, and every night he'd ask me if I was still up for going to Yarmouth and seemed really pleased when I said I was. The night before last, after dropping me back at the shops to get home before ten, we arranged to meet the next night at seven with all the rest of his mates and their girlfriends, then we'd be off. I was so excited, Connie, I hardly slept. Well, I didn't sleep, not a wink.

'I'd given me notice in already so all I had to do was collect me wages so I had some money to take with me.

As soon as I got home I quickly packed me stuff, dropped me case out of the bedroom window so Mam and Dad never saw me carrying it out, then had dinner like normal and went out as usual, saying I'd be back at ten. Only I wouldn't be coming back, would I?' She looked at Connie earnestly. 'I was going to send Mam and Dad a postcard from Yarmouth when I got there, honest I was, Connie. Not telling them I was with Johnny but with a girlfriend. I knew I'd have to face the music eventually when I came home after the season was finished but by then I thought me and Johnny would be a proper couple, maybe even married, and Mam and Dad finding out then didn't bother me.'

Babsy's face screwed up in devastation. 'Just as I got to the meeting place, Johnny and his mates were pulling off. There was another girl on the back of Johnny's bike. I couldn't believe it. He'd taken another girl in my place! I was so hurt, Connie, it was like my whole world had come crashing down on me. I don't know how long I stood there like an idiot, not knowing what to do. Then Franny and Josie turned up to meet their other pals outside the chip shop at seven.

'It was awful, Connie. I thought they were my friends but they both started laughing at me, saying hadn't I cottoned on that Johnny was just using me to make his girlfriend see that if she didn't change her mind and go to Yarmouth with him it was no skin off his nose 'cos he'd soon get someone else willing to go with him? He wasn't going to be the only lad without a girl tagging along. The house we stopped outside every night on his bike for a kiss and cuddle was his girlfriend's house.

'He used me, Connie. I gave up everything for him.

I've got no job and now I can never go home again, I couldn't face Mam and Dad and tell them all this 'cos I know they'd hate me for being so deceitful. I spent last night on a bench in Victoria Park and it was the worst night of me life. I was scared to death and badly wanted to go home but I just couldn't. I really believed Johnny loved me and wanted me to be with him. Oh, Connie,' she wailed, 'what am I going to do?'

She wrapped her arms around her distraught sister, pulling her close. 'Babsy, don't you realise what a lucky escape you've had? I dread to think what could have happened to you in Yarmouth. I know it sounds romantic, working on a fair at the seaside, but most of the sort that work in them places are rough types, Babsy, and a girl like you wouldn't have stood a chance with them. The money you earned wouldn't have paid for a nice room in a good hotel. You'd have been lucky to afford a room in a backstreet lodging house, and by the time you'd paid for food you'd not have had much left for 'ote else. I don't doubt for a minute either that as soon as Johnny Lowden found a woman more his sort he'd have dumped you like a ton of bricks, leaving you to fend for yourself. Remember how devastated you were to see him riding off with another girl on his pillion, leaving you behind? Well, how do you think you'd be feeling if he'd abandoned you in a strange town, miles from home, and more than likely with no money in your purse for your fare home? The kindest thing that man ever did for you was going off without you.

'You're going to face this like a grown-up, Babsy. I'm taking you home right now to put Mam and Dad's minds at rest that you're safe. Then you're going to tell them everything and face whatever punishment they dish out.'

Her sister pulled away from her, her face horrified. 'I can't, Connie. I can't!'

'You will, if I have to drag you all the way. We all love you, Babsy, and I hope this has taught you a lesson about how much we care.' Thinking of Val, Connie looked at her sister meaningfully. 'Some girls aren't so lucky as you, having a family that worries about them. I hope after this you'll appreciate yours more. I'm just going to get changed then we'll be off.'

By the time they reached the little prefab on the Wykes Road Babsy was physically quaking with trepidation over the reception she was going to receive. As it was, her parents were so overjoyed to see her safe and sound that she had been tearfully hugged and sat down with a cup of tea and a sandwich before they even demanded an explanation for her actions. They both listened to it in disbelief that their daughter could have been so easily duped into acting against her better nature by a man who had merely used her before callously discarding her. They were both keenly aware that this incident could have had a very different outcome. But Babsy had clearly suffered enough without the need for them to heap more punishment on her. It was best to put this all behind them and get on with the future.

As it was her day off the next day, Connie decided to stay the night and spend it with her family, showing Babsy some sisterly support. Irene and Vic had both their girls together under their roof and wanted to savour every minute of this rare occasion and make the most of it.

CHAPTER TWENTY

Eddie looked at her watch again. She frowned. It was a quarter to nine. Where was Gerald Sopworth? Their arrangement had been to meet at eight o'clock and she herself had been here since ten minutes to, having dressed very suitably in a light wool full-skirted dress of silver-grey with large black buttons fastening down the front to the waist. It was edged in black around the revered collar and turned-back three-quarter-length sleeves. On her feet she wore a pair of black suede court shoes. Now she had made her decision to learn the hotel trade, she was eager to get on with it and looking forward to accompanying the assistant manager on his rounds, keen to observe how he dealt with the staff and gain an insight into the way he handled any problems they put to him. She was also keen to meet the Head Chef so the enhanced menu could be implemented shortly.

Eddie looked at her watch again. It was now nearly nine and still no sign of Sopworth. She rose from her chair and walked out into the foyer. Several people were seated there reading newspapers; Mr Humphries the concierge seemed to be ticking off a waitress; Miss Harbin behind the reception desk was booking out two guests; several elderly couples and two genteel single ladies were making their way into the restaurant for breakfast; Danny the day porter was standing by the lift looking bored rigid. There was no sign of the assistant manager.

She beckoned Danny over.

He came with a big expectant grin on his face. 'Yes, Miss Griffin?' he asked eagerly.

'Have you see Mr Sopworth this morning?'

He pulled a thoughtful face before shaking his head. 'No, Miss Griffin.'

'Could you go and check around a few of the staff for me and ask if anyone has seen him, please, Danny? I'll be in the office.'

'Yeah, sure, Miss Griffin. Won't be a tick,' he said.

She returned to the office and sat down again behind the desk. Absently she leafed through a sheaf of papers in the Captain's filing tray. Amongst other things, there were a couple of invoices he had paper-clipped hand-written notes to which told Eddie he was in dispute with the respective companies about their overpricing on one and a delivery shortage on another. There were also several quotes for services, including one from a laundry company on which the Captain had written 'do not believe this company can provide such a comprehensive service at such a low cost'; also a dozen or so letters from the general public enquiring after job vacancies the hotel might have. Obviously this was the Captain's work in progress and in his absence needed dealing with. Also on the desk was a pile of unopened post which had clearly been delivered in the Captain's absence. She wondered why Gerald Sopworth hadn't thought to take responsibility for this as he was covering for the Captain, then she reasoned with herself that he'd probably not yet had the time with all the demands on him. She felt annoyed with herself for not being able to assume more responsibility.

Danny came bounding into the office. 'No one's seen Mr Sopworth this morning at all, Miss Griffin.'

'Oh, I see. I wonder where he could have got to? Mr Sopworth lives in, I believe, so do you think someone should go and check on him? Do you know yourself which room he occupies in the staff quarters, Danny?'

'I don't but I can find out, Miss Griffin. Won't be a tick,' he said.

She could not help but smile after Danny had disappeared. He really was an obliging young man and so very eager to please.

Ten minutes later he charged back into the office, stopping abruptly before he crashed into the desk. 'Mr Sopworth's poorly in bed, Miss Griffin,' he blurted out breathlessly.

'He's sick? Oh, dear. Does he need a doctor fetching?'

Danny shrugged. 'Dunno. I knocked on his door and he called to me to come in like he was dying. I told him you'd sent me up to check on him. He said to tell yer he's really sorry but he's been up all night with a dose of the runs.'

Eddie looked at him non-plussed. 'Excuse me?'

Danny looked back at her, confused. 'Excuse yer what for, Miss Griffin?'

'No, not excuse *me*. I meant, excuse me for not

understanding what you meant by . . . what did you say . . . a dose of the runs? What is a dose of the runs?'

'Well, it's when yer can't get off the lavvy, Miss Griffin. In one end and out the other.'

Eddie did then get his meaning. 'I understand perfectly now, Danny. Mr Sopworth is suffering from a stomach disorder. I suppose in that case bed is the best place for him.'

'He said ter tell yer he's sorry, and if he's feeling any better he'll come down later.'

'Thank you, Danny. You've been very helpful.'

''Ote else I can do for yer, Miss Griffin?'

She smiled at him. 'No, thank you. You'd better go back in case you're needed in the foyer.'

Immediately he'd left she picked up the telephone and dialled the room service number. When they eventually answered she requested they send a jug of fresh water and a glass up to Mr Sopworth's room. Always the best cure for stomach disorders. She got the distinct impression from the long pause she received before the young man on the other end responded that he was rather put out at being requested to do something for another member of staff.

There was a tap at the door then and Mr Vickers came in armed with a cheque book. 'I'm very sorry to bother you, Miss Griffin, but I was hoping Captain Fosedyke would be back. As he's not I find myself in a dilemma. He's the only official hotel signatory, except for yourself, of course. I can't delay payment on these outstanding accounts any longer or we risk having services withheld. I wondered if you'd be very good enough to sign these for me so I can get them in the lunchtime post?'

She had never signed a cheque before, never had to, and suddenly felt very important. 'Yes, of course I will oblige, Mr Vickers.'

Handing the cheque book across to her, he said, 'There are three separate cheques, Miss Griffin, covering the laundry, the telephone and the coal merchant. Er ... and I was surprised to learn we'd had a change of bank account, Miss Griffin. We've had the other one since the hotel opened its doors and ... well, I was wondering why it'd suddenly been changed? It's not as if we've moved to another bank, is it? The new account is with the same one we've always banked with.'

'The bank manager advised the change,' she said evasively, and quickly added, 'The telephone bill is for rather a lot of money. Do we spend that amount on hotel telephone calls each month?'

'Well, not all of it is hotel business directly, Miss Griffin. Quite a proportion of it is for guests' telephone calls which we pass on to them in their bills, plus an additional charge to pay for our switchboard operator's time.'

She felt foolish for not knowing. She hadn't realised that because she'd never studied a bill when staying in a hotel herself. All she'd done on booking out was to endorse it and the account had then been forwarded on to her father's office for settlement. She signed the cheques and handed them back to Mr Vickers. 'Anything else I can do for you?'

'Well, I was wondering how matters were progressing towards finding a replacement for Miss Stephens when she leaves us in two weeks' time to get married? Before Captain Fosedyke had his unfortunate attack, he informed me he had whittled down the applicants to the last two. He had interviewed one he wasn't that impressed with but was hopeful a Mrs Driffield was going to fit the bill. He was seeing her, I understand, on the day he took ill.'

The woman Connie had mistaken for herself, Eddie was reminded. It was really coming home to her that the hotel manager had a lot to deal with during the course of any working day. She looked at Mr Vickers thoughtfully. Obviously replacing his accounts clerk was very important to him and would keep the work his department handled flowing smoothly. If bills weren't paid, services could not be supplied to enable them to cater for guests. Mr Sopworth would hopefully be fully recovered from his own illness by tomorrow but whether he was able to give this matter his urgent attention with so much else outstanding was doubtful. To Eddie it made sense that Mr Vickers should take over the employment of a replacement clerk himself as he was the one who was going to be working with the successful applicant.

She relayed her thoughts to him and he looked pleased to be given this new authority and hurried away to deal with it.

Eddie felt satisfied that she had resolved this situation by using her own common sense, and as a result eased the assistant manager's workload just a little. It made her feel she had contributed to the running of the hotel in some way.

She sat for a while wondering what to do with herself now her plan for learning the business faced a setback.

She supposed she could have a walk around the hotel to check if everything was in order, but then she wouldn't actually know if it was, would she? She'd just have to hope no problems were experienced by the staff today that needed management decisions.

She got up and made her way to the office door, looking out into the foyer. A handful of guests were visible but nowhere near as many as she felt there should be. This meant the lowering of the tariff was not as yet showing the results she had hoped it would, but maybe she was expecting too much too soon.

The hotels she herself had stayed in usually had foyers buzzing with a constant stream of people coming and going, an army of staff continually catering to their needs. Its rooms fully booked way ahead, the Connaught should be turning away people, not desperate to find ways of enticing them through its doors. She was in no doubt that her plans for redecoration, along with the restaurant changes, would have done much towards enhancing its appeal. Well, maybe the redecorations could not take place as matters stood at the moment but certainly the changes to the menu could be implemented. If she had found any need to address Jess her cook over a matter to do with the preparation of a meal or a dinner party she was arranging, she would have paid a visit to the kitchen to talk to her about it. She didn't need the assistant manager to arrange for the Head Chef to come and see her, she could go and see him. She was keen to view the kitchen that catered for the guests and introduce herself to the staff who worked in it. As yet she hadn't done so and her need to see the Head Chef was a good opportunity. It was now a quarter to eleven so Chef would be on shift.

Entering the double swing doors that led inside the kitchen, Eddie stopped short on seeing the scene that greeted her. Four young men were beavering away at separate long wooden tables, in the process of preparing food. A kitchen assistant, her back to Eddie, stood at the huge sink over on the other side of the room, up to her elbows in sudsy water, washing up a pile of dirty dishes. Another kitchen assistant was coming out of a door at the side which seemed to be the dry store, carrying a huge sack of flour. Eddie's attention, though, was riveted on the huge man stomping around, arms flailing wildly, screaming out abuse. If this wasn't shocking enough to her, she flinched in further shock as he stopped by one of the young men to slap him around the back of his head and bellow, 'How many times have I told you, you stupid fucking idiot, to use the margarine for the roux and not best butter?'

Cowering, the young man spluttered, 'But, Chef, it ain't right . . .'

'Don't you questions my orders or I'll have you out of here so quick yer feet won't touch the floor *and* I'll make it my business to see no other kitchen takes you on, so any hope you've nursed of qualifying as a chef, you can forget. Now put that butter back . . .' He suddenly stopped his tirade, sensing Eddie's presence, and turned his head to glare across at her. 'And what the hell are *you* doing in my kitchen? Get out!'

Eddie stared back at him, astounded. Apart from the fact that she was appalled at his treatment of the staff, she had never been spoken to in this way by anyone and did not appreciate his manner towards her. 'I don't appreciate your attitude . . .'

Before she could finish Gordon Stimpson shouted, 'And I don't appreciate *you* being in *my* kitchen without me inviting you. I don't know who the hell you are or what yer doing here, and I don't give a damn. Now, get out!'

Eddie realised all the staff had stopped work and were looking across at her. Humiliation flooded through her. She made to turn and flee this awful situation, and especially this odious man, when suddenly it struck her that as the owner of the hotel this was her kitchen, not Chef's, and she had every right to be inside it should she choose to be. She had known Jess felt the kitchen back at the family house to be her domain but she had always treated Eddie with the greatest of respect and made her feel welcome should she pay a visit. This appalling man could at least have afforded her the courtesy of asking who she was and what business she had in the kitchen, and then if it was deemed unfitting she should be there, ask her politely to leave.

Her face tight, she said, 'If you would allow me to introduce myself? I am Miss Griffin, the owner of this hotel.'

His fat-lipped mouth snapping shut, he stared unblinkingly back at her. So this was the female owner he'd heard about, was it, the one who'd suddenly decided to show an interest in her hotel? He'd worked here for nearly twenty years and never known the owner even poke her nose through the front door in all that time. Why the sudden interest now? She was a good-looking piece, he'd give her that, but if she thought that just because she was the owner it gave her *carte blanche* to enter his domain whenever she felt like it then she had another think coming.

'Nice to meet you. Well, now yer've seen all yer want to see, if yer don't mind we're trying to prepare the lunches,' he said dismissively. Just then the back door opened and an older woman bustled in. Chef immediately spun round to face her and yelled across, 'You needn't think *you're* getting any help today 'cos I've got things I need Denby to do for me.'

Gertrude Braddock's face was instantly wreathed in anger. 'You know I can't make all the cakes and buns for the high teas *and* prepare the puddings for the evening meals by meself. Denby is my assistant, you've no right to keep commandeering her. Why do you need extra help anyway? It ain't like yer run off yer feet, the meals going out this kitchen ain't half what they used to be. You just like to make my life as difficult as you can because you're a nasty piece of work, that's what you are, Chef Stimpson.

'Well, Denby's working for me today, whether you like it or not. If you don't watch out I'll go and see the owner now she's on the premises, have a word with her about you. And I'll mek sure she listens to me, which I'm sure she will 'cos I've heard she's a nice woman.' She suddenly sensed Eddie's presence and looked across at her. 'Hello, me duck, was there something yer wanted? Guests ain't allowed in the kitchen, yer know.' And she added scathingly, 'Chef's orders.'

Gordon Stimpson swung around to face Eddie, his face showing disbelief that she was still here. 'She's already been told that no one but kitchen staff is allowed in *my* kitchen, without *my* say so, so if yer don't mind, Miss Griffin, I asked yer to leave,' he shouted.

Eddie's hackles rose then. She put up her chin and said, 'I do mind. I should remind you, Chef Stimpson, that this is *my* kitchen and it is I *myself* and not *you* who says who is allowed inside it. I wish to speak to you, *now*.'

He seemed utterly amazed that she'd dared to challenge him and Eddie could see he was fighting to control another eruption of ill temper. 'Get back to work, the lot of you,' he barked at his staff before coming over to join her. 'Look, I'm sorry, Miss Griffin, yer just caught me at a bad time. I have me work cut out trying to get this lot to meet my high standards. What did you want to see me for?' he asked through clenched teeth.

'I'm not happy with the menu.'

'Not happy? What do you mean, yer not happy with it?'

'I feel we don't offer enough choice. I would like you to come up with suggestions for additional dishes. I'd like us to offer at least five, preferably six, choices at each sitting.'

He was looking stunned. Offering extra choice would mean so much more work on his part and he was happy with the way things were. But most importantly the offering of extra dishes would require him to produce things he was not properly trained to cook with his limited culinary skills. If this woman was expecting anything more involved than roast meat and boiled vegetables, basic soups and sauces, to hell with her. The Captain had told him he was instigating the broadening of the menu after food restrictions were finally lifted after the war and many more ingredients became readily available. Thankfully for Chef that initiative had never been given the go ahead by the owners, for whatever reason, so his fears at that time of being shown up proved groundless.

This woman, though, was the owner and therefore in a position to sanction what she was asking him to do. She could actually sack him if he appeared to refuse, and he didn't like the thought of that. Another place of work might not bring with it the nice little sideline he had going for himself here. Then a thought struck him and a sly smile quirked his lips. Before, when the Captain had approached him with a similar proposal, he hadn't had a talented commis like Neal Richmond working for him. Richmond could come up with some ideas for new dishes *and* cook them all if he wanted to keep his job, which Chef was positive the lad did or he'd have left long ago. Miss Griffin herself would be under the impression it was all his work and he'd get the recognition, and maybe even a pay rise.

'I'll get on to it, Miss Griffin. Oh, er . . . and maybe in future you could warn me about any visit to the kitchen so I can make sure I'm available to deal with whatever yer need me for.'

'I'll make sure I do, Chef. May I expect your suggestions this afternoon?'

'I'll see what I can do.' There was a hint of defiance in his voice.

Eddie returned to her office, smarting at the man's offhand manner. There had been nothing in the least engaging about him and she didn't like the thought of him working in her hotel and dealing roughly with her staff. This was a matter she would place high on her agenda to speak to Captain Fosedyke about on his return. The Chef and head receptionist would make a good pair, she thought. Still, the implementation of the enhanced menu was underway and that was what was most important to her.

The telephone rang as soon as she entered the office and she hurried around the desk to seat herself and answer it. Minutes later she replaced the receiver and gave a deep sigh. The caller had been Mr Froggitt, the estate agent, to inform her that matters regarding the sale of the house had progressed swiftly and by the middle of next week they would be in a position to finalise the transaction via the solicitor he himself had instructed to work on Eddie's behalf. She felt she should be gratified that at least the fraudulent mortgage and outstanding debts Stibley had left them with could be settled and her father's good name restored, but that didn't stop her feeling sad that the house that had belonged to her grandparents, then her own mother and father, and been her own home all her life, would now be lost to her for ever.

Her head drooped. She felt it was incredible that only a matter of a week or so ago she had been living a carefree lifestyle, adequate finances at her disposal to do whatever the fancy took her. Her father had been able to spend his day doing what entertained him – his twice-weekly round of golf with his long-standing friend Harvey; a visit once or twice a week to his gentlemen's club; the long solitary reading sessions he seemed to enjoy so much studying the array of topics he found of interest; his monthly trip to the office in town to confirm his business interests were indeed running as smoothly and as profitably as his office manager had fooled him into believing they were. She and her father had been totally oblivious to the dreadful revelations looming over them.

'Oh, darling, you look as gloomy as I feel,' a voice broke into her thoughts. 'Be a dear and order me a large gin and tonic as I most certainly need one. And I think you ought to have one yourself, judging by the look on your face.'

Eddie's head jerked up in surprise. 'Phee!' she exclaimed. Then her face broke into a broad smile and she jumped up from her chair to run around the desk and hug her friend fiercely. 'Oh, Phee, how wonderful to see you.'

'I'm glad someone is pleased to see me,' she said, returning her friend's embrace. 'Father certainly wasn't.'

Eddie pulled back and looked at her quizzically. 'You're supposed to be in France. I wasn't expecting to see you for another three weeks at least.'

'Neither was Father.' Sophia undid her sable coat and sat down sedately in a chair before crossing her legs. 'Oh, you should have heard him go on when I arrived back late last night! I eventually made my escape to bed, thinking he'd be better disposed in the morning to appreciate why I couldn't stay in France any longer, but I was mistaken. As soon as I arrived down for breakfast he started on again, and Mummy wasn't any help as she was as displeased to see me back as Daddy, only not for the same reason.

'He didn't like the thought that he was paying for staff to look after us but we weren't there so they were idling around with nothing to do. And Mummy was wild because she was feeling so much better after her bout of flu she'd decided to come out and join Geraldine and me because Daddy, it seemed, was paying her absolutely no attention through the murder trial taking up so much of his time, and Mummy's lover is away himself at the moment, holidaying with his own family, so she was at a loose end and . . . well, anyway, they were both getting at me so I've left them to it and came to see you. Hopefully when I get back later they'll have something else to distract them.'

'Why did you cut your stay short?' Eddie asked her.

'Because I just couldn't put up with that little madam's attitude any longer.'

'The little madam you're referring to I take to be Geraldine?' said Eddie, going around the desk to resume her seat.

'Who else? It was quite apparent she didn't want to go on holiday with me and she acted most disagreeably from the moment we set off. After three days of looking at her miserable face and her not talking to me at all, most of the time with her nose in a book, I'd had enough and made arrangements to return home. When I told her to go and ask the maid to repack our things, that was the first time I saw a hint of a smile. I have to say, I wasn't particularly enjoying being there myself. None of the usual crowd I mix with were in residence this year, though where on earth they have all gone to I've yet to find out, so no promise of any parties or social events whatsoever. To top it all the weather was appalling. It rained for the first two days, and yesterday I woke up to find it overcast so one couldn't even take the sun by the pool.'

'But the weather would probably have picked up, Phee.'

'Most probably, darling, but Geraldine's sulky mood didn't look like it would and I wasn't prepared to put up with it any longer. It will be a long time before I agree to spend time in my daughter's company again. I don't know where she gets her selfish streak from, I really don't. It has to be from her father's side. Is that gin and tonic on its way, Eddie dear?'

'It's a bit early in the day for alcohol, Phee, even for you. I'll order us a pot of coffee.' Ignoring the look on her friend's face, she picked up the telephone and dialled the room service number. When they eventually answered she placed her order and replaced the telephone receiver. 'The coffee is on its way. So where is Geraldine now?'

'Where she always wanted to be and that's staying with her friend on her father's boat on the Norfolk broads. This friend has a brother a little older than herself and Geraldine, I understand. Need I say more, Eddie dear?'

She smiled. 'No, I get the picture.'

'So,' said Phee, looking at her keenly, 'I thought you and I could go and spend a few days in London. Stay at the Strand Palace, take in a couple of shows, do a spot of shopping. Henry Greenwood is throwing a party for his daughter's birthday and absolutely everyone is going. I had thought I'd miss it because of the France thing but now we can go, can't we? It'll be such fun, darling. Go and throw a few clothes in a suit-case and we can take a taxi to fetch my things then catch the one-ten train, be in London about four and on the town at seven!'

Eddie was looking at her, astounded. 'Phee, have you forgotten the small matter that I'm broke?'

'What? Oh, that, yes, it had slipped my mind. But don't worry, darling, I'll just charge everything to Daddy's account so the trip will be my treat.'

And Phee's father would be delighted when the bills come in, thought Eddie. 'Phee, you've obviously for-gotten I have a hotel to start learning to run.'

'Start learning to run? What on earth are you talking about? I thought it was just your father that's deranged at the moment. Have you forgotten you've staff to run the place for you and you're just overseeing the renova-tions? They don't need much overseeing anyway. You give the workmen your instructions, and a few days later you inspect the work in progress to check they're carrying it out to your satisfaction. If not you give them hell until they do do things the way you want them doing. How much of your day does that take up?'

Eddie realised then that there was much she needed to bring Phee up to date with that had transpired during the four days she had been away. She proceeded to tell her friend.

When she had finished Phee looked at her, stunned. 'Goodness me, darling, you have been through the wars. As if you hadn't gone through enough already before I went away. I'm so sorry to hear there is no change in your dear father. I'm sure he'll wake up one morning quite soon and his memory will be quite restored. Mind you, in *Random Harvest* Ronald Colman lost his memory in an accident and it took him absolutely *years* to regain it, and during all that time his poor wife ... played by Greer Garson, such a beautiful woman I've always thought. I do rather resemble her, don't you think, Eddie? ... Anyway, he had no recollection of his wife at all, and the poor dear had to pretend she was just his secretary so as to be near him. I can't remember how he regained his memory now. Oh, goodness me, don't tell me I'm losing mine? Yes, I remember now ... it was something to do with returning to a house he and his wife had lived in before he'd lost his memory and as he walked through the gate it all suddenly came back to him and then he and his wife lived happily ever after.

'That's what will happen to your father, darling, trust me. He'll wake one morning shortly and be back to normal, you'll see.' Without pausing for breath Phee continued, 'Oh, darling, what bad luck that some nasty little thieves should steal all your house contents from under your nose! Some cheek, you have to admit? Oh, but that really has put paid to your plans to do up this place. And it needs a spruce up quite badly, darling, doesn't it?' she added tactlessly. 'The boiler is about to blow up you say and other urgent repairs need doing ... Do you really think lowering the prices of the rooms and putting more choices on the menu are going to have much impact, darling?'

'I have to try something, Phee.'

She pulled a thoughtful face. 'Yes, I suppose you do.'

Eddie sighed deeply. 'Oh, Phee, I am so disappointed

I haven't the means to start redecorating. I know that would have done a lot towards getting this place back on its feet and earning properly.'

Phee looked at her. 'Well, how long is it all going to take, do you think, for you to learn to run the business then get it earning money for you? I want you back with me again. I mean, it is rather exciting having a friend who owns a hotel, but not if she's no time to come shopping with me, or to go to parties, or do anything we used to do together, in fact.'

'Oh, Phee, how should I know how long this will all take? I wouldn't bank on it being very soon.'

'Oh, really? Oh, dear, what will I do with myself? I have other friends, of course, but one's best friend is rather special. They understand one, if you know what I mean.' She looked deeply thoughtful for several moments, then picked up her handbag, uncrossed her legs and stood up.

'Where are you going?' Eddie asked her. 'The coffee should be here any minute.'

'Sorry? Oh, I've no time for coffee, darling, I've something to do. I'll be back later.'

With that she abruptly hurried out. Eddie stared after her, wondering what she had suddenly remembered she needed to do, considering she had been prepared to go off to London at a moment's notice should Eddie have been in a position to accompany her. The waitress then arrived bearing a tray of coffee for two. Eddie thought she might as well enjoy it.

Having drank three cups and eaten several biscuits she leaned back in her chair and closed her eyes to allow herself to think clearly without any distractions.

She really needed to come up with more ways to bring guests through the doors or getting the Connaught back on its feet could take for ever. No fresh ideas came to her, though. Then it seemed as if maybe what she was proposing to do was futile, and instead of putting herself through the agonies of trying to make this hotel profitable again she should cut her losses now and admit defeat. Harvey would still help her sell the place if she asked him, she knew he would. Her shoulders sagged despairingly as she felt everything close in on her. She saw her father, years ahead, trying to live on their dwindling resources. The next thing she knew someone was shaking her and she opened her eyes to find Phee staring down at her.

'I do believe you were asleep, darling. Never mind, you're awake now. You remember Giles Arbuthnot, don't you, Eddie dear? Yes, of course you do, you met at the Arklands' garden party ... oh, I don't know when. Times flies, doesn't it, dear, but a few years ago. It was at the Arklands' garden party, wasn't it, Giles, that we met?'

Eddie then realised her friend had brought someone with her and looked across to see a short, unremarkable-looking, middle-aged man standing before her desk. His face was familiar though Eddie couldn't quite place him. Phee was standing next to him, her arm hooked through his. She was inches taller than him, and much to Eddie's shock was gazing down at him adoringly.

'Whenever you say we met then that's when it was, my sweet,' he said to her, picking up her hand to kiss it.

Phee beamed broadly at Eddie. 'It's an amazing

coincidence, darling, but Giles is the owner of several companies and one of them, can you believe it, is an interior design service. Well, as you have a little job you need doing, and as Giles's company is in the business of undertaking such little jobs, I thought, why not reacquaint you two? Giles darling, why don't you go and have a look around while I have a quick word with Eddie? You know, women's talk, and I would so hate to bore you.'

He patted her hand, reached up and pecked her cheek. 'Don't you be long now, sweetness, because I'll miss you.'

She blew him a kiss. 'No more than two minutes, I promise. Now, shoo! Off you go.'

'Phee, what's going on?' Eddie demanded as soon as Giles was out of the door and earshot.

'Well, it's obvious, darling. You need a job doing and Giles is in a position to do it.'

Eddie stared at her friend in amazement. 'Have you gone totally mad, Phee? I have no money to pay for the work.'

'Oh, darling, don't worry about that. How much can a few pots of paint cost? Anyway, Giles is absolutely loaded and can afford to wait. I've told him your situation and he's happy to help out a friend of mine. If you're that bothered about it, just bung him a few quid now and again and pay it all off when your new guests start piling in. I'm sure when the place has been done up the bank will see what a good investment the hotel is and advance you a loan against it. You said yourself that a revamp would do marvels for getting punters inside the doors.

'Anyway, darling, Giles won't badger you for money, not while I'm keeping him sweet he won't. He won't risk upsetting my dearest friend, which of course would upset me. He wouldn't want to do that, I can assure you. The man is besotted by me and has been for years. I've lost count of the times he's begged me to marry him. Every time I bump into him, in fact.'

'Oh, Phee, you've agreed to go out with him just to get him to redecorate my hotel. That's what you've done, isn't it? Oh, but I remember Giles now and it wasn't at the Arklands' garden party we met him, it was at a Christmas ball at the Grand about twenty years ago. He plagued you all night to have a dance with him and you refused him each time he asked and were quite rude to him, I remember. You told me you couldn't stand the man. Said he bored you silly. Told me he reminded you of a Toby jug. You said you wouldn't entertain him if he was the last man on earth. I can't let you do this, Phee. It isn't fair to Giles for a start.'

'You can't stop me, darling. One has to make sacrifices for one's friends, Eddie dear, and I know perfectly well you would do the same for me if I was in need. If getting this place looking splendid again stops you from wearing that worried frown and frees you up to accompany me for some of the things we used to do together, then it's well worth the few weeks I'll have to play love birds with Giles. I can assure you he isn't complaining, and neither am I. Giles is fine as someone to take me out while there's no other man on the scene.'

This was the answer to Eddie's prayers. It was the

miracle she had been praying for. She was in no position to turn down such an offer. It didn't look like Phee was going to give her a choice anyway. 'Oh, Phee, I don't know how to thank you for doing this for me.'

'Actually, darling, it's not just for you, I'm doing this for Giles too. My agreeing to let him court me will make him realise I'm absolutely the wrong woman for him. Then he'll become unbesotted with me and go off and find himself the right woman, settle down and have a dozen children and live happily ever after! So come along and let's give him an idea what we want this place to look like once it's all finished, and hear what suggestions he has. Then he can get on with organising his men to do it all, but more importantly you and I can go out somewhere together tonight. Oh, no, not tonight as I promised Giles I'll have dinner with him. Oh, what a bore. But never mind, it's all in a good cause. I feel as if I'm doing charity work. Goodness, I nearly forgot.' She opened her handbag and pulled out a bulky envelope which she thrust at Eddie. 'This should help get you a new boiler. Of course, I've no idea how much one costs so I took a stab in the air about how much money to ask for, but hopefully there'll be enough left over to do some more of the urgent repairs.'

Mystified, Eddie opened the envelope and gazed at the bundle of notes inside. 'My God, Phee, how much is there here?'

'Five thousand.'

'What? How on earth did you lay your hands on this amount? It's a fortune, Phee.'

'Hardly a fortune, darling. Although I wouldn't say

no to having it in my purse while wandering around Harrods. Mummy gave it to me.'

'Your mother *gave* it you?'

'Yes, she did. With just a little persuasion on my part. I told her I needed some of my inheritance now as I'd got myself into a little spot of bother over a gambling debt. Rather inventive of me, don't you think, Eddie, considering the only gamble I ever take is a small wager on Ladies Day at Ascot? I'd sooner line the pockets of the owners of Liberty or Selfridges than the pockets of the bookmakers. Anyway, I told Mummy I had learned my lesson and would never gamble again, but if my debt wasn't paid by today then it would be a funeral she'd be stumping up for so either way she'd need to hand the money over. I said that was the real reason I'd returned from France. I'd thought by going I could escape my debt here, but then I realised that the people I owed the money to would involve Daddy as they knew who I was and where I lived. Daddy's reputation was bound to suffer and that wasn't fair of me so I came back to face the music.'

Eddie was staring at her, stupefied. 'And your mother believed you?'

'Well, obviously, dear, you have the evidence in your hands. Take that worried expression off your face, Eddie. Five thousand is nothing to Mummy, Grandmother left her oodles. My grandfather was *the* Mr Pickles of Pickles Ointments, have you forgotten, darling? Grandmother spent all her married life looking after Grandfather who worked twenty-four hours a day and never took her anywhere, so when he died she sold the business for a fortune and was determined to have a bloody good time in her dotage. She travelled all over the world, staying in the best places, but there was still plenty of money left to leave to Mummy when she passed on. So she doesn't need Daddy's money, she's plenty of her own.'

'Well then, why does your mother stay with your father? I mean, she's always got a lover according to you and . . .'

'Oh, darling, Mummy loves him,' Phee cut in. 'The lovers she takes are just a distraction to keep her occupied during the times he's so busy with his work he forgets to pay her any attention. Just like my grandmother loved my grandfather and why she put up with him for all those years of being hardly more than a housekeeper to him. Unlike Mummy, Grandmother would never have dreamed of taking a lover while my grandfather was alive to ease her boredom, but she certainly did after he died – and she was seventy-five when she became a widow!

'Now put that money away safely, dear, and let's go and find Giles. I need to keep him champing at the bit until this place is all spick and span again.'

CHAPTER TWENTY-ONE

Connie had a wonderful day off with her family. In an effort to settle her sister back home and ease the trauma of Johnny's betrayal of her, Connie and her mother had persuaded Babsy to accompany them to town to have a browse around the shops. Connie gave her sister credit for outwardly seeming to enjoy their excursion, playing along with her mother and sister by mentally spending a fortune on unaffordable items that caught their eye. Inwardly Connie knew it would take a while for Babsy to get over the man she had naively thought herself in love with. Connie did know, though, that this incident had brought home to her sister just how precious the love of a good family was, and that she would not be so quick in future to enter into risky relationships.

Babsy's main worry now was that she had no proper friends and no job. She proclaimed that she wanted a change, to do something different from factory work, something that would engross her like Connie's job did her, but she had no idea what to try next. Connie and her mother had told her not to worry, something would present itself, and they would do their best to help her find something that interested her. Inwardly they both believed this was a tall order as Babsy hadn't really shown a leaning towards anything in particular. But a good job would help take her mind off her mistake, afford her new acquaintances who would hopefully become friends, open new doors leading away from undesirable people she had become involved with.

Connie was so enjoying her time with her family that she left it until the last possible minute to return to her room and it was one minute to ten-thirty when she went racing around the back of the Connaught to let herself in by the staff entrance before Harry Glebe locked up for the night. To her dismay she found the door firmly shut. Harry must either have locked up early or else her Timex watch was slow. She stood in the gloom of the yard and wondered what on earth she should do now? There was no room-mate to look out for her as yet. Regardless she tried the room service kitchen window and, although disappointed, wasn't surprised to find it firmly secured. She supposed the only option she had was to go around to the front entrance and hope she could catch the night porter's attention, if he was there and not walking around the hotel as he did several times a night to check all was well.

As she made to retrace her steps around the building, she noticed one of the two large sashed kitchen windows and stopped to look at it. Was it latched? It was very unlikely that the kitchen staff had neglected to secure it but worth a few seconds out of her way to try.

On closer examination, Connie spotted a small gap at the bottom of one of the windows. She couldn't believe her luck. Lifting her eyes skywards she whispered, 'Thank you, Lord.' All she had to do now was heave up the heavy frame enough for her to climb through and she was home and dry. That, though, was harder than it seemed. The window was a huge one, so the bottom sash would be very heavy, and the sill was at least five feet from ground level which meant she would need something to stand on so as to be able to get her hands inside the gap and use all her strength to push the bottom sash up.

Scouting around, Connie found a stack of empty wooden beer crates stacked ready for collection by the brewery. With one upturned crate positioned under the window, she clambered on to it. Thankfully she was high enough to tackle her task. Handbag in the crook of her elbow, she eased her upturned palms through the gap and heaved upwards with all her might. Time had warped the frame and opening it was not a noiseless operation. Connie cringed as the window groaned and juddered upwards, hoping she wouldn't attract anyone's attention. Finally the gap was wide enough for her to get through.

Grabbing hold of the inside of the window ledge, she lifted up one leg and swung herself inside, bringing the other up to join it, then manoeuvred herself to stand inside the big pot sink below the window. She then gingerly stood up in the sink and slowly turned around to heave down the bottom sash and fasten it. That done, she lowered one leg down on to the floor. That foot now on solid ground, she made to lift the other out of the sink but it wouldn't budge. The heel of her shoe had somehow wedged itself tightly inside the plug hole. Despite Connie's efforts to free it, it was stuck fast. With one leg on the floor and the other bent inside the sink, it was impossible for her to ease her foot out of her shoe and free herself.

'Oh, God,' she groaned aloud. What on earth was she going to do? She couldn't stay like this all night until the breakfast staff came on at six and helped release her. There was no point in screaming for help either because Harry Glebe would never hear her cries from this distance away.

Suddenly she heard a sound nearby and stiffened. Someone else was in the kitchen. Her heart thudded. She tried to turn her head and falteringly called out, 'Who . . . Who's there?' Then froze in mortal fear as she realised someone was moving towards her. 'I said, who's there?' she cried again.

'Shush, Connie,' a voice whispered back. 'It's me, Neal Richmond.'

She could see his dark outline beside her. 'What . . . what are you doing here at this time of night?'

'Let's get you out of your predicament first. Put your arm around my shoulder,' he ordered her. She did as he told her and, supported by his weight, felt one of his hands on her ankle, the other around the heel of her shoe. 'Right, now try to ease your foot out of your shoe,' he instructed her.

Aided by Neal she was able to wiggle her foot until it slid out of her shoe and then lift her leg over the side of the deep sink. Neal twisted her shoe about in the plug hole until the heel came free and then handed her shoe to her.

'Thanks,' said Connie off-handedly, embarrassed that this man had found her in such a compromising situation while at the same time mortally relieved he had come to her rescue. Slipping on her shoe, she straightened up to look at him quizzically. 'What are you doing in the kitchen at this time of night?'

'You should just be glad I was,' he replied evasively. 'I take it you arrived back late, found yourself locked out and noticed the kitchen window hadn't been shut properly? You could have done yourself serious damage if you'd slipped,' he said as if he was really concerned for her.

'Well, thankfully I didn't,' she replied, more snappily than she meant to. She shivered and glanced hurriedly around. The kitchen equipment hanging from its hooks appeared slightly threatening, and long shadows cast by the weak moonlight shining through the windows gave the whole place an eerie atmosphere. She eyed Neal suspiciously. 'Why exactly are you in the kitchen at this time of night, Mr Richmond?'

'Just . . . er . . . making myself a cuppa.'

'In the dark? And usually we use the room service kitchen for that.'

He stared at her. Since their last embarrassing meeting he had been dreading bumping into her again but at the same time desperately hoping he would so he could make some sort of amends for his thoughtless remark. He still had the strong feeling Connie was his sort of woman and a possible future lay in store for them, provided of course she was attracted to him in the same way he was to her. Despite the dimness of the kitchen he could tell her eyes held suspicion. If he was not truthful with her as to his reason for being in this particular part of the hotel so late he knew she would think him up to no good, and her opinion of him sink even lower.

As Connie stood waiting for his answer, the thrill that had shot through her on first meeting this man was rekindled. She quickly reminded herself of his reaction when Harry had teased him about fancying her. Well, he might not be attracted towards her but that didn't stop her feeling drawn to him, though she'd rather there was a plausible explanation for his presence here and not the shady one she suspected.

She heard him take a deep breath and say, 'I'm here at this time of night because I'm keeping watch. Have been for the last couple of nights, in fact. I'm hoping tonight's the night. It's no fun hiding in the dark for hours on end, worried someone like Harry Glebe might catch me and demand to know what I'm doing.'

She frowned quizzically. 'Watching for what?'

He took another deep breath. 'Because I think . . . well, not think, I *know* the Head Chef is thieving on a grand scale and I was hoping to catch him at it. Then I could do a deal with him, get him to stop making the kitchen staff's lives a misery by threatening to expose him if he didn't agree to my proposition.

'Okay, I know resorting to blackmail isn't exactly the right thing to do, but neither is the way he's getting away with treating us. I'm not bothered for myself, I can put up with his abuse for another couple of months until I can qualify, but I don't like the thought of leaving my colleagues behind to face what he dishes out to them each day.'

Neal Richmond was clearly a good man and Connie felt it was a great pity he didn't have a fancy for her as she really would like to have got to know him better. He had just told her he would be leaving soon so there was no hope for them anyway. It was a coincidence, though, that he should have his suspicions about his boss while she had similar ones about the assistant manager.

'May I ask how you came to suspect Chef was up to no good?' she asked Neal.

'Well, I'd have to be stupid not to realise that the amount of food that comes into this kitchen doesn't all go out on the guests' plates, and neither is all that's over sold as pig swill or thrown away. Besides, when I was cleaning out the dry store the other morning a man came to the kitchen door and asked for Chef. When I said he wasn't on shift yet the caller said something about having an arrangement to meet him that night about twelve but wanting to change their arrangement for the next night instead. Tradesmen don't call at night, do they? Well, not normal tradesmen. It was obvious to me the business this man was referring to must be underhand dealings between him and Chef. Why are you asking anyway?'

'Oh, well . . . it could be something and nothing but I have a feeling the assistant manager's up to no good too.'

'Oh! And what makes you think that?'

'Well, it's not much to go on, I admit, but there was a peculiar incident the other day over a missing vacuum cleaner. I swear blind I saw Mr Sopworth with it but he made me look an idiot by denying he'd ever been in possession of a vacuum. I know the cleaner who's responsible for it is really worried she'll be blamed.

'Then another time I was having five minutes' fresh air sitting in the hole in the wall behind the dustbins when I saw Mr Sopworth come out of the staff entrance carrying a heavy box. He locked it inside one of the store rooms and was going about it very suspiciously – you know, looking around to see if anyone was watching him, that sort of thing. I suppose it could all have been perfectly innocent but somehow I don't think so. I couldn't check what was in the box to satisfy my curiosity because he locked up the store room after him.'

Neal frowned thoughtfully. 'Oh, I see. Not much to go on, I agree, but enough to have you bothered all the same.'

Connie pulled a face. 'If both Chef and Mr Sopworth are stealing hotel property it's not fair on Miss Griffin, is it? It's her they're stealing from. And it's not fair on the rest of us staff either. If the management is aware that something underhand is going on but is not sure who's doing it, that means we're all under suspicion. Even if it turns out that Mr Sopworth is innocent, you still know Chef is a thief. It's your duty to put a stop to his stealing.'

Neal looked at her hard then nodded. 'Yes, you're right. But I'm still not happy about reporting a fellow worker to the boss and him probably landing in jail, no matter how much I detest that colleague.'

Connie pulled a face too. 'Neither am I, not at all, so let's hope a threat from us will be enough to put a stop to whatever they're up to.'

'Us?' queried Neal.

'Yes, us. I'm in on this too now. Having two people catch either of them out and threaten to spill the beans unless they quit has more chance of success, don't you think? I'll help you nail Chef and you can help me with Sopworth, 'cos I'm going to be watching him like a hawk from now on. Anyway, I like Miss Griffin. She comes across as being very fair and I don't like to think of her being fleeced.' Connie frowned. 'It's a pity I can't look inside that store room now to see what Mr Sopworth put there. Then I could put my mind at rest about him one way or the other, provided the box is still there, of course, and he's not already got rid of it.' Then a thought struck. 'Oh, maybe I can have a look now without Mr Sopworth or anyone else asking me what I'm up to.'

'How, if the store room's locked?'

'Keys unlock doors, don't they? You lie low in case Chef shows up and . . . well, I hope he doesn't before I get back. Won't be a minute.'

With that she vanished through the service door, leaving Neal staring after, wondering what on earth she was up to.

It was a good five minutes later that Connie stole back into the kitchen and made her way over to him. 'Coast still clear?' she whispered.

'It's been as quiet as a graveyard!'

'Good, 'cos I really want to be here when you catch Chef at it. If he doesn't show tonight, I'll stand guard with you every night until he does. Right, come on,' she urged him.

'Where are we going?' he asked as they arrived at the back door leading into the yard and Connie shot the big bolts to top and bottom and turned the key in the mortice lock.

She clicked her tongue in exasperation. 'To have a look at what's inside that shed, where do you think we're going?' She turned to face him, holding her open palm out towards him.

In the gloom he could just make out the shape of

several long metal keys. 'I take it they're the outside store-room keys? How did you get hold of them?'

'From the cupboard in the manager's office. The keys are all labelled "outside store room" followed by a number one to four. I've no idea what number relates to the store room we're after so I've brought all the keys.'

'Oh, God, Connie, you took a risk! Did Harry Glebe not see you? What excuse would you have had if you'd been caught in the foyer at this time of night, or even worse the manager's office?'

'I'd have thought of something. Anyway, he didn't see me 'cos he was asleep. I was banking on him being engrossed in his newspaper but asleep was even better. Come on, let's get this over with.'

The first two keys they tried did not fit but the third turned easily and they pulled open the door and peered inside.

'I can't see anything, it's too dark. Did you think to bring a torch?' she asked Neal.

'No, I didn't, did you?' he snapped.

Connie shot a look at him. 'I was only asking. There's no need to get shirty. Do you smoke?'

'I hardly think this is the time to have a cigarette . . .'

'I don't smoke,' she interjected. 'I was after a match.'

'Oh, I see,' he cut in, delving inside his trouser pocket. Pulling out a petrol lighter, he flicked his thumb on the igniting wheel. A flame flared and, holding the lighter out in front of him, he stepped inside the store room and glanced around in the gloom. 'Is this the box you were on about?' he whispered across to Connie.

Stepping inside the store room, she peered down to look at it. 'Yes, I think it is. I wonder what's in these others at the side of it?' she said, noticing another three stacked close by.

'Is this your missing vacuum?' Neal asked her, the flame from the lighter now illuminating it. 'In fact, there are two vacuums,' he added, noticing another.

Connie squatted by the boxes. 'Can you put the lighter down here?'

He did as she asked.

Opening the first box, she gasped when she saw the contents. 'It's bottles of spirits.' She quickly opened the other three. One contained a dozen bottles of wine; another bottles of cleaning fluids; the largest box of the lot an assortment of items including several silver-topped salt cellars and matching pepper pots, three silver-plated Georgian-style coffee pots, matching milk jugs and sugar basins along with silver serving trays.

Closing up the boxes, Connie straightened up. 'Been very busy it seems has Mr Sopworth. I'm no expert but this lot altogether would fetch a few pounds from the right sort of buyer.'

'Like the bloke who came looking for Chef the other morning?'

'Yes, someone like him.'

'Well, at least you've had your suspicions about the assistant manager confirmed. It's what we do about it that we have to decide now. Let's lock up this room and you get the keys back before Harry Glebe wakes up and awkward questions are asked.' He looked at his watch. 'It's after eleven-thirty. If tonight is the night Chef's arranged to do business again then any time now he could be putting in an appearance. I was hiding in a dark place by the side of the range. I had a good view of practically all the kitchen from there and hopefully no one could see me. That's where I'll hide again. What about you?'

'Mmm,' said Connie distractedly. She'd really hoped she had been wrong in her suspicions of the assistant manager. Now she had the problem of what to do about her discovery. 'Oh, don't worry, I'll find somewhere,' she finally replied.

Having relocked the store room they had just re-entered the kitchen and secured the back door when a sound reached their ears.

'Someone's outside,' Neal urgently whispered, a look of panic on his face.

Then a tap sounded on the kitchen door and a voice whispered, 'You there, Stimpson?'

Neal grabbed hold of Connie's arm and pulled her across into the dark shadows by the wall at the side of the huge range. 'Shush,' he mouthed to her as they both squatted down.

Another tap sounded on the door. 'Oi, Stimpson, you there?' The voice had a hint of agitation to it. 'Fer fuck's sake, where the hell are yer? I ain't got all night.'

Just then one of the double swing doors opened at the other end of the kitchen and someone entered, padded softly to the outer door and turned the key in the lock.

Protected they dearly hoped by the dark shadows, Neal and Connie held their breath, terrified of being discovered. They were both thinking that it was all well and good planning to be detectives, but now they actually were being detectives it was a different matter.

A voice was heard to say, 'Oh, it's you. Where's Stimpson?'

The visitor came inside the kitchen and the outline of two men facing each other could dimly be seen.

'How would I know? I arranged to meet Chef here the same time as you, a quarter to twelve. It ain't quite that time yet but that don't mean we can't get *our* business out of the way.'

Connie recognised the voice as belonging to Sopworth.

'I thought you two was partners?' he was asked by the visitor.

He laughed. 'All's fair in business. Stay there while I bring my stuff over and you can tell me how much you're going to give me for it all. Be advised, I've a figure in mind and I ain't accepting no less.'

'Yeah, well, we'll see what calibre of stuff you've got first.'

'It's quality stuff and you won't be hard up to find buyers for it,' said Sopworth complacently.

Just then the double swing doors were heard to open again and another set of footsteps, heavier this time, were audible. 'Eh, what's going on? I hope you ain't double-crossing me, Sopworth?' hissed the new arrival as he joined the other two. 'We made a deal, we share the proceeds of whatever we accumulate in exchange for me introducing you to my contacts.'

'You've got a suspicious mind, Chef,' said Sopworth to Stimpson. 'I was just going to fetch my stuff so our man here could start assessing the price he's willing to offer us. Why don't you fetch out what you've got and let's be getting this over with,' he said, pulling a set of duplicate keys he'd had cut out of his pocket.

The chef gave a grunt and turned to make his way

over to the cold store. He pulled open the door and disappeared inside.

'What do we do?' Connie mouthed to Neal.

'Wait until they've done the business and the other man has gone then we'll tackle Chef and Sopworth,' he mouthed back.

She nodded in agreement.

Chef returned with a whole side of beef slung over his shoulder. The visitor laughed as Chef slapped the meat down on the table nearest him. 'How the fuck do you get away with covering up that?'

'It's easy when yer know how,' Chef laughed. Then he made his way back to the cold store to return seconds later labouring under the weight of a box. 'A round of Cheddar, two-pound block of best butter, a cooked ham, assorted joints of meat and a couple of fresh chickens.' Putting the box on the table, he disappeared inside the dry store room.

Meanwhile Sopworth had brought into the kitchen the two vacuum cleaners and two of the boxes from the store room Connie and Neal had found. He had gone out again to fetch in the last box when Chef returned with a sack of flour, sack of sugar, and catering-sized boxes of tea and coffee.

'Right, what's yer verdict?' he asked.

'Twenty quid the lot.'

'Twenty quid?' whined a dismayed Sopworth. 'Weren't worth all our trouble for a tenner each.'

'Fuck off!' spat Chef at the man. 'If yer think yer getting all this lot for twenty quid, yer can think again. The side of beef on its own's worth a tenner. The drink too. Those silver coffee pots you'd get three or four pounds each for, a fiver with matching milk jug and sugar bowl. Them vacuums are worth ... what ... twenty quid each at least.'

'Why do you need me to sell them on for you then if you could get that much yerself?'

Chef grabbed hold of the fence's lapels and pulled him up until his feet barely touched the floor. 'Just offer us a reasonable price, yer thieving bastard.' Then he let go of the man who stumbled backwards and fought to right himself and keep his dignity. 'No need to get violent, Chef, just passing a comment,' he blurted, straightening his shabby suit. 'Thirty-five and that's yer lot.'

'Forty-five and yer've a deal,' Chef responded.

The man gave a disdainful sniff. 'Yer drive a hard bargain. Okay, forty. And that's me final offer.'

Chef spat on his hand and held it out to the other man who reluctantly shook it. 'Another meet in a week,' said Chef. 'Same time, same place. Can't promise what we'll have between us but you can rest easy we'll mek it worth yer trouble.'

'Er ... well, yer can count me out,' said Sopworth. 'I'm leaving tonight once I've got me money.'

Chef spun round to face him. 'Yer leaving? But we've got a nice little earner going here. I can manage without yer, like I did before yer came to work here, but we make extra with what you can get hold of that I can't.'

'Yeah, well, it's time for me to move on and what I've made tonight will help keep me for a while,' said Sopworth evasively. 'So if I can have me share, I'd appreciate it,' he said, holding out his hand.

Connie's rage had been mounting to a head while she watched the scene being played out before her. On hearing Sopworth's announcement it spilled over. Before Neal could stop her she'd jumped up, shouting, 'You're not going anywhere, Mr Sopworth! That stuff isn't yours to sell and you're going to put it all back!'

The three men spun round to face her, shock on their faces.

'What the fuck . . .' cried Chef.

'What are you doing here?' spat Sopworth.

'What's going on?' their stupefied accomplice demanded.

Neal, stunned senseless by Connie's unexpected action, hurriedly gathered his wits and came to join her. 'You heard the lady. This lot is all being returned else . . . else . . . we'll fetch the coppers and Miss Griffin will hear what you two have been up to,' he threatened. 'I'd run while you can,' he suggested to Stimpson and Sopworth's accomplice, and before Sopworth could stop him he had lunged forward and snatched the copied keys from out of his hand, putting them in his own pocket.

Chef's face contorted furiously as he clenched one fat fist and raised it in a threatening gesture at them both. 'You two are gonna be sorry you poked your fucking noses into my business,' he snarled, advancing towards them.

'Touch either of them and it's you who will be sorry, Chef Stimpson,' a warning voice announced from the service door.

They all froze and slowly turned to see who had just addressed them.

CHAPTER TWENTY-TWO

Edelina, accompanied by Harry Glebe, appeared out of the shadows to stand before them all. She was dressed in a long red velvet dressing gown and matching slippers. A stern-faced Harry Glebe in porter's uniform waved a rubber cosh menacingly.

In the gloom, under the impression that Harry was a policeman, the fence frantically proclaimed: 'I'm off!' He shot out of the back door at high speed. His pounding feet could be heard running down the yard and fading away around the corner of the building.

Edelina looked at the stricken Sopworth. 'I'm glad to see you've made such a swift recovery from your ailment, Mr Sopworth. I was actually quite concerned about you. What a waste of time on my part.' She turned and addressed Harry then. 'Mr Glebe, would you be good enough to escort Mr Stimpson and Mr Sopworth off my premises, making sure they take nothing with them other than their own belongings.'

Chef was goggle-eyed, the significance of this unexpected turn of events slowly registering with him. He'd not only blown an easy job, the likes of which he'd find it difficult ever to land again, but also his accommodation. Clutching at straws he blurted, 'Now hang on a minute, Miss Griffin, you've got this wrong. It was me and Sopworth that scuppered these two at it, not the other way round. It's them you should be escorting off the premises, not us.'

Sopworth couldn't give a damn about the loss of his job but he'd rather leave with his good name intact, if it were possible. 'Yeah, he's right, Miss Griffin . . .'

'Please don't waste your breath,' Eddie interjected, holding up a warning hand. 'Mr Glebe and I heard enough to be in no doubt whatsoever who was selling property that doesn't belong to them and who wasn't. Be thankful I am not getting the police involved, and that is purely because I feel the hotel could do without the bad publicity this would cause. Mr Glebe, would you please escort these men off my premises?'

'I most certainly will, Miss Griffin.' He motioned the two of them to accompany him, making sure they both understood he would use his cosh if necessary. As they walked past Connie and Neal both men shot them murderous glares.

As soon as they'd left the kitchen Eddie said to Neal, 'Would you be good enough to return the food where it belongs, please? The rest of the items can be replaced in the morning. Connie, would you very kindly make a pot of tea for us all, then both of you please join me in the office.'

'Yes, certainly, Miss Griffin,' they said simultaneously, going off in opposite directions to fulfil the tasks.

A while later Eddie took a sip of her tea and looked gratefully at the two young people sitting opposite her.

'I have much to thank you for, it seems. It was very brave of you both. How did you know what they were up to?'

Connie and Neal looked at each other. It was Connie who spoke up first.

'Mr Richmond suspected Chef Stimpson and I suspected Mr Sopworth. We just got to talking, like you do, and our suspicions sort of came out during the conversation. We decided to keep watch to catch them at it. Neither of us liked the thought of them fleecing you, Miss Griffin, or the possibility of losing our jobs if they ended up bankrupting you. If we had had our suspicions confirmed then we er . . . were . . . er . . .'

She looked at Neal for support as she couldn't very well tell Miss Griffin that they'd intended blackmailing the thieves into giving up their illicit activities.

'Well, of course, what we did then depended on what we found out,' he finished for her.

'Oh, I see,' said Eddie. 'Well, I have to say, I dread to think what those two have been getting away with, and would have continued doing, without your diligence. This hotel can ill afford any additional losses as matters stand at the moment.' She smiled warmly at them both. 'Thank you. I suppose it's difficult to prevent staff from operating the occasional illegal activity in an establishment as big as this but I trust most of them are like you, honest enough to turn away from temptation.'

'None of the ones I know would dream of doing anything underhand, Miss Griffin, I'm sure they wouldn't,' said Connie resolutely.

'I can vouch for the kitchen staff now Stimpson's

gone, and you could trust them all with your granny's best silver,' said Neal.

Eddie smiled. 'That is very reassuring.'

'Er . . . can I ask how you came to be in the kitchen tonight, Miss Griffin, and Mr Glebe? Did you suspect something was going on yourself?' Connie asked her.

After what had surprisingly transpired that afternoon through Phee's generosity, Eddie had been unable to sleep.

Positive a cup of cocoa would work its magic and relax her, she had got out of bed and quietly made her way down the back service stairs to the room service kitchen. Finding no milk in the cold cupboard there, she had gone to the door leading into the main kitchen. As she was opening it the sound of hushed voices reached her ears. Automatically thinking the place was in the process of being burgled, she had immediately closed the door and gone off to fetch Harry Glebe. He had been asleep, a matter she would deal with later. Together they had returned to let themselves quietly into the kitchen just in time to hear negotiations for the stolen goods taking place between the hotel's chef, assistant manager, and their accomplice, and had then witnessed the intervention of the commis chef and assistant receptionist.

Eddie explained and gave a deep sigh. 'This leaves me in rather a predicament over our senior staff shortages.' She suddenly noticed a sheet of paper on her desk and picked it up to look at it. It was the new menu suggestions she had requested from Stimpson earlier that day. He must have put them on the desk

after she had retired for the night to her rooms. She glanced down the list and her eyes lit up.

'Oh, just the sort of dishes I was hoping would be suggested. Potted shrimps, seafood salad, savoury rice ring, assorted soufflés, pork and ham pie, veal cutlets in pepper sauce, poached salmon in butter and dill, fillet steak . . .'

Her face screwed up in worry and she spoke her thoughts aloud. 'Oh, dear, I wonder how long it will take me to find another chef capable of producing such delicious dishes? It really is too bad Mr Stimpson was a thoroughly bad lot as judging by this list he was certainly a first-class chef.' She looked at the list again. 'And the suggestions for puddings sound just divine.'

Neal was listening to her happily, a sense of pride enveloping him. Without thinking, he said, 'Yes, when I approached Mrs Braddock she said she'd be delighted to get away from just having to cook boring roly-poly pudding and treacle tarts and that sort of thing. She says she's got some great ideas for different gâteaux that she'll run past you, if you want her to, Miss Griffin. She did say, though, that she'd need to be assigned a permanent assistant if she's expected to do more in future as she's run off her feet as it is. She said she wouldn't mind an apprentice to train as another *patissière*.'

'Then we must see about getting Mrs Braddock more help immediately. I'm sure there must be a willing girl somewhere who wants to learn a trade,' said Eddie.

Connie's eyes lit up. 'Oh, Miss Griffin, you wouldn't consider my sister for the position, would you? She's looking for a job.'

Eddie smiled at her. 'I would certainly consider your sister. If she is anything like you then she will make a valued addition to our staff, I have no doubt. We'll make arrangements to ask her in for an interview as soon as possible, and take it from there.'

'Oh, thank you so much, Miss Griffin.' Connie couldn't wait to tell Babsy about this wonderful opportunity for her.

Eddie was looking at Neal quizzically as something he'd said registered with her. 'Mr Richmond, did I hear you correctly when you said it was you who approached Mrs Braddock regarding the new menu?'

He shuffled uncomfortably in his seat. 'Well, er . . . yes, Miss Griffin, I did, while I was coming up with the main course suggestions like Chef told me to. He said I had to have them on your desk by the time I'd finished my shift this evening.' Suddenly an idea came to him. Dare he ask her? He'd be a fool to let such a golden opportunity slip through his fingers. He took a deep breath and suggested, 'I could help you out while you find a qualified chef to replace Stimpson, if you'd consider me, Miss Griffin?'

She looked at him, taken aback. '*You* are capable of producing all these dishes, Mr Richmond?'

'Well, yes, of course I can. I've tried them all out. I used to save up and buy my own ingredients then come down to the kitchen when everyone else had finished for the night and practise them. I made a few mistakes . . . well, a lot at first, I won't deny it, but practice makes perfect as they say. Doing this was the only way I was going to be any better than a roast and veg chef. I've got ambitions, Miss Griffin. Besides, I was going to

A LUCKY BREAK

have to be the one to cook all these new dishes anyway or I'd have been out of a job, according to Stimpson. I was excited at the prospect, truth be told.

'Look, Miss Griffin, why don't you let me cook you something of your own choice and prove I can do what I say?'

She was staring at him, appalled. '*You* were going to be producing these new dishes and Chef Stimpson was going to be taking the credit? And after you'd spent your own money and time perfecting your skills? That man is beneath contempt. Thank goodness he's gone, this hotel is well rid of him, and I have both of you to thank for that.' She leaned back in her chair and eyed Neal thoughtfully. 'Well, Mr Richmond, as far as I am concerned you are fully qualified as of now. If you'll consider the position of Head Chef, I would be happy to promote you.'

He was looking at her wide-eyed. 'Would I consider . . . You mean it, Miss Griffin? You want me to be your new Head Chef? I can come up with lots more new dishes to offer the guests, if you want me to?' he blurted. 'You can do wonderful things with brisket that melt in the mouth . . .'

'Enough, Mr Richmond,' Eddie cut in. 'I'm convinced you are the man for me. I trust you can start immediately?'

In charge of his own kitchen, at liberty to produce the mouthwatering dishes he'd always dreamed of creating, a happy staff working alongside him? Well, it was a dream come true. 'I'll start now if you want me to, Miss Griffin.'

She smiled. 'Tomorrow will be soon enough, Mr

Richmond. We'll go over the new menu then. And I will take you up on your offer to cook for me. Tomorrow night I'll be the first to sample something from the new menu. Surprise me with your choice.'

'Oh, Miss Griffin!' he exclaimed. 'It'll be my pleasure, and it'll be the very best meal you've ever had, that's a promise.'

Connie was staring at Neal longingly. This man was proving to be everything she'd ever wanted in a boyfriend. It was such a pity he didn't fancy her. She was pleased, though, that their adventure in the kitchen tonight had proved so fortuitous for him. How she wished something similar would happen for herself.

Eddie sat looking at the two employees before her, feeling a deep sense of gratitude that at least these members of her staff took pride in their jobs and had showed themselves to be real champions when they suspected criminal activity was going on. She felt pleased, despite the circumstances, that she was able to give the young man a chance to prove his worth, which she was in no doubt he would do.

As for the young woman . . . Connie Monroe was the person Eddie wanted heading her reception counter in future, she had no doubt of that. Eddie wondered what she could do to bring about this state of affairs. She could not sack Miss Harbin, it would not be right after her being in the post for so many years, and Eddie doubted there was another job the hotel could offer her that didn't actually bring her into contact with the guests. Would Captain Fosedyke, on his return, have the answer to this problem?

Captain Fosedyke . . . Now there was another

problem that faced her. She desperately needed a proficient manager to lean upon, to guide her through the host of new skills she needed to acquire if the hotel was to fulfil its potential again. But from the evidence she had seen Captain Fosedyke appeared to have done nothing to halt the hotel's gradual decline over the years. Nor did Eddie find his choice of staff reassuring. What she couldn't understand was that he'd been appointed by her mother who had, according to Ralph Waddington, carefully chosen someone who possessed not only the skills required to run such a hotel but had also shared her vision of creating a welcoming environment for its guests. Why had Captain Fosedyke seemed to stand by and do nothing to stop the decline of the Connaught? There were questions she needed to have answers to and she hoped he recovered soon so she could hear those answers. But more importantly she could not run the hotel without a knowledgeable person at its helm with her, and at the moment Captain Fosedyke was the only person she knew qualified to do that.

She made to ask Connie if any news of the Captain's return had been received from him, which for some reason had not been passed on to her, when she was stalled by the arrival of Harry Glebe.

'I've dealt with your problem, Miss Griffin. Both men are off the premises, and I can assure you neither will return in a hurry.'

'Thank you, Mr Glebe,' she said, and looked at the three of them. 'I would appreciate it if the situation surrounding the departure of the chef and assistant manager did not become common knowledge. It might then leak back to our guests and create the impression that their valuables are at risk here.'

They could all see the wisdom of that and nodded their agreement.

Harry Glebe sniffed uncomfortably. Shame-faced he said, 'That . . . er . . . predicament you found me in, Miss Griffin, when you came to fetch me tonight. I can assure you it won't happen again.'

Eddie felt positive the night porter had learned a lesson and his word was his bond. He would never fall asleep at his post again. Besides, she didn't want the problem of having to find another night porter when, apart from this one lapse, she had no reason to believe he was not good at his job. 'I trust it won't, Mr Glebe.'

He looked mortally relieved he wasn't going to receive severe punishment for falling asleep on the job and vowed he would never risk his job again by such behaviour.

Connie then remembered a predicament of her own. Digging the store-room keys out of her coat pocket she held them out to Miss Griffin. 'I ought to put these back.' She flashed Neal a look as though to say, 'And you need to dispose of the copied keys in your pocket.'

Eddie looked at them. She was too tired now and had too much on her mind even to ask what doors the keys Connie referred to were for or what part they had played in tonight's revelations. She felt positive she had been about to ask Connie something important but at this moment whatever it was escaped her. 'I trust you know where they belong?' She rose. 'If you'll all excuse me, I am going to retire.'

'Yeah, me too,' said Neal, standing up also.

'And me,' said Connie.

Eddie departed to return to her room, followed closely by Neal, Harry returned to his position behind the reception desk, but before she departed the office Connie automatically gathered the tray of tea things and returned them to the room service area for washing up in the morning by the kitchen staff. She was disappointed that Neal had not said good night to her. Still, they had been thrown together in extraordinary circumstances and she doubted their paths would cross much in the future. They hadn't before and now he was going to be kept very busy in his new job.

She was making her way up the service stairs towards her room when she found Neal loitering there.

His heart raced at the sight of Connie. He felt such an idiot standing there, looking like he was waiting for a bus. If he didn't ask her out now, though, he might not bump into her for ages again.

He opened his mouth to speak but Connie beat him to it.

'Can't find your room?' she said breezily. 'Anyway, congratulations on your new job. I'm sure you're going to win Chef of the Year next year. Excuse me,' she said, moving briskly past him. She pulled open the door leading to the female quarters and made to enter them.

'Do you fancy coming out with me, to help celebrate landing my new job, Connie?'

She turned and stared at him, heart thumping so loudly she felt sure he'd hear it. So he had liked her all along? Stupid man, she thought, putting them both through agonies because he couldn't summon the courage to ask her out. Well, she wasn't going to pass this chance up and risk his not asking again! Without hesitation she replied, 'Yes, I'd like that.'

A beam of delight split his face. 'Oh, that's great! I thought I'd blown it with you, I really did, with what I said to you after Harry Glebe's gibe. I never meant it like that, you see. It just sort of came out wrong because Harry had embarrassed me. I really like you, Connie. I wanted to ask you out the first time we met on these stairs only I couldn't find the nerve to.'

Her face lit up in a beam of delight. 'Really? I wanted that too, Neal. Well, we've some lost time to make up for, haven't we? It's going to be difficult seeing each other because of our shifts, but I'm sure we'll sort something out. My night off is usually a Wednesday. Now you're the boss in the kitchen, you can sort yours out to suit yourself, can't you?'

'Yes, I can, can't I? My night off will be Wednesday in future. Good night then, Connie.' He stepped towards her and hurriedly pecked her cheek before disappearing into the male quarters.

Connie's heart swelled with excitement and anticipation of things to come. She might not ever land her dream job in this hotel but she was positive it had already produced the man she was going to spend the rest of her life with. If putting up with Miss Harbin's ways was the price, then she was delighted to pay it. 'Good night, Neal,' she said softly after him.

CHAPTER TWENTY-THREE

Eddie smiled delightedly at her visitor. 'Uncle Harvey, how lovely to see you.'

After returning her embrace, he held her at arm's length, looking at her quizzically. 'What is going on out in the foyer, Edelina? Those workmen seem to be preparing the place for decorating.'

Her face filled with a look of excitement. 'Not just in the foyer, but in a block of five rooms on the first floor by way of a start. The workmen are all painters and decorators. There are two gangs of six. Once the foyer has been finished the gang working on it will proceed to do the other reception rooms. When the second gang has finished the first block of bedrooms, those rooms can then be let out at a higher rate and the men will start on the next lot of rooms until the whole hotel is finished. The restaurant will be the last room to be done. Of course it would have been more practical to close the hotel for the duration but unfortunately I cannot afford to lose the revenue and cover the staff wages. I just have to hope our guests will be understanding. I have lowered the room rates so I hope that may be compensation enough for stepping over dust sheets and paint pots. It shouldn't be for long, though, as Giles gave me the impression his men were very efficient. Oh, Uncle Harvey, it's going to look splendid when it's finished!'

'But I thought you hadn't the money to pay for the renovations after the theft of the house contents?'

'I haven't. I have my friend Sophia to thank for this.'

'In what way?'

'Phee has persuaded a friend of hers who owns a decorating business to do the work for me on spec. I'll pay what I can as it proceeds, and at the end whatever I haven't paid off I will borrow from the bank. They'll have a transformed hotel to guarantee the loan, it shouldn't be a problem.'

He was looking stunned. 'Oh, I see.'

'Not only that, Uncle Harvey, but Phee has also given me enough money to pay for most of the major repairs, in particular replacing the old boiler. She says it's a gift but I have every intention of paying her back as soon as I can. I'm so lucky to have her for my friend. She's saved me, she really has.' Eddie took a deep breath. 'Yesterday morning I sat in this office, trying so hard to think of ways I could generate new business and knowing that task was nigh on impossible without renovations taking place. Then Phee appeared and everything changed.

'It is wonderful, isn't it, Uncle Harvey? I know this hotel is going to be great again once the renovations are all finished and will afford Father and myself a good future. I know it may sound ridiculous but I have a feeling that my mother is with me in spirit, willing me on. Maybe I have that feeling because I knew how much this place meant to her.' She paused to narrow her eyes. 'After all his years of plotting and scheming, Mr Stibley may well be sitting somewhere in luxurious surroundings, toasting his success in ruining my father, but he couldn't get his hands on this hotel because it is mine, and what is mine is also my father's as far as I am concerned. So Stibley wasn't entirely successful in his aim, was he? Far from it. I just hope he finds out somehow and the last laugh is on him.'

Harvey looked at her for several long moments before saying, 'I have to say, you have totally surprised me, Edelina, I never thought you had it in you. That was my mistake.'

'I'm surprising myself, Uncle Harvey. I never thought I had it in me either. It's astonishing what you can do, though, when you are driven by need.'

He patted her arm affectionately. 'I couldn't be more pleased that everything is working out for you and that your future looks so much more promising. What is the news on Edwin?'

A flash of deep saddness crossed her face. 'No change, Uncle Harvey, but they do keep insisting that in matters of the mind it is still early days. It just feels like for ever to me, I do want him home.' Her face brightened a little. 'Although there are still no leads on the stolen house contents and I am getting the impression the police don't hold out much hope of ever bringing the guilty parties to book, there is news on the house. The estate agent telephoned me yesterday to say the sale should be finalised by the middle of next week. It will be a sad day for me, but at least the debtors can be paid off then and Father's good name restored.'

'Well, that is good news.'

'I just hope the new occupants appreciate the house as much as we Griffins did.'

'Oh, I am sure they will,' he replied with conviction.

'It's the future I have to concentrate on now, Uncle Harvey, not the past. It's ambitious of me, I know, considering my limited business skills which I do eventually hope to rectify, but I won't be happy until the Connaught Hotel is the best in Leicester and so busy we're having to turn away customers, just like my mother intended.'

Just then Connie appeared at the open door. 'I'm sorry to disturb you, Miss Griffin, but the foreman wishes to have a word with you.'

'Thank you, Connie. Please tell him I'll be along in a moment.'

'I can see you are busy, I'll leave you to it,' Harvey said to her.

Eddie looked disappointed. 'Oh, but you'll stay for some coffee? I'm sure the foreman won't keep me a moment.' She would hate Harvey to think his friendship was less important to her now the Griffins' once dire future looked so much more positive. 'I'd like to show you around and go over the colour schemes I've chosen for the foyer and the bedrooms that are being done first. Oh, and I'd like to tell you about the new menu we're trying out.'

There was astonishment on his face now.

'New menu suggestions? My, you are surprising me today, Eddie. I'd like to stay and have coffee very much, but unfortunately I have an appointment. This was just a quick visit to check how you were getting on, and of course hear the latest news on your father's progress. I'll pop in next week to see if you can find the time to allow me to take you for lunch. In the meantime you know where I am should you need me for anything, Eddie, but to be honest you seem to me to have everything under control.'

She looked thoughtfully after him as he departed. She might look as though she was in control but that was only because so far this morning no staff had come to her door with any problems to do with the hotel. That reminded her that apart from the foreman wanting to see her she had another matter needing her urgent attention, something that couldn't wait any longer if this hotel was going to function as she wanted it to in future.

The foreman's query dealt with, she hurried over to the reception desk.

A beady-eyed Miss Harbin saw her and elbowed Connie out of the way to get to her first. 'I have to say, I fully commend your decision to renovate the hotel, Miss Griffin. If I may make a suggestion? The foyer would look very grand in cream and brown. When I trained at the Dorchester in London the foyer was decorated in cream and brown-flocked wall coverings, with tasteful landscape paintings strategically placed.'

How uninviting and old-fashioned, Eddie thought, and felt positive the Dorchester's foyer would have been brought up to date by now.

'I appreciate your suggestion, Miss Harbin, but the colour scheme has already been decided upon. It is to be in shades of light blue for the foyer extending into all the corridors, and the lounges will be in pastel greens and yellows. A dark blue and cream carpet is being fitted in all the corridors.'

Thanks to Giles's negotiating with a friend of his who owned a carpet factory in Bradford, they were being given a trade price for this order and for the new bedroom carpets. Cream brocade drapes were being made for all the windows in the public rooms by a woman Giles employed, not to mention the individual bedrooms whose curtains would complement each room's new colour scheme.

Eddie's face had grown steadily paler as she mentally added up these costs as they spiralled.

Phee's prediction of a few pounds for paint had escalated enormously to a few thousand by now. Eddie was deeply worried but had been swept along by her desire for this work to take place and just prayed that when she was presented with the final bill, the bank would be as obliging as Phee insisted they would.

Amelia Harbin was smarting inside at this lost opportunity for ingratiating herself with the hotel owner. Blue was totally the wrong colour for the foyer of the Connaught Hotel. Far too garish. 'I'm sure you know what you are doing, Miss Griffin,' she said tight-lipped.

'To complement it all the reception staff . . .' Eddie paused and looked Miss Harbin fixedly in the eyes before adding '. . . will be kitted out in smart dark blue skirts and light blue blouses instead of those old-fashioned black dresses you wear now.' That had been Phee's suggestion. Eddie had thought it an excellent one and it could easily be financed from the money Phee had given her.

Miss Harbin was staring at her. 'I really think I should have been consulted over the new uniform I will be expected to wear, Miss Griffin. I don't wear skirts and blouses,' she said, with an expression as though she was being expected to wear something totally unseemly. 'Besides, my dress mode needs to reflect my position. I cannot be attired in the same style as the junior staff: that would not be acceptable.'

This woman really was difficult and obviously did not welcome change in any guise. Eddie was willing to compromise, though, to keep the staff happy, as long as it did not detract from the overall ambience she hoped to create. 'Well, maybe we can find a suitable dress instead for you, Miss Harbin. Are the temporary new tariffs in place yet?'

They were but Amelia was not exactly making them as public as she ought to be. 'I wouldn't say the reduction of the room rates has had any real impact,' she said as though to say, I told you so.

'It is far too soon for us to form an opinion surely, Miss Harbin?'

Her lips tightened even more. 'Oh, yes, well, I suppose.'

'You will do your best to make sure the tariffs are well publicised and spread by word of mouth, won't you, Miss Harbin?'

So she was to be reduced to actually dealing with the riff-raff the lowered room rates would bring in? Like hell! At least when the hotel's transformation was completed the room rates would reflect the calibre of clientele a woman of her own level should be dealing with. Miss Harbin smiled sweetly. 'You can rely on me, Miss Griffin. I heard gossip in the staff room as I came in this morning . . . not that I listen to gossip as a rule, Miss Griffin, but sometimes one cannot help but overhear conversations. What was being discussed was that Chef and our assistant manager have left.'

'You overheard correctly, Miss Harbin.'

'Well, I never had much to do with Chef but he wasn't, I understand, a very prepossessing character. His food was palatable enough, I suppose, if you like plain cooking, but when you have eaten at good hotels as I have then there really was no comparison. As for Mr Sopworth . . . well, I can't imagine what Captain Fosedyke was thinking of when he employed him. I suppose in the Captain's defence, when the job was advertised after Mr Aldwinkle retired there weren't many applicants to choose from. It's my opinion that's because the Connaught Hotel has a reputation for expecting high standards from its employees, and youngsters these days are not prepared to give their jobs one hundred per cent, you are in fact much safer sticking with the older generation. I expect you'll agree with me, you being the lady that you obviously are, Miss Griffin, that staff should be properly trained and come with the highest credentials? And as we are discussing unsuitable staff, I really would like an opportunity to speak to you about . . .'

Eddie was getting fed up with listening to her monotonous voice and cut in, 'I actually have an urgent matter to attend to, Miss Harbin. Can this wait if it isn't urgent?'

Amelia was incensed that another opportunity to be rid of Connie had been foiled. 'The matter I wish to discuss is urgent to me, but I suppose it can wait if you have more pressing matters to deal with, Miss Griffin.'

She certainly did. Like finding a hotel manager to handle the day-to-day problems that arose in the running of the hotel. 'Have you heard any word at all regarding Captain Fosedyke returning to work?'

'If the Captain had left such information with us we would have passed it through to you. I run a very efficient department, Miss Griffin.'

Oh, dear, Eddie thought. What could she do now but hope that somehow the staff would deal with their own problems in the interim? 'Well, should you hear anything, would you please make sure I'm informed immediately?'

'Of course, Miss Griffin,' she said stiltedly, insulted that her employer should think otherwise.

Eddie returned to the office and sat down. This really was a worrying situation, the hotel manager being off sick and she with no idea when or if he was going to return, and in the meantime no assistant manager to cover his responsibilities.

Eddie heard a tap on her door and looked up to see Connie framed in the doorway.

'Can I help you, Connie?' she asked, smiling.

The girl looked uncomfortable. 'I told Miss Harbin I was going to the toilet or she'd have wanted to know why I wanted to see you. I couldn't very well tell her I overheard some of your conversation or she'd accuse me of eavesdropping. But . . . well . . . I couldn't help overhearing you asking Miss Harbin if we'd heard word when Captain Fosedyke is expected back.'

Eddie looked at her hopefully. 'You have heard? When is he coming back to work, Connie? Soon, I hope?'

'Well ... that's just it. He isn't coming back, Miss Griffin.'

Eddie looked bewildered. 'What do you mean, he isn't coming back? But he's the manager. If he doesn't come back, I have no one to oversee things. Surely if the Captain's decided not to return, he should at least have had the courtesy to inform me by letter and then I could have started the process of finding a replacement for him. I certainly do not have a very high opinion of the Captain if this is the way he conducts himself!'

Connie was looking confused now. 'But Miss Griffin, Captain Fosedyke hasn't told you he's not coming back because ... well, you already know he's not. You dismissed him.'

'I beg your pardon, Connie? *I* dismissed Captain Fosedyke?'

'He told me when I went to visit him in hospital. He'd had a letter from you, hand delivered it was, I took it in to him myself. It gave him immediate notice, and it was such a shock to him that it caused his collapse.'

Eddie was staring at her, stunned. If Fosedyke had received such a letter it certainly hadn't been from herself. 'I must visit Captain Fosedyke. Is he home from the hospital?'

Connie nodded.

'Do you have his address?'

'I can get it for you, Miss Griffin.'

'Thank you, Connie, I'd be much obliged.'

As Eddie came down the last of the stairs into the foyer after collecting her coat her eyes caught sight of someone at the reception desk. Connie was dealing with him and Eddie stopped short as recognition dawned.

The man seemed to sense Eddie's presence and turned his head to look directly across at her. His face immediately lit up and he walked across to join her.

'How nice to see you. I never expected to bump into you again but that doesn't mean I wasn't hoping I would. How are you, Miss er ... ?'

Eddie knew it was most impolite of her not to tell him her name, but she was aware he was anxious for this information and, with devilment at play within her, she decided he could work just a little bit harder for it. She smiled warmly at him. 'I'm very well, thank you, Mr Gifford.'

He was impressed she had remembered his name. He just wished he knew hers. 'What a coincidence we meet again here. I hadn't thought this hotel to be to your taste. Are you here lunching again with your friend Miss Rymmington-Smyth?'

'Knowing Phee, she will probably turn up but I haven't any specific arrangement with her for lunch today. Are you lunching here yourself, Mr Gifford?'

He shook his head. 'I think the management would be well advised to have a look at their menu with a view to offering more choice and then I might do so.'

'Interesting that you should suggest that, Mr Gifford,' Eddie said, tongue-in-cheek. She was beginning to feel slightly unnerved. Mark Gifford was an extremely good-looking man and very charming, and she was finding herself more and more attracted to him. But she hadn't time for flirtation at this moment. She'd a very important task she must get on with. 'You will excuse me, Mr Gifford? I have an urgent appointment.'

He looked extremely disappointed. 'Oh, I was going to ask if you'd join me for lunch as I happen to know of a new restaurant that has opened on the Belgrave Gate. The food is very good, I hear.'

'It is, I can vouch for it. Another time maybe?'

'Er . . . yes. Look, if you'll just give me a moment to seek an answer to a question I came to ask the manager, maybe I could drop you somewhere? I have my car outside. While I'm driving you we could make arrangements for a more suitable time to meet.' He fixed her with his eyes. 'I'd really like to take you to dinner, if you're agreeable? I would very much like to know your name too,' he added, looking expectantly at her.

She felt a tingle run down her spine. She certainly did want to see more of him. Not that she had ever been short of admirers, but she could not remember when a man had last appealed so strongly. It was apparent he was not going to give up until she agreed, but he'd have to wait a little longer to find out who she really was. 'If you could drop me I'd appreciate it as it will save me getting a taxi. I'm not going far. And I can save you some trouble by telling you that I happen to know the manager isn't available.'

He looked frustrated. 'Oh, dear. I was hoping to find out some details about Mr Griffin's movements as I'd like an interview with him as soon as possible.'

'Maybe I can help you?'

'You know the owner?'

She smiled, 'I am the owner, Mr Gifford. My name is Edelina Griffin.'

He looked at her in total surprise. 'Judging by this place I'd totally expected the owner to be a very old gentleman or stuffy old lady, most certainly not someone like yourself.'

She smiled. 'I will take that as a compliment. What did you wish to see me about, Mr Gifford?'

'With a view to selling me this place.'

If he had approached her yesterday before Phee's intervention there was every chance Eddie would have snapped his hand off. Now she thanked goodness he hadn't. 'As you can see, I am in the process of renovations which obviously tells you that the hotel is not for sale.'

'The renovations are not too far underway, from my observations. I'm prepared to make you a good offer, Miss Griffin. I really am keen to have this place. It would make excellent office accommodation.'

Would she be a fool not to ask what sum he was prepared to pay? No, she didn't want to know. The thought of her hotel being turned into office accommodation was now unbearable to Eddie. She couldn't understand it but somehow the place felt like a part of her, that she was responsible for it and for all the people who worked inside its walls. She didn't care about the hefty bill the hotel renovations would incur. This place was now her home and it was here that her future lay. If she ever came to sell it would be as a very last resort. 'The answer is no, Mr Gifford,' she said with conviction.

His eyes sparkled keenly. 'I do admire a decisive woman. Should you ever change your mind, would you offer me first refusal?'

'I would. But don't hold out much hope of it.'

A humorous light flashed in his eyes. 'Oh, I never give up hope, Miss Griffin. If you can't manage lunch today, would you care to have dinner with me this evening? I would very much like to have your company.'

She looked at him and her eyes twinkled. 'No.'

His disappointment at such a flat refusal was apparent. 'Oh!'

A spark of humour flashed in her own eyes. 'I would very much like it if you'd dine with me, Mr Gifford. I'm sampling a dish from the new menu I'm implementing in the restaurant. That's if you don't mind being a guinea pig?'

He smiled at her winningly.

'I don't mind at all if it means I have the chance to get to know you better.'

CHAPTER TWENTY-FOUR

Reginald Fosedyke stared at Eddie in a mixture of astonishment and disbelief when she was shown into his sitting room a while later by a very stern-seeming woman who did not appear pleased that her charge was having his rest disturbed.

'Miss Griffin,' he addressed her politely, courteously getting up to greet his unexpected visitor. He was very conscious of what he felt was his own inappropriate attire. He was in a pair of crumpled pyjamas under an old dressing gown, unshaven, hair ungroomed. In all honesty, since his abrupt dismissal from his job and return home he had found his old high standards slipping.

He accepted her hand and shook it.

Eddie was shocked by the elderly man's appearance. Despite her opinion that as its manager he could have done much to halt the Connaught's decline, nevertheless she had gleaned the impression from the way people had spoken of the Captain that he was a smart sort of man, which was hardly the impression she was gaining now. She knew he was not long out of hospital after an illness but even so, not to be dressed at this hour of the morning! She did, though, sense his discomfiture that she had caught him in such a way and in an effort to ease this said, 'I can see my visit has come as a surprise to you, Captain Fosedyke.'

He cleared his throat and said stiltedly, 'Well, it has rather, Miss Griffin. I can't imagine what you would need to see me for as I no longer work for you. Er ... please won't you take a seat?' he offered, indicating a comfortable-looking armchair opposite the one he had risen from. 'May I offer you any refreshment?'

'No, I'm fine, thank you,' she said, sitting down and placing her handbag on the floor to the side of her.

Reginald dismissed the formidable-looking woman hovering by the doorway and seated himself facing Eddie.

'I do apologise for my housekeeper's manner,' he began. 'She makes me feel like a young child who needs permission to do anything. The hospital staff found her for me and she's strictly temporary until I find myself a more congenial companion, one who doesn't treat me like an imbecile.'

'You never married, Captain Fosedyke?' Eddie asked him.

'With due respect, Miss Griffin, when I accepted the job as manager of the Connaught I knew such a position came with certain demands on the incumbent but I never envisaged that it would come to consume as much of my time as it did. I was left with very little to devote to a social life for myself. I had, though, made a commitment to run the hotel as best I could and felt duty bound to honour that, despite the increasing difficulties I encountered.' He paused and added, 'I appreciate you haven't come here to listen to my domestic problems,' then eyed her quizzically. 'To what do I owe this pleasure, Miss Griffin?'

She took a deep breath. 'First, may I enquire after your health, Captain Fosedyke?'

'Well, it's very good of you. I've had no relapse, thank goodness, after my initial collapse, and the hospital is pleased with my progress. I have to avoid any situation that could cause a sudden drastic rise in my blood pressure, which it appears was what caused my collapse.'

'That is good to hear,' she said with genuine feeling. She looked at him closely. 'Am I right in thinking that what brought on your collapse was a letter you had received?'

His eyes took on a steely glint and he said gruffly, 'Well, that does seem to be what was to blame. Your dismissal of me came as rather a shock, Miss Griffin, after my long years of loyal service.'

'It's as much of a shock to me, Captain Fosedyke.'

He looked at her, bewildered. 'I don't understand.'

'Neither do I. That letter was not from my hand, Captain Fosedyke.'

'With due respect, it was signed by you.'

'The signature was a forgery. I never signed such a letter.'

He looked bemused. 'But who would do such a thing, and why?

Eddie knew exactly who had done this: Stibley. The fraudulent mortgage he'd taken out against their house had not been his final despicable act against the Griffins, the sacking of their hotel manager had. Eddie could only assume that Stibley had been clutching at straws.

Unable to get his hands on the hotel to dispose of it himself, he'd planned to see it diminish its value even further by sacking the hand at its helm.

'I think I know who sent you the letter, Captain Fosedyke, but I don't wish to disclose any more for personal reasons. I came here today to set the record straight as I cannot imagine what you must be thinking of the Griffin family, of me in fact as the letter was supposedly written by myself. I only hope you will accept my deepest apology for the way in which you believed yourself treated.'

He looked at her searchingly for several long moments before saying, 'I'll just say that your visit today has gone some way to sweetening the bitter taste all this has left in my mouth.' He paused and looked at her fixedly. 'I need you to know, Miss Griffin, that when I took on the job as manager of the Connaught, I took my commitment to do my best very seriously. I have done my best, but the last years have been extremely difficult due to . . . well . . . bluntly, having no back up from the owners whatsoever.

'When I was taken on as manager by Mrs Griffin, she had just completed the renovations and told me her dream was for the Connaught to be the best hotel in Leicestershire. I felt truly honoured Mrs Griffin had selected me out of all those who'd applied and I made a promise to her that I would never in any way make her regret her decision to employ me.'

His face contorted. 'It has grieved me beyond words to witness the hotel slowly deteriorate before my eyes after Mrs Griffin's painstaking efforts. I would beg Mr Stibley, your father's representative, for authorisation from Mr Griffin to allow me to carry out desperately needed redecorations and repairs but I never got the go ahead. In fact, any changes intended to modernise the hotel as tastes changed over the years were steadfastly prevented.'

Eddie was looking at him, horrified. What a terrible injustice she had done this man in thinking that he had stood by and done nothing to stop the decline of the hotel when all the time it had been Stibley. Who else?

She took a deep breath. 'Captain Fosedyke, I can only hope that you will accept my profound apologies for the difficulties you have been facing. I owe you a debt of gratitude for endeavouring to keep the hotel functioning when I fear it would have ceased long ago without a man such as yourself presiding over it. My mother chose well when she chose yourself.'

'I was a great admirer of Mrs Griffin. She was a charming, attractive, intelligent woman and I felt privileged to work alongside her. After her death . . .' He issued a sad sigh. 'Oh, so terrible that was, and your father and mother so devoted. I appreciated without question Mr Griffin's need for time to grieve and come to terms with his loss, but as I strove to keep the place going as best I could I never thought it would take forty years for a member of the family to show an interest in it again. That's why that letter, which you now tell me was a forgery, affected me so much. I gave my all to that hotel and felt devastated to receive my notice without warning, not even a please or a thank you for my loyal service. You can understand why I was angry, can't you, Miss Griffin?'

'Yes, I can, Captain Fosedyke,' Eddie replied

sincerely. 'It has been a long time coming but the Griffin family is finally taking an interest in the hotel again. Renovations are taking place as we speak and I am implementing changes to turn it back into a first-class hotel, one that my mother would have loved.'

His face lit up. 'Believe me, Miss Griffin, I had got to the stage where I never thought to hear such good news. I am just sorry not to be part of it.' He gave a despondent sigh. 'I hope you will consider the staff during these modernisations? All but a few have worked for the hotel for years, some nearly as long as I have. Employing the right staff has posed a continual problem to me, especially these last twenty years. Be honest, Miss Griffin, what bright youngster would see a career being forged for themselves in a hotel in such decline unless they had no other option?

'I was stuck with a chef who I knew treated his staff atrociously. I'd been reduced to taking him on originally at the beginning of the war as the chef we had then enlisted, and finding any qualified replacement was very difficult. After the war ended I searched high and low for a replacement so I could be rid of Stimpson but no one of any calibre would accept a position at the Connaught, for reasons I think you will appreciate.'

Eddie smiled wanly. 'You'll be pleased to learn, Captain Fosedyke, that Chef Stimpson is no longer employed at the hotel. A much more suitable young man is taking his place and the menu is being upgraded as we speak. Unfortunately Mr Sopworth too has proved most unsuitable and is no longer employed at the hotel either.'

'Oh, really?' said the Captain with interest. 'I am disappointed naturally, although again in Sopworth's case I had little choice but to offer him the position as he was the only one I interviewed who would accept the pay and conditions the Connaught offered. Soon after his commencement I began to realise he was not up to the job, but I wondered if I'd been wrong and not given him enough time to prove his worth after his show of quick thinking in getting me to hospital as he did.'

'I don't know how you came to the conclusion that it was Sopworth who took charge of getting you to hospital, Captain Fosedyke. It was all down to Miss Monroe and her quick thinking. I was there myself so I know.'

He looked utterly shocked at this information. 'It was Miss Monroe who came to my rescue? Well, she never took the glory when she had a chance to.' His face screwed up in disgust. 'Sopworth took the credit so I would be better disposed towards him and let him keep his job for a while longer? Despicable. I am very glad the man is no longer employed at the Connaught.

'What a lovely young girl Connie Monroe has proved to be, though. She'd already proved herself a very competent chambermaid and I had observed that the guests liked her when I found a moment or two to spare to observe her conduct in reception.' He gave a deep sigh. 'I should have had more time for the staff and their welfare in these last few years, like I did in the past. But after Mr Aldwinkle retired . . .

'I am rather ashamed to admit that I used to be very

quick at spotting staff who showed potential but had become so demoralised towards the end of my service that if Miss Monroe hadn't had the enthusiasm to push herself forward ... well, I am very gratified that one of my last acts as manager was to give her a leg up in her chosen career. I am gratified she chose the Connaught when I am positive another hotel would have snapped up someone like Connie Monroe.

'Despite everything else I had to contend with, I never had cause for concern about the reception department as Miss Harbin runs it very efficiently. I appreciate she is rather formal in her approach to the guests, though that was exactly what the hotel required of reception staff when Miss Harbin assumed her position. I was hoping to mellow that approach by giving her some personable young assistants. Still, I suppose I shouldn't be concerning myself about the hotel now.'

Eddie's mind was racing. It was not fair that this elderly man should be left with any feeling of failure after the decline of the hotel he'd managed. He'd done his best against overwhelming odds and one vindictive man's obsession with ruining the Griffin family. It was not right that Stibley's actions should blight the rest of this innocent man's life, and, selfish or not, she herself needed Captain Fosedyke back on board again as the caring and efficient manager he obviously was.

Would he be willing to return, even for a short while, until she was better able to run the hotel or else found another manager of his calibre?

Taking a deep breath, she said, 'You will be a difficult man for me to replace, Captain Fosedyke. I have no doubt you have done an exemplary job in keeping the hotel running. Without your endeavours I'm sure it would have been forced to close its doors long ago. In all honesty, I would not know what specific qualities to look for in a replacement for you at interview. I am committed to learning the intricacies of running a hotel myself, but as you know it will take time, and also I need the right sort of teacher.' She smiled at him. 'A man like yourself, Captain Fosedyke. There is no one better qualified than yourself for the job. I appreciate you have reached an age when you are looking forward to taking things easier, but dare I hope you would consider coming back to the hotel in an advisory capacity for as long as you wish? I would understand if you refused my offer but would very much appreciate your considering it.'

He looked at her, startled. After having his every waking moment consumed in the drive to keep the hotel functioning and honour his promise to Roxanne Griffin, finding himself suddenly ousted without any warning had hit him hard. He might be seventy years of age but he wasn't an old seventy and still felt he had a lot to offer before he succumbed to retirement. Since his dismissal he had fought a terrible feeling of rejection, of no longer being needed, and with no family to support him had found the time stretching endlessly ahead a bleak prospect.

Over the years he'd often wondered how Roxanne's daughter had turned out. He supposed he had envisioned a spoiled young woman, the sort who'd never had to lift a finger to earn her living. He was gratified to see that in fact Roxanne's daughter was just like she had been: sincere, hard-working, genuinely concerned for the welfare of her dependants. It would be a privilege for him to give her the benefit of his vast experience in the hotel trade and help her on the path towards making the hotel great again.

CHAPTER TWENTY-FIVE

Back at the hotel, Connie was humming happily to herself as she collated the breakfast and newspaper orders received so far that morning. She was feeling very excited. As she had left her room that morning to start her shift she had found Neal waiting for her on the landing at the top of the stairs.

His face lit up on seeing her. 'I was hoping I'd catch you,' he said, not revealing he had been waiting for the last half an hour to make sure he did. 'You know I'm cooking Miss Griffin a meal tonight so she can see for herself what a great chef I am?' His eyes twinkled humorously. 'Well, I was wondering, if I cooked extra would you like to eat with me afterwards?'

Of course she would, she was thrilled that he'd asked her, but it wouldn't do to look too keen. 'Oh, you want to poison me too, do you?' she laughed. Then looked at him seriously. 'I'd like that very much.'

'That's fantastic. Come down to the kitchen about seven. I'd really like it if you were there as my lucky mascot while I put the finishing touches to the new dishes, and you can give me your opinion before they're taken through by the waiters.'

Just then a man arrived at the counter. He put down

a well-used case by his feet and leaned heavily on the counter top. He was smartly but cheaply dressed. Running one hand through his sparse hair, making what he did have stick up wildly, he grinned at Connie.

'Get us booked into a room quick, will yer, sunshine? I've had one hell of a journey up from London. Talk about slow boat to China . . . this was the snail pace to Leicester! The train was delayed so many times, for God knows what reasons, that a two-and-a-half-hour journey took nearly five hours. I need a couple of hours' shut eye before I have to get ready for my performance at the Hippodrome tonight. It's Variety Night. I do a few jokes, sing a few songs, dance a little . . . that sort of thing. Never been to Leicester before. Only got this booking 'cos Dickie Valentine pulled out with laryngitis. Let's hope his bad luck is my good fortune, 'cos keep yer fingers crossed, a talent scout will be in the audience and the next gig for me is at the London Palladium!

'Me agent usually gets his assistant to book my sleeping arrangements but this gig being such short notice she never had the time. Don't usually stay in a hotel . . . well, can't actually afford to . . . but the couple of guest houses the taxi driver took me to were fully booked and time was running short. Then the driver said he'd heard this place had reduced the price of its rooms, and if I didn't mind stepping over some paint pots in the foyer it could be just the ticket. I told him I'd slept *on* paint pots during my time, when things were really bad, so stepping over a few wouldn't bother me. So I'll have your cheapest room, please. Just the one night.'

Amelia Harbin came up to them both. She gave a hurried glance around the foyer before looking at the new arrival with a haughty expression. 'We're fully booked.'

Connie gasped. The hotel was far from fully booked. Miss Harbin was blatantly ignoring Miss Griffin's instructions that anyone who chose to stay at the Connaught was to be afforded every courtesy. Miss Harbin had lost the hotel goodness knows how much profit in the past by carrying out this practice and obviously did not intend to stop. She was clever too in making sure that Miss Griffin did not catch her at it. Connie had noticed her check to make sure the proprietor wasn't around before she had told this man he wasn't welcome. Connie could not let this continue. She wasn't stupid and knew that the hotel was not doing nearly as well as it could. This man's money was as good as anyone else's. Connie could not stand by and knowingly let Miss Harbin get away with what she was doing.

'Excuse me, Miss Harbin, I forgot to tell you that the lady who had booked room 160 telephoned to cancel so that room is free now,' she lied, and before Miss Harbin could say anything grabbed a reservation card from under the counter and placed it in front of the guest along with a pen.

Smiling welcomingly at him she said, 'If you'd like to fill that in, sir, I'll get the porter to show you up to your room. If you wish your fire lighting please telephone down and we'll arrange a chambermaid to see to it right away for you. Anything else you need to make your stay comfortable, you just have to ask and we'll do our best for you.'

Connie was fully aware of Miss Harbin's eyes boring into the back of her head and was so thankful that a retired Major and his wife arrived then and Miss Harbin had to go off and deal with them.

'Major Bright, Mrs Bright, how good to see you back again. You haven't booked? Oh, that's no problem. Yes, we are having the place renovated. I agree, it's long overdue. The owner sought my advice on the colour scheme naturally. I thought blue would be very elegant, and she agreed. Of course, I appreciate that your stay may be disrupted by the work being carried out so, as valued guests of long standing and as a show of good will on my part, I will reduce the price of your room.'

Connie could overhear all this as she dealt with her guest and felt it a shame that Miss Harbin could not show the same courtesy to everyone who turned up.

As soon as Connie had despatched her guest with Danny the porter Pamela came up to her. 'Message for Mr Willett,' she said, handing her a piece of paper.

'Thanks, Pamela. I'll type it out and put it in his pigeon hole.'

Pamela flashed a quick look behind her to check Miss Harbin was still engrossed in dealing with the Major and his wife. Satisfied she was, she turned back to face Connie and said, 'Did you hear her just now say to the Major and his wife that she agrees with the renovations, when all she's done since the work started is complain? And I heard what went on with that theatrical chappie. I think what you did was brilliant, Connie, and you're ever so brave, standing up to that old crow. What she's doing in picking and choosing them as get to stay here is wrong. Miss Harbin's off her head, she must be, to think she's a right to do what she is. She must be losing the hotel so much money.'

Connie nodded. 'Yes, I know, and it worries me. Especially with what it must be costing Miss Griffin to bring the place up to date.'

'Shouldn't you tell Miss Griffin what Harbin's up to? It's not just the money, it's the damage she does by hurting people's feelings. It doesn't help the hotel's reputation, does it?'

Connie looked worried. 'I can't do that, Pamela. I might not like the woman, in fact she's the bane of my life, but I can't have her sacking on my conscience. I've just got to hope Miss Griffin catches her out. Trouble is, she's clever is Miss Harbin. She's been caught once by Miss Griffin turning a customer away and was put in her place, so you can bet she'll make sure she's not caught again so easily.'

'Well, we can only hope a miracle happens and she is. I for one would be overjoyed to see the back of her and get a decent senior receptionist as our boss. Anyway, you're in the dog house good and proper with her this time, Connie, with what you just did.'

'Listen, Pamela, my days on reception were numbered the minute I started my trial. Miss Harbin doesn't think I'm good enough for the job because of my background and nothing I say or do is going to change her mind. She's determined the receptionist who gets taken on permanently will be someone of her choosing, whose ideas on how reception is run are the same as hers.'

Pamela looked downcast. 'Well, I hope you don't leave the hotel altogether, Connie. You and I have become friends and I'd miss you. Anyway, now you're courting Neal Richmond, if you did leave seeing each other would be harder, considering the shifts you both work.'

Connie gawped at her. 'How do you know about me and Neal?'

Pamela smiled. 'You know nothing is a secret here for long. I overheard him talking to one of the breakfast chefs in the corridor when I arrived. They didn't see me. I heard Neal tell the chef that he was cooking a meal for you tonight and wanted to make sure it was special because *you* are special. He was asking the other chef's advice very earnestly.' Pamela grinned and gave Connie a nudge in her ribs. 'I got the impression he's thinking along the lines of a future for you and him.'

Connie's face lit up. 'Neal said I was special?'

Pamela nodded. ''Course, the breakfast chef ribbed him about wedding bells and all that but Neal didn't seem to care a jot. He was more interested in where he could get hold of some candles.'

A surge of excitement swirled in Connie's stomach. She'd been hoping that Neal felt the way she did and having it confirmed by Pamela heightened her nervous excitement over the evening ahead. Her red and green boat-necked dress was the one she would wear. She knew she looked good in it and Neal would be sure to recognise she had made a special effort for him.

Just then the postman arrived. Nodding a greeting at the two women, he put a pile of post on the counter.

'Thank you, Bernard,' Connie said.

'You're welcome, ducky.' He made to depart then stopped, leaned across the counter and said, 'See her?'

He pointed a finger in Miss Harbin's direction. 'In all the years I've been delivering post to this hotel, she's never once said good morning or thanked me, just looked at me as though I should be honoured she'd allowed me to come inside to deliver me post. But you . . . well, your smile and your welcome brighten my day like you wouldn't believe. See yer tomorrow, me ducky.'

'See what I mean?' said Pamela. 'If you went such a lot of people would miss you. I'd better get back to it,' she said, flashing a look behind her to see if Miss Harbin had noticed she wasn't at her post.

Having sorted the stack of mail into piles, Connie was then putting guests' correspondence into the appropriate pigeon holes when her eyes settled on the empty box assigned to room 140. Connie stopped what she was doing and frowned. She had booked Miss Weaver in several days ago and it was suddenly striking her that she hadn't seen the woman since. It was odd as Connie always made a point of addressing the guests when she could, to enquire if they were enjoying their stay, as they passed in and out of the hotel close to the reception desk.

She wondered if there was any reason why she hadn't caught sight of Miss Weaver. The welfare of the guest suddenly became of paramount concern to her. She was probably worrying unnecessarily, but all the same in her need to make sure all their guests were safe and well while under the hotel's roof she would pay a visit to Miss Weaver's room to satisfy herself nothing bad had befallen her. It would be her lunchtime soon and she would do it before she went through for her meal.

A couple of minutes before her lunch hour started Connie held her breath as she saw a stony-faced Miss Harbin making her way towards her. Her actions of that morning were about to be brought up and Connie knew Miss Harbin was not about to thank her. But just as her superior opened her mouth to address Connie she caught sight of Eddie entering through the revolving door and planted a stiff smile on her face as the proprietor approached them.

She smiled warmly at the two receptionists. 'Have you encountered any problems while I've been out?'

Connie knew better than to upstage Miss Harbin and kept her own counsel.

'Everything has run as efficiently as it always does, Miss Griffin,' she responded.

Eddie was relieved to hear that. 'The workmen aren't hindering you too much, are they? Hopefully it won't be too long, three or four days at the most, before they have finished in the foyer. We've not had any cancellations due to the upheaval, have we?'

'A couple, Miss Griffin. Guests who felt they should have been warned they were being expected to put up with the inconvenience of workmen and didn't think the rate reduction was compensation enough. They went elsewhere, but that was only to be expected. Most of the arrivals since work started have been perfectly accommodating when we've explained what's happening and have apologised for any disruption it may cause.' Miss Harbin flashed a dark look at Connie before addressing Eddie once more. 'We've had at least one new customer booking in this morning who was more interested in the price of the room than anything else.'

'Oh, that *is* gratifying. Well, let's just hope that once word gets out that the hotel has had a facelift as well as offering an improved menu, trade will pick up and then this work will all have been worthwhile. Thank you both for doing your best while all this is going on. All the staff have been marvellous, I'll have to find a way to show you all my appreciation.' Eddie made to hurry off to her office to check for messages then turned back. 'Oh, I know you'll be pleased to hear that Captain Fosedyke is fully recovered and returning to work tomorrow.'

Amelia was delighted to hear it as the first thing she was going to get him to deal with was resolving her little problem on reception.

'Oh, that is good news,' said Connie sincerely.

Eddie made to depart again, then remembered something else. 'I shall make sure I speak to Captain Fosedyke regarding the arrangement of an interview for your sister, Miss Monroe. It's important Mrs Braddock has the right person working for her and I am very hopeful your sister will suit her. I'm sure having another Monroe working for us would be a real boon for the hotel.'

Connie appreciated the compliment. 'Thank you, Miss Griffin.' She felt sure Babsy would jump at this chance to learn a good trade under the expert tuition of Mrs Braddock, and it was just the right job for her, in the right sort of atmosphere, Connie felt, to help her sister recover from her recent trauma, an opportunity for her to mix in new circles and forge a far more rewarding future for herself than the one she had nearly found herself facing.

'It's *you* who should be thinking of applying for a kitchen job, not your sister,' hissed Miss Harbin as soon as Eddie was out of earshot. 'Because, I can assure you, with the Captain returning tomorrow your trial on reception will soon be coming to an end.'

Connie smiled politely at her. 'I'll go for my lunch then, Miss Harbin.'

'Don't be late back,' she snapped. 'I'll be watching the clock.'

Connie went off to do her errand before she took her meal. Arriving at Miss Weaver's room she tapped lightly on the door. Within seconds it swung open and an expectant face looked into Connie's. On seeing who it was Miss Weaver's face crumpled in great disappointment. 'Oh! I thought . . .' She paused then asked Connie anxiously, 'What did you need to see me about?'

Connie smiled warmly at her. 'Nothing in particular, Miss Weaver. I hope I haven't worried you by paying a visit, that wasn't my intention. It's just that I hadn't seen you going about like I do the other guests and wanted to check you were all right, that was all.'

'Oh, I see. Well, that's very nice of you. But as you can see, I'm fine.'

With that she shut the door.

Connie stared at the door, frowning. Something was very wrong with Miss Weaver. She looked as if she hadn't slept for days and her eyes held a haunted look. A lesser person would have walked away, let her get on with it, but Connie knew instinctively the woman on the other side of that door was deeply distressed over something. If Connie could help her in any way she would. She knocked on the door again. When she received no reply she knocked again.

It swung open. 'What is it you want now?'

'Is there anything I can do for you, Miss Weaver? Look, I beg your pardon if you think I'm sticking my nose into your business but it's obvious to me there's something the matter with you. And . . . well, it's my duty as a receptionist to do what I can for all our guests.'

The guest stared at her for several seconds then to Connie's shock dissolved into a flood of tears. 'Oh, I don't know what to do, I really don't,' she moaned.

Connie gently took her arm and said to her kindly, 'Why don't we go back into your room and let me telephone room service to send you up a tray of tea?'

'A cup of tea won't solve my problems. Besides, I can't pay for it. I can't pay for my stay at all. I don't know what to do, I just don't.'

Inside the room Miss Weaver sank down on her bed to bury her face in her hands, quietly sobbing. Closing the door behind her, Connie went across and sat down beside her, placing one hand gently on the distressed woman's arm. 'Do you want to tell me about it, Miss Weaver?'

She dropped her hands and looked at Connie through tear-filled eyes. 'I shouldn't have come here. I knew when I booked in I couldn't pay for the room but I was so hoping they would see their way . . . Oh, it's useless! Mr Rogers would be turning in his grave if he knew how they were treating me.'

'How who was treating you, Miss Weaver?' Connie gently probed.

'Mr Rogers's nephews, that's who. He'd no children

of his own. He never married and his sister's boys were the only family he had left. He was really good to them over the years, but when it came to him needing help from them they turned their back on him.' Her shoulders sagged miserably. 'I'd worked for Mr Rogers for forty years when suddenly last week he died. Oh, he was a lovely man. I so enjoyed doing what I could to keep his house comfortable and prepare him nice meals, always made sure his clothes were pressed just the way he liked them. Mr Rogers was so appreciative of what I did for him, he never forgot to thank me.' She paused to take a handkerchief from her dress pocket and blow her nose.

'Trouble was, Mr Rogers was very hard up these last years as his business failed and he was forced to retire. The money he'd left to live on wasn't that much so he couldn't afford to pay me a wage. But he couldn't look after himself, and I couldn't just up and leave him after all those years of working for him. His house had come to be my home too. We came to an arrangement. In exchange for my continuing to do all I'd always done for him, he said that if anything happened to him I would receive a lump sum out of the sale of his house to help get me settled in a little rented flat and leave me something in the bank to live on till I found another job. Mr Rogers told his nephews of our agreement and they promised to honour his wishes when the time came. But they never had any intention of doing so. As soon as the funeral was over they told me to pack my belongings and go. The house is on the market.' She gave a violent shudder and a fresh gush of tears poured down her face. 'Not only have I lost a very good friend in Mr Rogers, I've lost my home as well. I never married and I haven't any relatives living now, no one of my own to turn to.'

Connie's heart went out to this poor woman. She seemed so genuine, and how callous those nephews of her late employer were to turn her out into the street after she'd loyally served their uncle for practically all her working life. 'So,' she said, her mind racing, 'it's a job and somewhere to live you urgently need, Miss Weaver?'

'Not only that,' she sniffed, 'I have to find the money to pay my bill here. I deserve to go to prison for what I've done. As I said before, I knew I couldn't pay before I booked in but I wasn't thinking straight at the time and I desperately needed somewhere to stay after being thrown out. This place was the first I passed. I was so hoping the nephews would change their mind when they'd thought things through. I let them know where I was and have been sitting here ever since, waiting for them to leave a message or come and see me here. I thought . . . hoped . . . prayed it was one of them when you knocked on the door, I really did.'

Suddenly an idea struck Connie. Captain Fosedyke had told her he was looking to employ a housekeeper. Would Miss Weaver suit his requirements? Connie felt sure she would, if the position wasn't already taken. In her urgent need to help this woman, as well as to resolve a problem for the Captain in the process, she blurted, 'I might know of someone who's looking for a housekeeper. It would be a live-in position, I under-stand.' Immediately afterwards she could have bitten her tongue off as she remembered Captain Fosedyke was now returning to work so his need of a house-keeper might not still be uppermost in his mind. But Miss Weaver was looking at her so hopefully Connie couldn't bring herself to tell her she might be sending her on a fool's errand.

'You do? Oh, do you think I might be of interest to them?'

'Er . . . well, it wouldn't hurt for you to pay them a visit. The gentleman I have in mind is a Captain Fosedyke. He really is a nice man. If it doesn't work out then in the meantime I may be able to come up with another solution to your problem.' The hotel might have a position Miss Weaver would be suitable for and offer her a room to go with it. As far as she knew all the female staff quarters were occupied except for the vacancy created by Val's departure in Connie's own room. She would really have preferred a room-mate of around her own age but wouldn't mind sharing with Miss Weaver if it meant resolving her problem. Hopefully one of these possible solutions would come to fruition. She hoped so for this lady's sake.

'But I still have to pay my bill and I can't,' Miss Weaver said anxiously.

Connie patted her arm reassuringly. 'Well, let's take one thing at a time.'

'I'll go now in case someone else beats me to it,' she said, jumping up to collect her coat and handbag.

Connie gave Miss Weaver the Captain's address, remembering it after acquiring it for Miss Griffin earlier, and wished her good luck.

As she ate her lunch Miss Weaver's plight was upper-most in Connie's mind. So much so that several other members of staff gave up trying to have a conversation with her as they were getting nowhere. Connie was not even aware of Neal slipping through the door that led from the main kitchen until she felt a nudge in her ribs and jerked her head around to see him sitting beside her, looking at her expectantly.

She stared at him blankly for a second then her face lit up in recognition. 'Oh, hello, Neal.'

'I asked what you thought of your lunch?'

'Did you? Oh, this shepherd's pie is very good. Chef Stimpson's wasn't bad, I have to say, but this is so much tastier.'

He gave a disdainful tut. 'Shepherd's pie is made with lamb, the one you're eating has beef in it so rightly it's called cottage pie. You will have to get your food facts right if you're going to be going out with a chef, Connie.'

She liked the idea of going out with a chef, especially this one. 'Did you make it?'

'I supervised Brian who was using my recipe.' He scraped a hand through his shock of red hair and asked her anxiously, 'Does the pie meet with your approval then?'

'It certainly does, Neal. There's something extra in it. What?'

He winked at her. 'Can't give my secrets away, Connie, you should know better than to ask a chef that.' Then he looked at her fixedly, seeming to drink her in, and said huskily, 'Mind you, Connie Monroe, there is a danger I could end up telling you everything you ask me.'

She felt herself redden in embarrassment. This man

433

liked her, he really did. The feeling was reciprocated. She felt a desperate urge for him to kiss her but their first kiss should be something special, just between them, not observed by at least fifteen other members of staff who were eating their lunch in the staff room. 'So . . . er . . . how has your first morning in charge gone?'

'So far, so good.' He grinned at her cheekily. 'I've not poisoned anyone yet as far as I know. There's so much I want to do to make life in the kitchen easier for the staff.'

'I'm sure they will appreciate that. How did they take to the news that Stimpson has gone and you were in charge?'

'Oh, Connie, can you believe my staff are actually singing as they go about their work? I have to say I was a bit concerned as to how they would take the news of my appointment, but I needn't have been. A couple of the lads raised me on their shoulders and paraded me around the kitchen while the rest of them cheered.' He pulled a face then. 'I am a bit bothered about tonight . . .'

'Oh, you've no need to be,' Connie cut in reassuringly. 'You'll bowl Miss Griffin over with what you prepare her if this pie is anything to go by.'

That wasn't what Neal was anxious about. Impressing Miss Griffin was very important to him, but it was his date with Connie that was causing him concern. It wasn't very romantic, conducting it in a kitchen. Still, he would do his best to make the occasion as memorable as possible as he intended this date to be the first of many. He had arranged with the head waiter to bring a table through from the restaurant and was going to set it nicely with a candle in the centre as a romantic finishing touch, and he hoped she'd like the expensive bottle of wine the head waiter had recommended and Neal had bought, dismissing its cost as to him Connie was more than worth the price.

'What are you preparing for Miss Griffin to sample tonight?' Connie asked him, interested.

'Beef Wellington. Or to the lay person that is fillet of beef in light flaky pastry. Steamed vegetables and *duchesse* potatoes.'

'Sounds wonderful,' said Connie, her mouth watering.

He was glad she liked the sound of it as that was what she would be sampling too. 'You were miles away when I came in. Something on your mind?' he asked.

She was pleased he had noticed and thought enough of her to ask. 'Just a bit worried about a guest, but I'm sure it'll all work out.'

Not caring if others in the staff room witnessed what he was about to do, he leaned over and pecked her cheek. 'I'd better get back. See you about seven.'

She smiled up at him. 'I'll be there on the dot.'

Connie was surprised to find no sign of Miss Harbin when she arrived to take her place behind reception. Immediately she arrived, Pamela unplugged her earphones from the switchboard and dashed over to her, a broad grin on her face. 'You just missed all the fun, Connie. Oh, it was a joy to witness, it really was.'

'What was?' Connie asked her. 'And where is Miss Harbin?'

'Gone shopping.'

'Shopping?'

'About fifteen minutes ago, Major Bright came down and informed Miss Harbin his wife had discovered she'd left her toiletry bag at home and was in urgent need of the things inside it. He handed Miss Harbin a list and told her to see the items were bought immediately. Miss Harbin said she would instruct her assistant to go out for them as soon as she returned from lunch. He told her that was not good enough as his wife wanted the items as soon as possible so she could ready herself for a civic function they were attending this afternoon at three. Also Boots the Chemist, which is nearer to us, wouldn't do either as there was a special soap that Mrs Bright uses that only certain chemists sell. The only one they knew of in Leicester was a little shop at the bottom of Church Gate. Miss Harbin had no choice but to go herself and leave me to man reception until you came back from lunch. Oh, her face, Connie! It was a bloody picture.'

Connie grinned. 'I wish I could have been here. But then it would have been me who was sent out so I am grateful I've been spared that. Look,' she said, nodding her head towards the revolving door, 'it's started to pour down. I hope Miss Harbin hasn't got an umbrella with her.'

Pamela giggled. 'You are wicked, but a good drenching is the least that woman deserves after the way she treats you. Oh, there's me switchboard buzzing, better get back! You enjoy the peace while you can, Connie, 'cos Miss Harbin's going to be in a foul mood when she returns and it's you that'll take the brunt.'

Connie had no doubt of it.

A while later she had just sent some guests happily on their way to Marshall and Snelgrove's department store to purchase evening gloves when she saw Miss Weaver come through the revolving doors and make her way over. The look on her face told Connie all she needed to know.

'Your trip to see Captain Fosedyke was successful, I take it, Miss Weaver?'

'Oh, yes, it was,' she enthused in delight. 'The Captain is such a nice man with a lovely home. It'll be such a pleasure for me to look after him. It's a nice room I'll have for my own quarters too, and he says I can make it mine however I want to. It's important to him I consider his house my home for as long as I choose to work for him. We had a good chat and got on ever so well. Yes, I know I'm going to get on well with the Captain like I did with Mr Rogers. Oh, I am so lucky! I woke up this morning with a dreadful fear on me I'd end up in a place for down-and-outs, and now look at me. I have so much to thank you for, and the Captain did ask me to say a big thank you to you too for sending me along, but also that he would thank you in person himself when he sees you next.'

Connie was so pleased that she had been able to bring these two people together. Then she noticed Miss Weaver was looking perplexed. 'Is there anything the matter, Miss Weaver? Is something about your new job worrying you?'

'Oh, no, dear, nothing about my new position worries me at all. It's just . . . well, it's the matter of my bill here. When you book out of a hotel you have to settle up, don't you? But I can't.' She looked at Connie anxiously. 'It was on my mind to ask the Captain for an advance on my wages but I've no idea how much my bill comes to and I was worried what my new employer would think of me for asking such a thing before I've even started my job. Do you think . . . dare I ask that the hotel will trust me to settle my bill as soon as I can, even if I have to do it over a matter of a few weeks? I promise I have no intention of not paying. I wish I had something of value I could leave as security but I haven't.'

Connie's mind was racing. She knew this woman to be genuine but also knew the hotel rules stated that accounts were to be settled in full upon departure, the same way as all hotels operated. She felt sure though that this situation must have happened in the past. She knew Miss Weaver was anxious to pack her belongings and return to Captain Fosedyke's to begin her new life. Nevertheless, Connie herself had no authority to endorse Miss Weaver's departure without settlement of her bill. She was just about to tell her she would have to wait until Connie's superior returned, however long that might be, when she saw Miss Griffin coming out of the restaurant and making her way towards the office. In Miss Harbin's absence, and with no manager or assistant manager available to her, Miss Griffin was the next person in line who could authorise this situation. She also had a feeling that the proprietor would be far more sympathetic to this woman's plight than Miss Harbin.

Excusing herself to Miss Weaver, Connie went to see Miss Griffin.

'Hello, Connie, what can I do for you?'

'I'm sorry to bother you, Miss Griffin, but Miss

Harbin's gone out to get some urgent shopping for a guest and I'm not sure how long she'll be. I've a situation that needs a manager's sanction.'

'Oh, I see. Well, I will help you if I can,' Eddie said cheerfully.

Connie, mindful not to gossip about Captain Fosedyke's private business, said, 'I have a guest wishing to book out but unfortunately she's found she can't pay her bill. She's ever so upset about it. She's a lovely woman, Miss Griffin, and she's promised me faithfully she'll settle up as soon as she can if we'll trust her to. She will, I know she will.'

'I see. What is the usual procedure in a situation such as this?'

'I'm not sure, Miss Griffin, it's not happened before while I've been working on reception.'

Eddie was glad to hear this as the hotel couldn't afford to wait extended periods for bills to be settled on a regular basis. 'Well, it's obvious to me you think Miss Weaver will keep her word and that is good enough. I'm sure I don't need to mention that you must get all the relevant details from her. Please tell her we'll look forward to receiving settlement as soon as she finds herself in a position to, and that we also hope she has enjoyed her stay at the Connaught Hotel.'

'I will, Miss Griffin, and thank you.'

Miss Weaver was sent happily on her way to start her new job as housekeeper to Captain Fosedyke, and it was a very relieved Connie who clipped a note onto her unpaid bill and put it in Miss Harbin's tray so she could explain to her superior what had transpired on her return.

It was an hour later that Miss Harbin appeared and judging by the look on her face she was not a happy woman. Her wet hair was plastered to her head, helping to accentuate her already sharp features. As she reached Connie she thrust a carrier bag at her and ordered, 'Find the porter and tell him to take this straight up to Major Bright's room. If you can't find him, take it up yourself. Hurry up about it!'

Connie took the bag from her. 'Yes, Miss Harbin.'

As it was, Connie could not locate Danny so took the bag of toiletries up to the Major's room on the second floor herself and was presented with a shilling for her trouble, which she wasn't sure whether to hand over to Miss Harbin or not, so she decided if the Major had given it to her then it was hers.

Arriving back behind the counter she was immediately accosted by Miss Harbin who was holding Miss Weaver's unpaid bill in her hand, Connie's handwritten note attached to it.

'This bill was in my tray. Your note states Miss Weaver is returning to settle it?'

'Yes, that's right, Miss Harbin, I was going to explain to you . . .'

'Don't interrupt when I'm talking,' she cut in sharply. 'You have no jurisdiction to authorise such a thing, Monroe. You should have had this woman wait for me to return and deal with it.'

'Yes, I know, but . . .'

'Will you stop interrupting when I am talking? I am the senior receptionist and only I or management have the authority to sanction a guest's being allowed to leave the premises under such circumstances. You are well aware of hotel rules so there is no excuse for your actions. I will not have a junior receptionist working under my charge any longer who undermines my position. Miss Griffin will have no choice but to have you off the premises immediately for such breach of protocol.'

'But, Miss Harbin . . .'

She held up a hand in warning. 'Don't waste your time begging me to give you another chance. Your unsuitability for the position was glaringly obvious right from the start and I have just been given more than enough evidence to prove I was right. Maybe now management will listen to me in future as to what sort of person qualifies as receptionist material. Get your things together and wait here until I return.' She thrust her face into Connie's and said mockingly, 'I trust you can follow that instruction? You don't seem intelligent enough to follow any others I've given you.'

Without waiting for Connie to respond, she spun on her heel and headed off to confront Edelina in the office. Without knocking on the door she marched right in and launched into her attack.

'Miss Griffin, I find myself in an intolerable position. I cannot work with Miss Monroe any longer. I wish to part company from her with immediate effect.'

Eddie, who had been studying a list of new wines she was thinking of introducing to complement the improved menu, looked askance at her.

'Oh, I see. Well, I am of course very sorry to hear your announcement but if you insist that you cannot continue working with Miss Monroe any longer, I will have to accept your wishes.'

Amelia puffed out her skinny chest, a look of deep satisfaction on her face. 'Well, I'm naturally very gratified you understand what has driven me to this decision.'

'I have no choice but to, Miss Harbin, you've made your intentions very clear. All that remains is for me to wish you well in the future and thank you for your past services.'

Amelia stared at her, stupefied. 'You're thanking *me* for *my* past services?'

Eddie looked puzzled. 'Yes, of course I am. Is it not the courteous thing for me to do in the circumstance of your terminating your employment?'

Miss Griffin had got it all wrong. It wasn't Amelia herself terminating her employment, she was insisting Connie Monroe's be terminated.

Just then Phee breezed in. She gave a surreptitious glance at Amelia Harbin as, slipping off her gloves, she sat down. 'I haven't called at a bad time, have I, darling?'

'No, of course you haven't, it's always lovely to see you, Phee. Miss Harbin has just handed in her notice and I am wishing her well in her future.'

Phee looked at Amelia. 'Oh, really? So another hotel is to get the benefit of your experience, is it? Remains to be seen what they'll make of you. I expect you'll be wanting to get off, don't let us keep you.'

Amelia's mouth was opening and closing, fish-like. 'Well, I . . .' Oh, God, her mind screamed. This was not supposed to be happening. It was the Monroe girl who was supposed to be leaving, not herself. What on earth was she going to do? There was nothing she could do in the circumstances but to stick to her guns. Well, she'd show them! She would leave and see how long it took Miss Griffin to realise what a mistake she had made in allowing her to go.

Phee put her gloves on the desk as Amelia banged the door behind her. 'I never liked that woman. Her resignation has saved you from having to get rid of her. What made her decide to leave so suddenly?'

Eddie gave a shrug. 'I don't know. I suppose I should have asked. Oh, dear, this makes me realise all over again how urgent it is for me to learn more about this business so I know I am dealing with every situation correctly. Thank goodness I have Captain Fosedyke back on board, his wealth of experience is going to prove invaluable to me in future. Anyway, Phee, to what do I owe the pleasure?'

She looked hurt. 'Do I need an excuse to come and see my best friend?'

'Not at all but I've a feeling you're here for a reason. I know you, Phee. You get a certain look in your eye when you're after something, and you have it in your eye now.'

'Yes, well, you are right. I do need a favour. Please say you'll agree to join Giles and me for dinner at the Adelphi this evening with a group of his friends? If they're as boring as Giles then I will most certainly need you there to keep my sanity intact.'

Eddie looked at her, troubled. 'Oh, Phee, if you're already regretting your decision to encourage Giles . . .'

'Don't fuss, darling,' she cut in. 'How can I regret doing something so vital for you? But you can pay me back by doing something for me. So we'll expect you at eight for cocktails at the Red Circle Club before we go on to join Giles's friends.'

'Well, I can't, I'm afraid.'

Phee stared at her. 'You can't?' Her face fell. 'Why ever not, darling?'

'Because I already have a dinner engagement.'

'You have? Oh, how thrilling,' she exclaimed, eyes sparking keenly. 'What's his name, darling?'

'What makes you think it's a man, Phee?' Eddie said cagily.

She tutted. 'Oh, don't be silly, Eddie, of course it's a man, and one you have an interest in judging by the pink spots in your cheeks.' She leaned her elbows on the table, rested her chin in her hands and looked at Eddie fixedly. 'So, spill the beans? I'm not going anywhere until you do.'

She took a deep breath. 'Mark Gifford.'

Phee pulled a face. 'Mark Gifford? Do I know him? Oh, yes, I do. He's the rather delicious-looking man we met when we came to inspect this place for the first time.' She grinned. 'Oh, you dark horse. You're not supposed to keep secrets like this from me. How long have you been seeing him?

'I haven't kept this from you. Dinner this evening is our first date together.' Eddie looked at her, concerned. 'You don't mind, Phee, do you?'

'Mind? Why should I?'

'Well, you were rather taken with him yourself.'

'Yes, I was, and I would much rather it were me he was taking to dinner tonight, but as it's not I'd rather it be you than anyone else. I shall want to know all the details tomorrow, darling. You have a wonderful time.' She pulled on her gloves and stood up. 'Well, I suspect your evening will be far more interesting than mine.' And she added, her eyes sparkling mischievously, 'I'll keep telling myself it's all in a good cause. Toodleooo, darling.'

As soon as she'd departed Eddie picked up the telephone receiver.

Back in reception, Connie braced herself to receive her notice. She watched a drawn-faced Amelia Harbin stalk right past her to gather her own belongings together and march across to the staff room. Connie looked across at Pamela who shook her head and gave a shrug as though to say, I don't know what's happening either. A call came through then. Concluding it, Pamela turned to say to a still confused-looking Connie, 'Miss Griffin wants to see you in the office.'

She gulped. There could be only one thing Miss Griffin would want to see her for after Miss Harbin's interview with her and that was to relieve her of her reception duties. Her heart sank. Despite Miss Harbin's harsh regime, she really would miss her job on reception.

A minute later Connie knocked tentatively on the office door and entered when she heard Miss Griffin summon her.

'You wanted to see me, Miss Griffin?'

'Yes, I do, Connie. Miss Harbin has decided to leave the hotel's employ with immediate effect. That leaves me with a vacancy for senior receptionist which I thought you might like to try out for? Let's see how you feel you'll cope, although I myself feel very confident you will excel in the position. All we need to do then is seek a suitable replacement for the assistant's place, which I will ask Captain Fosedyke to attend to when he returns tomorrow.'

Connie could not believe it. Was she dreaming? Had Miss Griffin really just told her that her nightmare of a boss had left and Connie was to be her replacement? No, she must have misheard. 'I'm sorry, Miss Griffin, could you please repeat what you just said to me, only I didn't quite catch it properly?'

Eddie looked at her knowingly. 'Oh, I think you heard me perfectly, Connie.'

'I did! You really mean that Miss Harbin has left and you want me to be senior receptionist?'

'Yes, I do.'

Connie stared at her wildly. 'Oh, I . . . I . . . don't know what to say, Miss Griffin.'

'"I accept" would be a start. I can't think of anyone more suitable than you to take up the position.'

Connie was thrilled beyond belief. 'Really?' she blurted. 'Oh, Miss Griffin, then yes, of course I accept.'

What a day this was turning out to be, and the best was still to come. She had her evening with Neal to look forward to.

CHAPTER TWENTY-SIX

Framed in the office doorway, Eddie looked out into the newly refurbished foyer and a feeling of satisfaction swept through her. The transformation that had taken place here over the last six weeks under the expert guidance of Giles and his team was startling. They had managed to create the welcoming relaxed atmosphere Eddie had hoped for to welcome future custom. The renovations were not yet complete as the third-floor redecoration was still underway and the restaurant had yet to be tackled, but already the hotel's profits were showing a marked improvement as larger numbers of guests were coming through the doors. Eddie was now more optimistic that when the final bill for the work was presented to her she was going to be able to settle it with a much smaller loan than she had at first feared.

She knew that the increased profits were not just down to the redecoration but that the number of people choosing to eat in the restaurant had doubled, thanks to the delicious menu Neal and his staff were now offering. Business was in fact increasing daily as word spread wider, and according to Captain Fosedyke's inside information the likes of the Grand and the Bell, the Connaught's main competitors, were already beginning to feel concern over losing trade and looking at ways they could halt the stampede.

Eddie smiled as she witnessed Connie and her new assistant dealing with several new arrivals at the reception desk. What a good choice she had made in appointing Connie to the position that had been left vacant by Amelia Harbin's departure. The young girl was proving such an asset to the hotel, her personality just right, Eddie felt, to afford a warm welcome to anyone choosing to stay under their roof.

Eddie saw Captain Fosedyke approaching her and smiled a greeting.

'You'll be glad to hear Mr Harper has agreed to start a week on Monday and is very satisfied with the terms and conditions we have offered him, Miss Griffin.'

'Oh, that is good news. Thank you so much for finding him.' She looked at her acting manager in concern. 'This doesn't mean your services are any less vital, Captain Fosedyke, I still need your help in learning the hotel trade.'

'Oh, Miss Griffin, you don't need to learn much more than you know already. You have amazed me the way you've picked it all up. You've been a pleasure to teach, you really have.'

She was surprised herself how much she had learned over the last few weeks under this man's expert tuition. In fact, at a push, with the aid of the new manager they had just appointed, she felt she could probably manage to resolve any problems that were presented to her, or at least know who to turn to amongst her staff to sort matters out. She wasn't willing for the Captain to feel that his presence was no longer required, though. Not until he was ready to leave himself. But she was aware that this man was now in his seventies and he'd been on the premises since seven-thirty that morning, on the go non-stop helping her to keep her hotel running smoothly. He must be feeling tired, but pride would prevent him ever admitting the fact. Choosing her words carefully, she said, 'It's such a lovely day outside . . . just a thought, but why don't you make an early afternoon of it?'

'But you might need me, Miss Griffin.'

'There is nothing I envisage happening that we can't handle between us. Please accept my offer of an early finish by way of a thank you for all the hard work you have done for me since your return.'

He looked pleased at her compliment, and in fact he would like to get home. He had a reason to now. The bleak welcome his empty house used to afford him on his return after a hard day's work had been transformed completely since Miss Weaver . . . Florence . . . had been there to welcome him back. There was always a hot meal waiting for him, a blazing fire to toast his feet by, her pleasant company in the evening, chatting or just sitting quietly, sewing or knitting. In fact there was a military band playing this afternoon in the Abbey Park bandstand that he would very much like to see. Such occasions he'd never been able to attend before due to his work regime, but now he could. In fact there were many other pursuits he would once merely have like to have followed, and now could. He wondered if Florence would like to accompany him. The thought of her company pleased him. It couldn't hurt to ask.

'Well, if you're sure, Miss Griffin, I'll see you in the morning.'

Eddie walked back into the office and sat down behind the desk. Alone and unobserved she stared blindly across the room. How much her life had changed during the last few weeks, had changed in fact out of all recognition. Eight weeks ago . . . was that all? It seemed so much longer to her. It seemed incredible in the light of the devastation he'd caused the Griffins, in particular her father, but in truth she did owe Stibley a debt of gratitude. Thanks to his vendetta she had been forced to find qualities within herself she had never realised existed, and had had it brought home to her how unrewarding her previous existence had actually been. Not knowing any better, she had enjoyed her daily social whirl then, but shopping for a new dress or attending a charity event, trips to the theatre and weekends with friends in the country, had never left her with the sense of satisfaction she experienced now when retiring to bed after a hard day's work. And without Stibley's actions she would never have met Mark.

Her heart raced as she thought of the man she had fallen head over heels in love with over the last few weeks as their relationship had developed. He was proving to be everything she had ever hoped to find in a man but had begun to think she never would as time had passed. Besides his striking good looks, he was intelligent, smart, and made her laugh as well as being very caring and considerate. More importantly, Eddie believed that she was the sort of woman he had been looking for, too. He was certainly giving her that impression anyway. She had a feeling that Mark was going to be the man she would spend the rest of her life with. She hoped so.

Until now, though, she had not been able to bring herself to tell him of her father's ruin by his former employee, or that he was now in hospital suffering from a mental breakdown. She'd feared, probably unwarrantedly, that he would think less of Edwin for allowing this to happen to him. But now she'd decided she knew him well enough to trust him with this terrible secret and intended to divulge it all to him over dinner this evening. She hoped too that when her father finally met Mark he would approve of him.

She sighed deeply as she thought of her father. The lack of any progress towards regaining his faculties, despite the treatment the hospital was administering to him, was causing her great concern. He had been this way for eight weeks now. Surely there should be some sign that he was going to revert to the person he had been before the shock of finding out about Stibley's betrayal? She had faith enough in the medical profession to believe that they would do all they could to help her father, had no choice but to believe it. Looking ahead to his recovery she had decided that the two small flats at the back of the hotel that had once provided accommodation for the hotel housekeeper and manager but which were now full of junk would be cleared. With certain improvements they would make better living quarters for her and her father than the hotel's rooms and she intended to have the work done to make them habitable as soon as the money was available. Meanwhile all she could do was carry on ensuring that the hotel thrived and would support them in the future.

Another thing struck her then. She realised she hadn't seen anything of Harvey since he'd come to pay a visit on her unexpectedly a few weeks ago and she'd informed him of her good fortune in securing help with the hotel's restoration. He had spoken of returning but she had been so busy since then, one day rolling into another, it was only now she realised that so much time had passed without an appearance from him. She wondered if he was all right. She must find time to pay him a visit to check on him.

The telephone ringing on her desk jolted her out of her thoughts and she reached over to pick up the receiver. 'It's the *Leicester Mercury* for you, Miss Griffin,' Pamela informed her.

What would a reporter working for the *Leicester Mercury* want with her? she thought as she asked Pamela to put the caller through to her. Then it struck her. It must be that they wanted to do an article on the hotel's renovations. The publicity could bring welcome benefits as the newspaper had a wide readership covering the whole of Leicestershire.

'My name is Mr Green and it's about the notice,' the person at the other end informed her.

'Notice?' she queried. 'What notice are you referring to, Mr Green?'

'The one for insertion in tomorrow's publication then as per instructed to run all next week, announcing the closing of the Connaught Hotel. Only we have a problem with the actual date of the hotel's closure on the form that the clerk wrote out when you or your representative came to place the notice at our offices. Our typesetters can't decipher if it's a three, a five or an eight, so we aren't sure if the closure date is the thirteenth, fifteenth or eighteenth of this month. We wouldn't like to make a mistake, Miss Griffin. If you could just confirm the correct date we can get on with putting the notice in the paper for you. And may I take this opportunity of extending to you our sincere apologies for the mistake by the clerk who took your order.'

Eddie was frowning, perplexed. 'But I have authorised no such notice. The Connaught Hotel is certainly not in the process of being closed down. Not my Connaught Hotel anyway. And I have to say I am not aware of another Connaught in Leicestershire.'

'Oh, I see,' said Mr Green. 'This is most confusing. The form definitely states the Connaught and that the order was placed by a Miss Griffin.'

'I do not know what form you have in front of you, Mr Green, but I can assure you I certainly did not come into your offices nor have I sent a representative to place a notice in your newspaper that my hotel is closing. This is either a mistake or a hoax.'

'Oh, I see. Well, I do apologise, Miss Griffin, for any distress I may have caused you. Good day.'

Eddie looked puzzled as she replaced the receiver but before she had time to think about the matter any further the office door shot open and Phee raced in. 'You have to save me, Eddie,' she announced, looking perturbed.

'Why, what on earth is wrong?' Eddie demanded.

'I have an awful feeling that Giles has something on

453

his mind and that he wants to take our relationship further. I'm so worried he might spring it on me when I least expect it. I need to avoid him until I can think of some way I can reply that won't devastate him too much when I decline his offer. I might not feel like that about him, darling, but he *is* rather a dear. I thought I'd be safe here. I'm sure I remember him telling me he had business out of town today, but I just noticed him coming down the stairs as I made my way across the foyer and shot in here hoping he hadn't seen me.'

'Giles told me himself when he arrived a short while ago that he'd had business out of town today but had concluded it early so he came here to check on the progress of his men.'

There was a knock on the door.

'Oh, my goodness, it's him!' Phee exclaimed.

'Well, he's probably come to give me a progress report as he always does after an inspection visit.'

'I can't see him at the moment,' she insisted in hushed tones. 'Get rid of him, Eddie,' she mouthed. 'Shout that you're indisposed and he should come back later.'

'I couldn't be so rude, Phee, not after all he's done for me.'

'Some friend you are,' she snapped, flashing her eyes around in search of a hiding place.

She spotted her best bet and dashed around behind Eddie to squat down behind the desk just as the door opened and Giles entered. He looked surprised to find that the only occupant of the room was Eddie.

'Didn't I just see Sophia come in here?' he asked her, looking puzzled.

'Oh . . . er . . . had you arranged to meet her, Giles?'

'No, I just thought I saw her. Must be my eyes playing tricks on me.' He settled his portly frame into the chair to the front of the desk. 'My men are getting on well. They should have finished the third floor by the end of next week and all that remains is the restaurant. We'll need to get together sometime and confirm you are still happy with the colour scheme we originally settled on. I hope you're pleased with the results so far, Eddie?'

'I most definitely am pleased, Giles. I'm so fortunate that Phee was acquainted with you and brought us together. I would also like to ask if it would cost much more to freshen up the staff living quarters? I paid a visit up there for the first time earlier this week and, I have to say, I was appalled by what I found.'

'I'm sure we can come to some arrangement. I'll have a look at them the next time I come, and sort out a price.'

Eddie was painfully conscious of Phee crouched beside her and worried Giles would discover her presence and be hurt when he realised she was hiding from him. Eddie noticed he'd suddenly become distracted and asked in concern, 'Is anything the matter, Giles?'

'Pardon?' He gave a deep sigh. 'Actually there is. I have a problem and have no idea how to go about solving it without hurting her feelings. I would so hate to hurt her feelings, I really would.'

'Hurt whose feelings, Giles?'

'Sophia's. I know she's fond of me, you see, and . . . well, I have always admired her greatly, worshipped her, in fact, thought she was my ideal woman. When she agreed to allow me to escort her I was one happy man. But . . . well, since we have been courting and I've got to know her better, she has rather slipped off the pedestal I'd placed her on, if you understand me?' He paused to look at her, shamefaced. 'I've met someone else.'

Eddie looked at him in surprise. 'You have?'

He nodded. 'I met her here at the hotel, in fact.'

'You did?'

He nodded again. 'I don't know whether you remember because you were rather busy yourself at the time with hotel business but two weeks ago I came to meet Sophia here as we'd arranged, only she never showed. Later she told me it had been somewhere else we had arranged to meet but I'm still convinced it was Sophia who was wrong and it was here and not where she insisted. Anyway, I had been waiting over an hour and had given up on her coming. I thought I'd pay a visit to her house to see if she was at home in case she had been taken ill or something. When I passed the guests' lounge on my way out I saw people having tea there and found myself feeling rather peckish. I decided to order some and continue to Sophia's house afterwards.

'The only vacant seat was at a table already occupied by a lady who said she didn't mind in the least my joining her when the concierge asked her. Well, we got to talking and one thing led to another and I found myself asking her to join me for dinner that evening as it didn't look to me like Sophia would be accompanying me. I feel so very guilty as I have been seeing Frances ever since. She is such a dear lady and we have so much in common, which I now know that Sophia and I don't have.' He gave a worried sigh. 'I don't know how to break off my relationship with Sophia without hurting her; I'm sure she will be distressed. I can't go on like this. What I'm doing isn't fair to Sophia in the least. I'm acting like the worst kind of cad and not proud of myself at all.' He looked wretched. 'I cannot imagine what you must think of me as you're her dearest friend, but who better to advise me on how to approach this?'

'Oh, I see . . . well . . . would you like me to break this news for you, Giles? I'll do it very gently, I promise. I'll make sure I convince her you had no intention of misleading her but you must follow your heart. Better to end your relationship now than let it carry on and her be more hurt than necessary.'

'Oh, Eddie, would you? I'd be so grateful, I really would. It would be such a load off my mind, I must show my appreciation to you somehow.'

'There is no need, really.'

'Oh, but I must,' he insisted. 'I know . . . you're not to worry about settling my bill for the renovations until you are absolutely in a position to pay it comfortably. I'll also give you an extra discount.'

'I couldn't expect you to do that, Giles,' she exclaimed in astonishment.

'Oh, I insist. I have to do something to restore your faith in me after what I've just told you.' He stood up. 'I'd better go. I'll be back in a couple of days for another inspection visit and to get together with you before we make a start on the restaurant.' He looked at her in concern. 'You will be gentle with Sophia, won't you, when you tell her?'

457

'I promise, Giles.'

'Thank you so much.'

As soon as the office door clicked shut on his departure Phee shot out from behind the desk, exclaiming, 'Well, really! Of all the cheek.' She moved around the desk to sit down in the seat just vacated by Giles.

Eddie looked surprised. 'But, Phee, it was always your intention to make Giles realise his love was unrequited, and for him to find someone far more suited to him than you ever would be.'

'Was it? Oh, yes, so it was. Well, I suppose I have achieved what I set out to do then. I'm pleased for Giles and really hope he's happy with his new woman. But how *dare* he carry on with someone else behind my back?'

Eddie looked incredulous. 'Phee, you have a nerve accusing Giles of playing around behind your back when you have been doing exactly the same to him, and not just with one man but a string of them.'

'Oh, yes, well, I suppose you have a point. I ought to forgive him just the one woman,' she conceded graciously.

'I can't take him up on his offer of an extra discount though, Phee, not under the circumstances. I would feel so deceitful, knowing what I know.'

'Well, you have no choice but to accept it or you'll have to explain why you're not going to and then the truth behind my agreeing to see him in the first place will come out and think what hurt *that* would cause him!' Phee's face suddenly lit up. 'Anyway, this means I don't have to find an excuse for not seeing him this weekend now. I was rather running out of excuses and was on the point of asking you to help me come up with some new ideas. Well, I don't have to now, do I? Are you busy at the weekend, darling?'

'Yes, I am. Apart from working here as hotels do not shut at weekends, I am having some time off on Sunday. Mark is taking me for a run into the country in his car. The Peak District was mentioned, and lunch at an inn he knows of near Dovedale.'

'Oh, that sounds so romantic!' said Phee, resting her elbows on the desk and looking at her friend keenly. 'I am rather miffed he chose you over me. I suppose it's too much to hope that he has an unattached brother?'

'Sorry, Phee, it is too much to hope. He's told me he's an only child like myself. His father is a widower, I do know that.'

'Father!' She gave a disdainful tut. 'When I get so desperate I have to look towards the older generation, I will let you know. Anyway I have been invited to the Crawshaws' country pile for the weekend to join a shooting party through Roddy Fultenham. You remember him, darling? His father made a packet after the war selling army surplus stock. Roddy and I had a little thing going at one time, never anything serious. It finished when I took rather a fancy to a pupil in Daddy's chambers, but that didn't work out because Daddy found out and caused such a fuss . . . anyway, I'm considering giving Roddy another chance but there is the little matter of his current girlfriend. If I get my way, and I *do* like to get my way, after this weekend she'll be off the scene. I bumped into Roddy at the tennis club yesterday and he invited me along. There's quite a crowd going, it should be fun.'

'Have you shot before?' Eddie asked her, not at all liking the thought of Phee let loose with a gun.

'No, darling, so everyone will need to hold on to their hats, won't they?' she said, laughing. 'Pity you're seeing Mark or you could have come along.'

It was not Eddie's idea of fun and she was thankful she had her own plans for the weekend by way of excuse.

Then she remembered the telephone call she had received from the *Leicester Mercury*. 'Oh, Phee, as if I haven't got enough to worry about after the hospital informed me this morning they're going to try electro-convulsive therapy on Father, I had a strange telephone call just before you arrived. It was from the *Leicester Mercury* who seemed to have received a notice that we were closing the hotel.'

'The hotel is closing? You never told me that, Eddie. And after all this work Giles has done for you.'

'But that's just it, Phee, I never sanctioned such a notice.'

'You didn't? Well, it's a mistake then.' She flapped a hand. 'The papers are always making mistakes. Don't you remember a few years back when my engagement to a Phillip Mackintosh was announced and everyone was telephoning to congratulate me? I'd never even met the man. The newspaper had my name mixed up with another Sophia Smyth. How they had come to add the Rymmington Lord only knows. I can only guess a silly little clerk had got it mixed up somehow with an article about me attending a charity event that was in the paper the same day. There's obviously another hotel called something similar to the Connaught . . . the Consort or something . . . somewhere in Leicestershire that is closing down and owned by someone with a name that sounds like Griffin . . . Riffin or whatever, you know what I mean. Not being able to read the form properly, they found out the nearest-sounding name to what was on the form which happened to be this place.'

'Oh, do you think so? It would explain their mistake, I suppose.'

'Darling, stop fretting. It's the poor man whose hotel is really closing down who will have the problem when people turn up to stay and find no room at the inn, so to speak, because his announcement of its closure never got into the paper.'

'Well, that could be so but I did worry it was a nasty hoax by either Mr Stimpson or Mr Sopworth to get back at me for discovering their little tricks and removing them from my premises.'

'Well, if you are right their little game hasn't worked, darling, so be thankful.'

Eddie smiled at her. 'Yes, you're right.'

'And, darling, try not to worry about your father. The doctors wouldn't be giving him this treatment if they didn't think it would help to bring him back to normal. I should think one look at those ghastly probe things they're about to stick on him would be enough to bring anyone to their senses.'

Eddie looked at her. Sometimes Phee was completely oblivious to what she was actually saying. Her description of what Edwin was facing had now made Eddie feel even worse about it all.

Phee, though, was looking at her expectantly. 'Giles

mentioning tea has made me realise I'm a little peckish myself. How about you treating me to a cream tea?'

Eddie needed something to distract her at the moment and liked the sound of Phee's suggestion. It would also afford her the opportunity to try a selection of the new cream cakes Mrs Braddock was now making along with her assistant, Connie's sister, with whom Mrs Braddock seemed very happy. Captain Fosdyke had taught Eddie that much could be gleaned by evesdropping on guests' comments, especially their grumblings over something they weren't happy about. It gave the hotel the chance to put the matter right before it became a real issue. It would also give her the chance to learn the public's opinion on the new décor . . . all very favourable, she hoped.

CHAPTER TWENTY-SEVEN

Three evenings later Connie and Neal were hurrying around the back of the hotel with only a few minutes to spare before Harry Glebe did his lock-up rounds. They had been to a skiffle club in a basement under a building in the Market Place, and along with the rest of the crowd of youngsters packing the airless smoky room had had a great time tapping their fingers on the round table tops in time to the beat of the latest trend in popular music and sipping on glasses of warm beer.

As they neared the staff entrance Connie suddenly pulled Neal to a halt.

'What's the matter?' he asked her, then put his arms around her and pulled her close. 'Oh, a kiss and cuddle you're after, are you, Connie Monroe?'

She pushed him away. 'Not right at this minute. Neal, I'm sure I've just seen people going in at the staff entrance.'

He gave a shrug. 'Well, they're probably staff like us.'

'I know it's quite dark but I didn't recognise any of them. Besides, I don't know of any of the live-in staff who dress like the women I just saw. I've got a feeling something's not right. Come on,' she urged him.

He had no choice but to do what she commanded. Together they dashed over to the staff entrance and ran up the winding narrow back stairs. On reaching the attic staff quarters they still hadn't come across anyone.

Connie looked at Neal, perplexed. 'If it was members of staff I saw, we would have caught up with them coming up the stairs. Whoever it was must have gone into the hotel corridor on one of the floors.'

'Are you sure you're not mistaken?'

'No, Neal. I'm positive that as we came around the corner of the hotel into the yard I saw three women and, I think, a man entering by the staff entrance.'

'Well, maybe they're guests?'

'Guests use the front entrance not the staff one, Neal.'

She had a point.

'Come on,' she urged again, grabbing his arm.

As he ran after her down the stairs, he asked, 'Where are we going?'

'To check the corridors. I need to put my mind at rest, Neal. We don't want strangers wandering around willy-nilly.'

As Connie poked her head around the door leading on to the third-floor corridor she saw that it was empty and immediately proceeded down the stairs to the next floor, closely followed by a now panting Neal. He was fully convinced they were on a wild goose chase but thought enough of Connie to humour her. Poking her head around the door leading into the second-floor corridor, Connie was taken aback to see three gaudily dressed women, each accompanied by a man, about to enter three separate rooms. She recognised none of them as guests she had booked in.

She dashed down the corridor and ran towards them. 'Excuse me, but who are you?' she questioned.

The six people spun round to face her, along with Neal who had now caught up with her and stood at her side.

'What's it got to do wi' you?' one of the women demanded. 'If yer don't mind, we want to get into our rooms.'

'Yeah, sod off and bother someone else. I'm paying for 'er time,' slurred a very drunken man, clinging on to one of the women and swaying dangerously.

Connie was positive none of these people had come to reception and booked rooms earlier in the day, or any time in fact. She would remember. But the three women had keys to the rooms they were about to enter. So someone had booked them. Connie wasn't stupid. These women were prostitutes, the men with them clients. Before the women could protest Connie had snatched the room keys from their hands.

'Oi! Wadda think you're playing at?' one of the women hissed at her, launching herself at Connie in an attempt to take the key back.

Neal intercepted and pushed her away. 'Watch yourself, lady, or you'll have me to deal with,' he said, protective of Connie.

Clutching the keys tightly in her hands she said, 'You're not plying your trade in this hotel, I'll be damned if you are.'

'But he said for a backhander we could,' one of the women answered, looking perplexed.

'Who did?' Connie asked, bewildered.

'The chap who approached us last night with his proposition. Told us he was the manager of this place and said we could have a nice little earner going between us if we was prepared to give him a back-hander. He gave us these keys earlier tonight as pre-arranged and said we could use the rooms between ten and twelve. He told us how to come in the back way. Well, lady, we'd be stupid to look such a gift horse in the mouth. 'Course, we jumped at it, didn't we, gels?'

'Yeah, we bloody did,' the other two agreed.

The well-lubricated men with them were becoming agitated. 'Eh, come on, can we get on wi' this, I've to get 'ome to me missus,' one of them urged.

Whoever the man was who'd approached these women it was certainly not Captain Fosedyke, Connie knew that without a doubt. He would never do such a thing.

Just then a guest poked his head out of the door opposite and, bleary-eyed, demanded, 'What on earth is all this noise about? People are trying to sleep.'

'I'm sorry, sir.' Connie spun round to address him. 'Er . . . er . . . these guests have been to a fancy dress party and found themselves on the wrong floor. I'm just helping them find the right rooms.'

The guest glanced the women up and down in dis-belief that anyone would want to dress up like women of the night, fancy dress party or not, then said, 'Oh, I see. Well, hurry up about it. I've a conference to attend in the morning and I need my sleep.'

'I apologise, sir. Please sleep well.' Connie spun back

to face the group before her. 'Out, now,' she commanded them.

'Listen to the lady,' Neal backed her up.

One of the women scowled at her defiantly and snarled, '*You* can't chuck us out! We've an arrangement with the manager and we've got his permission to be here.'

Connie glared at her. 'I don't know who the person was who struck this deal with you but he was definitely not the manager of this hotel.'

Just then Harry Glebe appeared. 'What's going on?' he asked Connie and Neal. 'I was just in the middle of doing me lock-up and checking round when I heard this commotion.'

'These people need escorting off the premises, Mr Glebe, and if they refuse, telephone for the police.'

The threat of police was enough to have the women looking worried. 'All right, all right, we're going. I'll fucking do for that manager if I ever see him again,' one of them snarled.

'Not if I get to him first,' another said furiously. 'Wasting our time like this. He said we'd have no trouble. Might 'ave known it were too good to be true.'

'Come on, gels,' the third one ordered. 'Time is money and we ain't gonna mek it in this place.'

'Where we going?' one of the men asked as his arm was grabbed by the woman he was with and he was yanked along behind her.

'Up a back alley, where do yer think?' was her answer.

Connie and Neal watched as Harry herded the six of them back by the way they had entered.

'Captain Fosedyke would never have done this,' said Connie.

'No, I agree, he wouldn't. Do you think we ought to tell Miss Griffin what we've just put a stop to?'

She blew out her cheeks. 'Well, I suppose we ought to. First, though, I want a look at the reservations book, to see what names those rooms were booked under. Hopefully I can remember who actually booked them, and then at least I might be able to tell Miss Griffin who it was and she can take it from there.'

They had just arrived in reception when a hammering at the front door alerted them. Thinking it was guests arriving back after a night out, Connie went across to open the door and let them in.

She found two uniformed men outside.

'Police,' one of them announced.

Wondering what on earth the police could be paying a visit to the hotel for, Connie stood aside to allow them entry.

'What can we do for you, officers?' she asked in the foyer.

'And you are?' the older and more official-looking one asked her.

'I'm Connie Monroe, head receptionist, and this is Neal Richmond our chef.'

'Is the manager on the premises?'

Connie shook her head. 'But the owner is.' Or she hoped Miss Griffin was in her rooms and not out. 'What's going on, officer?'

'Would you fetch the owner, please, miss?'

A few minutes later a bewildered Eddie, accompanied by Mark and now Harry Glebe who had returned from his rounds, joined Connie and Neal. They were all looking at the policemen quizzically.

'I'm Miss Edelina Griffin, owner of the Connaught,' Eddie introduced herself, holding out her hand in greeting to the officer she assumed was in charge. 'What can I do for you, Inspector?'

He accepted her hand and shook. 'Well, Miss Griffin, we've received a telephone call from a guest staying here who says he knows you're allowing certain rooms in this establishment to be used for illegal activities between the hours of ten and twelve at night.'

'I can assure you, this hotel does not sanction any such behaviour,' said Eddie, insulted. 'What sort of illegal activities are you implying?'

'Prostitution, madam.'

Eddie was struck speechless.

'I am sure there has been a mistake, officer,' Mark said.

'If there is then we'll apologise but you must appreciate, sir, we have to follow up such reports. We need to check on the rooms reported to us as being in use. First I'd like to see the reservations book.'

'Be my guest,' said Eddie. 'Connie, would you furnish the officers with the keys to the rooms supposedly being used for these illegal activities?'

The officer told Connie the room numbers reported to them by the guest who had called them. Connie gulped. The keys were in her pocket. Nevertheless she slipped behind the counter and made it look like she had unhooked them from the box on the wall.

Ten minutes later the officer in charge looked at Eddie apologetically. 'Well, everything seems to be in order. The rooms are empty and obviously haven't been used this evening for any purpose at all. Do you have any idea who this Mr Smith is who reported they were being used for prostitution?'

'I remember him coming in,' said Connie. 'He said the rooms were for himself and his wife, daughter and mother-in-law, all paying a visit to Leicester on a shopping trip. He filled in the booking forms and I handed over the room keys. I asked him if he wanted the porter to take up their baggage and he told me they'd see themselves to their rooms as he could see we were busy, which I thought was nice of him as we were at the time.'

'I see. Well, there is no sign of Mr Smith or his family in any of those rooms. So whether this is a set up, like you're claiming, or you were just lucky we haven't caught you out, I couldn't say. We will be keeping an eye on this place in future. Good night, Miss Griffin.'

After the policemen had gone Connie relayed to Eddie what had transpired a short while before.

Ashen-faced, she gasped in shock as Connie finished her tale. 'Oh, my goodness! If those women had been caught in our rooms entertaining their clients the police would have shut us down. I can't thank you enough for your diligence, Connie, Neal. Oh, thank goodness you returned when you did tonight and saw those people coming in.'

'I was just doing my job, Miss Griffin,' said Connie.

'Thank goodness you take it so seriously. You'd better go to bed. I'll see you both tomorrow. And thank you so much again.' After they had departed, she looked at Mark. 'Who would do this to me? First the newspaper announcement informing the public the hotel is closing down, and now this on top of it.'

He looked at her gravely. 'Someone wants to cause you a lot of damage, Eddie, it seems to me. Have you any enemies you can think of? Although I can't think of anyone who would nurse a grievance against you myself,' he said sincerely.

'I can only think of Sopworth or Stimpson. Neither was very pleased his sideline was put an end to, and of course they both found themselves out of work. But would either of them go to such lengths to pay me back?'

'Well, the main thing is that whoever it is behind these incidents, they didn't succeed, darling. Let's be thankful for that.'

'Oh, I am. I shall instruct that the back entrance is to be locked at all times and keys will be cut for all the live-in staff so they can let themselves in. We have to put a stop to anything like this happening again.'

'Can I get you a drink, Eddie?' he asked her.

She smiled appreciatively at him. 'No, thank you. I know you want to get off. You have an early business meeting in the morning and all this has held you up.'

'I'm glad I was here, not that I could do much but by way of support anyway. If you're sure you'll be all right? I do want to be fresh and alert in the morning. We have a meeting which is rather important as my father and I are hoping to close a deal for an old warehouse by the canal. With work it could then be sold on as a possible factory or suchlike, with a nice profit for us. The present owner is a wily character who I've no doubt would fleece his grandmother out of her last penny if he could, so I'll need my wits about me.' He looked at her in concern. 'Darling, don't let this upset you. The plan was foiled, that's the main thing.'

'Yes, I should be happy about that. But I'm not happy about the police keeping their eye on my hotel in future.'

'Look at it as a safeguard. Should any criminals you might think are innocent guests try to use this place for any reason, the police keeping an eye out will put a stop to it before any damage is done to your reputation.'

She sighed. 'I suppose that's one way of looking at it.'

He pulled her into his arms and kissed her tenderly to which she willingly responded.

'We're still on for dinner tomorrow night?' he asked.

She smiled. 'Of course.'

CHAPTER TWENTY-EIGHT

Three days later Eddie was abruptly awoken by persistent knocking on her bedroom door at just after six in the morning. Mindful of her father's forthcoming ECT later that morning, she had slept fitfully and was slow to wake. She fumbled for her dressing gown which was draped over the counterpane and pulled it on before opening the bedroom door to find a frantic-looking Harry Glebe outside.

'What on earth is the matter, Mr Glebe?'

He flashed a glance up and down the corridor. 'You'd better come, Miss Griffin,' he whispered.

'Come? Come where?'

'It's the kitchen, Miss Griffin.'

'What about the kitchen?'

'It's . . . well, it's overrun with vermin!'

A while later, in the redbrick early-Victorian building on the outskirts of the city, a hospital orderly entered a room.

'Morning, Mr Griffin,' he said, approaching the man sitting on a bed staring out of the barred window opposite him, his overcoat across his knees. 'You all set then?'

Edwin turned his head to look at the man before him blankly.

'I'm taking you for a walk, Mr Griffin.'

'I can't go for a walk, I'm waiting for my wife. She'll be here soon.'

'Oh, we've had a message from her. She's waiting downstairs for yer.'

His eyes lit up. 'She is?' Edwin stood, placed his coat over his arm and followed the orderly out.

They proceeded through a maze of corridors, down a flight of stairs, and as they were passing an open door the orderly stopped, poked his head through the doorway and addressed those inside: 'I'm just taking Mr Griffin for his *walk*. I won't be long.'

'Oh, Nev, we've just had a message come though to say they ain't ready for yer yet. Doctor's been held up. You'd already gone to fetch Mr Griffin so it was too late to stop yer. Leave him out there, he's harmless enough, and come and have a cuppa while yer wait. They said they'll ring us when it's time to take the patient through.'

'Oh, right yer are,' Nev responded. 'Could just do with a cuppa.' He turned to face Edwin who was standing by him. 'Now you sit yerself down there for a minute.'

'But my wife . . .'

'Oh, she'll be along shortly.'

Edwin sat down on one of several shabby chairs lining the wall. Nev disappeared inside the office.

Edwin glanced around him. This corridor wasn't familiar to him. What was he doing here? Where was Roxanne? He seemed to have been waiting for such a

474

long time. The man had told him she was waiting down here but he could see no sign of her. Just then a door opened across the corridor and Edwin's hopes soared, thinking Roxanne had finally showed up, only for them to plummet again on seeing a stranger walk past him to enter an office. What Edwin had noticed, though, was that the door opposite led outside. He had seen a glimpse of sky as the man had come through before he'd shut the door behind him. Suddenly Edwin had had enough of this. He must have got the meeting place wrong. Roxanne would be waiting at home for him.

He pulled on his coat and buttoned it up, then headed for the door and let himself out.

The guard in the gate house at the entrance to the hospital called 'Good morning, sir' to him as he caught sight of the distinguished-looking, smartly dressed man walking purposefully past the gate-house window.

'Good morning,' called Edwin as he passed through the hospital gates.

A short distance down the road from the hospital he stopped walking and stood staring around, perplexed. He didn't recognise this area of town at all.

'You all right, me duck?'

His head jerked around to see who had addressed him and he stared, bewildered, at the young woman facing him. She was dressed most oddly, Edwin thought to himself. The fitted, sleeveless dress she wore was bright yellow and finished at her knees. Most unbecoming for a lady, in his opinion. Roxanne's clothes were ankle-length and she wore bright colours in the evening for social occasions but never in the day. Neither did Roxanne's clothes hug her figure in such a way as this woman's did, although his wife was a very shapely woman. This woman, though, looked pleasant enough.

'You look lost,' she said to him.

'Well, I think I am,' he replied. 'I need to get to Stoneygate. Could you possibly point me in the right direction?'

She pulled a face. 'Stoneygate? Never heard of it. Oh, yes, I have. It's that posh area off the London Road where all the nobs live. That's miles away from here. Tell yer what, there's a taxi firm just down the road. You can't miss their little office, it's got Winchester Taxis painted on the window. You look to me like you can afford a taxi,' she said, glancing him up and down. 'They'll help you out.'

As Edwin was making his way to the taxi office Mark came hurrying into the hotel office and stopped short. 'Eddie, what's going on? I came as soon as our secretary gave me the message that you needed to see me.'

She had been cradling her head in her hands. She jerked it up and he saw her red-rimmed eyes.

'Oh, Mark, I'm so sorry to bother you but I needed to talk to you. I hope I haven't interrupted anything important? It's just that I can't believe what's happened, I really can't . . .'

He rushed around the desk to take her in his arms, cradling her protectively. 'Is it your father, Eddie? I know you're worried about his treatment today.'

She had momentarily forgotten about that. 'No, Mark.'

'Then what is it that's upset you so much?' he demanded.

'Oh, Mark,' she cried. 'One of the breakfast chefs on his way into work this morning noticed a large piece of cardboard placed against one of the kitchen windows. He couldn't understand why it was there so automatically pulled it off and found a huge hole had been cut out of the glass behind. When he looked inside the window he could see that the kitchen was swarming with vermin and cockroaches.'

Mark gasped in horror.

'The chef summoned Harry Glebe who came to fetch me.' Eddie was pacing backwards and forwards before the desk, wringing her hands. 'Oh, Mark, I didn't know what to do. I sent Harry to fetch Captain Fosedyke and it seemed such a long time until he arrived. As soon as he did he took charge. He didn't need to tell me this was sabotage. But who did it? Who would do this to me, Mark?' she beseeched. 'Captain Fosedyke said at all costs we must keep this from the guests but we urgently needed to get the fumigators in. It was too early for them to have started work so in the meantime the male staff who were around bravely went into the kitchen, as carefully as they could to guard against possible escape of the vermin into the rest of the hotel, and tried to catch as many as they could.'

She paused momentarily to give a violent shudder. 'That's when the maggot-infested meat was found also. Slabs of it had been thrown through the hole in the window to land all over the kitchen. Captain Fosedyke had managed by then to contact the men from the fumigators who said they'd come urgently. I went and fetched Connie down and asked her to waylay any guests going into the restaurant for their breakfast and . . . oh, I don't know what excuse she'll have given them but she assured me she would deal with it. Then the men from the Ministry of Health turned up.

'They'd received an anonymous message at their offices about the appalling state of our kitchen and the danger it posed to guests' health. They had come urgently to investigate because of the serious nature of the tip-off. I did my best to explain to them that we'd been sabotaged. Captain Fosedyke assured the Ministry men the fumigators were on their way and that we'd be rid of all the vermin and the kitchen sanitised from top to bottom, but they said they had no choice but to shut us down and would call back in ten days for another inspection. They did warn me though that they wouldn't necessarily allow us to reopen then unless they were absolutely convinced there was no vermin remaining.' Face deathly white, she looked at him and implored, 'Who would do this to me?'

He shook his head.

Just then a knock sounded on the door and Connie came in. 'Just to let you know, Miss Griffin, the last guests have just left and as far as I know none of them has heard about the problem in the kitchen. I told them the owner had decided it was best to close the hotel for a couple of weeks while the renovations were being finished off.'

'Did they believe you?' Eddie asked worriedly.

'They had no choice really, Miss Griffin. The guests booking out today anyway weren't too upset when I promised them a free meal the next time they returned after we'd opened up again. I hope you don't mind I did that but I felt I had to offer them something. Most of the longer staying guests weren't very happy at being turned out at such short notice but after I'd promised them a complimentary night's stay the next time they came they were a bit nicer about it all. I hope I did right, Miss Griffin?'

'Yes, you most certainly did, Connie. I appreciate your trying your best to salvage what you could out of this awful situation.'

'The fumigators have turned up and Captain Fosedyke is dealing with them.'

'Thank you, Connie.'

Eddie's shoulders sagged despairingly as Connie departed. 'Oh, Mark, I cannot believe either Sopworth or Stimpson would stoop to such levels to pay me back for sacking them.'

He scraped a hand through his thatch of thick dark hair and exhaled sharply. 'Well, someone wants you shut down very badly, Eddie.'

She looked at him. Yes, someone obviously did. Then she gasped in shock as a terrible thought struck her. No, her mind screamed. It couldn't be Mark himself. No, surely not? But he had wanted this hotel to turn it into office accommodation. That's how they had met. Had he wanted it badly enough to go to such lengths? And he had told her he was a man who liked to get his way. Was it in fact the hotel he had been referring to all along and not, as she had thought, his desire for her? Had their relationship all been a sham on his part so as to be close to her, to find ways to reduce her to the point of selling the hotel?

Mark was staring at her quizzically. 'Why are you looking at me like that, Eddie?'

The shrill of her telephone made her jump and she grabbed up the receiver to answer it. She listened frozen-faced to what the voice at the other end told her and without uttering a word dropped the receiver back into its cradle.

It was very evident to Mark that Eddie had just been given terrible news.

'What's happened now?' he demanded.

'It's my father. They can't find him.'

'What do you mean, they can't find him, Eddie?'

'He's gone. Left the hospital somehow. He was being taken down for his treatment and they weren't ready for him. The orderly left him sitting on a chair outside the office while they waiting for the summons to take him through to the treatment rooms. That's the last they saw of him. They've got a search party out for him. They're informing me out of courtesy and asked that should he by any chance turn up here, would I let them know immediately?' Her face twisted. 'Oh, God, where is he? He's sick, Mark. At the moment my father thinks he's a young man and my mother is still alive.'

'He'll make his way here to you, Eddie, like the hospital said he might,' he tried to reassure her.

'No, he won't, Mark. Remember what I told you the other night when I was explaining to you all about Father's employee and his frauds? My father doesn't know I've moved into the hotel.' Her mind was thrashing wildly then another thought struck her. 'He thinks he's not long married to my mother and that they live in our old house. Father isn't even aware I've had to sell it. That's where he'll go, isn't it? He'll make his way there thinking my mother will be inside waiting for him.'

He grabbed her arm. 'Come on, I've got my car outside.'

CHAPTER TWENTY-NINE

As Mark's car sped smoothly down Knighton Road, a highly charged Eddie willed it to go faster. She was desperate to find her father and keep him safe. Just then she spotted his thin upright figure disappearing through the wrought-iron gates leading to the imposing property that until only a matter of weeks ago had been Eddie's home all her life.

'There he is!' she cried to Mark as he stopped the car behind another already parked outside the house. The second it drew to a halt, she jumped out to rush over to the gates, calling out, 'Father! Father, it's me, Edelina . . . Eddie.'

'Oi, you!' a male voice shouted at her out of the window of the car Mark had parked behind.

She spun round to address him. 'I beg your pardon?'

'D'yer know that man that's just gone in there?' he asked.

'Yes, I do. He's my father. Why?'

'He scarpered off wi'out paying his fare.'

'I'll see to it, Eddie,' Mark shouted to her, diverting to thrust a pound note through the window at the man. 'Keep the change,' he called as he rushed to follow Eddie through the gates.

Halfway down the drive she stopped and glanced around her. 'I can't see him, Mark. Where's he gone?'

'He must have gone around the back.'

'What if he's let himself in at the back door? Oh, I don't know what the new owners are going to think if they suddenly see a stranger walking through their house and treating it as his own. I'll have to knock on the front door, explain as best I can what's happening, and hope they're the understanding sort.'

Running the rest of the way, she arrived at the front door and rapped the brass lion's head knocker. Seconds later a plain-looking woman dressed in a maid's uniform answered the door.

'I'm very sorry to bother you but is your master or mistress at home?' Eddie asked her.

She nodded. 'Please come in.'

Eddie and Mark followed her inside the wide entrance hall.

As soon as she stepped over the threshold a great sense of familiarity overwhelmed Eddie, a feeling she was coming home after a long holiday. Her eyes immediately settled on the ornate Victorian glass chandelier vase that sat on the half-circle walnut table by the stair wall. She'd always had a fondness for it . . . and suddenly she froze, spinning round to face the maid who was about to ask the visitors' names so she could inform the master who was calling on him.

At the look on Eddie's face the maid asked her worriedly, 'Is there anything wrong, madam?'

'This furniture . . . all these things . . . where . . .' Suddenly she stopped abruptly as a voice reached her ears. She knew that voice. Knew it well. But what was he doing here? Her eyes located the half-open door from which the voice issued. It was getting louder as the person it belonged to moved closer.

'Well, that ploy this morning worked better than the last two we tried,' the voice was saying. 'A few more tricks like that and we'll have her begging us to take the hotel off her hands. You played your part well today and here's your money as promised. I'll contact you when I need you again.'

'Madam, what's the matter?' the maid asked Eddie, the haunted look on her visitor's face greatly concerning her.

Mark too was worried about her. 'Eddie, what's wrong?' he demanded.

Eyes wild, she blurted out, 'Oh, Mark, this furniture . . . that voice . . .'

Suddenly the man who'd been talking appeared out of her father's old study accompanied by another man. Eddie recognised him too. The men were shaking hands. Suddenly the larger of the two sensed their presence in the hallway. As he recognised Eddie his eyes bulged in astonishment. 'What . . . what are you doing here?'

'It's what *you* are doing here that I want to know, Uncle Harvey?' A movement from the back of the hallway alerted her and she saw her father coming through the kitchen door. 'Father!' she cried. 'Oh, Father, there you are.'

Harvey looked appalled to see his old friend Edwin heading towards him.

Eddie meanwhile made to rush to her father but froze rigid at the look on his face. She had never seen such an expression on anyone's face before. It was as if he'd seen a ghost, mingled with disbelief and horror. His eyes were fixed on the man with Harvey. Without warning Edwin suddenly launched himself forward and before anyone could stop him he had the other man up against the wall and was shaking him violently.

'Why, Stibley? Why did you do what you did to me? What was it you thought I'd done to you for you to seek such revenge?'

'Get him off me! Get him off!' Stibley was screeching as the back of his head rhythmically contacted the wall.

Mark leaped over to Edwin and restrained him.

Without her eyes leaving Harvey, Eddie went to her father's side and placed one hand on his arm protectively. Then she demanded, 'Uncle Harvey, what is going on? What are you doing in our house and why is all our furniture here? And why is my father calling Mr Whittle "Stibley"?'

Having gathered his wits after his unexpected attack on his person, Frank Whittle was gulping nervously. 'I'll be off,' he announced, attempting to make a dash for the door.

Mark, though, was too quick for him. Letting go of Edwin, he made a dive for Whittle, holding his shoulders and pulling him backwards. 'No one is going anywhere until Edelina has had her questions answered,' he said, pulling Frank Whittle around to land back beside Harvey.

Mark then commanded him, 'Edelina asked you some questions and she deserves to hear the answers.'

An evil glint sparkled in Harvey's eyes. He smirked. It was as if he was a different man from the one Eddie thought she knew. 'You want answers to your questions, Edelina, my dear? Then I will give them to you, and it will give me a great deal of pleasure. It's about time you knew the worth of the man who fathered you. Why don't you all come into *my* study and make yourselves comfortable?'

With that he turned and walked calmly back into the room he'd just vacated.

They followed to find Harvey leaning on Edwin's desk, the one that had supposedly been stolen by bogus removal men. He wore a smug expression on his fleshy face. As Eddie fixed her eyes on this man whom she had always found so kindly, so caring, a suitable friend for her beloved father, she felt she was looking at a stranger.

Mark sat Edwin down in a chair, then addressed Harvey. 'Well?'

He swelled out his chest, fixed his eyes on Edwin. Wagging one podgy finger at him, he hissed, 'You thought I would let you get away with it. Stand by and do nothing. Well, you were wrong. She was mine . . . *mine*, you hear? She would have married me if you hadn't stolen her.'

Eddie gasped, clasping her hand to her mouth, frozen in shock to realise that Harvey was referring to her mother.

'You had a hold on her somehow, you must have, or why else would she have settled for you when she could have had me?' Harvey continued. 'You were nothing but a common plumber. What could you offer her? You hadn't a pot to piss in. You wanted her money, that's all you were after. Thought I was fool enough not to know that. I loved her, *really* loved her. She was everything I'd ever dreamed of in a woman. I came from the same background. I was educated, a medical professional like my father before me. I came from good stock. She was happy with me, I know she was, until *you* came along. Before I could do anything to stop it you were married. You made sure that happened damned quick, didn't you, Edwin. Why? I'll tell you why. Because you were terrified she would realise what a terrible mistake she was about to make in tying herself to you and come back to me, the man she should really have been with, until you blinded her to the truth.'

His face twisted into a look of repugnance. 'Have you any idea how it was for me, seeing the woman I adored in the arms of another man, her looking at him the way she should have been looking at me, that other man at her side in bed where I should have been? Then I had to endure the fact that she was carrying this other man's child, the one that should have been mine. Giving birth to that child killed her. It was *you* that killed her, Edwin, you gave her that child. You robbed me of everything I ever wanted by causing Roxanne's death. You had no right to anything you got through it because it should all have been mine.

'Well, I might have lost the woman I worshipped above everything and feel my life was now meaningless without her in it, but I was damned if I was going to turn my back on what should have come to me as her rightful husband. I made a vow to myself that I was going to avenge Roxanne's death and put you back in the gutter where she found you, and I didn't care how long it took me to achieve it.'

He gave an evil laugh. 'You were like a lamb to the slaughter! Being the ignorant man you are you easily accepted that I was your devoted friend. Getting rid of Murgatroyd was easy. One small push in the back and he was down those stairs without knowing what had happened. With him off the scene, my way was clear. I was already acquainted with Frank Whittle. We will call him by that name though it's not his real one, of course, just as Stibley isn't. We'd met while he was serving a sentence in prison and I'd been called in to replace the usual dentist for a few weeks while he was ill. We got quite friendly, didn't we, Whittle?' he said, flashing a glance at the man standing rigid by the window, listening apprehensively to Harvey's confession.

Harvey immediately returned his wicked eyes to Edwin, sitting in the chair across from him, his hands clenched in his lap, his face a mask. 'Whittle was in prison for crooked accounting and pocketing the paltry gains. Unfortunately for him his then employer had far more of a business head on him than you ever had, Edwin. You don't mind me telling them your nasty secret, do you, Whittle? Too bad if you do. He told me as we chatted while I attended to him that he was due for release soon. Luckily for me it turned out to be two days after Roxanne died. I met him at the prison gates and put a proposition to him. One you gladly accepted, didn't you, Whittle, as you knew only too well that with your history it was unlikely you'd get a decent job.

'You readily accepted the services of Whittle, or Stibley to you, Edwin, on my subtle recommendations so he could take care of your inheritance from Roxanne while you grieved for your terrible loss. Well aware of your ignorance in business matters, I was confident that once Whittle proved himself indispensable to you, you'd be convinced the business was safer in his hands than in yours and then we'd be free to do what we wanted, for as long as we wanted. Whittle was happy with his cut of the deal and I was more than happy with what I was getting, but you see on my part it wasn't all down to the money I felt should have been mine by rights. It was really about my need to reduce you to the position you were in before you set your cap at Roxanne. Would still have been in if you had not wormed your way into her affections and fooled her into marrying you.

'I don't need to go into the intricate details of how we achieved your ruin, Edwin, you already know them. So do you, Edelina. In a nutshell, over the years, under my watchful eye, Frank fleeced you out of everything you gained from your marriage to Roxanne and we shared the proceeds. In the meantime, you can't begin to imagine the pleasure it gave me to be living very comfortably on my share of Roxanne's money which Frank was handing over to me as he siphoned it away. When eventually our dealings were revealed, I knew the police would never be able to trace anything back to me, my name was never used in any of the official records, and by that time Whittle would have been long gone so no chance of collaring him either.

'I haven't run my dental practice for years. Why would I need to toil when I'd more than enough coming in to make me a wealthy man . . . wealth I should have had anyway as Roxanne's husband? I kept the premises on and set out as a dental practice by way of a front. I eventually bought this house, the one that should have been mine all along, and wouldn't rest until I was living inside it like I should have alongside the woman I loved, with money I'd taken from you ... and the added bonus as it turned out of the house's contents too,' he added, puffing out his chest proudly.

'The time came when there was nothing left for me to claim back and Edwin needed to find out the real truth about his financial situation. Except for the hotel which was in your name, Edelina. I was fuming that despite all the schemes I'd come up with and got Whittle to execute, there was absolutely no plausible excuse I could come up with to fool Edwin into handing over the deeds so we could dispose of it and pocket the proceeds. I always thought that the one thing I would have to concede defeat on. The only saving grace was that, over the years, through Whittle I had made sure it became as worthless as I could make it. No investment whatsoever was made in it and no changes to the way it was run.

'Then it seemed my wish to acquire everything would be granted after all thanks to your reaction, Edwin, on learning the extent of my vengeance on you. I couldn't have wished for a better outcome. With you in the mental institution, Edelina would be easy prey for me.' Harvey's face screwed up nastily and his evil glinting eyes settled on her.

'But you shocked me, Edelina. I never thought for a moment you would consider running the hotel yourself. I never thought you'd have it in you to succeed.

Getting rid of the manager seemed like a master stroke as with no one to help you, just like your father, you'd run the business into the ground. Wrong of me now, I admit, but I was convinced that once you realised just what you had taken on you would come begging me to help sell the hotel and hand me the signed deeds. I was furious to learn that your friend had come to your rescue, and it looked very likely you would make a go of it. But, regardless, I wasn't about to give up so easily.

'You should have just handed me the deeds when I offered my help to you in the first place, Edelina, then you would have spared yourself all the heartache you have recently suffered and will do in the future, my dear. I warn you now, I will not rest until I render that hotel as worthless as I can and you are forced to concede defeat and get rid of it. I vowed when I learned that my beloved Roxanne was no longer that I would ruin the man I knew to be responsible for her death. Sorry, Edelina, but that includes you too as you are his daughter.'

'You're mad,' she whispered.

'Mad?' Harvey laughed. 'My dear, it takes a clever man to execute all I have and get away with it. You don't think Whittle was intelligent enough to come up with the schemes to steal all your assets, do you? He's no more than a crooked bookkeeper, I was the real brains behind it. I told him what to do, and how to do it, and he did. And do you think it was easy playing the part of a devoted friend to a man I despised, wanted to spit at every time I looked into his face? Let me assure you, it wasn't.'

'You won't get away with it, I will see to that on Edelina's behalf.' Mark spoke up.

'Oh, so you have a champion, my dear? How nice.' Harvey smirked at her sarcastically. 'Have you not been listening to me?' he spat at Mark. 'There is nothing you can pin on me for any of this.'

'But you forget, sir, we have your partner in crime here,' Mark told him. 'I appreciate Mr Griffin innocently signed various documents under the impression that his manager was acting in his best interests and that we will never be able to prove he was tricked into doing so, but the bank manager can confirm Mr Whittle was impersonating Mr Griffin and when it is proved that the signature on the mortgage taken out against this house is a forgery . . .'

'Then what?' Harvey cut in sardonically. 'How will they prove Whittle was working ultimately for me? It's his word against mine that we were in league, and any prosecution brought can only be brought against him, not me. I will be free to carry on my plan to get that hotel shut down.'

Fury was building inside Frank Whittle. 'I was ready to disappear, you know I was, when we'd cleared out all Griffin's accounts and got the money from the mortgage. But when you realised there was a good chance you could get the hotel after all, I agreed I'd stay and help you finish your job out of a sense of loyalty to you. After all I've done for you, you'd let me take the blame for this on my own?' he shouted.

Harvey Crankshaft laughed at him. 'You only agreed to my proposition in the first place because of all you stood to benefit from it. I'm no fool,' he hissed. 'You knew the risks.'

Whittle's fury erupted as he saw the grave possibility

of his facing another long term in prison. Before anyone could stop him he had stepped over to the desk, grabbed Edwin's paper knife, and screaming, 'You bastard, Crankshaft!' plunged the knife into Harvey's chest. He then made a bolt for the door, knocking the maid flying, before fleeing from the house.

The room's remaining occupants all stared down at Harvey Crankshaft's lifeless body.

CHAPTER THIRTY

Much later that evening, Edwin looked deep into his daughter's eyes. 'I need you to believe, Edelina, that I really thought that man was my friend. I was so in need of one after your mother died. I truly believed everything he helped me with was done out of his friendship for me.'

'It's all right, Father, I understand, I thought Harvey was a friend to me too,' she whispered.

Edwin's shoulders sagged despairingly, his handsome face creased with the deep emotional pain that was consuming him. 'When your mother died it was like the end of the world for me, I could not think of a life ahead without her in it. The only thing that kept me from ending it then was that our child needed me. It was you who gave me a reason to live, Edelina. Your welfare was the only thing that mattered to me. Anything else held no interest for me whatsoever.'

'Oh, Father,' she uttered, a lump sticking in her throat.

'I was so grateful at the time, Eddie, for Harvey's recommendation of Stibley. I trusted his word completely that he knew the man to be upright and with the highest credentials. I was really convinced that your inheritance was safer in what I thought to be his expert hands than in my own because of my inexperience in business. I was convinced I could serve you better after your mother's death by being at home, with you, trying my best to raise you in the manner she would have wanted.'

'You were a good father to me, you still are, I couldn't wish for better.'

He gave her a bleak smile. 'By the time it became apparent to me that your need for parental closeness was no longer so acute, I was convinced the business was prospering without me and thought it best to leave well alone. Stibley or Whittle or whatever his real name actually is seemed to be doing so well for us.'

'I understand why you did what you did, really I do,' Eddie assured him. 'It wasn't your fault that you didn't know what was going on behind your back. Between them they were very clever about making sure you never got an inkling. Remember, they fooled me too, especially Un . . . Harvey who was the main perpetrator.'

'Oh, Eddie, that is no consolation to me. When all is said and done I let them take your inheritance.' Edwin's face was distraught. 'It doesn't seem likely that we will get any of it back, from what the police said.'

'But there is always a chance they will find Whittle. If so we could get back what's left of his cut. As for Harvey, I didn't wish to see him dead but at least now we know he won't pursue us any longer. As he has no relatives left alive, Mark has told me Harvey's estate will most probably go to the Crown. I know I speak for you too when I say better the Crown has it to help the people of this country instead of its funding Harvey's twisted ideas of revenge. And he didn't get away with quite everything, did he? We still have the hotel, Father. Be thankful we have that. After all, it was the thing Mother prized the most, and I know she would want us to make it work.'

'Yes, you are right, Edelina, she would,' Edwin said softly. 'You do believe me, Eddie, when I say that I had no idea at all Harvey felt the way he did about your mother? Absolutely no suspicion there could be any ulterior motive behind his business suggestions. I acted upon them because I respected the fact that he was an educated man which I am not. But that difference in backgrounds between your mother and me was never an issue for either of us. We loved each other.

'The only small glimmer of comfort I feel right now is the fact that on your mother's death I had the hotel transferred into your name because I knew how much affection Roxanne had for the place and that she would have wanted her child to have it. But also I had the deeds transferred because the hotel, more than anywhere else, held so many memories for me of your mother. It was a way of avoiding further grief if I divorced myself from it as much as possible. There were many times I tried to tell you about it but I was frightened you would want to become involved in it like your mother had been, and maybe want me to help you, and that would have meant me having to go there and revisit the place in which I'd seen her so happy. It would have been like losing her all over again. I was stupid to worry about that, Eddie, I realise that now. The hotel was her place and that's a comfort really, it's as if Roxanne is still with us in a way.' A gush of tears filled his eyes. He faltered, 'I still miss her so much, Eddie,' then let go of his daughter's hands and stood up. 'Please excuse me, my dear, I am so tired, I must go to bed.'

Eddie rose and took her beloved father in her arms. Hugging him tightly, she wished him a good night's sleep.

As soon as he'd left the room, Mark came over to Eddie from where he had been standing by the window and took her hands in his.

'Oh, Mark, I know this sounds awful but in a way I'm glad for today's events because they have brought my father back to me. He will be all right, won't he?'

'Of course he will, he has you. And you, Eddie, will be fine because you have me.'

'Oh, Mark,' she sighed, collapsing into his arms. 'I have a confession to make to you, and I feel so guilty about it.'

'You don't need to tell me, I already know.'

'How do you know?'

'I saw the way you were looking at me this morning just before you received the telephone call from the hospital. I told you when we first met that I wanted the hotel badly, and when you told me it wasn't for sale I said I wasn't a man who gave up easily, so I don't blame you for thinking all the trouble at the hotel could have been at my instigation. But it wasn't the hotel I was referring to, Eddie, it was not giving up on you.' He looked at her closely and lovingly. 'There are other hotels that can be turned into office accommodation, but I knew as soon as I met you there was no other woman for me.'

She smiled tremulously. 'I'm glad to hear it, Mark, because I've always known you were the man I was waiting for.'

CHAPTER THIRTY-ONE

Eddie proudly watched the steady stream of guests, dressed in evening attire, chatting and laughing together as they made their way through into the restaurant for the first of the many dinner dances the hotel planned to hold.

She felt a gentle squeeze of her hand and turned to look into the eyes of the man she loved.

'You didn't expect so many people to attend, did you, Eddie?'

She shook her head at Mark who was looking devastatingly handsome in his smart evening clothes. 'There are far more attending than I'd dreamed of. I would have been delighted if half the tables were filled but as it is we haven't a spare seat. Six months ago when I woke up to discover the kitchen infested with vermin I feared the hotel would lose its reputation for good. I am so fortunate that through the staff's hard work, Harvey's act of sabotage failed.'

'Eddie, do you not think that your employees' show of loyalty is down to their respect for you? My darling, finding out the truth about your father's so-called friend was devastating for you but we all admire the way you have fought back and forged ahead with your plans for the hotel. Within six months you have almost reached the stage where you are having to turn people away because every room is full. Considering you had no prior business experience you deserve a big pat on the back. I know I never had the privilege of meeting your mother but I feel positive that she would have been proud of you, Eddie.'

She smiled at his compliment.

Just then Connie approached them, looking lovely in a red chiffon knee-length cocktail dress. 'Miss Griffin, Neal has asked me to come and tell you that everything is fine in the kitchen, just in case you were worried Oh, yes, and the band has arrived and will be ready to start playing as soon as the meal is finished. They're in the staff room getting changed and I made sure they've all got a drink.'

'I much appreciate your thoughtfulness, Connie, but may I ask what you and Neal are doing working when I purposely made sure the shifts were organised to allow you both the night off? I want you to help me celebrate the first of many of these functions, but also to thank you for all your hard work in contributing to the success of the Connaught.'

'Neal worked hard to ensure all the food preparation could be tackled in his absence, but just wanted to make sure the staff were coping all right as he worries about them. And that gave me a chance to lend a hand where I could because I know how important tonight is to you, Miss Griffin. As soon as Neal's satisfied everything in the kitchen is up to his standards we're going to take our places at our table.'

A beam of delight spread across Connie's face. 'My

mother looks beautiful in the new dress she's made 'specially for tonight and my dad looks so smart in his suit. She's asked me to pass on her thanks for the complimentary tickets you gave me for my family. Mam's not been to a posh do like this since she can remember and she can't wait to get my dad on the dance floor.' Connie added, giggling, 'Though whether she will remains to be seen as my dad says he's got a bone in his leg! Our Babsy looks so pretty too, and her and Melvyn the commis chef she's got together with since she started work here seem to be getting on so well together.' Mischief glinted in her eyes. 'I wouldn't be surprised if there's an engagement announced in the near future.'

As Connie hurried off, Eddie looked at Mark and said, 'It wouldn't surprise me if there was another engagement announced first, between Connie and Neal. You only have to look at those two to see their feelings for each other.'

'Oh, darling, don't you look positively dazzling tonight? I knew I was right to make you decide on the silver off-the-shoulder number,' Phee exclaimed to Eddie as she breezed up to them, looking stunning herself in a black satin, heavily sequinned and strapless evening dress. Then, looking at Mark, she tilted her head and with a wicked glint in her eye, said, 'And *you* look absolutely ravishing, darling.' Leaning closer she whispered, 'Should you decide to change your escort for the evening, you know where you can find me.'

Just then a tall, distinguished man approached them.

'Ah, at last, my father has arrived,' said Mark, going over to greet the new arrival.

Phee's eyes sparkled with interest. 'Oh, my goodness,

you didn't tell me that Mark's father was as devastatingly handsome as his son.' She gave a secretive smile. 'To think, Eddie dear, that I dismissed this hotel as a hunting ground for my next husband.'

Seconds later Eddie watched her, arm-in-arm with Mark's father, making their way into the restaurant together.

'Well, it looks as if I don't have to worry about finding a companion for my father this evening,' said a laughing Mark.

'Nor for the foreseeable future, if I know Phee and read that look in her eye correctly,' commented Eddie. And thought to herself that an older man such as Mark's father, with the means to finance her extravagance but also the maturity to handle her, might just be what Phee needed in her life. 'Talking of fathers, we had better go and join mine or he'll be wondering where we are. And after I had such a job prising him away from fixing that leaking sink in one of the guests' rooms, for fear he'd never be ready in time.' She smiled. 'I see people looking at me strangely every time they learn the hotel plumber is my father.'

'It doesn't matter what people think if he's happy in what he's doing, Eddie.'

'My sentiments exactly. I know that his contribution towards the success of our hotel is making him feel needed and has helped him a lot in getting over Harvey Crankshaft's betrayal.'

'Good evening, Miss Griffin.'

Eddie turned her head to see Captain Fosedyke with a pleasant-faced, middle-aged lady on his arm and smiled at them both welcomingly.

'May I introduce Miss Florence Weaver?' Reginald said proudly.

Eddie shook Florence's proffered hand. 'I hope you both have a very enjoyable evening, especially you, Captain Fosedyke, after all your hard work in helping to bring this occasion about.'

'It was my pleasure, Miss Griffin.' He looked at his escort and smiled at her warmly. 'We certainly intend to enjoy ourselves tonight, don't we, my dear?'

Florence smiled up at him coyly as they made their way towards the restaurant.

'Oh, my goodness,' said Eddie when the older couple were out of earshot. 'I have a feeling it's not two engagements we will be celebrating soon but three, and I couldn't be more pleased for all of the couples concerned. Shall we go through ourselves now, Mark?'

'Before we do, may I ask you to join me in the office for a moment, please, Eddie? There's something I want to give you.'

Without waiting for her response he took her hand and steered her through the remaining guests and on into the office.

Shutting the door behind them, he pulled a large brown envelope out of his jacket pocket and held it out to her.

'What is it?' she asked, taking the envelope from him.

His eyes twinkled. 'Why don't you look inside and see?'

Curiously, she undid the flap of the envelope and pulled out what seemed to be an official document. Even more curious, she opened it out and studied it. Then she gasped as she realised what it was.

'Oh, Mark!'

He smiled at her. 'The deal was finalised today. You and your father have your home back again. I should also mention that I secured all the contents also.' He looked at her searchingly. 'Eddie, I hope you will accept this as my wedding gift to you? But first . . .' Then he took a small box out of his pocket and opened it up. Inside glistened a solitaire diamond ring. His voice husky with emotion, he looked at her expectantly and said, 'I sincerely hope, my darling, that the rush of engagements the hotel is about to witness will not stop at three?'

She smiled back at him radiantly. 'I think we can safely say there'll be a fourth,' she told him, and slid her arms around his neck to hold him close to her.

Now you can by any of these other bestselling books by **Lynda Page** from your bookshop or *direct from the publisher.*

FREE P&P AND UK DELIVERY
(Overseas and Ireland £3.50 per book)

Evie	£6.99
Annie	£6.99
Josie	£6.99
Peggie	£6.99
And One For Luck	£6.99
Just By Chance	£6.99
At The Toss Of A Sixpence	£6.99
Any Old Iron	£6.99
Now Or Never	£6.99
In For A Penny	£6.99
All or Nothing	£6.99
A Cut Above	£5.99
Out With The Old	£6.99
Against the Odds	£6.99
No Going Back	£5.99
Whatever It Takes	£5.99

TO ORDER SIMPLY CALL THIS NUMBER

01235 400 414

or visit our website: www.madaboutbooks.com

Prices and availability subject to change without notice.